THE
REICH
MUTINY

THE REICH MUTINY

WILLIAM REYNOLDS

LitPrime Solutions
21250 Hawthorne Blvd
Suite 500, Torrance, CA 90503
www.litprime.com
Phone: 1-800-981-9893

Published by LitPrime Solutions   07/13/2022

ISBN: 979-8-88703-021-0(sc)
ISBN: 979-8-88703-022-7(hc)
ISBN: 979-8-88703-023-4(e)

Library of Congress Control Number: 2022911646

CONTENTS

CHAPTER 1

THE REASON

December 23, 1939

At Child's Restaurant on 34th Street in New York City, a man entered, shook the snow off his shoulders, and took his usual seat at a designated table on the main floor.

The waiter approached the table.

"Good evening, Mr. Becken."

Frank Becken looked up, his face losing its look of anxious pre-occupation as he spoke.

"How's it going, Terry," he said to the waiter. "Just bring me a cognac for starts. I'm expecting a guest."

Please, don't ask any questions, Becken thought, as he stared down at the table cloth, let's skip the youthful enthusiasm for once.

"What was it you told that communist at the Bund meeting the other night?" Terry said. "Let's see, 'pity the man that is unwilling to lay down his life so future generations can have a better one,' was that it?"

"Yes," Becken said rudely.

"Imagine the pig saying Herr Hitler was merely a political accident. Accident hell, he changes the world."

As a tremendous belch roared up from Becken's gut, his small, steely eyes cast downward, his hands fidgeted in his lap, and his jowls, shiny with oil from the warmth of the dining room, flushed crimson.

To those that knew him, Becken's various maladies were familiar, but no less embarrassing when manifest.

"I'll get your drink," Terry said with a slight bow of his head.

The waiter left and returned with a snifter of cognac.

Frank Becken swirled the cognac around in the glass as he absently watched Terry rub the table down in long strokes.

He felt more comfortable with Terry going about his business.

There would be time for ideological discussions, always time these days, but for now he only wanted to enjoy his drink in peace, a marvelous drink cognac, filling his head. He hoped the drink would settle his stomach and even calm his hated flatulence, which had flared up since he had learned that he was to meet with Erich von Ullman of the German embassy.

Across the dark room, over the sea of faces, against the wall to his right was a huge mirror with an ornate golden frame of Corinthian design........ as one might see in a bordello, Frank imagined.

He saw his image in that mirror, the small eyes staring back at him amid the other moving heads, amid the other people, who were oblivious to himself, a woman with black lace from a hat over her dark eyes and full lips, a man in a double breasted suit, the cigarette girl, swaying past with lithe legs and a dreamy look.

And he mused that it must be the eyes that gave him his

strength, his will, his intellect, that which inspired other men towards the cause. For certainly Frank Becken was not a handsome man, not by any means, he decided—the cheeks too plump, shiny, pock-marked from his acne condition in his teens, and the mouth, the thin lips almost invisible next to the massive cheeks.

It's a miracle, he mused, that I have a pretty wife.

Just like so many other obstacles in his life, his appearance was a thing that he had to overcome.

"I didn't mean to sound rude," he said to Terry. "I am preoccupied......... my guest, it's very important."

"No problem, sir, I understand."

He watched as Terry prepared the table—the clean, white tablecloth with the neatly folded cloth napkins, the utensils newly polished, the crystal wine goblets, the various condiments in china bowls. His wife would enjoy such a table.

On nights such as these, he missed her more than ever, and assuring himself that the rows they had over the Bund and the time it took from their family were merely a passing phenomena, Becken turned to his drink.

With his first sip of the cognac, he felt better. The long legs of Annette, the cigarette girl, moved towards him. He threw his head back, killing the drink, and in the same motion that he slammed the snifter to the tablecloth, he raised a forefinger to Terry, indicating another. The cognac filled his chest, gave him courage.

"Annette, when will you let me buy you dinner?" he said, marveling at her smile, which lit up her face and made her French eyes smaller.

"Any time, Mr. Becken, how about a cigar?"

"After my guest arrives and we've finished talking. Then I'll have a smoke, and you and I will have a chance to talk."

"Swell," she said, again granting her radiant smile, and Becken feeling the power of that smile over him, the smile given too easily to be sincere. He watched the corner of the smile as it approached her scrunched up shoulder, and with a swaying motion of her black skirt, she turned, the black laced stockings moving among the tables.

As he took his second drink, he chastised himself briefly for setting a pace which would take him into a third drink before Ullman arrived. His doctor had warned him of drinking too much. It did nothing to help the heart murmur Becken had since childhood, but Becken had shrugged the advice off.

Becken was a well-known financial consultant in New York. His exterior facade was that of a stock broker and investment analyst, but anyone, who understood Frank Becken, would have to understand his politics.

His parents had been German and had come to the United States ten years before the first World War. Becken had grown up with the German language, his parents having never mastered anything but the most broken English. Another barrier that Becken had overcome was his tongue. In many ways, by the time he had reached his mid-teens he had interpreted for his father and mother, the American world, that sprawling English-speaking arena, that lay outside the fifteenth ward in their German ghetto, outside his father's cocoon of a tailor shop. Becken hated that shop, and he despised his father's coddling of the rich customers.

He fought his way into the local gangs, and again overcoming his lack of physical prowess, became a numbers runner, then an accountant. Always a part of, yet on the periphery of the American gangland struggles, and finally acquiring enough money to attend NYU, Becken had received his business degree. Frank Becken became a stock broker.

He had pleased his father, that same father who had taught him his harsh German tradition, who had laid the groundwork for the boy's inner steel, who had schooled him in the ways of the Fatherland, and like so many German fathers, had educated Becken on the humiliation of Versailles. Every German must have a strong father, Becken thought, as he sipped his cognac.

Three weeks after his father had died of a heart attack, Frank Becken had joined the German American Bund.

His prediction had been correct. He was into his third cognac when he saw Erich von Ullman enter the restaurant.

Becken shook himself out of his stupor as he watched Ullman's tall figure approach the table.

"Here he is, sir," said the waiter with his customary aplomb.

"Thank you, yes."

The man slipped off his black overcoat and hat and sat down. He was a balding man with iron gray hair, combed neatly down the sides of his head. His stiff white shirt with gold cuff links, the immaculately folded handkerchief in his pocket, and his compact manner in holding his head and body absolutely erect added to the overall impression of sterile efficiency.

His features were thin. Beneath wire-rimmed spectacles Ullman watched Becken with small eyes.

Becken quickly ordered for both men. Cordials served with salad and spaghetti, followed by veal cutlet with house wine.

As Becken spoke, Ullman watched and smiled, as if even in the process of ordering dinner, he was keeping his host under close scrutiny.

"You order as if we were celebrating," Ullman said with a dismissing wave of his hand. "Considering what has happened, I think we have very little to celebrate."

"People are starving just outside that door, Ullman, I don't intend to be one of them, no matter what happens. Don't panic."

Ullman's mouth tightened, and he had the appearance of one who was trying to suppress a rage.

"Herr Becken, you are being held accountable......"

"Don't talk down to me, Ullman. What happened last week is the result of your own orders. If we're going to talk business, skip the bullshit. You're out in left field."

Ullman's face softened. "Left field?"

"Never mind," Becken said, smiling.

Ullman leaned forward. "The F.B.I. break-in endangers your operation."

"Why state the obvious? In my mind we have two choices.

Continue what we are doing or close up. Which do you want?"

The two men were interrupted when one of Frank's customers, a Roy McDonald of the New York Times stopped at the table to lament the stock market situation, which Frank assured him would improve with events in Europe. McDonald, pleased with Becken's recent advice to invest in I.G. Farben, the German chemical conglomerate, ignored the fact that Becken had not introduced him to his distinguished guest and left the table when Terry showed up with the first course.

"Privacy seems to be a problem here," Ullman observed as Terry poured the wine.

Becken smiled as he shrugged. "Customer..... what can I do?"

When the waiter left the table, the conversation continued.

"My superiors point out....."

"Why do you always take that tone with me?" Becken said, the cognac adding to his courage. "Just tell me what you want. There is no need to talk about your superiors, as you call them. I will gladly take my orders from you."

"It is difficult to speak to you when you are so defensive."

"Forgive me, Herr Ullman, but I don't want to be anyone's scapegoat. We're doing the best we can. You have to know that."

"No one is interested in your excuses," Ullman said evenly, "no one."

A half-eaten string of spaghetti fell from Becken's mouth.

"You're hiring too quickly and carelessly," Ullman said, raising an eyebrow. "You are bound to have hired informers."

Becken's round face flushed with anger.

Ullman placed the tips of both fingers together.

"Your life must be simplified. You are much too friendly to too many people."

"I'm a business man. I have business contacts."

"You are a stock broker and a bookmaker. Your gambling operation puts everything we are working for in danger."

"You're talking about my silent partnership at the Varsity."

"You know exactly what I'm talking about....."

"I have to scratch out a living."

"Not even the break-in downtown is that significant in itself," Ullman said. "Merely a nuisance, just as it will be if you are linked to a petty gambling charge. The government will bog you down with personal problems, which will distract you from our goal."

Ullman took the tips of his fingers apart, intertwined his fingers and folded them inward, cracking his knuckles as he spoke.

"It makes me very nervous, Becken, to see your rotégés at the Varsity showing up at Bund meetings. I have heard that your new friend made quite an impression on Fritz Kuhn."

"Who do you mean? Maxwell? He speaks his mind. Any crime in that?"

Ullman pushed his plate back, his spaghetti not touched. "Are you telling me that you invited him yourself?"

"Absolutely."

Ullman ran his hand over his balding head, down his cheek, and stared with his small eyes at Becken, as if to discern the slightest sense of betrayal in his manner. He again placed his fingertips together as he leaned forward.

"Is it possible that you actually believe in this Maxwell fellow? I'm told he makes a very poor first impression."

Becken belched uncontrollably. "Would you lay off?" he managed to say. "I trust this man. He's my friend and associate. I invited him because he was curious....."

"The F.B.I. will come at you through your bookmaking business. It will be very soon. In short, close up and don't tell me any more sad stories about your family. You may be right about Maxwell. But be suspicious of associates who have a sudden interest in attending three Bund meetings, introduce themselves to almost everyone there, ask all manner of questions, then, just after the break-in, leave town."

"He went home for Christmas," Becken said. "You're totally off base. Tommy Maxwell is one of my best friends. If we've been infiltrated, it isn't by him."

"I only refer to him as a general example. Watch who you are trusting."

Becken laughed with exasperation. "Eat your spaghetti, Ullman. The main course will be here soon."

The two men continued to argue. Ullman reminded Becken that the German American Bund, once only an organization formed to help German immigrants, was the only official organization supporting Hitler's recent invasion of Poland—the single event that would mark the beginning of the Second World War.

Becken maintained that the American public, which he felt he could gauge through his stock market channels, while in general disapproval of Adolf Hitler, were distracted from world events by the Great Depression. Becken described Americans' mood towards the war as that of morbid curiosity and worry, rather than horror.

At this Ullman vehemently reminded Becken of the Bund's orders from Berlin. The Bund was to antagonize Americans against the British declaration of war against Germany. Through a massive propaganda campaign they were to support an isolationist stance.

Over the last two years the German American Bund not only

contained their normal German nationals, but members of the Pacifist Left, anti-Semitic elements, and intelligence operatives of the Third Reich.

Passing occasionally with coffee, Terry noticed the familiar, confidential manner each man took with the other, but he also noticed, in both Becken and Ullman, the fleeting nature of their familiarity, the men at times stepping back and watching one another with the same degree of trust in which a stranger views another in a hospital elevator.

"You continually refer to yourself as a business man," Ullman said with a cordial nod. "We expect you to be far more." Becken bristled.

"What are you driving at?"

"Your friends. Control them."

Becken drained his glass before answering. "You are referring to Maxwell."

"Not just Maxwell, but any of them. Our struggle requires that we make hard decisions. If the individual figures into the general good, then so be it, but if the individual gets in the way...."

Ullman's hand gestured in the air in slow circles as if to finish his sentence.

"Clam it," Becken said with a half-burp. "Enough said. Now let's get to further business."

The waiter rolled the food cart up to the table. Both men had veal cutlet and shared a carafe of red wine. The meal was sumptuous, and neither man spoke until they had finished eating. Over the dessert of macaroon pie and ice cream, the discussion continued, centering on the coming propaganda activities of the Bund for the next month.

This accomplished, both men relaxed over a cup of coffee before Ullman stood up and pulled his brim hat over his eyes.

"Thank you, Herr Becken," he said as he shook hands. "If there is any need to contact me sooner, you know the procedure."

Becken smiled at the subtlety. "I doubt if it will be necessary," he said.

As he watched Ullman duck his head into the snow at the restaurant's entrance, he held his coffee cup for Terry. The waiter filled it.

"I trust everything was satisfactory," Terry said with a slight bow.

Becken stared off, absorbed in thought. "Yes, quite satisfactory, as usual Terry. Here, keep the change."

"Thank you sir."

Two women entered the restaurant, and Frank Becken watched them giggle and knock the snow off their shoes and bobby socks.

Annette, approaching with the cigarette tray, saw the pensive look on Becken's face and turned the other way.

Glad now that she had not spoken, Becken thought of her last utterance, "Swell." His eyes swooned upwards. Where could that infernal expression come from? He thought. Everyone says it. The swell of the sea, perhaps.

And with the thought of the sea, he remembered a night last week when, like tonight, he had questioned his situation, even his very identity. He had been at a friend's house, overlooking the quiet, night waters off Long Island Sound, hearing the waves, like thoughts, rhythmically lapping the shore.

He preferred to see all things in terms of the sea. The sea violent far away, while at home now, like the Sound waters, relatively calm. Americans were no more affected now by the war than was a school of fish, twitching in unison to a distant clap of thunder.

His friend, Tommy Maxwell, had been with him that night.

Both men had tired of their host's guests inside and had come outside to smoke a cigarette. The twinkles of passing freighters had shone on the calm Sound.

As he had done many times before, the young Maxwell had tried to to back Becken off.

"Don't try to conform me to your principles," he had said.

"Personally, I have no principles." Becken had not wavered. He had talked of Germany's cause, of Hitler's doctrines. He had told Maxwell of the life his father had in Germany, of his coming to America, the sea offering an escape from the tyranny of economic and spiritual humiliation.

Despite Becken's inspired pleas, his friend had remained unimpressed.

The fraulein in the evening dress was at the piano now. She played a composition from Liszt.

Ullman's words stuck in Becken's mind. The conversation about Maxwell had bothered him.

Frank had spoken with assurance to Ullman regarding Maxwell's loyalty. And whereas Becken was certain Maxwell would never betray him, he was not so certain that he would return. As he stood and put on his coat, he asked himself why he had stuck his neck out so far for Maxwell. He buttoned his coat and smiled to himself.

He had always had a gut instinct about Tommy Maxwell. To try to explain it was as vague as explaining any friendship. He supposed it was Maxwell's youth that appealed to him. It was a time for the young and the vital. Such was Hitler's assertion.

And yet as Frank Becken left his table and paid his bill, he could not shake the gnawing doubt within him, that perhaps he too was as Maxwell pretended to be—devoid of selfless principles.

Becken's life in the last three years had been one of a survivor.

Many of his comrades had been annihilated by the crash of 1929.

Becken had done what was necessary; he had scraped money in any way he could, had turned to bookmaking, even sold hardware part time, and most of all, maintained his German investments—I.G. Farben and the Krupp armaments.

He put on his hat and entered the cold air. Lowering his hat as he walked, flecks of snow touched his chin.

The weather had been much like this when he had put Maxwell on the train five days ago. Their conversation had been light and friendly, and as Maxwell had entered the train, Becken remembered his feeling of reassurance.

He shrugged. Probably needs time to think, Becken surmised, no better place than on a train.

December 28, 1939

At three o'clock in the morning a man sat on a train. As the car rocked in the darkness, he ran his hand over the seat. He looked at his watch, grimaced, and reached into the left inside pocket of his coat. He found a small metal flask and turned it up. The scalding whiskey warmed him. He capped the flask and put it in his pocket. He had blonde hair which hung in a lock over his forehead, a nose which was slightly crooked from having previously been broken, and a thin mouth with a slight overbite.

Again he looked at his watch. The train was bound for New York city, scheduled to arrive at six-thirty in the morning.

The man's name was Tommy Maxwell, age twenty-eight. He was returning from a Christmas visit in Murphy, North Carolina.

He squirmed in the seat and looked out the window. He saw his dim reflection in the rushing landscape. He knew he would appreciate home more after he was away for another three months or so, and he could not blame his parents for worrying. After all, he had made drastic changes in the last year.

> *The rain droplets on the vibrating*
> *window, creating trembling pockmarks, on*
> *the blue, sleeping faces—eyes closed, mouths gaped.*

A man with a newspaper across the aisle said, "World's in a hell of a shape."

Maxwell had not answered.

He stared out the dark window and remembered the conversation with his father only three days before. He was not sleepy. Besides, he had promised himself he would sort it all out.

The conversation had ocurred on Christmas day 1939. Tommy Maxwell and his father had excused themselves from dinner, as the women, Tommy's mother and sister, had started the dishes. The two men had walked into the woods behind the house. The air was crisp and the woods smelled of smoke from the fireplace. The two men smoked and continued an argument, whose stages had reached levels disturbing to the women inside.

"This is no time to quit a job," his father said.

The smoke from the cigar moved upwards against his spectacles. On the horizon Maxwell could see the vague purple outline of the Smoky Mountains.

The day was overcast and the mountains steeped in clouds.

"Answer me, damn it," repeated his father.

The two men walked a few more feet into the woods, and if it were not for the hobbling limp of the old man's stiff leg, they would have kept perfect step, as if they had mimicked these exact steps hundreds of times.

"I've been up there over a year now, dad," Tommy Maxwell said.

"So why all the secrecy? Tell me that."

"What's the point? You wouldn't approve anyway."

"How do you know?" But his father stopped as his son held up his right hand and let it fall, slapping his thigh. This was the gesture he used when indicating that the conversation was in a rut.

They passed the oak tree to the right of the path, its great trunk descending to its tantalizing tangle of exposed roots, over which both men had to struggle as they proceeded up the familiar way.

"What happened?" asked his father. "Why don't you come back where you belong?"

"Why do these things matter so much to you?" Maxwell said. "I came home to see you and the family and to enjoy Christmas."

"Fine. Enjoy it then," his father said with disgust.

The sun peeked through the clouds above. Maxwell stared at the golden patches of light on the ground.

"Take back your old teaching job here," his father said. "That's what you want."

Maxwell smiled, looked off, and shook his head.

"Why do you always seem to know more about wwhat I want than I do?" he said.

"You're nearly thirty years old and still have no respect for us."

"I have plenty of respect for you and mom both," Maxwell said. "It's the other way around."

"What in hell are you talking about?"

"You still treat me like a child," Maxwell said, angrily flipping ashes from his cigar.

"Look at George and Michelle," his father said. "They're happy. They enjoy marriage, kids…."

"My brother and sister aren't me," Maxwell said as he leaned his head forward. "Can't you understand that?"

His father looked away. "What about Elaine?" he said. "You had it made……."

"Oh yeah?"

"You had an excellent job at the high school."

"Right and what else?"

"Come on, Tommy."

"I just don't see the point," Maxwell said.

But his father continued. "You were engaged to be married, then out of the blue….."

And again Maxwell raised his hand and slapped his thigh, turning away in disgust, as if the words were causing him physical pain.

"Yeah, that's right. You don't want to hear it," his father said. "Well, you're going to hear it anyway."

"Good," Maxwell said. "Tell me about my life. Tell me all about it."

"I will."

"Good, go ahead," Maxwell said.

"And out of the blue you quit your job and try to convince everyone it's a leave of absence."

"It is a leave of absence."

"And what in hell is in New York:" his father asked in a tone of accusation.

"Graduate school."

His father snorted. "You aint in school."

Maxwell stopped and wheeled around. He started to speak, then turned up the hill.

"Don't walk away from me," his father said.

Maxwell stopped and wheeled around. He started to speak, then turned up the hill.

"Don't walk away from me," his father said.

"Maxwell stopped, took a deep breath and turned around.

"This conversation gets endless," he said.

"Are you afraid to tell me the truth?" his father said as he threw down his cigar and smashed it into the dirt.

"Where are you getting your money? Who's supporting you?"

Maxwell did not answer.

The silence was punctuated by a slow roar of wind as the sun was again shrouded. The landscape was filled with racing shadows. The men began walking back towards the house.

"Don't you see?" his father said. "Your teaching job could keep you from being drafted."

"Why are you worried about that? You went, didn't you?" Maxwell paused, looking down at his father's stiff leg. "You did your duty in the great war."

"That's fine," his father said, quietly. "You're a pacifist. I've never argued that point. It's your right."

His father straightened his glasses on his nose. "It's still because of what happened when you were a kid, isn't it?"

"Come on, dad, you know better than that."

"No, you've said so before. It's because of what happened when you were a kid, isn't it?"

"Come on, dad, you know better than that."

"No, you've said so before. It's because of what happened when you were fourteen. Dammit, Tommy, what do we have to do? Do we have to beg? We've said we were sorry. Are you going to punish us for the rest of our lives?"

"Come on, dad, that's not it….."

"You're lying. What about all the good years we've had, the thousands of things your mother and I have done for you? Do all those count for nothing?"

"What do you want from me, dad?"

"For God's sake, come on home. Your mother needs you. If you are against the war, that's your prerogative…."

"And become a sod buster like my brother?"

"Take the easy way out," his father said, his voice pleading. "They don't draft teachers.

"I doubt if that will be true. There are plenty of women to teach."

"You've answered none of my questions," his father said.

He looked at Maxwell's mouth, at the cruel, pursed effect it took when closed.

"It's a woman, aint it? You got some whore."

"Just shutup," Maxwell said angrily. The old man rea hed out and grabbed an arm.

"You may beat hell out of me," he said. "But I aint gonna take that from you. You talk that way to me again and I'll knock the shit out of you."

Maxwell stepped back, stunned by his own anger and feeling that familiar regret. Looking into his father's tired eyes, he put out a hand and touched the old man's shoulder.

"Look, I'm sorry. It's just that......."

"I don't want it like this," Mr. Maxwell began.

"You know I love you," Maxwell said. "It's Christmas now."

"It's hard for me to accept that you love your mother and I when you treat us this way."

"What way?" Maxwell said, resuming his defensive tone.

"What way?" his father mimicked.

"What does it matter, Dad? I'm safe. Things are fine with me," and he stopped, watching the movement of the thick layer of cloud surrounding the nearest mountain. A bird rustled in the brush behind him. He saw the rusty pump handle to the side of the house, watched it as if mesmerized. A patch of birds fly overhead. He shook himself as if roused from a deep sleep.

"I keep things from you to protect you," Maxwell said, and stopped, fearing that he had already said too much.

"So that's it. It's that goddamned Bund."

"Don't start that again. I don't want to talk about it."

"The Bund's nothing but a bunch of grown men playing Halloween," his father said. "You're intelligent enough to know that."

"These people are my friends," Maxwell said stiffly. "They mean as much to me as our church friends mean to you."

"You need to be back here with your old friends," wheedled the old man.

Maxwell grunted. "Not again."

"Working somewhere."

"Please."

"What's wrong with your old friends?"

"Nothing, not a damn thing."

"You need a job, that's your problem."

"I got a job."

"Yeah, and you're real proud of it too. I mean something legal."

Maxwell kicked a clod of dirt to the side.

"This country's been good to you, young man," the old man said.

"Yeah, sure, and look what the hell it's done for you….."

"We got a roof and food."

"Right. You got that, dad, and what the hell else you got?"

The old man looked quickly to his right. This was the equivalent of his son's slapping his leg.

"You're getting off the point, Tommy."

"No, you are," Maxwell said. "I'm sorry, dad, but I can't do everything your way."

They moved out of the tall woods towards the back of the house.

Maxwell smelled the old wood from the tool shed as he passed it—the shed with its familiar rusted horseshoe nailed over the door, with the same piece of cardboard placed behind where the side wdow of the shed had been knocked out three years before Maxwell had left home. He moved past the shed and the knee-high chicken houses, over the white splotches of day-old chicken droppings to the back porch.

The house was a typical North Carolina farmhouse, painted white with a front porch swing in front, a fireplace, and a screened-in porch in the back which faced thick woods that descended down a steep ridge to the house.

As the two men parted, Maxwell entered the house and was assaulted by the same smells. The fire burned merrily. On the other side of the room was a Christmas tree. He started to light a cigarette, but when hearing his mother moving in the kitchen, he put the cigarette down.

His mother didn't approve of smoking either. He stretched his legs and looked at a picture of an old plow horse on the wall.

"Does Elaine like pumpkin pie?" his mother asked from the kitchen.

"Yes," he said, "as far as I know."

At mention of his former fiance whom his parents had taken the liberty to invite over for custard, Maxwell sighed, thought what the hell, and lit a cigarette.

"Are you smoking?" his mother said from the kitchen.

"Yes," he said, s he walked to the small table with the radio. The broadcast was saturated with mop-up operations in Poland.

Maxwell listened for a time, the cigarette sending a vertical line up, bisecting his face.

"Why don't you turn that off, Tommy," his mother said. "I'm sick of hearing all that."

He became lost in thought. Ever since he had left home, it was always the same when he came back. The constant proddings and interrogations made him wish he had not come home at all. His mother and father seemed to be only existing together. Guess he got stuck with the deal like everyone else, Maxwell thought. He could already picture the evening meal—his brother and sister straining not to mention anything about Maxwell's decision to leave teaching. And Elaine's presence would only complicate things more. He looked at the Christmas tree with the crystalline angel atop it.

I will always be a child to them, he thought. He sighed again. He was thinking that he was a liar, and although lying seemed to be the only prudent way out of his dilemma, he was still disgusted by it. He knew that even his pro-German statements to his father were partially an act. True, he had been exposed to these ideas, but he was not sure how much he believed them. And why he chose to appear more pro-German to his parents than he actually was he did not know. It merely felt like the right thing to do. It gave them a reference point into his mind. And he would pull the same act with Elaine tonight hen everyone had gone to bed. The truth would be too painful. He felt confused and very tired.

A crash and wail of iron—the same blue faces

The train jolted hard to the right. Maxwell started. He had been in a deep sleep. He looked at his watch. It was not yet five o'clock. He must have dropped off for a few seconds.

What had jolted him out of the throbbing darkness of the diesels he could not say. Out of the window his eye remained unbothered by a sign of a town or needle of light from a house. In rhythm to the churning diesels the moonlight trembled and shimmered over a great bare field.

He decided to stay awake and watch in the dawn. He knew he would arrive in New York shortly after daylight.

Once when the train slowed down outside a small town, two derelicts entered the car in long overcoats, one with a pull down hat, the other bareheaded with a patch over his eye.

Maxwell knew immediately on seeing them that they had hopped the train, and he amused himself, watching the interplay between the two men and the conductor, who was determined to have them thrown off. Near Jersey City the train ground to a halt and the two men ushered off.

Maxwell laughed to himself. Times were hard. The two bums were probably making their way to New York to seek their fortunes. And what could they find there but thousands more like themselves, homeless and destitute.

Maxwell lit a cigarette.

He thought of his boss, Frank Becken. For a year now Maxwell had run Becken's pool hall and small bookmaking operation. It had started out innocently enough when Maxwell tended bar for Becken in one of his smaller holdings—a bar off 89th called The Rathskellar. It was a place where Becken often came with his friends, mostly from the German sections of New York. In a year Maxwell had found himself running a bookmaking operation which helped fund the propaganda machine of the German American Bund.

The peach light of the sun on the horizon. A small baby was crying fitfully towards the front of the car. Maxwell watched the young mother rock and feed the child.

He was thinking of his conversation only three days ago with his former fiance—Elaine Cory. How had he come so far in only a year?

First, a school teacher with all the trimmings, he thought, and now this. He laughed to himself.

The baby began crying again. His mind swum in memory.

Elaine Cory was a beautiful girl. Maxwell had always thought so, even from the time that they were high school sweethearts. On Christmas night, after his parents had gone to bed, he had watched her face as she talked. Her hair, as always, was dark and curled and her large eyes shone with animation. After he kissed her for a time, thei lights glinted off silent tears, as Maxwell reached a point of discussion he had been postponing for a long time.

"It's not that I don't love you," Maxwell said, touching her arm.

"What is it, then?" What am I supposed to think?" she said.

They sat on the hearth next to the fire.

"It's just doesn't make sense," Maxwell said.

"What? The fact that I want to be normal, that I want children?" she said, shifting her hips on the hearth.

"You know exactly what I'm talking about," he said.

He stopped and watched her face. He felt ridiculous. She was hanging on his every word, words that he was carelessly throwing out.

"What is coming will not allow ties like marriage to exist," he said.

"Come on, Tommy," she said.

"After it's over, perhaps, but not now." He reached up and touched her ear, then ran his fingers through her brown curls.

"What is coming?" she sighed, for she already knew what his answer would be.

It seemed she had heard it forever.

"The war's coming, Elaine."

At mention of the word, she knitted her eyebrows in a way which had always weakened Maxwell and threw a prim shoulder up towards her cheek as her head turned in disgust. She was wearing a white dress with tiny blue tulips printed over the smooth material which clung neatly to the sleek line of her legs and her small, but well-formed breasts. She was sitting on the hearth.

She leaned back slightly.

"Don't talk to me about war," she said. "That's not what's bothering you and you know it."

"We can wait."

"Wait for what? I'm twenty-four years old."

"If our relationship is sound, it can stand any test," he said, pulling back.

"You don't really believe that," she said.

"It would be no good with me away all the time. Don't you see?"

"And where do you have to go?" she said. "What's in New York? You don't have a job there. What am I supposed to think?"

"I'm in a period of transition," he said.

She was crying now. Silent tears trickled crookedly down her flushed face, her flesh the color of a pink rose, and as she wept, she managed to hold her head high, wearing that flush in a manner irresistible to Maxwell. Tiny wisps of hair reflected the fire.

Maxwell held her behind the neck. His prominent nose wrinkled slightly as he spoke. "Come on, now, Elaine," and he kissed her repeatedly, feeling at first the soft wetness of her cheek, then her tongue as her mouth opened wider. He had begun to ease slightly onto her on the hearth, when she stiffened and pushed him back.

Glancing to the side, she picked up her cup of boiled custard and took a sip, flicking her tongue over the corners of her mouth.

"Not now, Tommy."

"Not now," he repeated to himself as he stared off past her.

"I'll ask you again. What am I supposed to think?"

"We must be disciplined," he said, finally finding the word which filled the void of silence.

"Discipline, is that all you ever talk about?"

He looked into her glistening eyes. He put his head in her lap, feeling her fingers lightly stroking his temple.

"Oh, Tommy, you are such a little boy. You always have been."

"Why do you say that?" he answered wearily.

"You're just drifting through life," she said, "looking for some kind of adventure." With her fourth finger she wiped a tear from her cheek.

"Something that probably doesn't even exist."

"That's enough," Maxwell said, sitting upright.

"What's the matter?"

"I won't be patronized," he said. "That's all I get around here."

Her eyes half-closed, she stared down into her custard, as if the answer lay in the small, crystal cup.

"We're both talking too much," Maxwell said. "Let's sit on the couch."

She followed him over and sat down, her hips a small distance from his. He rapidly closed the space between them, putting his arm around her shoulder.

They sat for a time, watching the fire as the big log began to catch, sending shuddering orange sheets over the room. The Christmas lights on the tree slowly blinked.

"So where dos this leave us, Tommy?"

"Like I said, sometimes we analyze ourselves too much, rather than just letting things happen naturally."

He mustered a warm smile, boyish and precocious, looking her directly in the eyes.

She read the look and smiled.

"You always did have the nicest crinkles in your eyes," she said.

She had barely gotten the last word out when he kissed her full on the mouth, then her cheeks, eyelids, and neck. With his right hand he slowly massaged her back in slow circles, toying playfully with the zipper on the side of her dress. They kissed for a time, and when her breathing got heavier as he bit gently on the nape of her neck, with his left hand he gently kneaded her left breast. She began to respond. He ventured his fingers to the folds of her dress, and each second expecting a "no", he gently slipped the material upwards. So slowly did his fingers move, that it was a full five minutes before the dress was completely over her hips, the fire fluttering over her sleek legs and panties. He began to massage between her legs through the sheer, silky material. He helf his breath. In all their years this was as far as he had ever gotten. He took his time, staring at the fire as if the subject under his massaging fingers were only of passing interest.

"Not here, Tommy," she whispered, but she lay her head back on the couch.

She was wet now. As softly as he could manage, he gently pulled back the elastic from her thigh and put his fingers inside over her coarse hair.

Suddenly she tightened, gave a virginal shudder, and twisted away. With a quick motion she pulled her dress back down and sat straight up.

"No, Tommy, not now," she said, as he started again. She took a deep breath and began straightening her hair.

"I knew it was too good to be true," he said.

"What do you mean?" she said. "You know how I feel about that...... not until we're married."

"Right, I remember now."

"Come on, Tommy. I just......."

"Don't bother to explain," he said. "It's just one of your Christian virtues. Let's see, honesty, chastity, what else?"

"Tommy don't."

"Don't worry. I won't." He laughed without mirth.

"I'll tell you what you told me," she said. "We must be disciplined. If our relationship is good, it can stand any test."

Maxwell's eyes bulged and he bolted from the couch. He hated it when she turned his words back at him. He viewed it as a cheap, womanly trick.

"It's time for you to go," he said.

"It that's all you want from me......."

"Oh, come on, Elaine," he said. "You're like nobody else. We've been dating for years. What do you expect?"

"Get your coat."

"Tommy."

"Get your coat and get thee to a nunnery," he said, laughing bitterly.

"So you've read Shakespeare. I'm very impressed."

She had her coat now, her pocketbook over her arm. She was not crying, but her mouth was tight with anger.

"Elaine," he said, and then seeing that she expected the apology that he was getting ready to make, "never mind, let's go."

The conductor's uniform moves past, his gold watch

Reflecting early sun, moves silent

The train jolted in the half-light. The only things visible were the silhouettes of passengers across the aisle and the glow of a cigarette.

Maxwell again had fallen asleep. He was thinking of Elaine and re-living some muddles version of their conversation. It seemed in the rocking car, in and out of the throes of slumber, two phrases continued to sound in his mind—"Tommy, you're just drifting through life" and "I'm just in a period of transition."

He squirmed in his seat and looked out the window.

A man across the aisle shifted and grunted.

As the man shifted again, the newspaper on his seat fell into the aisle.

Maxwell saw the headline—Mussolini-Hitler Clash Over Non-Agression Pact.

He watched the abandoned boxcars and the vast scrapyards on the outskirts of the city.

He had become obscure in the last year. Something had snapped—family, friends, career, all thrown aside.

He lit another cigarette. Yes, he thought, one conversation changes a man's life.

Maxwell remembered the night, much like this one, nearly a year ago, when he had left for New York unannounced, and as he drifted in and out of the fringe of sleep, just as he had done a year ago in another railroad car, he re-lived the talk he had had with Reeves Ferguson, his principal.

The date had been June 1, 1938. Things had changed drastically since that day. As he re-lived every word and gesture, he pulled frpom the inner pocket of his tweed coat a small, metal flask. His friend Oscar, who made the finest local "corn" in Murphy, had given him enough for the trip. "Just enough to keep me warm," Maxwell said.

The flask was cold on his fingers as he turned it up, the scalding liquid sliding down his throat and sending rushes of warmth up and down his limbs.

June 1, 1938. He would never forget that day.

It had been warm, one of those radiant Spring days in the mountains surrounding Murphy high School. The teachers were all in the best of moods, winding up small bookkeeping matters such as inventories of classroom desks or the counting of text books. It had been the last day of school, and everyone was celebrating the coming of summer. The end-of-the-year conference with the principal was for eyeryone else a pat-on-the-back session—merely a formality.

Maxwell's conference had been scheduled last. Except for the custodians, everyone else had gone.

Behind the principal's desk was a mural, painted by students. Maxwell watched it as he entered the office. The heading over the mural read: "America the Beautiful". The mural was one of those patriotic cliches which rendered crude images of Cherokees dancing in circles upon painted mountains, buckskinned settlers gazing over distances with their hands over their eyes, and jumbled battlefield depictions between redcoats and revolutionaries.

Maxwell sat in the soft, leather chair.

The principal Reeves Ferguson was a short, squat man. He was thirty-five, with hair slicked back in two prominent wings on the sides of his head. A half-smile continually played around his otherwise wan features, as if constantly grimacing at the sun. He stood and shook Maxwell's hand in a compact, measured way. He sat down and opened a file. Everything about him was the picture of bureaucratic propriety, from the dark, pin-striped suit he wore to the neat stack of papers on his desk. It was rumored that his wife, who was the daughter of the school system's lawyer, had been instrumental in getting Ferguson his job. He began his words in the same slow, even tone with which he always spoke.

"In reviewing your file, Tommy," he said. "It's obvious that you're an excellent teacher of history."

"Thanks."

"Let's see, awarded teacher of the year by the Optimist Club your second year, Coach of the Year in Wrestling your third year." He looked up.

"You quit coaching last year," he said, looking slightly to the side as if remembering a detail that had escaped him. "I believe you and Coach Davis had a run-in."

"You've known that for a long time," Maxwell answered. "We spoke of it at length."

"So that's why you stepped down from your coaching position.

"Okay, what's on your mind?" Maxwell said bluntly. "You seem to be driving at something."

The smile passed from Ferguson's eyes, as if reluctantly relinquishing the comfort of overture.

"These elements concerning your coaching, while inconvenient and at times distracting in no was take away from your abilities in the classroom. You certainly have the ability to affect students. There's no doubt as to your popularity. We'll discuss the content of your teaching in due time....but, for now....there is an unfortunate, shall we say, incident."

Maxwell felt his stomach fall. He knew what was coming. And yet he had to say it.

"What are you talking about?"

"You don't know?"

Maxwell stared at Ferguson's smiling face, then at the mural behind the desk.

"The other night in Mason county. Surely you remember, or were you too drunk?"

Maxwell did not answer.

"Regardless of that," Ferguson continued. "Sheriff Oliver was lenient because of your professionl."

Maxwell started to speak, then stopped.

"A profession which may no longer be suitable for you," Ferguson said.

Maxwell swallowed. "Mr. Ferguson, I made a mistake. I readily admit that. It won't happen again..."

"You're absolutely right. It won't happen again."

Maxwell stared through him.

"Under the present contract," Ferguson said, "it is clearly stipulated that a teacher may be let go on the grounds of moral turpitude."

Maxwell was blind with anger.

"That's not what the contract says," Maxwell said.

"Oh really."

"The law passed by the State legislature last year says that nothing in a teacher's private life may be infringed upon," Maxwell said.

"You're wrong."

"Unless he is convicted of a felony, and I was not charged," Maxwell said.

"There is another directive," Ferguson said.

"Or unless it affects his teaching, which it hasn't."

"The last stipulation is subject to interpretation," Ferguson said.

Maxwell bolted from his chair. He was enraged to the point that words escaped him. He pointed his finger at the oval face and finally managed to say, "I know my rights."

"I'm determined to have you removed," Ferguson said calmly.

"What's come over you?" Maxwell said, taking a step forward.

"Sit down." Ferguson closed the file. His plump cheeks were flushed. "No, you're right," he said. "Perhaps the incident in Mason County isn't enough, but other incidents concerning your teaching have recently been brought to my attention." Ferguson began tapping his pencil on the desk as he talked.

"You're popular, but it seems that your religious views have crept into your teaching."

"What views?"

"Views that are entirely unacceptable."

Ferguson took a deep breath, sighed, and opened a manilla folder.

"On April 14 Judy Sharpe complained to her mother that you were teaching some rather odd interpretations of Christianity's function during slavery."

"What of it?" Maxwell said coldly. "It concerned the reasons slaves were only allowed to read the Bible."

"Explain the theory."

"I won't go into it now."

"I'll bet."

"All history is subject to interpretation," Maxwell said.

"Would you call yourself an atheist?"

"That's none of your damned business."

"An agnostic?"

Maxwell did not answer.

"Your silence is adequate to convince me."

"Of what?"

"Of the fact that your views are not conducive to what our children need in the classroom."

"Bullshit."

"What did you say?"

"You heard me," Maxwell said.

"I think it would be wise for you to resign."

"And what if I won't?"

Ferguson leaned forward and folded his hands. "Then I'll be forced to bring these matters before the board."

"I have a right to believe any way I want."

"But not the right to indoctrinate our children."

"I don't indoctrinate anyone…." And once again words failed him. The conversation had stunned him.

Ferguson sat back and swiveled his chair against the tile. One of the wings of his slicked back hair now faced Maxwell, the forefront of what had become the hideous mural.

"I'll inform the board as to my position," Ferguson said. "You can fight it if you want. Perhaps you'll survive," he said, his chair making a shrill scrape on the tile as he again turned to face Maxwell.

"But believe me, if you stay, you'll wish you hadn't. You know what I can do."

"It wouldn't have anything to do with my coaching would it?" Maxwell added in as sarcastic a tone as he could muster.

"That's completely beside the point," Ferguson said. Then he stopped, leaning back in his chair as he evened his gaze at Maxwell.

Maxwell took advantage of the silence to look around the room. The stillness of the overhead fan just above, the sterile shine of the filing cabinets, the pale sunlight coming through the window to the right, revealing a blizzard of dust particles, and the gaudy painting behind Ferguson's face—everything added to the impression of cold, efficient sterility.

"I love teaching," Maxwell said in a voice barely audible off the cold echo of the tile. "Working with kids."

"Ferguson placed his fingers together and leaned forward, again speaking in that slow, measured tone. "It takes more than just the love of teaching. A good teacher has to have some sense of community. He has to be a role model."

"You're going into your little speech now," Maxwell said.

"I don't have to take that."

"You're just like all the rest of the elected clerks," Maxwell said. "You're not human. I told you something about myself…"

"Listen."

"No, you listen. I tell you something human and you respond with one of your pat speeches. You're not a man. You're a machine."

"I can see there's no talking to you," Ferguson said.

"If you want to be rid of me, you'll have one hell of a time," Maxwell said.

"I know the law."

"Ferguson smiled. "There are unwritten laws. I don't like you, and you know what that means."

"Yeah, I know what it means."

"Life can be made very hard around here for someone who's not wanted."

"The kids want me."

"You don't work for the kids."

"Who do I work for then?" Maxwell shouted. "It sure as hell aint for you."

"You work for this community, but the problem is that you're a missing piece. You don't fit."

"Prove it."

"I see no point in continuing this discussion."

"Neither do I," Maxwell said. He got up and started out the door.

"By the way," Ferguson said, "all your senior classes will be taken from you. I'll switch you to basic ninth grade social studies. That I can do."

Maxwell had not waited for the rest. He had slammed the door so hard that he thought the glass might shatter.

But it was over now. It was December 28, 1939 and he was on a train, in the dim light of morning bound for New York, and best of all, he had his little flask. He shook it—half empty. He turned it up again, feeling it tingle his nose and water his eyes, causing the light outside to blur.

During the summer after Ferguson's conference, Maxwell had decided upon a leave of absence. It had accomplished two things. First it had assured him of respectability in both his parents' eyes. Second, it had taken away Ferguson's momentum. He had put everything on hold. He was leaving merely to further his education. He had the guaranteed option to return. The decision to take a leave of absence had come in an instant.

And what of it, thought Maxwell, who lit a cigarette against the grayness.

If it hadn't happened that way, I never would have met Frank.

Maxwell had blamed most of his misfortunes on small town life, so he got what little money he had and entered Long Island University in New York.

Three months after arrival, he dropped out. He had always dreamed of being on his own, and he found it exciting, being on the fringe of the law. He called it "his period of transition" but he knew it was far more. He began to think of his mistress in New York.

He stretched and heard voices at the other end of the car. A couple was snuggling and talking.

Must be nice, he thought oh well, Julie is waiting. I wonder what they are talking about, must be the war, it's all anyone talks about any more.

The train arrived at 7:14 in Grand Central Station. Maxwell grabbed his single bag and blended into the crowd that moved between two trains. Red caps hurried by with luggage.

At the end of the track a man stood, scratched an unsightly melanoma on his nose, and lit a cigar. The man folded a newspaper under his arm and followed at a safe distance. He watched Maxwell hail a cab, returned to the station, and made a single phone call.

By the time Maxwell arrived at the apartment Julie was gone. The place was strewn with nylons and her underthings hung on chairs, the bed, and door knobs. Maxwell knew he would see her tonight. Just the smell of her made him forget about Elaine.

Julie was twenty-three. She was five eight and had a voluptuous figure.

The beauty mole on her right cheek coupled with her dark eyes and coy smile did its number on Maxwell whenever he was around her. She fancied herself a singer and sang at the Stork Club on 89th.

Although Maxwell found her talents in bed far more developed than her talent for song, Julie held fast to her dreams. Both agreed that their relationship would never be serous, that it was one of convenience and good sex.

Maxwell's apartment was located on 116th just over a Chinese restaurant and pool hall where he worked.

Maxwell went downstairs, took two cups of coffee from the diner across the street, and went to work.

Larry had already opened up, and Maxwell went right down the steps and behind the cash register and counter.

"Look what the cat dragged in," shouted Larry, a tall man with pale features and acne-covered cheeks "Didn't expect you till tomorrow."

"What's that?" Maxwell said, pointing to a bald man in his mid-sixties who was mopping between the pool tables.

"Old man Murphy, who else," Larry said, as he counted a stack of fives.

"He stiffed us last week and Frank says he has to work it off."

"I don't see it," Maxwell said. He waved at the old man in a gesture of dismissal.

"It's what he says."

"I don't care what he says. Murphy said he would pay next week and that's good enough for me." The old man put on his hat, nodded at Maxwell, and left.

"Geez," Larry said as he looked up momentarily from his counting, "you got a soft spot somewheres. I guess in your head more than your heart. I was cutting the old man a break."

"He'll be ok. I'll take responsibility."

"That soft spot will get you burned someday. It aint good business."

"Any business is good business. Aint you heard?"

"Right, teach, whatever you say."

Larry finished his bookkkeeping and headed for the door.

"Don't let the door hit ya where the Good Lord split ya," Maxwell yelled. He burst into laughter. He was feeling better already.

As the regulars filtered in and the room filled with smoke and the balls began to pound against each other, he felt back in his element.

"Oh, by the way," Larry said, sticking his head inside the door. "Frank said to come out to his place tonight if you can. He said it was important.

Important, with a clown like you, geez, I don't know..."

The day wore on. By five o'clock the boys from the law school were drinking their set-ups and smoking their cigarettes as they played pool.

Maxwell got a kick out of them. They loved to gamble on football and the Notre Dame-Army game was coming up on New Year's day. By seven o'clock they were drunk, and Maxwell's relief showed up.

He counted the money and headed out the door to Frank Becken's house at 7;14 a man watched Maxwell ascend the basement steps of the pool hall and get into his green Chevrolet. As the car pulled away, the man, who sat in the black Ford in the law school parking lot across the street noted in a scratch pad—"exit proprietor two."

Darkness sifted down like ash on the various parked cars, the Chinese restaurant and laundry adjacent to the pool hall. The steps leading to the entrance of the apartments were occasionally occupied by tenants coming and going. But the man paid no attention to the tenants; merely scratched an unsightly mole beside his right nostril and stared at the pool hall steps.

At 10:16 a fat man in a pin-striped suit descended the steps.

He carried what looked to be a book satchel under his right arm. The man in the sedan noted on his pad- "10:14 enter first subject."

Opening the door of the car, he walked to the phone booth at the edge of the lot. As his dime trickled into the box, the agent watched a co-ed kiss her boyfriend outside the law library.

He heard the phone ring. A voice on the other end answered, "Yeah."

"Third proprietor and first subject are in," the man said. "It's started."

"Hold until relieved."

The agent put the phone back in its cradle and returned to the car.

In an hour Maxwell had arrived at Frank Becken's house, a large, white structure with a typical two seat swing on the front porch and a neatly manicured hedge bordering the front yard. He had to park several yards up the road since the small driveway and the curb in front of the house was already lined with cars.

When he knocked on the door and pushed it open, he heard the familiar accordion music coming from the back room. The furniture was stately and well-kept. Crystal figurines were arranged neatly on the mantle. The couch and matching chairs were made of the finest wood with red felt cushions, the carpet a deep green.

A woman with a light blue dress and chestnut hair greeted Maxwell.

"Come in," she said. "Here, Tommy, let me take your coat."

"Thank you, Cheryl." This was Frank Becken's wife.

"The others are in the back," she said as she walked away.

"I'm trying to get the kids down."

As he moved down the hall, he smelled sausage and strudel.

He made his way to a large room at the back of the house.

When he entered, there were shouts of welcome from the seven people, who were sitting about in the large, converted study, warming themselves by the fireplace, listening to the Victrola and talking. Two women smoked cigarettes with long holders while everyone nursed a drink made at the small bar near the window.

"What'll you have, Tommy?" Frank Becken said from behind the bar.

"Bourbon and ginger with a twist of lime."

"I knew it," Becken said. "Some people are entirely predictable."

The sight of Frank's amiable face with the plump, flushed cheeks, and the merry little eyes beneath the wire-rimmed spectacles immediately cheered Maxwell. He took his drink and sat in the chair at the corner of the room, taking in the general conversation. A lovely German immigrant named Helga sat in the chair next to him.

"So Germany owns Poland now," she said, her face beaming, "how exciting."

"Have a sandwich, dear," said the woman's escort, Mick, a burly, bald man. "Things are becoming too exciting.

England has declared war."

"Cheryl made these croissants," Frank said. "Please, everyone eat at least one or I'll have to devour them all."

"Delicious," Frau Arnold said. She had a dark complexion, and long, elegant arms. "You're the resident expert, Frank.

What will England do?"

"They will wage a war of sorts, but in my opinion an ineffective one."

"If England falls, do you see the United States entering the war?" Mick asked.

"No, not if she has any sense. Her position would be too untenable."

"I can't see this nation turning her back on the mother country," Maxwell said, at the same time laughing at his own expression and tossing his head back.

"It's good business," said Herman, the dark haired man across the room.

"You would be surprised at the amount of powerful American interests more than willing to invest in the new Reich," Frank said as he started to rise, then thought better of it. "That is the Bund's job. Neutralize the anti-German propaganda with our own. We must not be cajoled by Roosevelt into entering this war."

"Were you at the rally the other night at Sellersville?" Herman asked.

"No," Frank said as he began laughing. "But I heard about it."

"The police cordoned off three blocks and they had a hell of a time keeping the crowd back."

"Which crowd?" Frank asked.

"Not us, but the so-called patriots who had gathered to kick our asses. Anyway, when Fritz changed the map of Poland on the podium..." Everyone laughed.

"There were Polacks running everywhere," Herman exclaimed, waving his arms in the air.

Maxwell pictured the scene. He found no humor in it. He had been to one of the Bund's rallies at Madison Square Garden. He remembered how the rumors of a bomb in the Garden, meant for the Bund's speakers, had police crawling over the stage like ants. And although most of the Bund regarded the bomb threat as a scare tactic from Mayor La Guardia, the anticipation of imminent violence had given the speeches an edge of tension, which had constantly rippled through the crowd.

"Have you been to a rally, Tommy?" Helga asked, straightening her back against the chair.

"Yes, once. The one at the Garden." Again everyone laughed.

"What did you think?" Mick asked.

"Honestly?" Maxwell said. "I found those fat men on the podium, wearing uniforms and saluting this spider on a flag ridiculous."

"Tommy's like a lot of people," "Frank said with an uneasy smile, "scared of spiders."

"The uniform commands respect in Poland, sir, I assure you," Mick said, his mouth now tight.

"It reminded me of a Ku Klux Klan meeting," Maxwell said, who insisted on finishing what he had started. "It's like my father said. They look like grown men, playing Halloween."

Mick took a quick step towards Maxwell.

"Easy, Mick," Frank said. "We're merely having a discussion. Everyone is entitled to an opinion in this house."

"Don't get hot under the collar. I'm trying to help.

Ceremony and militarism mean nothing to Americans." Maxwell shrugged and laughed.

"Jeepers," Frank said, "little Tommy's been talking to his daddy again."

"Shove it, Frank," Maxwell replied. "You can leave my father out of it. You guys are men, just like the Americans, the Germans, everyone, and men have the talent for one thing. Men kill. Just like yourselves, they find all sorts of grand reasons for killing, but the result is always the same. I support the Bund only because they're the only group in this country who's actively speaking for complete neutrality in this huge sarcasm of a war."

"They say the Poles started the war with their border violations," Mick said, who appeared extremely nervous and was now standing again, leaning over Helga.

"That is subject to debate," Maxwell said.

"Some people say the SS drubbed up the border violations," Helga said.

Maxwell was more interested in Helga's breasts, which were straining against her black gown.

"Jewish lies," Mick yelled as Helga's breasts bounced with alarm. "Don't you know propaganda when you hear it? If you believe that, Helga, you believe the Dies Committee too."

Helga puckered her lips, sat back, and sipped coffee.

"All this talk about the Jews," Maxwell said as he swallowed a finger sandwich in one bite. "Do you really believe all that?"

"I admit it's a little embarrassing," Frank agreed, as he handed Frau Arnold a fresh drink. "But with anything you have to take the good with the bad. But you're right, Tommy, the Jewish position needs softening."

"The way of the Jew is leading this nation to Communism," Mick shouted.

"Bullshit," shot Maxwell. "Racist statements only detract from what the Bund must stand for. The Bund is an American organization."

"Tell that to the Dies Committee."

"Kuhn has said so himself a hundred times....."

"Is Kuhn betraying us?" Helga asked.

This brought a rampage of talk at the woman, as the conversation shifted to the charges, recently brought against the president of the German American Bund, Fritz Kuhn. The Dies Committee, which had been formed to investigate whether or not the Bund was a Nazi spy organization, had failed to gather any substantial evidence. The fact that Fritz Kuhn had known Hitler in Munich in 1923 and had visited him in 1936 failed to produce concrete evidence that the Bund was an extension of Nazism. Kuhn had continually insisted that the Bund was an American organization.

"The great land of the free and the home of the brave seems very, shall we say, 'flexible' when it comes to the almighty legal system," Frank said.

"Tell Cheryl to fix strudel next time," Mick said with a yawn. "And since we're on the subject......"

"What subject?" Maxwell asked with mock seriousness.

"Does this party have a goddamned agenda or what?"Helga laughed.

"The F.B.I have seized their papers so they can fabricate their lies," Frank said. "And I think Cheryl knows how you feel about her strudel."

In late October the F.B.I. had broken into the downtown headquarters of the Bund and seized funds and certain documents. From these documents there had arisen charges that Fritz Kuhn had misappropriated 5,641 dollars of the Bund's funds.

"I don't care what you say, Mick," Helga said, who was as determined to inflame everyone as Maxwell. "It's bothersome to hear that our leader is spending our money on his women."

When everyone began speaking at once, Frank stood up.

"Helga, you're a pretty thing," he began. "But you are like the rest of these ignorant Americans. You actually believe in the infallibility of the legal system. You believe you have rights, my dear. You have no idea what's going on."

The conversation centered on the incident recently reported in the local papers. Two infiltrators of the Bund testified in court against Kuhn, stating he had used the mis-appropriated money to buy furniture for his mistress.

"He's right, Helga," Maxwell said. "In this country when the authorities want you out, they tag you as immoral.

I've been so labeled for quite a while now," comically raising his eyebrows, Groucho Marx-like.

Helga laughed, obviously charmed. "You don't seem so bad."

"Oh yes," Maxwell said, with a wink. "It's all in the files, a morals charge. The good Christians will go for it every time. There's nothing they like better than sex scandals. It reaffirms their superiority over the rest of the world."

Helga threw her shoulder to her cheek. "Oooh, so you are capable of a sex scandal," she said with a teasing smile.

"The F.B.I. plays it smart," Frank said. "They infiltrate the Bund with an elevator operator and a petty bartender, illegally seize some documents, then have the two pimps complain that Kuhn is betraying the membership."

"They're succeeding nicely," Mick said, who suddenly found himself agreeing with everyone.

"It's the American way," Maxwell said. "They'll tie up the Bund with adverse publicity concerning this hoax of a trial and the populace will lap it up, moral turpitude I think they call it. Believe me, I speak from experience."

"Tell me more about your experience," Helga suggested.

"Enough, Helga," Mick said.

"Hitler's regime is the only nation that officially observes the laws of evolution," Mick continued. "The fit will survive and dominate, and only the fit deserve to survive."

"And suddenly only Germans know where a millennia of millions of years are taking us," shot Maxwell. "What hogwash."

The conversation went on in fits and starts for another hour.

At midnight all of the guests had left. Maxwell had started to leave when Frank stopped him at the front door.

"Don't leave. I told Larry to tell you."

"What?" Maxwell said, turning to face Frank.

"I need to talk to you. Wait here. Fix yourself another drink if you like. Let me say goodnight to Cheryl and I'll be right back out."

Maxwell wandered into the kitchen and poured himself a glass of white wine. He went back to the study and sat by the dying embers of the fire. The fire reminded him of his conversation with Elaine, but he shook the feeling off.

Frank entered the room behind him. He held a steaming cup of coffee.

"Can I fix you a cup?" Frank asked.

"No thanks."

"So what did you think of Frau Duncan?"

"Frau Duncan?"

"Helga, dummy."

Maxwell started to answer when he saw Cheryl enter the room.

She wore a light blue night gown and her chestnut hair hung half way across her face. Her eyes were swollen as she apparently had just awakened.

"The baby's crying again," she said. "How long are you two going to be?"

"I'll be in a while," Frank said. "We've got something to discuss."

"There's always something to discuss," she said as she moved down the hall.

The thin blue figure of Cheryl in the nightgown gave Maxwell a feeling of tranquility. Was that why he gravitated to Frank?

He admitted to himself that he envied his life.

"Look, I feel like I'm in the way here," Maxwell said.

"Nonsense," Frank said, who took off his spectacles and briefly rubbed his eyes. When he replaced the glasses, his eyes took a stern, fixed gaze.

"We have problems," he said.

"What do you mean?" Maxwell asked.

"What can you tell me about this new guy, Mark?"

"Nothing. I barely know him. You hired him."

Maxwell was normally in the pool hall on Tuesday nights.

Three weeks earlier Mark had filled in and overseen the regular crap game in the back room.

Frank began rubbing his palms together. "Yeah, I know I hired him," he said. "I was hoping you had gotten to know him."

"He works nights," Maxwell said. "What else is there to know?"

"He mentioned the Bund meetings the other day in passing," Frank said, again removing his glasses.

"So?"

"Did you mention the meetings to him?"

"Hell no, I've barely talked to the guy."

"He's a pimp then."

"What are you talking about?"

"A government informer."

Maxwell laughed. "You've been hanging around these cloak and dagger types too much. What makes you think that?"

"No one in the center knows about the Bund meetings here but you. If you haven't told him, then he knows from someone else."

"I don't know, Frank," Maxwell said in a mocking tone.

"Is the game on tonight?"

"You know it is," Maxwell replied. "Listen, Frank, aren't you getting skiddish? The government doesn't give a damn about us. So we print and distribute a few tracts?"

"Things are changing," Frank said. "Over the last week I've been followed."

"Let them follow. What can they do?" Maxwell asked.

"You aren't really that naive, are you?" Frank said.

"They'll padlock our place, throw you in jail for one. You do realize our activities are illegal."

"So what do you want me to do?"

"Fire the son of a bitch first thing tomorrow."

"Consider it done," Maxwell said. "What reason do I give him?"

"Don't give a reason. Just do it."

Maxwell put down his drink. "I don't operate that way," he said. "I've been treated that way before."

"So have I," Frank said, thrusting his glasses angrily onto his nose. "Just do it. Governments are known to take definite stances towards organizations like ours."

"Can the corn, Frank. There's such a thing as freedom of speech."

Frank burst into laughter. "Please. The right doesn't exist. The only freedoms you have are those that step on nobody's toes."

"Whatever you say."

"By the way," Frank said, nudging Maxwell with his elbow.

"Back to Helga, attractive breasts, eh?"

"She's lovely," Maxwell said. "But her dainty talk about war— Christ."

"Look...."

"I'm getting sleepy. Got to go."

"How can you talk the way you do? You've been in the Bund....."

"I've come to a few meetings," Maxwell broke in. "That's all. I'm a pacifist. That's the only attraction I have to your precious Bund."

"You've been talking with your father again."

"What the hell you know about my father?"

"What you've told me. Don't you see that there are causes in the world that are worth giving up a leg for?"

"Are you speaking of my father?" Maxwell asked.

"Only as a general example. What if your father had been singled out to pay the debts of the world, as so many of my own relatives have in Germany over the last twenty years?

The French and the British were responsible for the last war, not Germany. You know the truth."

"Listen..."

"I agree that your father's sacrifice was a joke, but believe me, Tommy, there are things worth fighting for.

When people are oppressed, they have the right to raise up their backs. Hitler's the first leader with the genius and the guts to do it, without compromise," his voice rising with emotion.

"You're rolling, Frank. He has compromised pretty definitely with the Russians."

"All right, but you get the point. We're odd ducks in this country, Tommy. We have no rights. You'll soon see that.

You of all people ought to know. You told me how you lost your teaching job. Where were your rights then? No sir, only the mainstream robots have rights. The right to be dehumanized."

Maxwell put on his coat and lit a cigarette. "I've got to go," he said. "I'm keeping you from Cheryl."

Frank walked as far as the front porch with him.

"Listen," he said. "Mark is fired, right?"

"Yeah, sure," Maxwell said, feeling a sudden need to get away.

Frank grabbed Maxwell's arm. "Look my friend," he said, moving within inches of Maxwell's face, "you're one of the few people in the world I can trust; we have differences, but we're more alike than you think. What you have to understand is that with what is coming, there'll be no sitting out. You'll have to take a stand. You may need to change the nature of your activities."

"What are you talking about?"

"A number of us may have to go underground for a time.

Some will go to Canada. I need a courier, a man to transfer people and sums of money. Need a job?"

"You got to be kidding," Maxwell laughed.

"It'll pay quite handsomely."

"Hey, Frank," Maxwell said, grabbing his friend's arm.

"Get hold of yourself. You ought to be in the pictures."

The two men shook hands and Maxwell left.

It started to snow. Flurries swirled and disappeared in the headlights of the car. Maxwell turned on the radio and listened to the slow music.

During the last moments with Frank he had felt overwhelmed by all the conflicting ideas within him. He found it odd that he had begun to agree with Frank to the point that he now found himself.

He felt that old feeling—a feeling that in the last few years became more frequent, and ever stronger—that is, he was haunted by a cramped sensation—all the people, furniture, ideas, too much—he was happier now, on the road, in motion, between, away from family and friends, undefined and contemplating only the sights and sounds of his motion, feeling the life of the engine under his foot—hypnotized by the swirling snowflakes, caught in their furious whirlings, in an illusion of stillness, aswarm in the beams of his headlights.

By the time he arrived at 116th Street the snow was slanting down in earnest. He parked his car on the curb just in front of the quaint Chinese restaurant next to the pool hall. Above the restaurant were the windows of his apartment building. A soft, orange glow shone in the end room directly over the restaurant. She was there.

With difficulty he headed down the stairs into the pool hall.

In the parking lot across the street the two policemen noted the time on their scratch pad—"enter proprietor two." They watched him descend the steps.

As Maxwell entered the pool room, the sight was typical of all Tuesday nights. Four men were occupied on the tables and Mark was leaning back behind the counter with his feet propped up as he read a comic book. A cigarette smoldered in the ashtray.

"Everything o.k.?" Maxwell said, as he saw the feet come down and Mark go for his comb, nervously combing back his brown hair while he talked.

"Yeah, sure, how was your trip?"

"Fine," Maxwell said, as he walked behind the counter into the back room. The smoke was thick around the circle of shouting men and three women, their earrings dangling and shining off the glaring overhead light.

Maxwell noticed Martino tipping a flask as he wiped the sweat from his forehead.

"Oh hell," Maxwell said. "Mike's on a run; he's drinking the long gulps."

The chatter and sound of dice on concrete stopped momentarily to acknowledge Maxwell's presence.

Normally, Maxwell would watch for an hour or so, but he could not forget Julie. He figured she would welcome him back right. It had been all he could do to walk past the apartment, knowing she was there.

He walked back into the hall, saw Mark with his feet propped up again, and headed back out. He told himself that nothing was going to happen tonight, and he didn't have the stomach to fire Mark. Frank hired him, he thought, let Frank fire him. He seems like an alright Joe to me.

When he got to the top of the steps, he felt the butterflies return to his stomach. His thoughts turned entirely to Julie.

"Damn," said Detective Tipps as he watched Maxwell exit the hall and enter the apartment building. "Missed that one." He scrawled angrily on the pad, "Exit proprietor two."

"Who says?" his partner said.

"We can't get him up there," Tipps said.

"The hell we can't. He ran out of the pool hall and we pursued."

They laughed. "Thirty minutes to go," Tipps said into the radio.

The two squad cars and paddy wagon acknowledged.

"What are we waiting for?"

"Just seeing if more fish arrive," Tipps said.

The apartment was just as Maxwell had left it, the clothes and nylons strewn about and except for the soft light on the dresser near the window, completely dark. In the soft light Maxwell could see Julie.

She sat in front of the dresser in a sheer bathrobe. One long, elegant leg rose up out of the robe, her heel planted on the dresser. A slight turn of her head indicated she had heard Maxwell enter, but one would have had to have watched closely to notice it. As she gently ran a razor down her upper thigh, slowly disposing of the lather in a small bowl of water on the dresser, the red neon of the laundry flashed over her smooth face. She wore only a bra and panties under the robe. She had a beautiful figure. Her breasts protruded and strained at the bra and her hips were in perfect proportion to her thin waist. As Maxwell approached, she turned her head lazily and smiled, displaying her even teeth. Maxwell loved her mouth. There was the slightest excess of flesh on her lips, and her habit of slowly sucking them into her mouth and releasing them before speaking always set him aflame.

"How was your trip?" she said as she yawned and dipped the razor.

He leaned down and kissed her. "It was fine. Here, let me do that for you."

He took the razor and gently ran it up her thigh. "So how was Elaine?" she said, her smile revealing a hint of anticipation.

"Her same old traditional self."

She laughed in that gesture of abandonment that he loved, tossing her head slightly to the side, causing her hair to bounce slightly.

"Poor Tommy," she said, her eyes half closing with the light movement of the gentle razor. "He had what every man dreams of, a virgin, and he don't even want it."

Maxwell smiled. Their relationship had always been this way. They spoke openly of any affairs they might have and continued to maintain what they had established from the first, that their relationship was a temporary one.

A horn blew outside. Maxwell noticed the red light playing off her skin.

"Does that feel good, baby?" he asked.

She lit a cigarette, inhaled, and formed an "o" with her mouth as she slowly blew out.

"Ummm, you know it does."

Maxwell looked down at her panties as he dipped the razor and ran it up again, this time on the last vein of lather, bringing the instrument up between her legs.

"You know what my director said to me today?" she said.

"What did he say?"

"He said I projected well."

"He said that?"

"Ummmmm, yeah, that's what he said."

"What else did he say?" Now Maxwell was running the back side of the razor up the entire length of her leg.

"That's all. You think he was lying?"

"Probably."

"Listen," he said, gently taking the razor and lifting one side of her panties up next to her thigh and seeing the black hair leap out, her beautifully full bush revealing only a hint of the pink lips beneath. "Don't you want to shave that?"

She slowly put the cigarette out. She put her other leg down and with a lazy motion slightly spread her legs. A slight smile played around her mouth.

"You think it needs it?" she said.

"It's up to you."

She looked down at herself, then directly into his eyes.

"You might cut me."

"Yeah, exactly what I intended," he said. "But not with this." He threw the razor aside as he flipped off the light.

She jumped into his arms, her open mouth accepting his.

He put his hands over her breasts, slipped the robe over her shoulders and unclasped her bra. She pulled her mouth back, as she felt his hands moving her huge breasts up and down in the darkness, finally his warm mouth over one of her stiff nipples. She began panting. "So what are you going to cut me with?" she managed to say.

He swept her off the floor and began stumbling over the clothing and shoes which were strewn on the floor towards the old bed at the other end of the apartment.

She laughed. "I must say that Elaine didn't do a very good job."

"To hell with her," he said, as he dropped her on the bed and slid down her panties and began lowering his zipper.

They made love in the usual fashion. At first slowly tantalizing each other, he with his mouth between her legs, then flipping over on his back as she reciprocated, her fleshy mouth stretching as her flicking tongue did its work.

This last thing always excited her, and she would get on top, slowly straddling him at first, then moving her hips in a lazy, circular fashion, and finally finishing with bouncing abandonment, finally screaming as they both reached their peaks together.

They lay for a time, he kissing the nape of her neck and smelling his own breath against her moist skin.

"Why is it that you're so good?" she said.

"You make me good."

"It isn't true. I've had plenty of men and none like you.

Why do you have to be so good?"

"What do you mean by that?" She didn't answer, but he knew what she meant. He felt the same way. They were going in different directions, he told himself. He was going nowhere and she was striving towards that singular career.

He fell asleep.

He had slept for only a short time when a sound awoke him. He staggered up in the darkness. Then he saw the flashing red light in the window.

He ran to the window. Below were two police cars and a paddy wagon. Mr. Harvey was being helped into the van as the black woman in the red dress was occupying two officers.

"Let go of me," she screamed as she kicked at one officer.

Mark was leaning against a streetlight, talking to another policeman.

Maxwell had seen enough. He bolted for his clothes in the darkness.

"Where are you going?" Julie said as she sat up and rubbed her eyes.

"We got company," he said as he struggled with a shoe.

He quickly pulled his shirt over his arms without buttoning it and grabbed his overcoat. He ran to the window.

The last woman was being ushered into the van. Mark was still talking to the one officer while two others ascended the apartment steps.

"Don't turn on the light," Maxwell said as he ran to the door.

"I've heard of screwing and running, but this is ridiculous," she said.

He closed the door behind him and ran on tiptoe to the end of the hall and around the corner. He paused for a second. He heard the feet on the steps. He heard the first knock. He was lucky. They were starting with the first apartment. They would have to check two more before getting to his. He tiptoed to the soiled window, which he raised with a gentle rattle of glass. He hoisted himself out onto the black fire escape which led down behind the building. No longer worrying about noise, he pounded down the iron steps in the darkness, finally jumping six feet over the rail into the garbage-strewn alley below. After running three blocks down, he cut between the shoe store and the Golden Bough Restaurant and into the pale light of Lenox Avenue.

The snow slanted into his face.

Finally satisfied that he was not being followed, he cut into the Wine Cellar, an all night bar. His feet were cold.

He had dressed so fast that he had forgotten to put on socks.

He put a dime into a phone near the entrance, dialed a number, paused and spoke.

"Frank, I'm at the Wine Cellar, get your ass down here now."

Outside, the snowflakes—perfectly crystalline in form, symmetrical in their random order, intricate in their myriad composition—whirled furiously through the orange halo of lamplight, in happy motion— exploding onto the pavement below.

And the train roars through the darkness. I decide tosleep in the sound of the diesels, surrendering to the rocking car, to the sounds of wheels, exploding on the rails.

CHAPTER 2

Maxwell loved Ottawa.

He had been the first one up this morning, the first among his four friends, who had all agreed that a three day hunting and camping trip would do everyone good, the first among the gray haze of dawn to rustle, start the fire blazing under the pyramid of wood, and the first to check the trout lines, which had yielded breakfast, and after attending to the breaking of camp, the first to start on the trail upwards, taking the point, again tracking the elk herd they had trailed for three days, leaving the remnants of the camp fire below twisting up like a blue vine.

Behind him, fighting the uphill trek, Frank Becken walked, his brown squares on his morning jacket huge now below his great jowls. Even from the height from which Maxwell viewed him, Becken's face streamed sweat and shone crimson like a small, bobbing radish. Looking back, Maxwell smiled. He had Frank out of his element. Becken, who had so guided Maxwell's own life in the last year, now strained against the hill, straining for the question that both he and Maxwell had long expected.

The raid at the Varsity had chased Maxwell from New York.

Instead of becoming a courier for dissidents, Maxwell had become one of the dissidents himself. And although he faced only a meager charge of running an illegal gambling operation, he had no intention of facing any charge. His life, he decided, was complicated enough as it was.

So Maxwell had been relegated to what was called the Ottawa lodge, a huge log cabin which easily housed eight or better in the midst of the Canadian mountains. His comrades were three: Richard Thibadeaux, a Cajun explosives expert, just out of Hoboken Prison, Gabriel Coss, a disenchanted Puerto Rican stevedore, and David Brouse, an orphaned socialist from up state New York with a sharp wit and teeth that were rotten down to their little, dark nubs.

Earlier in the morning, Maxwell had said with his mock New York accent, "Geez, guys, one look at you fucks and I know there ain't no hope for me. Frank wants to ask me a question. I wonder what it could be?"

"Cut the bimbo bullshit, Tommy," Coss had said. "You know what he wants."

Thibadeaux jogged the steep trail to catch Maxwell. Tommy had not turned around, but had kept his eyes straight ahead on the trail above, only knowing of Richard's presence by the feel of hot breath on the back of his right elbow and by the pungent smell of body odor.

"Hey man," Thibadeaux said, with a wide horse grin. "How you making?"

"Doing fine."

"Why don't you slow the pace? Ooowee, look at Frank, man. He be dyin' you don't slow down."

Thibadeaux was a good four inches taller than Tommy. He had dry, well-combed black hair, dark skin with a yellowish tint, and a large mouth with big teeth.

"If he wants to slow down, why doesn't he say so?"

Thibadeaux laughed. "You know him, man, he proud. Look at him, babe, he be dyin', him."

"He suggested this damn trip so he could ask me something," Maxwell said as without missing a step he pounded out a cigarette and lit it. "If he's got to set me up for it, it must be a hell of a question."

"You know what he be wantin'."

"Yeah? And what's that?"

"Word is we be moving to Nordland, down in Jersey."

"Tell Frank we'll stop in fifteen minutes."

Thibadeaux stopped, lit his own cigarette, and waited for Becken to catch up.

Alternating bands of light and shadow played off Maxwell's face. He kept his eyes to the summit, a good three hundred feet above. He was ready to get to the top, ready to see open space, more mountains, the woods on the upward trail were too close now, making Maxwell feel claustrophobic.

Nordland, Maxwell thought, so that's it. He remembered a vague reference Becken had made to Coss last week about a Camp Nordland in New Jersey. Coss had been discussing the imminent east coast shipping strike, that was being organized by John Lewis's C.I.O.

"I often talk to Lewis myself," Becken had said. "The labor problems going on in the C.I.O. will work right along for what we are training for at Nordland."

"Kiss my ass, man," Gabe had said. "You tell me the F.B.I. ain't going to know who's behind it when ships start blowing up in their bays? Labor, my ass."

"Enough said," Becken had said.

Maxwell laughed to himself as he shifted his back pack, feeling the butt of his Winchester in his ribs.

So this is what it's come to, he thought. I knew it.

Ever since Roosevelt had signed the Lend-Lease agreement with Britain, everyone in the Bund had been enraged. It was evident that the President was trying to get the United States into the war in order to end the Depression. And although Maxwell knew that Germany would never declare war on the United States (since there would be no strategy for such a war), he also knew that Lend-Lease could not be tolerated.

Britain was on the verge of collapse, but all concerned knew what an American supply line would mean.

As he reached the top of the hill, Maxwell noticed that many of the small virgin trees to the right had been bent or broken. Three piles of fresh excrement lay beside one of the broken trees. The elk herd had been through here yesterday, probably heading for the water of LaConte

Lake below. More than anything Maxwell had wanted to go far enough in to see Lake LaConte, which originated from fresh water springs.

He had enjoyed his respite from the city. And although he missed Julie and had plans to see her, he relished the feeling the Canadian mountains had given him. They made him remember, made him feel just as the Smokies did at home.

How many times he had been on hunting expeditions with his father in those mountains he could not count. Maxwell remembered his admiration for his father in those days, that same father who had taught him how to track, shoot, and field dress a deer, and who had, even with his leg stiff and dragging along the trail, never missed a trip and never fallen behind, never feigned fatigue.

The summit yawned before him now, the trees giving way to egg-white light.

"Tommy say we stopping, oh, in 'bout fifteen minutes or so," Thibadeaux said, as Frank passed him.

"To hell with that," Becken said, his half-stooped figure continuing on ahead. "I'll die in fifteen minutes." Brouse laughed behind Thibadeaux. "This was your bright idea, Frank."

"Don't remind me."

"Hey, babe, we all know why you come all the way up here this week. If you want Maxwell with us at Nordland, just ax him. You don't gotta have to agree to shit like this. Hell, I'm a city boy too, me."

"How can you run your mouth as much as you do and still breathe up this fucking hill?" Frank said.

Thibadeaux is right, Becken thought. No use coddling Maxwell. Just ask him and accept his answer. That damned Ullman. It's his fault.

Becken and Ullman had talked after their meeting at the Astoria with representatives from the C.I.O., General Motors, I.G. Farben, and International Telegraph and Telephone. The prospects of business in the new Nazi Europe had been the reason for the meeting. Ullman had answered questions concerning the war in the Atlantic. Of special concern was whether or not the Germans had built enough U boats and how they planned to cope with Lend Lease when there was a standing order in the German Navy not to fire on American vessels.

After the meeting, Ullman still had enough energy to scrutinize Becken's end of the operation.

Does death start by feeling like there is this huge bubble in my chest? Becken thought, as he felt a sharp pang also in the back of his leg.

His ever-present flatulence had worked itself up from his stomach, in the form of heartburn, and in what Becken pictured to be a huge, pressurized bubble, now pressed outward in his chest.

He remembered how he and Ullman had argued that night, how when they had again come upon the name of "Maxwell," and Ullman had insisted he be recruited as a sub-agent, Becken had burst into laughter.

"I could see his face now if I asked him," Becken had said.

"His background fits perfectly."

"Not compared to anyone we have at Nordland."

"You're wrong," Ullman had said as he had stretched his fingers and closed his small eyes.

"If Maxwell can be trusted, he is the perfect candidate. Do you think he agrees to be a courier only for money?"

"He is a pacifist, that's all."

"Precisely. And you think that because he is not a criminal, he cannot work for us? You could not be more wrong. It is necessary that we hire specialists, a necessary evil.

But the most effective agents come from the mainstream. Men with a void in their lives. They will act out their loyalty in order to fill the void. Maxwell is the perfect candidate for Operation Kaninchen."

Kaninchen was German for "rabbit", and Becken wished he could now spot a rabbit, any excuse to stop and rest.

If I die on this goddamned trail, Cheryl will never forgive me, he thought, as his eyes swooned upwards to where Maxwell stood. Although his wife and kids had left him a month ago and moved to Connecticut with her mother, Becken still thought of them as his and had no doubts they would reconcile.

His foot slipped on a rock, and he temporarily lost his balance, the solitary figure of Maxwell above, vibrating and swaying athwart the sunlight at the summit.

As Maxwell waited among the waist-high rhododendron and mountain laurel, he drank in the view before him. Giant shadows of cloud ran fleetingly over the mountains' folds below. Beyond the next mountain lay Lake LaConte, its blue surface reflecting the bright, summer sunshine in dancing jewels of light.

While he waited for the others, Maxwell pulled from his left shirt pocket the letter Julie had sent him from his father.

And indeed as he read, nothing ever surprised him. He told himself that even before he had seen it, he had already guessed the letter's content, almost to the word.

Dear son,

We are writing you at the post office box you gave us two years ago. God only knows whether you will get this. We do not know where you are and you have made no effort to contact us.

Actions speak louder than words.

You must know that you have broken mine and your mother's hearts.

Maxwell heard the wind in the mountain laurel, its leaves glistening with sunlight and movement as the rhododendron's petals clapped together.

When in his youth, the mountain laurel would bloom in the Spring back home, Maxwell remembered his mother's putting two or three of the white blooms in her light hair. Her eyes had shown with happiness then, not to be compared with the spark of bitterness and resignation which silently grew in them over the years. Common to good Christian women, he thought.

If it is your professional situation that keeps you from coming home, please reconsider.

I heard about your situation from Reeves Ferguson and am working in your behalf. Some of our friends at the church have offered their help when and if you decide to return.

Wisps of cloud moved like specters between the great mountains' folds.

Come back and face your problems. Don't be a coward. A man faces things like a man. A coward runs away.

I know you are against the war. If you are worried about being drafted, come home.

Re-join the church and declare yourself a conscientious objector. Your refusal to enter the church since that day when you were fourteen is stupid pride. Use what is at your disposal.

Maxwell had not read the rest. Before arriving at the section of his father's letters that always read, "With all our love," he wadded the letter quickly and threw it into the space before him, seeing the wind catch it and sending it whirling downwards into the trees.

How his father had always misjudged him! Why did he continually ignore the fact that Maxwell no longer considered himself a Seventh Day Adventist, not since that day? The Adventists' history had always been one of conscientious objection to all war, a premise which Tommy's father, along with other Adventists in Murphy, had ignored with the outbreak of the First World War.

He looked below him on the trail. How ridiculous was the contradiction that among the whispers and hints of his surroundings, he was made aware that there were men, whom he did not know, who were shaping his path, men who, for whatever reasons, believed in his abilities, while those with whom he was more familiar expressed only doubt.

"A coward," Maxwell allowed himself to say aloud, as Frank Becken pushed past Richard Thibadeaux and with his forearms jiggling, emerged out of the shadows of the trail below.

Maxwell prepared himself for the question that Frank would ask him. He already knew the question; had already formed the answer.

"Hey, pandejo, slow the fuck up," Coss yelled from below.

CHAPTER 3

March 22, 1941

The short man hunched over the wheel of the taxi cab. He looked at his watch. He was hungry. He had not eaten all day; he could never eat on the day of a "kill." His alert eyes darted up to the rear view mirror. The other taxi was behind him; his partner's engine still running--the white smoke rising up behind the cab.

Again the cabby put the binoculars to his eyes. The night was cold. Spring had not come to New York. The usual stream of people was moving in front of the Taft Hotel on Broadway and Times Square. The cabby watched the paper boy on the curb and again looked at his watch.

The short man inhaled and exhaled with a long sigh. He saw the cream-colored wheel fog as his breath hit it. It had to look like an accident. He was in a society that still recognized the rules.

He felt the vibrations of the idling engine tingle up in his hands and arms. He loved Fords.

How long he had waited he could not say. Leaning his head back in a tired motion, he lit another cigarette and looked up at the concrete skyline.

He glanced at his watch. The target was a full six minutes late now. Or had the paper boy missed his cue?

The light changed at the crosswalk.

The boy, who held the papers aloft while he shouted over the adjacent stream of people on the sidewalk, dropped the bundle of papers in both his right and left hands. As he stooped down to pick up the papers, the man in the black overcoat walked past him to the intersection.

The cabby flicked his lights off, then on, and waited until the cab behind him did the same.

There was no time to lose. He threw his cab into gear and gathered speed. His timing had to be perfect. When he was within a block of the intersection, he floored the accelerator.

The cab lurched forward.

The pedestrian, apparently hearing the engine's roar, and seeing the sudden headlights bearing down on him, squared off, facing the cab. Just as the cab neared, he leapt to the left.

The cab had only clipped him, knocking him in a spinning pirouette onto the pavement.

A woman screamed from the sidewalk as the first cab sped away. The man was reaching for his hat and trying to hobble up when the second engine, as if in echo to the first, was upon him. The second cab burned no lights and as the man was unable to rise, pathetically holding an arm over his eyes, the cab struck him viciously, the back tire, crushing his head.

The two cabs raced from the intersection. Three people ran out to help the pedestrian. The paperboy picked up his papers and walked away.

The crumpled brim hat, which lay beside the body, was soaked in blood.

CHAPTER 4

November 16, 1941

Seven months later Frank Becken pulled into the wooden garage behind his house. As he neared the back door, a shiver ran down his back. He put the key into the tumblers and entered the dark kitchen. He paused in the darkness, smelling the familiar odor of his house and listening for any foreign sounds. He turned on the light. He went from room to room, turning on lights until every light in the house was on.

Mere paranoia, he continually told himself, as he got to the front living room, which looked bare since his wife had taken the furniture.

He headed to his study in the back of the house, sat down at his desk and got out his cognac. It seemed the only thing that would calm his nerves. He poured the first glass and threw it down his throat, poured a second and took a slow sip.

Ever since the murder of Erich von Ullman, Frank Becken had begun to fear for his life. Only an hour after he had met with Ullman at the Taft Hotel on the evening of March 21, 1941, Becken had heard of his friend's death. Becken had been at Child's Restaurant when the waiter brought the phone to his table.

Bruno Wilhelm had been on the other end. "Ullman is dead.

Run down in front of the Taft by two taxi cabs."

Becken had not spoken. He had merely hung up the phone and rushed home.

Although the death was described as a hit-and-run mishap in the papers, members of the Bund knew differently. British agents had engineered Ullman's assassination. Becken had believed that he was next. Since Ullman's death, he had lost fifteen pounds. He had become a bundle of nerves. He was nearly relieved that Cheryl had taken the kids to her mother's in Connecticut.

At least they are safe, he thought, as he gulped his second drink. He looked at his watch--8:14. Bruno Wilhelm was to arrive in twenty minutes.

With his second drink he had regained his courage. He leaned back and took a deep breath.

"Fortunes of war," he said aloud.

He remembered Ullman's words that night at the Waldorf Astoria: "Britain will be dispensed with in a matter of weeks."

Things had not worked out that way.

In early 1941 the war had raged over the skies and in the waters of the English Channel. The German forces were frustrated on two major counts. First, they had not produced proper landing craft for a land invasion in England. Second, the British had developed radar. Luftwaffe planes could be tracked within one hundred miles of English air space and their courses determined early. English Spitfires intercepted them before they knew what had hit them.

If Hitler had allowed Admiral Karl Doenitz the one hundred extra U boats he had requested, Britain would certainly have been lost. Heady from his quick seizure of power in Germany and his lightning conquests of Czechoslovakia, Austria, Poland, Denmark, Norway, and France, Hitler concentrated on the war on the ground and in the air. It was a critical mistake, nearly as mis-spent as was to be his fanatical thrust eastward into Russia.

Meanwhile, the German-American Bund carried on its clandestine propaganda with unabated fury.

It was almost 9:30 when a stout, burly man of forty entered Frank Becken's house. He did not leave until 11:16 that evening. The man's name was Bruno Wilhelm. The two men sat in Becken's study, drank cognac, and talked incessantly. By ten o'clock Becken was drunk.

"Why are you so damned edgy?" Wilhelm said, his suntanned

forehead deeply lined above two prominent lobes above the bushy eyebrows. "The Addis Fritsch letters come to you, so what?"

"You don't understand," Becken said. "I directed the contact in Lisbon to cease communications to me."

"How did you code it?"

"I told you once," Becken said as he slurred his words. "I said that my business is suffering from a lack of cash.

I went on to say that they should not send mail to me again, but to contact my relatives who were doing better."

"Did you mention the Ullman murder?" asked Wilhelm.

"Of course I mentioned it," Frank said, standing up and jerking his body with disgust. "I mailed the letter to Herchenhaun. I stated plainly, 'Larry dead. Killed in accident on Times Square.'"

"This cognac is delicious," Wilhelm said, as he poured the bottle into his shot glass. "So what's the worry? Your instructions were followed. The coded instructions for Operation Kaninchen are coming to me."

"Go over the details once more," Becken said.

Wilhelm sighed. He had been over the plan a half dozen times in the last hour.

"Okay, but this is the last time. Kaninchen will take place in three distinct places--Amagansett, New York, Ponte Vedra, Florida, and Morgan City, Louisiana. Near all three of these places German U boats will land their contingent of agents. We will receive them and get them to safe houses.

At the landing in Louisiana, not only will we receive agents, but two Americans will be picked up and taken to France for further training."

Becken held up a hand. "Have you chosen the two candidates?" he asked.

"Not yet."

Bruno Wilhelm was in charge of training at Camp Nordland in New Jersey. Operation Kaninchen was a full six months away, and according to Wilhelm, the trainees were far from ready.

"How is Maxwell working out?"

Wilhelm gulped down his drink and shrugged. "One day he shows a great enthusiasm for learning, the next day I expect him to quit."

"He's a good man," Becken answered. "He's come a long way, don't you think?"

"He's more interested in his writing for the Advocate than for sabotage," Wilhelm said, gesturing with his large hand.

"I want you to stay on him," Becken replied. "He's one of your top candidates."

"Okay, so everything is going according to plan."

"Except for the Fritsch letters," Becken said as he shifted in his seat. "It just doesn't make sense."

The name of Addis Fritsch was well-known among inner circles of German espionage. It was the alias of SS commander Reinhardt Heydrich, the infamous butcher of Prague.

"So Heydrich is in contact with you," Wilhelm said casually. "Has he mentioned Kaninchen?"

"Not directly. He doesn't have to," Frank said. "The references are indirect, but with the British getting inside us like you know they are, I'm afraid of a leak."

Bruno moved his glass around the table in small circles.

"If Japan pulls the U.S. into the war, the British will be the least of our worries."

"But that's not what really disturbs me," Frank said, leaning forward. "Fritsch or Heydrich is SD. He is head of SS intelligence. This is an Abwehr operation. His letters hint that I should brief him on Kaninchen. It's as if he's spying on the Abwehr."

Wilhelm laughed and rubbed his chin. "I train men and follow orders," he said. "Where the Abwehr leaves and the SS begins is of no concern to me and neither should it be to you."

"There is too much communication about this," Frank said.

"Keep your eyes open or we'll end up in jail or lying in some gutter like Ullman."

"Don't get jaundiced," Wilhelm said. "Is there any reason to believe the letters are not authentic?"

"No."

"Are you also receiving instructions from Herchenhaun?"

"Exactly," stated Becken with a tone of frustration. "And that's what's bothering me. Herchenhaun is my Abwehr connection. You know that. Now tell me why in hell I should be briefed by one intelligence service, the Abwehr, and then turn around and report my activities to another."

"So you think the SD is monitoring you."

"Not just me, but the Abwehr operation," Becken said with a wide expression. "If they are so concerned about Kaninchen, why can't Heydrich ask the Abwehr himself?"

"I admit. It doesn't make sense," Wilhelm said, suddenly scratching his head as if puzzled. "Unless there is a purge developing."

"What kind of purge?"

"How the hell should I know?"

"All these intrigues are too much for me......here, pour you another."

"You'll be as drunk as I am after this one," Frank said with a thin smile.

"I usually prefer beer as you can tell by this gut."

"Never developed much of a taste for it," Becken replied.

"But you see what I'm getting at."

"I understand your concern."

Frank paced again to the window. "Dammit, don't tell me you understand. Give me advice. I have no one else to talk to."

Wilhelm snorted and belched after taking a drink.

"If you are sure the Fritsch letters are authentic..."

"Of course they are. The British aren't that much inside us."

"Then your only choice is to obey orders and brief Heydrich on Kaninchen. Let the Abwehr and SD work out their own differences. If Heydrich is spying, he has his reasons."

"But your theory is that a purge is developing between the two intelligence agencies."

"I don't get paid to theorize. My job is....."

"Goddammit, don't give me some mechanized response."

"My opinion is that SD does not completely trust the Abwehr. You remember how the SS took care of the SA back in '34?"

"Yes, but that was before the war."

Wilhelm threw up his hands.

"How can I possibly know? I would imagine......I don't know what to say."

"Shit. It makes me nervous. It's bad enough that we have the British and Americans to worry about. Now the SD is meddling in our affairs."

Wilhelm scooted up his chair.

"You're not getting yellow, are you?"

"Fuck you."

December 7, 1941

In Bridgeport, New York, the dimming sky shone on a sea resort called The Breakers. The resort occupied both sides of the two lane with the hotel on the shore side and the lounge-restaurant overlooking the sea. Tommy Maxwell parked his car in front of the hotel and crossed the highway. It was twilight. As the wind tossed his hair back, he heard among the laughter of voices, the cry of gulls, the crashing of sea waves, and the moan of distant traffic, the sound of a woman's voice in song, her tone deep and soporific. As he followed her sound and neared the entrance to the restaurant, her words became more distinct.

> So leave me tomorrow
> I'd rather not know
> Just please keep me talking
> It's much better slow
> And leave me as you go.....
> Goodbye

The first thing Maxwell noticed on entering the lounge was the piano player. He wore a white tuxedo, and his black hair was parted down the middle. The singer, a girl with a purple evening dress and white gloves to her elbows, sat before a red velvet curtain. Her thin limbs were motionless as her voice rose above the murmur of the guests.

Maxwell lit a cigarette. The flickering orange of the lighter revealed his face. The sinews of the jaw muscles were drawn a fraction tighter. He had lost ten pounds. Otherwise he looked the same.

Then he saw Julie.

Her hair was the color of honey. She wore a red dress with a thick white sash. A cigarette extended from her slender fingers. In her lazy manner, as she reclined and listened to the singer, he could tell she had noticed his presence, yet she did not acknowledge him. She sat by the window facing the sea below.

He made his way through the tables towards her.

"Hello Julie," he said quietly.

She did not answer, but appeared more erect as she sucked her lips into her mouth, then released them. He saw her eyes dart upwards to the cocktail waitress.

"Bourbon and ginger with a twist of lime," Maxwell said.

They made small talk and soon were into their third drink.

"So where were you?" he asked.

"When I heard? Getting ready for work. Where were you?"

"At camp."

She smiled faintly. "So you finally have quit being mysterious. Camp is it?"

"Nordland."

"Nordland. So that's it." She laughed.

"Look, never mind."

"It's okay," she said. "But why do you have to lie to me? Don't bother to deny it. I know you've been lying."

Maxwell shrugged, looked down at the table cloth, then back into her eyes, as if to admit his fault.

"It is so demeaning to be lied to," she said, her huge eyes holding him, mesmerized. "Especially by you. We were so close, back in the old days."

"You mean the days of tuna fish sandwiches and beer."

As Julie laughed, her smile causing her eyes to light up, illuminating a constant play of animation on her face, an elderly lady walked by with her husband and recognized in Julie immediately the look of adoration and wonder that typifies young women in love. The elderly woman smiled at the young couple, glanced questioningly at the sea outside the window, and seeing her husband gesturing to their own table, shed her initial feeling of nostalgic sadness and went to her seat.

Maxwell and Julie spoke in an intimate fashion for over an hour before Maxwell finally got the courage to say, "You act as if you want me to move back in."

"Do I?"

"Maybe I'm wrong."

"Is that what you want?"

"I miss you. Don't you miss me?"

Julie looked towards the sea, hiding her eyes from Maxwell.

She stared for a time at the half-moon, its reflecting light forming a giant "V" over the shimmering waves.

"Then move back in, Tommy."

Maxwell looked to the side, produced a cigarette, and lit it.

"You're like so many men. Afraid of commitment."

"You know we had an understanding at the time, Julie. You were as afraid of falling in love as I was."

"Once you've been burned already....."

"All right, all right, we've discussed your situation with your parents before."

"What do you mean?"

"You know. The guy that was supposed to marry you. The abortion. Your career."

"I guess we've both been running away. Me no more than you."

"We have tonight," he said, a slight smile in his eyes.

"That's as much as anyone can say on this day. Even husbands and wives."

They talked for a time about Pearl Harbor, as so many Americans did on that day--drifting in and out of the subject, shifting first to personal matters, then to the events in Hawaii, unable to divorce their personal fates from those of the Americans, who had only that morning been attacked and defeated.

And as always, when Maxwell talked to Julie, the overall effect lay not so much in the sense of her words as in an overpowering effect her demeanor had over him, that is, he was taken in by a force, an intangible energy between each of their faces, arising from the interlay between the light in her eyes, the flush of her skin, and the shape of her mouth.

"Maybe you need to teach again. I bet you were a good teacher."

"I was."

"You could teach again if you wanted. No one can stop you."

"Women teach."

"Who says? Is that what bothers you? You're in a profession dominated by women."

"I don't know."

"Is teaching not good enough?"

"Not now," he said. "Maybe someday, but not now."

"If I had your education. It's my biggest limitation.

I often wonder if directors keep me around for my acting ability or for my body."

"You're beautiful. It's a blessing."

"Right. Any more funny stories?"

"Men respond to your body. You don't discourage them. Far from it."

"Are you jealous?"

"Not much."

"I'm not ashamed of my body like all the good Christian women," she said, purposely using one of Tommy's terms.

"Thank God," Maxwell said laughing with that precocious sparkle in his eyes that she loved.

"I know all about you, Tommy, you know that, don't you?" she said. Maxwell shifted uneasily.

"There are a world of things you don't know about me," he said. "And it would be wrong of me to tell you the truth."

"You don't understand," she said, folding her hands in front of her and never taking her eyes from him. "I don't care about all your little political intrigues. That's your little game. Men are all little boys. I understand that.

Just don't think you can lie to me. It's insulting."

"You're perceptive."

"It's one of my faults," she said, sucking her lips into her mouth to moisten them, then releasing them. "Sometimes I wish I were not so perceptive. It has caused me a lot of pain in the past."

Maxwell smiled. "Okay," he said. "I'm sorry.

It won't happen again. And you're right about 'my little games' as you call it. The last few months I've felt like my wheels were spinning. I don't know. It all seems stupid now. I guess I've lost track of myself."

She reached across the table, touching his wrist. "You seem sad," she said.

"Yeah."

He looked down at the sea. He was thinking of Pearl Harbor.

"How many ships did they say we lost?" Julie said distractedly, as if straining for conversation.

"You've heard the radio," Maxwell said with a dejected tone.

"Practically the whole damned Navy, five ships sunk completely, many more damaged, hell, I don't know......"

"Shouldn't that make you happy?"

Maxwell started. He watched the orange lamp for a time at the adjacent table. He was thinking of Frank's warning that Julie might be an F.B.I. plant, but he had never believed that and had continued to see her periodically.

"No, it doesn't make me happy."

She smiled.

"Then what does make you happy?"

"I think you know."

She laughed. "You better order some oysters then."

"I've never needed them before."

She smiled again, her eyes glistening slightly. "You said just a drink....."

"I always say that."

"Just one last time before you go to war!" she said. "I guess that's the mood of the day, huh?"

"I don't believe in the cause," he said. "Roosevelt knew ahead of time they would attack. He must have. It's just too neat...."

"It doesn't matter," she said, and as she spoke, he watched the sea below. "I know things.......that's why I agreed to meet you tonight. I've always sensed something about you. My mother once told me that a gypsy hypnotized me when I was young.....anyway....."

"Come on, Julie."

"No, listen, just give me the benefit of the doubt. I know you better than you think, Tommy Maxwell."

"If you think I'll go running off to kill Japs like the rest........"

"No, you won't do that. Something else will happen."

"What's that?" he said, feigning a yawn, hoping she would get the message.

"Listen to what I say, Tommy. Why are you laughing?"

"I don't know."

Julie began laughing too. "Come on, Tommy, I'm serious. Now wipe that smile off your face."

"Okay, okay, it's natural I suppose."

"What?"

"The desire to be God. Everybody has it. That's what mankind is all about."

"Hanging around all your German friends. You should know."

"They're no worse than your acting friends. They just take a different form."

"Anyway, I don't care if you believe me or not."

"Okay."

"Here goes."

After they both burst out laughing, finally gaining control, Julie spoke.

"Something extraordinary will happen to you. I've always felt that way......you're so different. What makes you that way?

Some people spend their whole lives trying to be different, but not you, you just are."

He lit another cigarette, releasing the smoke in two parallel streams out his nostrils. "It was what happened between me and my father a long time ago," and even as he said this, his own words surprised him. He had never spoken to Julie about his father.

"What was it?"

"I'll tell you someday."

"Someday is now. I won't see you again," she said, "or if I do, it will be a very long time......after everything is over."

"Look Julie, I told you....."

"But you don't understand. It doesn't matter what you think. I feel it."

"Feel what?"

"What's your sign?"

"Aries. You know that."

She smiled. "The warrior."

He laughed and leaned back in the chair. "Julie, always the dramatic actress."

"You know it's true," she said. "You won't stay out. You know you won't. You can't escape your nature."

"You sound like these clowns I've been hanging around," he said. "People are born to be this and that. I've never believed that. Now how about dinner?"

He rapidly changed the subject. They ordered seafood and more drinks. As they ate their meal, he was unable to take his eyes off the black sea below, nor could he deny the piercing effect her words had on him.

At two o'clock Maxwell and Julie lay in bed in the hotel across the two lane from the lounge.

He rubbed the back of Julie's neck and felt her body relax.

He could not forget the earlier conversation, and he began to question her again.

"So you're convinced that I'll be something extraordinary," he said, trying to sound as if he were joking.

She began to sniffle. "It's very good with you."

"Why are you crying?" Maxwell asked, turning her face to his.

"The world's coming apart. Haven't you heard?"

"Yeah, I've heard," he said grimly.

"People are going to die.......it will go on for years," she said.

"Who can say?"

"Come on, Tommy, don't kid yourself."

"It's the only thing that keeps me going. I have to believe that, you see."

"You were going to tell me something earlier," she said.

"About your father."

"Never mind."

"You promised."

"Forget it."

She raised up and looked him in the eyes. "For the strangest reason I feel that some day I'll see you again," she said.

"Here we go with the gypsy," he said.

"No, really, there are orbits people get on. And I believe that certain people......no matter how many years have passed, will see each other again. Do you believe that?"

"Maybe."

She turned over and put her hips against his crotch, straightening her back against him as a cat would do on a window pane.

"Kiss my back," she said. It was one of her signals. He immediately started kissing her up and down her back until she began to breathe hard. She got down on all fours, her huge breasts swaying back and forth. She reached behind her and felt that he was hard and with very gentle fingers helped him inside.

December 8, 1941

Maxwell drove in the early morning fog. The fog came off the sea to his left and swirled like a legion of apparitions in his headlights. He had quietly risen from Julie, kissing her softly on the nape of her neck, dressed and tiptoed out of the room. At the desk in the lobby, he had paid for the room, including a breakfast in bed for her.

He had not wanted to say goodbye. He had left a note on the dresser. "Maybe some day."

As the fog burned off to the morning sun and patches of blue appeared over the ocean to his left, his car gathered speed. He had to get back.

Again the solace of motion--the happiness attendant to the feeding of the white lines beneath his machine--he was sure that something was wrong with him, in that despite the pleasures of physical intimacy, pleasures he continually sought, there was simultaneously within him--in the moments after sexual union, in the glow of closeness-- the dream of solitude, of again stealing quietly from her bed and embrace.

He sought the balm of movement, forever longed-for, defiant of any category or definition.

He reached into his glove compartment for the half-filled bottle of bourbon. This was early even for him. He threw his head back with a long gulp. The whiskey slid down his chest, burning his nose, his mouth opening with a sigh. That familiar numbness in his head returned, blunting out clear thought as he capped the bottle and slammed the glove compartment shut.

There was no way to know what to expect when he arrived at Camp Nordland. Pearl Harbor was a fact. War was now a reality. Yesterday when he had heard the news, he had been plunged into the depths of depression.

He looked at his watch. Two hours to New Jersey.

As the day cleared off, as the lines of the two lane fed beneath the hood of the Chevrolet, he struggled with a question. Was he afraid of making a decision? Had what he agreed to do been merely a fantasy?

He pounded the steering wheel with his fist, causing the car to swerve slightly.

As the two hours passed, ominous, dark clouds traveled east over the land to the sea. By the time he reached New Jersey, the sky was spitting rain.

Maxwell arrived at Camp Nordland by 9:11 a.m. After a quick breakfast at the mess hall, he hurried to his cabin to find a man who had become his best friend, Richard Thibadeaux.

Camp Nordland was a New Jersey farm, a cluster of shacks spread across thirty acres. In the days before Pearl Harbor the camp was the headquarters of the Bund and the site of rallies on weekends. Before war was officially declared, Americans had abounded at the camp. Visitors ranged from those that actually supported or sympathized with the Bund's message to F.B.I. informants to the curious.

But today the mood was different.

Maxwell found Thibadeaux lying on the bed in the cabin, flicking cigarette ashes into an empty soup bowl.

"So," shouted Thibadeaux. "You pop her sweet cherry, you?"

Thibadeaux smiled in his normal way, the long, horse-like face sporting wide teeth.

"I forgot what an ugly son of a bitch you are," Maxwell said. "Especially in the mornings. I guess after a good night's sleep, a man just ain't ready for the shock."

Thibadeaux lit another cigarette before speaking. Maxwell lay on his own bed.

"Didn't expect to see you back," Thibadeaux said.

"Why not?"

"Hell, after yesterday, half of us gone. Got cold feet. By the way, how you toes feeling?"

Maxwell lit a cigarette of his own and stared out the window.

"So what it gonna be?" Thibadeaux said. "You in or out?"

"I don't know."

"Hell, ain't nobody forcing you to stay," Thibadeaux said, as he shifted on the bed.

"If there would be an assignment, anything, I might consider it, but this waiting around."

"Frank said more training later."

"Do you believe everything Frank says?" Maxwell snapped.

"No sense getting testy with me, Tommy," Thibadeaux said, sitting up stiffly.

"It's getting boring. Hell, the food stinks. I feel like I'm in prison."

"I can tell you ain't never eaten no prison chow, you."

Again Maxwell did not answer, but merely sat up and stared out the window. The day was gray and cold.

Thibadeaux was right. Indeed, no one was forcing him to stay, and for the life of him, he could not explain why he carried on with this charade. During the previous months he had spent the days with his writing, and the nights, doing as Frank wished, training for sabotage.

The training included courses in the handling of TNT, the sabotage of bridges, the de-railing of trains, and underwater demolition. Further training included the making of molotov cocktails and the firing of various weapons. Maxwell was quite proficient with a rifle. He had gotten to the point where he could stitch a silhouette at two hundred yards, four out of five shots with iron sites. He had taken a course in setting underwater mines with eighty day timers as well as lessons in projecting fake distress transmissions into the Atlantic and falsifying reports of phantom U boats.

It was this last task, not the sabotage, Frank assured him, in which he would be most involved.

Of the fifteen recruits that were trained, Maxwell and Thibadeaux were singled out as the top candidates for further training. Maxwell watched Gail enter the mess hall.

He heard Thibadeaux laughing behind him.

"Hell fire, don't blame you for leaving," Thibadeaux said as he stood up and stretched.

"Who said anything about leaving?"

Get outta here, grits, how I'm gonna believe you staying?"

"Oh, I guess you're a fucking mind reader too?"

"What you talkin about, grits?"

Maxwell laughed. "Would you give me a break with that grits shit? Why don't you learn to talk anyway?"

"Talk. Shit. I speak least two languages good. French and American. How many you speak, grits?"

"American, huh?" Maxwell said with a shrug as he laughed.

"I repeat the question. When you leavin'? Everybody else is, you know. War be declared on Germany this week. You ain't gonna gain no advantage staying. Shit, it's the other way around. You got everything to lose, you."

"How do you figure that?"

"You different than me," Thibadeaux said. "Got a home and a family to go back to."

"The point is that no one will be going to their families in the next few months. They'll be signing up in order to go overseas and be slaughtered. All dead patriots."

"So go to Canada."

"Everyone will be involved," Maxwell said. "No neutrals."

"Wrong, grits," Thibadeaux said with a smile. "I a neutral. Hell, I be working for the only political party in the world, and no, it ain't no Nazis--money. But not you, no.

You the noble type. You like to be telling yourself you got the cause when actual you just like me and everybody else."

Maxwell frowned and shook his head. He felt very confused.

"All I can say," Thibadeaux said. "If you taking the lamb, make your decision fast. Shit, before long they ain't gonna be no choice."

December 9, 1941

At six thirty a.m. four police cars parked outside the gate to Camp Nordland. Within a half mile of the entrance the cars had extinguished their lights.

Sheriff Dexter McClure, a burly man with a thick neck, led sixteen men into the camp. McClure was the tallest of the men, who but for two uniformed deputies, were dressed in civilian clothes.

The other thirteen men had been deputized yesterday after the injunction issued by Joseph Canton ordering the closing of Camp Nordland.

McClure's temples throbbed as he neared the first cabin.

"Okay, Jake, you and Martin roust them out," he said, belching whiskey, "and tell those sons of bitches to quit laughing."

Two men in plaid shirts and wearing sidearms entered the first cabin. A clamor of shouting began inside followed by a banging and laughter. Three people emerged in nightshirts, two men and one woman, all shivering in the early morning chill.

"Who in hell you think you are?" the bald man in the nightshirt said.

"Jake," ordered McClure. "That one talks again, cuff him and put him in the car. Mario, Thompson, take the next cabin. We'll go two at a time and assemble them here. Stop that laughing."

McClure watched with satisfaction as his orders were carried out.

Camp Nordland had long been an embarrassment to his community, long believed to harbor traitors and spies, all hiding behind the Constitution of the United States.

Three more men were shoved into the darkness. It would be first light before all the campers were assembled.

Maxwell lay in his bunk, watching the gray line of cigarette smoke curl towards the ceiling. He had told Thibadeaux nothing, but he had decided to leave camp for home.

As Richard had predicted, Congress was contemplating war on Germany. Bob Smith and Gail Maroni, virtual radicals before the Japanese attack on Pearl Harbor, had become disillusioned and departed. Only the hard core loyalists to the Bund remained.

Maxwell continued to tell himself that he was neither a coward nor a procrastinator. For weeks now he had been yearning for an assignment, but now he felt apathetic.

He told himself that he had not been home for Christmas in two years and that now seemed a good time to go. Although the prospect of retreating back to his mundane existence depressed him, the idea of staying in this country as a German operative seemed far worse. As he had told Frank numerous times, he felt improperly trained and he was not about to go into the venture ill-prepared.

Maxwell and Thibadeaux were to meet Frank in Connecticut on Christmas Day to finalize their plans for further training. But privately Maxwell was remembering the train schedule home.

In the next bed Thibadeaux grunted, sat up, and flicked on his bedside light.

"What the hell you doing, you?" he said, as he reached for a half-eaten sandwich beside the bed.

"Just thinking," Maxwell said.

"Thinking about what?"

Beyond the sound of their voices there was laughter, just on the edge of hearing. Thibadeaux glanced to the window, then looked back at Maxwell.

"You really believe there is an assignment?" Maxwell asked.

"Frank say so."

"Then why haven't we been assigned?"

"You in some kind of hurry?"

"You know I am," Maxwell snapped.

"Ain't in no bigger hurry than I am," Thibadeaux said, who rubbed the left cheek of his long face, as if monitoring his beard. "And I ain't so sure you want an assignment."

"Kiss my ass."

"What I mean is you stay for different reasons than me."

Maxwell sat up and stretched.

"Go on," he said.

"You like writing in that book you got. That's your big thrill, I say fine, but it ain't my kind of item."

"What did you think of the last article?"

"The one about easing up on the Jews wasn't it?"

Maxwell laughed. "Hell, you can read, can't you? It referred to how the British invented concentration camps in the Boor Wars."

"Right," Thibadeaux said, whose droll look over his horse-like face caused Maxwell to burst into laughter.

"You really don't give a shit, do you?" Maxwell said.

"Not about your writing, no."

"At least you're honest."

"Like I'm saying, if it good for you, go. Me, I'm different. Ain't got no good education. Frank promised me a job, something that pays. What the hell you doing here, hell, I don't know, if I had your education..."

"I'm a student of history," Maxwell said smiling and already anticipating Richard's answer. "What better time is there to write about it?"

"You a damned clown," Thibadeaux said. "You straddling the fence. You don't even hate Jews like the rest of these nuts, you."

"My point of view is different....."

"Please, grits, no long, sad stories," interrupted Thibadeaux.

"Next time I'll write an article on one of your second story jobs," Maxwell said. "Then I'll find out for sure if you can read."

Thibadeaux laughed and flicked his ashes.

The door burst open. Maxwell leapt up. Two men, one of whom laughed in a cackle, strode in.

"Get up and get outside,' said the shorter of the men.

"What the hell is this?"

"Shutup," said the skinny one with the beard and the gap in his teeth. "Get outside."

"What tree did you fall out of," Maxwell said.

The fat one pushed Maxwell, at the same time poking his face so close that Tommy could smell onions on his breath.

"Maybe you don't hear so good," the deputy said, laughing and grabbing Maxwell's arm. "Outside."

Both men started to grab an armpit when Maxwell threw his arms forward. "I can walk," he said.

When the men arrived at the mess hall, Maxwell had drawn a beat on the situation. Amid the gravel yardway and occasional puddles, nine deputies were standing in the yard while a tall man read from a piece of paper to the camp members who had been gathered in the circle of officers.

"We the citizens of Carney, New Jersey and acting on the injunction passed on 12-8-41 in the district court of the honorable Joseph Canton, hereby order the closing of Camp Nordland along with the immediate vacating of all said premises....."

"You can't do that," Judi said, the short-haired blonde in rolled-up jeans who seemed, even as she spoke, to have forgotten what she was going to say.

"Who's the slut?" yelled the fat deputy, before he laughed.

"Don't talk to her that way," Maxwell said.

"Since there are seventeen people here, you are in violation of the injunction and hereby ordered off this camp."

"You take your hereby's and stuff them up your butt, you," Thibadeaux said. "We ain't heard of no injunction."

"You've heard it now, buddy," said the skinny one who pushed Richard, but Thibadeaux dodged back and kicked, catching the deputy on the side of the leg.

One of the deputies to Maxwell's right reached for a gun.

"Hold it," said the tall one. "Put that away. There's a better way. And shutup laughing."

He walked up to Thibadeaux and started to turn when he suddenly wheeled and popped a jab into Thibadeaux's right eye. The two deputies doubled over, cackling.

"There, Luke, grab this bastard's arm, stand him up for me."

It took a few seconds for the two men to pin Thibadeaux's arms behind him. The tall one gauged the distance to Richard's face when Maxwell sprang at him. He grabbed the tall one's wrist and wheeled him around.

A heavy weight came down on Maxwell's shoulder, and he felt the ground under his palms. A scurry of feet, and two other deputies jerked him up and pinned his arms back just like Thibadeaux's.

"Hey, there's no need.....'

"Shutup," screamed the deputy. "Or you'll get the same."

Maxwell was jerked around and he heard the cracking sound behind him of Richard getting hit; heard laughter.

The Sheriff was in his face. He had very thin lips and a thick neck.

"Let me tell you one thing, asshole," he said, laughingly, poking his finger in Maxwell's chest, and barely able to contain himself. "Better still, let me show you how we feel about Nazi's."

The spittle hit Maxwell cold on his neck. Laughter.

"Hey, sorry about that, asshole, let me wipe it off."

The next thing Maxwell remembered was Richard's face and the dizzying feeling of being lifted off the ground by two men.

He shook his head.

"You okay?" All the men were laughing.

The gravel spun and wavered below him.

"Yeah," Maxwell answered, but as soon as he spoke, he could feel his jaw was broken.

"Now get your shit and get out."

They arrived at Frank Becken's farm in Connecticut and were taken by Frank to a local hospital and subsequently treated---Thibadeaux for minor abrasions on the face and Maxwell for a broken jaw. The doctor said that Maxwell's teeth would be wired together for three weeks. Becken reported that the two men were injured in a minor traffic accident.

It was not until they were in Frank Becken's Ford that they had a chance to speak at length.

Thibadeaux and Frank sat in the front while Maxwell lay out on the back seat. He had a throbbing headache which caused his eyelids to pound each time he closed them. Occasionally he looked at the passing lights in the rear window or at the back of Frank's thinning scalp. The rain hit the windshield in a steady slant.

"A lot of things have changed," Frank said. "Several people that were with us a week ago have already left. The damned Japs have thrown a monkey wrench into everything."

"Japs or no Japs, both Tommy and me tired of sitting on our butts, us," Thibadeaux said.

"No more sitting around now. Things are moving fast," Frank said. He paused and lit another cigarette before continuing. "I told you guys all along that you would be trained further."

"Nuts Frank," Maxwell managed to say through his wired teeth. "You call that training? I barely know how to light a match."

"We've done the best we could under the circumstances," Frank said. "Things will be happening soon in New York, but I've got a bad feeling about it. There are too many holes in the organization. That's why I'm sending you two elsewhere."

"Where's that?" Thibadeaux asked.

"Never mind, 'where's that,'" Frank said. "There's one thing I want to know first. Are you guys with us or not? I understand things have changed. A lot of feelings have gotten hurt by Pearl Harbor. All I ask you is to tell me the truth.

Are you in or out? If it's yes, fine, if no, it doesn't matter, we'll go our separate ways with no hard feelings; that's the way I feel about it."

"I'm in," Thibadeaux said without hesitation. "As long as the money's right, you can count on me, babe."

"Good. What about it, Tommy?"

And the trembling patterns of the rivulets of rain on the back window of Frank's car brought memory swimming up, as a bright fish from the depths of a dark sea. Why the rain on the window caused the sensation or to what degree the situation in which he found himself contributed to memory he could never discern. Just as the smell of pencil shavings in a sharpener bring back memories of that first school room, so did the rain in violent, small, vibrating streams, like veins in a spasmodic muscle, stimulate the remembrance of that night--the night like so many memories of childhood, perceived from the distance of Time in a swoon of phantasmagoric, hallucinatory impressions.

Raining that night, Maxwell thought, raining just as hard.

Memory always perceived that night as a haze of purple velvet, occasionally illumined by brilliant flashes of light.

Even at fourteen he felt the power of the mountains at night, even in the rushing darkness as the storm approached.

The rain on that country road near Murphy, North Carolina.

Recalcitrance was new to him then. His recent rebellion of sneaking down the lattice-work at nights had brought no repercussions. He had never been caught. The boy had run to his barn and fetched the pack of cigarettes that he hid in the pile of hay. He smoked one a night during his short, nocturnal walks.

And if it had not been raining that night, he would never have ventured near Forsyth's Feed Store. If it had been raining earlier, he would never have snuck out. But the storm had come suddenly as often happens in the mountains.

As he walked, the boy had savored the rushing wind, the illuminating flashes that lit up the great purple walls, followed by the low rumble of thunder.

When the rain first began to spit, he knew he only had a few moments. He remembered during hunting trips with his father how these mountain storms behaved--sudden, violent, and brief, as oftentimes happens on the sea.

As the rain and lightning increased, he broke into a run. He was almost to Forsyth's Store. When he got to the porch, he walked up the steps and sat under the tin roof. He sat for a time, watching the sheets of light revealing the wall of mountains.

He recalled a camping trip with his father and how they had to make a bon fire and keep torches lit to discourage a bear that had become too brave. His father was a brilliant huntsman but had never had a desire to shoot a bear. Lost in the dream of the woods, swooning with the light of the bonfire, an occasional citing of the bear at the edge of a thicket, the beast's wild eyes orange against the fire, the boy had lost all track of time.

In the same manner, as he sat on the porch, neither did he notice the small, twitching avenue of light behind him inside the store. Not until the storm had all but ceased and Tommy had risen had he heard the bumping sound, as the figure inside had stumbled into an object as he moved in the darkness of the store.

The boy looked again. The light had shone from behind the register then quickly shut off.

The fear had been sudden and his feet tangled as he started to bolt from the porch. He fell headlong off the porch before getting back up. He tasted and smelled the earth. The rain had stung his face as he ran. He had relaxed into a jog when he heard the heavy thud of the running footsteps behind him. The fear had seized him again as he gathered speed, his heart pounding up into his ears. Then the heavy body upon him, tackling him, grabbing him, one iron-like fist coming down cold on his cheek. You ain't going nowhere, boy," came the familiar voice. "Yep, you'll have to learn the hard way." Again the fist had come down. The boy locking part of the blow. Then the strong grip under his armpits and the familiar voice saying, "Come on, Tommy, you was caught."

He remembered the bright ceiling light of the police office, shining down in small circles off the head of Reverend Hough, the town preacher. He remembered how strange it had seemed--the feel of the cruel downward blows and the impression of that overly kind face, like an aged cherub.

"Roy," the familiar voice said. "I was just happening by the feed store when I saw this light inside. I went to the porch and saw the light go out. I don't know if he heard me or not, but the next thing I know, he comes out lickety split, running as hard as he could. When I caught him, he tried to strike me."

It would become the boy's most vivid and prevalent image, the ceiling light off that small desk in the jail, the longest night of his life. His father's face, in that glaring light, humiliated, yet respectful as the preacher told the story.

Maxwell remembered his own silence, and in his silence an admission of false guilt.

And after all the beatings by his father, he remembered how he nearly believed it himself--he was a "thief," a "sneak."

The boy had almost come to believe the lie himself, for the truth that the preacher, the Reverend Hough, had actually been inside the feed store seemed too preposterous.

Yet months later, the truth continued to assert itself. The boy realized that the town preacher had been robbing the store himself, that he had done the only thing he could have done upon being discovered by a teenager. He had blamed the entire thing on the boy.

Years later, after the Reverend had moved away, Tommy Maxwell still refused to set foot in the church.

He watched the rivulets of rain against the back window.

"Tommy, you okay?"

"Yeah."

"Did you hear my question?"

"Yeah, I did."

"Well, what about it?"

As Maxwell spoke, he tried to ignore the whistling and spitting sounds he made while trying to talk through his wired teeth.

"I'll tell you one thing, Frank," he said. "I ain't been real happy in the last few weeks. It's been a lot of screwing around for the most part. And I'll tell you further that after Pearl Harbor, I had plenty of doubts. I hadn't even told Richard, but I was planning on being home for Christmas....." he paused, trying to formulate the right words.

"But here's the dope," he said, his eyes growing smaller. "I been spit on and ass-kicked for the last time by the good, Christian law-abiding Americans. I'm in."

"The worm do turn don't it?" Thibadeaux said.

"All right," Maxwell said. "You said we had orders."

Maxwell lay down again and listened as Becken talked.

"In four weeks both of you will be supplied with driver's licenses and social security cards. You will board a bus to Morgan City, Louisiana. You'll both be given enough money to last until you can get some jobs. Only temporary, mind you. You will live at separate addresses and meet at an agreed-upon place each month."

"Each month?" Thibadeaux said, leaning up. "How much longer do....."

"Just shutup and listen. You'll be receiving further training, but you'll have to follow orders in the mean time.

Security is the biggest factor for a few months. The less you know, the less you'll have to tell. Everything has to be on a need-to-know basis from now on. You'll be leaving as soon as Tommy's jaw is healed."

The darkness vibrated and throbbed. A few miles later Maxwell fell into an uneasy sleep.

June 20, 1942

In a small, dimly lit New York hotel room a man huddled over a phone. The room was dark, but for a single light that burned on the bureau. A warm breeze blew in the open window, the sounds of the city occasionally swimming off the canyons of hotels, which lined the street below.

The man had thinning blonde hair, which was etched in gray along the temples. He wore small spectacles, had thin lips and extremely pale skin, especially for summer. He picked up the phone once, then slammed it down. He jerked his glasses off and jammed his fists into his eyes. He stared fixedly at the darkness of the room, lost in thought.

The man was George Johann Dasch. On June 13, he had landed with two of his comrades on a beach near Amagansett, New York. He had crossed the Atlantic in a German U-boat U-502 out of Lorient, France.

As Dasch stared into the darkness, he tried to make sense of the last three years of his life. Although he was a native German, he had spent ten years in the United States and even married an American girl.

Business interests had called him back to Germany, where in 1939, he had been trapped by the war.

The condition of becoming a German saboteur had been his ticket home to his wife. The two months of training near Hanau, Germany had been rigorous.

He and his comrades had boarded U-502 in Lorient, France on May 30. Their job had been to go ashore in the U.S. get into a big city, and after a month of having disappeared, secure a job in one of the shipping factories on the Eastern seaboard.

The confines of the U boat had been oppressive. Tubes and pippins' encroached from every angle. Men lived on top of each other, unable to shave and bathe properly due to a lack of fresh water and long periods of submergence. Enroute to the U.S.

U-502 had sunk two tankers, and Dasch had experienced being hunted by destroyers, had felt the cold, steel deck plates as he listened to the horribly shrill beat of the Asidic.

On the last night of his voyage, when he and his comrades were taken ashore amid the dunes of Amagansett, New York, luck had not been on their side. The saboteurs, dressed in bathing trunks, had been spotted by a lone coastguardsman, who was making his nightly rounds on the beach.

The young sentry had questioned the three men about a large bag they had been dragging up the beach. Although the youth had accepted over three hundred dollars in cash as a bribe to keep quiet, Dasch had seen betrayal in his eyes.

The next day the papers had been full of the reported incident of a U boat citing near Amagansett. Apparently the guardsman had reported the meeting on the beach and a number of men had gone to the beach and seen a long, dark object in the water, just miles from the landing spot.

A subsequent search of the beach turned up a bounty for the shore patrol. In a marlin-sealed case, buried in a sand dune, were casings of explosives, in huge black chunks, made to look like coal. Also found were reversible civilian clothes and 100,000 dollars in U. S. currency.

The hunt is on, Dasch thought, as he ran both hands through his hair. He thought of his wife. Is it possible that I will never see her again?

He walked to the window and stared down at the thin line of street between the dark brick of the city's walls.

Occasionally a car's lights meandered down the avenue. He leaned on the sill, again entertained the idea of jumping, then turned from the window with a disgusted laugh. He did not have the guts.

He tried to re-think the whole thing. He had been over it a hundred times.

There was no way out, either way he went. If he did not act, if he disappeared and tried to hide, the Abwehr would find him, and his life would not be worth a dime. If he surrendered to the U.S. authorities, he may hang. Even still, this was his best bet.

He would come clean. He would turn State's evidence. He could give them names and addresses, and he would give them details of his training, the movement of U-boats, everything.

He had been trained for a desperate mission, and upon arriving in America, discovered he had no stomach for it.

He paced to the other side of the room and back again.

Should he go to see his wife before he turned himself in?

No, better not to involve her. He had been dead for Sarah for the last three years, so why not remain that way? His confinement in prison would be long, but if he turned State's evidence, his confinement would have a goal. If the war ended with a positive result for the U.S. he may serve a suspended sentence.

We will do anything to live, he thought. Just so we can get up in the mornings and piss.

He did not know why he was going over all this again in his mind. He had made his decision days ago. And whereas his attempts at turning himself in had been futile, he was determined to go through with it.

Twice now, he had contacted the F.B.I. by phone and on both occasions they had cut him off, thinking him to be a crackpot.

He walked into the bathroom and turned on the small light over the mirror. He straightened his glasses as he watched his face in the mirror. True enough, he looked to be an insignificant weasel.

He laughed, slammed his fist down on the sink at the thought.

He made his way through the darkness of the bedroom and turned on the light. Frantically, he threw his clothes into a grip.

He had decided upon his course of action. He would make his way to Washington D.C. and see J. Edgar Hoover himself. It was the only way to save his life. He was convinced of that. He would make someone believe him.

Paying no attention to the noise, he stormed out of the apartment into the hall.

What was happening to his nerves? He raised his head and sniffed the air. He smelled the U boat. It seemed no matter how much he bathed, he could not get the stench of confinement from his nostrils.

Once on the street, he hailed a cab and directed it to the bus station.

In three days he would give his full confession. The confession of George Johann Dasch would lead to the incarceration of eight men, six of whom would be executed. It would set off a series of circumstances affecting hundreds--events as strangely related and illogical as the fortunes of war.

June 24,1942

On a lonely highway near Morgan City, Louisiana Frank Becken drove alone. The closer he got to the sea, the thicker the fog became. He slowed to fifteen miles per hour.

The last thing he wanted was to drop a tire off on a sandy shoulder and go tumbling into the swamp.

He kept his car radio turned up, waiting anxiously for the next news broadcast.

The big band song faded out and the broadcast aired precisely on time.

"Our lead story.....Trial has been set for George Johann Dasch and his team of Nazi agents who were arrested by the F.B.I. on June 25. Dasch and seven other unnamed suspects are charged with espionage in relation to two U boat landings at Amagansett, New York and Ponte

Vedra, Florida. According to F.B.I. sources, the German U boats landed secretly on June 6 in New York and June 17 in Florida.

Nazi saboteurs were put ashore with hopes of infiltrating into the country and sabotaging Eastern shipping lines to England. The F.B.I. investigation was led by......."

Becken listened to the rest of the broadcast in a slow boil. Nothing new had been added to previous accounts.

The broadcast, rather than dwelling on the trial at hand, concentrated on the expertise of the F.B.I. in crushing the German spy ring.

Becken knew differently. He knew that the capture of the incoming agents had been more the result of blind luck than skill.

He lit a cigarette and wound through the fog. He thought back over the disastrous events of the last two weeks.

Only days after the Amagansett landing, Dasch turned State's evidence. All of the agents that had landed in New York and Florida were tracked and incarcerated, their pictures in Life magazine.

Becken already knew how the trial would turn out. It would be held and completed in a great hurry. Dasch and Ernst Peter Burger, another American, who had turned State's evidence, would be given prison terms, while the rest of the agents would be quietly sentenced to death and hanged.

Becken smashed his cigarette into the ashtray and turned off the radio. The road climbed onto a dune, overlooking the sea. He cut off the engine and rolled down the window. In his headlights he saw the sign--Beach Area, Do Not Drive Beyond This Point.

He turned out his lights, locked his car and climbed over the dune. He began walking east along the beach.

As he walked, he put the misfortunes of the past weeks behind him. His mind was on Operation Kaninchen. In forty-eight hours, a third U boat landing was to occur not twelve miles from his present position. Not only would German agents be put ashore, but two Americans were to be taken aboard the U boat and transported to Lorient, France for training.

Becken stopped. He watched the fog roll in, looked through that great, gray phantasm, now like transparent gauze, which obliterated the crashing sea.

"Nacht und Nebel," he said to himself. He ruminated, as he belched deeply, over recent events.

Reinhardt Heydrich, head of the SS intelligence agency, the SD, was dead. He had been killed outside of Prague by an allied assassination team--a team, who had known precisely when the "butcher of Prague" would leave the city in his Mercedes convertible, a team, who knew precisely what route he would take, a team, who had attacked the car with machine guns and a hand grenade.

Despite the hole in his side, Heydrich had emerged from the wrecked car, firing his lugar at his fleeing assassins.

The grenade, that had pierced his side, contained infected horse hair. Days later, after the Reich's best surgeons had been flown to the scene and pronounced that the Protector was recovering from his wounds, Heydrich developed a new set of symptoms. The horse hair had contained spores of Anthrax, and Heydrich later died of the fatal cattle disease.

The sea crashed in. Becken listened to the foam sizzle on the sand.

It was Becken's belief that the assassination could not have occurred without, at some level, supplied information from the Abwehr, the Wehrmacht's branch of military intelligence. He knew the Abwehr had been monitoring British experiments with bacteriological warfare off a Scottish isle.

But why would army intelligence engineer the murder of the head of SS intelligence?

The sea moaned in the fog.

Members of the allied assassination team had taken their escape route through the town of Lidice, where they were hidden for two days. Three days after the assassins had left, SS detachments entered Lidice. The men, women, and children were promptly separated; the men were lined up against a schoolhouse and summarily shot. The women and children were sent to concentration camps; the pregnant women sent to Ravensbruck for abortions and executions. As a reprisal for hiding

Heydrich's killers, the entire town of Lidice had slipped into what Hitler called the "Nacht und Nebel" or "Night and Fog."

The fog poured in over the evanescent sea.

Becken would brief Maxwell and Thibadeaux tomorrow.

He had not seen them in two months. He belched uncontrollably. A drink sometimes mollified his hated flatulence.

He had been drunk a lot in the last six months, but he would be sober when he talked to Maxwell tomorrow.

He at least owed him that.

June 24, 1942

The first thing Tommy Maxwell heard that morning was the sea.

Its rhythmic waves crashing on the beach seemed intermingled with his fitful dreams. He rolled over and felt bits of grime between his own body and the cold concrete. How could he have slept here?

As he pulled himself up to an elbow and saw the sun, shining brightly through the porch screen, he felt the drunkenness in his head.

Reluctantly he pulled himself up. He could see the green waves pounding the beach behind his cabin. The tide was coming n, and he felt like a swim.

The screen door opened with its accustomed creak, and Maxwell stooped down with sluggish difficulty as he undid his shoes. He wore a tee shirt and jeans. His hair was close cut, yet matted, and his face had a two day beard.

As he walked slowly towards the sea, he watched the gulls' lazy passings' at the green water. They appeared to be in suspended animation at times, before they swooped down in a quick splash for a morning's fish.

He felt the waves on his toes, shivered as he waded waist deep, then dove into a four foot breaker. He went down, then emerged, wiping water from his eyes and tasting the salt. He loved the sea. It had been the most bearable element of his last six months.

As he trudged back towards his small, white cabin, he tried to remember what had happened last night. He had been drunk before, but never this drunk, and never to the point that memory failed him.

When he reached the beach, he changed his mind. Down the beach to his right, a mile away, the old man fished as he did every morning.

Maxwell had never spoken to the old man, nor did he know from where he came. He guessed that he belonged to the lighthouse, which lay at the end of a peninsula, that extended out to the sea for five hundred yards, like a white finger.

Just like this morning, Maxwell would walk towards the old man, watching the sway and bend of the cane pole, as he surf-fished.

Once he had even gotten close enough to see the bottoms of his rolled-up trousers as he stooped down, putting a hook through the eye of a minnow.

Maxwell had never spoken to him. He envied his serenity, his apparent contentment.

A half mile up the beach from his cabin, Maxwell turned around and headed back.

Memory swam up in Maxwell's sluggish head. Right, he thought, now I remember, Thibadeaux and the girls are inside.

A vague remembrance that Thibadeaux and his two Cajun girlfriends were in the cabin caused Maxwell to quicken his step.

He brushed the sand off his feet on entering the screened-in porch where he had slept. He quietly opened the back door.

The cabin was a small affair, the only cabin for miles, located at the end of a dirt road, which wound serpentine through the south Louisiana marsh. The trees surrounding the cabin were draped with Spanish moss. When Maxwell had first been shown the place by Frank, he figured it would be a good place to write, perfect solitude.

He moved into the dark living room. Beside the couch, on the hardwood floor was the remains of a broken whiskey bottle, shining in the dim light like a hundred diamonds. Maxwell paused. He could not remember.

In his bedroom he saw Mercienne, the thin Cajun girl that Thibadeaux occasionally brought over for him. She lay naked under the sheets, one of her breasts exposed, the small aureola rising and falling in the gray light.

When Maxwell saw her thin features, he remembered last night.

He began to feel sick. His lovemaking had left much to be desired. He had thrust into her violently, with careless abandon, as if to take out on her the frustration of the last few days. Now he was remembering, and as he remembered, he wished he could forget again.

In the small bathroom, above the medicine cabinet was a key. He reached up and got it and opened what looked to be a towel closet.

He opened the door and stepped inside, locking himself in. He had to duck his head to get in the closet, until he reached the area where the wall had been knocked out, opening into a small office. To the left was a typewriter, a desk, and a fluorescent light. Maxwell turned on the light. The empty space in the corner had been the place for the transmitter and receiver.

After the Amagansett Incident had hit the papers, he had destroyed the equipment in the swamp.

Those nights, alone with his transmitter, had been his only touch with the war in the last six months. Of course, he read the papers, but there were holes in the reports. It was hard to separate propaganda from fact.

It had been a year ago that Maxwell had heard the news. Like the rest of the world, he had been stunned.

On June 22, 1941, German armored divisions had crossed the Polish border into Russia. For a year now the German war machine had remained unchecked, survived a Russian winter, and was inflicting heavy casualties as its long, steel arm spear-headed into the heart of Russia. 1942 would go down in history as the turning point of the war. Events were coming to a head in several theatres. The German war machine continued to advance in the east as the Japanese were doing in the Pacific.

America was beginning to mobilize her own machine.

He told himself in times of uncertainty that operations like Kaninchen must not fail. Both sides were reaching the apex of their power. The Battle of the Atlantic was in a precarious balance.

Maxwell continually told himself that destruction of supply routes to England held the only hope for peace. If Britain fell, the Allies' morale and resolve would crumble. They would be forced to negotiate. One thing was certain. Germany was penetrating successfully on all fronts. In Russia she was winning victories daily, while in the Atlantic, her U boats had so successfully cut off supplies to England, that onlookers expected the capitulation of Britain shortly.

Alone at nights, Maxwell would sit with his transmitter and receiver. Over that dark sea, the voices bounced, as if they were in the same room--the voices of sea captains, conversing on U boat sightings, the projections of the shore patrol on nearby action in the Caribbean, and only on occasion, from far away over that darkness, a muffled German voice, answered by another.

He did not speak much German, and neither was he to report any evidence of U boats in the vicinity. His instructions had been to monitor the courses and dispositions of tankers in the area.

Every morning, his first task was to hike into the swamp, where at an appointed place--a small metal box under a large tree--he left his findings in a sealed envelope. The messages were written in code, as in the case of those he would receive in the same place. The now familiar handwriting fastidious, the messages terse.

Strange as it may seem, despite his pacifist leanings, Maxwell felt that he was missing out. His monitoring of the war became as envious and obsessive as the rest of the civilians left behind.

One night, two weeks ago, while in a bar in Morgan City, he had overheard a story of a shore patrolman, who had been stationed near New Orleans. The patrolman had been on a routine beach patrol, when he had heard a tremendous explosion, which had rumbled in from the sea like thunder. Knowing that the war was being waged over the horizon, he and another patrolman had climbed in a small plane, where they were to witness the sinking of the Eva Marie by two German U boats.

"There she was," the patrolman had said, "burning from stem to stern, oil all in the water, and survivors, black in the water. The two U boats just sat and watched.

Hell, you could see the crew standing on decks. It was a helpless feeling. We were afraid to get too close, afraid they would open up with their deck gun. We couldn't even throw a rock at them."

As Maxwell rummaged in his desk for a cigarette, he remembered how he had envied the patrolman.

He found a half-smoked Lucky Strike and lit it. He sucked the smoke in, feeling dizzy again as he exhaled. The bucket of ashes still lay to his left. When he finished his cigarette, he threw the butt into the bucket. The bucket represented all that was left of a manuscript on John Reed, on which he had been working for three years.

Never was any good, he thought.

The more he had read his manuscript, the more weak it became. He had stopped writing entirely a month ago, in direct proportion to the increase in U boat activity near New Orleans.

The closer he got to the war, the more he realized how his writing paled in comparison.

Peaceful patitudes, he thought with a sarcastic laugh.

He stood up quickly, felt the drunkenness in his head, and began to remember. He walked out of the cubbyhole, into the bathroom, locking the closet behind him.

Mercienne still slept, curled into a different position, her rounded hips outlined in the sheet. She had witnessed the culmination of his frustration last night, a frustration that had started with the news of George Johann Dasch, with the spread in Life magazine, detailing the names and photographs of the incarcerated Nazi agents.

Maxwell wandered into the living room. Again he watched the sunlight from the window, playing off the dazzles of broken glass. He went to the kitchen, fetched a broom and dustpan, and returned to the glass. The whiskey was sticky under the broom.

The Dasch incident had forced the issue. No longer was Maxwell in control of his life, no longer did he walk the precarious balance between the author and saboteur. The cards had been played. The Dasch confession dramatized the fact that Tommy Maxwell was a traitor and a spy. As far as he was concerned, he was a wanted man. For Maxwell, now more than any other time, prison and a possible death sentence were as far away as a knock on the door.

He and Thibadeaux had argued about it last night.

"Frank calls and you don't even try to pin him down,"
Maxwell had said in a loud voice.

Thibadeaux had laughed and put his finger to his lips.

"Will you lower your voice, boy? The girls in the kitchen."

"To hell with you," Maxwell had said, turning from Thibadeaux in disgust and pacing the floor with the half-filled whiskey bottle in his hand. "You shouldn't have brought them here anyway. You don't know what you're doing."

"What do that mean?"

"Look, Richard, maybe your idea of a good time is going to prison," Maxwell had said, his eyes bulging slightly.

"After all, you've already done a stretch, but it ain't gonna be my career. Now get them the hell out."

Maxwell had already been drunk, swaying as he talked.

"Come on, Tommy, you over- react. Frank coming tomorrow. He have us a way out the country, him."

Uncontrollable rage came over Maxwell, inspired by the culmination of several elements at once--the Dasch incident, the burning of his manuscript that day, the mention of Frank's name, and the non-compliance of Thibadeaux. With a quick motion of his arm, he sent the bottle shattering onto the floor.

Thibadeaux looked lamely at the broken bottle and said, "Why you do that?"

Maxwell stared at Richard for a moment, then at the two women who had come to the kitchen door to watch.

He burst into laughter, staggering towards Mercienne.

""To hell with it," he had screamed. "Eat, drink, and make with the women."

Everyone had laughed and the party had continued.

Mercienne had been compliant, as usual, and Maxwell, in his drunkenness, mechanical.

He missed Julie more than he cared to admit, and he had been very close to calling her on different occasions.

Maxwell cleaned up the glass, dumped it in the kitchen garbage, got a wet cloth from the sink, and wiped up the sticky hard-wood floor. He went back to the kitchen to make coffee. He had just lit the gas stove when he heard footsteps behind him.

Richard Thibadeaux wore long shorts and an undershirt.

A cigarette protruded out the corner of his wide mouth. His long face was unshaven.

"Making coffee?" he said, as he searched the upper cabinet for an unopened bottle of bourbon. "Need something to sweeten the mud?"

He found the bottle, opened it, and took a long drink.

Maxwell turned and said, "No thanks."

Thibadeaux noticed that Maxwell was fixing breakfast.

"Hell, the girls do that."

Maxwell waved his hand. "After making an ass of myself, it's the least I can do."

"You get breakfast ready," Thibadeaux said, leaning back, "I get rid of the broads, then we meet Frank."

"Are you going to be drunk when he gets here?" Maxwell asked.

Thibadeaux moved the bottle in slow circles on the table.

"Don't know what he say, but I tell you how I going to spend my day. Packing. I ain't about to be in no Life magazine, me."

Maxwell was the first to eat. He made up his favorite concoction of eggs mixed with sausage bits.

While Thibadeaux and the girls finished their breakfasts, he again walked out to the beach. He sipped on another cup of steaming coffee. The coffee cut into the drunkenness. He would be sober by the time he had to meet Frank.

He watched the sea. The day was windy with white caps appearing just hundreds of yards from the beach. The gulls were farther out now over the green waves.

He loved the sea.

He guessed at what Frank Becken would say.

Frank had come to represent change in Tommy Maxwell's life. In the past he had asked for commitment; for a relinquishing of all excuses.

Maxwell had a morbid fascination with the traces of the war around him. Whenever oil and the debris of tankers would wash in off the great sea--oil-slicked lifejackets, ration containers, even sailors' hats--he found himself rummaging through the debris like a curious child.

He breathed in deeply. Yesterday had been a day of weakness. He had fumed for all he was worth about his situation.

He looked at that sea, at the churning green horizon. If Frank had come to ask what Maxwell suspected, he would not be disappointed. The waiting would be over. He would approach his mission with commitment and strength, with the discipline and courage of a soldier.

Mac's Pub was located on a side street in Morgan City.

A speakeasy with a dance floor at night, with the suggestive sign on the outside reading, "Ladies and Gentlemen Welcome," where at nights marital status or former bonds rendered as weak as the revolving, purple light over the dance floor--by day, the bar was largely unoccupied, the booths over by the big window, steeped in shadow, the mutterings of the two regulars at the bar, under the large face of Mac, befitting the nature of the shadowed booths, soporific and conspiring.

It was after ten in the morning when Maxwell and Thibadeaux entered.

Frank Becken, suppressing a belch, his chin tucked into his plump chest, forced an uneasy wave. Maxwell ordered three bottles of Jax beer before joining Frank.

As greetings were exchanged, Maxwell could not help but notice the change in Frank's demeanor since the last time he had seen him. Gone were the corpulent, reddened cheeks of

health and the small, merry eyes. Maxwell sat at such an angle that the white light of the outside reflected against Becken's glasses, his eyes not visible, thus highlighting the ugly, thin mouth, turned down at the corners, the pock-mocked, fat cheeks.

"Boy, Frank, you look rode hard and hung up wet," Maxwell said, surprised and repulsed by the sound of his own voice, with its tone of forced friendliness. "You're the changingest son of a bitch I've seen."

"No time for small talk," Becken said tightly. "You do read the papers."

Thibadeaux laughed loudly, leaning back.

"Are you drunk?" Becken asked accusingly.

"Couple of nips on the way," Thibadeaux said. "Only tipsy, Frank."

"Have some discipline."

"To hell with discipline," Maxwell said, "this Dasch thing has left us with our asses hanging out."

"Don't worry. You're leaving the country."

"Don't tell us not to worry. We get caught, we hanged like them others, us."

"How you been?"

"No time for small talk."

"You and the wife still on the splits, you?"

"Yeah, like I say, let's get on with it before this place crowds up."

"You say we're leaving the country. Brief us."

"You are instructed go to this spot where a vehicle will be waiting for you."

"Where the spot?"

"Five miles south on Highway 4."

"Lord Jesus, that pure swamp."

"An abandoned pickup will be waiting. The keys in the glove box. The rest is self-explanatory."

"Are we just running or is it a mission?"

"Both. I can tell you nothing else. You will be briefed."

"What about the money?"

"Same old Richard," he said.

"That's right, same old Richard," mimicked Thibadeaux.

"If I working for the Germans and....."

"Lower your voice.."

"No one can hear us. What's the matter with you?"

"Nothing," Frank muttered. "Nothing will be wrong if you're careful. Even when you leave the country."

Becken held up a hand. "Say no more. The money will be as promised. You now work for the greatest empire.....

"Goddammit," Maxwell said, "Take your parlor talk about Germany's destiny and the Bund's role in world peace and stick them up your ass, Frank. We're screwed thanks to you."

Becken's eyes twitched with anger.

"Grow up, Tommy, goddammit. You've gone in with both eyes open, and if you know what's good for you, you'll shutup and listen to what I have to say."

"Some people never learn. Okay, Frank, I'm listening again."

"Reinhart Heydrich is dead."

"Right, he's dead," Maxwell said, as he shoved his untouched beer aside and leaned on the table with both elbows." I read the papers too, you know. Personally, I never knew the guy."

"Who's Heydrich?"

Maxwell shook his head as he spoke and pounded the cigarette butt against the table before lighting up. "The head of the SD, SS intelligence, moron."

A tremendous fart exploded from Becken, whose face with its downturned mouth, pockmarked cheeks, and downcast eyes, despite Thibadeaux's laughter, held a look of resigned embarrassment--flushing now, as he spoke, the eyes invisible now as his head rose, the thick glasses reflecting the white light of the morning sun--the tone of his voice deep, atremble, monotone--as if trying to mollify, in a stoic sound, the ominous nature of his words.

"It's all coming apart," he said in a barely audible voice.

"If either of you has an ounce of intelligence left, you will both be quiet and listen. What I am about to tell you could cost me my life."

When Thibadeaux started to speak, Maxwell touched his elbow.

Becken reviewed for Thibadeaux's benefit the nature of Heydrich's death, including the details of the SS reprisals in Lidice.

"What you must understand," Becken said with sad eyes, "is that in times of war certain kinds of people become necessary, people who would be unacceptable under normal circumstances."

"You're talking about the SS," Maxwell said, as he watched Becken's small eyes move to the side, avoiding his gaze.

"Yes," he said, as he pinched his nose and hiccuped, "the Reichsfuhrer has taken an interest in Kaninchen."

"Himmler?" Maxwell heard his voice say.

"Heydrich contacted me through coded letters," Becken said.

This time his eyes looked directly into Maxwell's with a severe gaze. "He wanted to know all about Kaninchen. From me. It was as if he were spying on the Abwehr."

"So what? I thought you said he dead, him."

"It's coming apart. The allies could never have gotten him without inside information. I think even the Abwehr hated him, maybe feared him."

"You're speaking in riddles, Frank," Maxwell said, as he felt a trickle of sweat on his temple. "The Abwehr and the SS are all Germans."

"Don't be naive," Becken said with a sigh. "Germany has never been united under Hitler. Remember the Night of the Long Knives."

"What's that?"

Maxwell listened with a disinterested air as Becken reviewed for Thibadeaux the night of June 30, 1934.

It was Hitler's move against the head of the massive SA, Ernst Rohm, that first revealed the nature of the SS. Originally recruited as an imperial guard to protect the Fuhrer, and later evolving into a militaristic sect, and influenced by the fanatical Himmler, the SS grew in numbers and ideology.

Goering and Himmler convinced Hitler that an SA putsch was imminent. More importantly, Hitler became aware of a public resentment of SA strong arm tactics in the streets.

Frank's eyes, barely visible off the glare of his glasses, twitched as he spoke. Thibadeaux watched a girl outside the window, her skirt billowing in the sunlight as she waited for a bus.

"It was not that they did not have skilled assassins available, but the nature of the murders required no such finesse.

One man was killed in his home with a pick axe. Another hanged in front of his family inside his house, another shot in woods adjacent to his house. After the initial outbreak of violence, the official arrests and executions began. Rohm was not spared."

"I heard he queer and everything, him. What's this got to do with us?"

"Heydrich's death, I believe, temporarily saved the Abwehr."

"What are you talking about, Frank?"

Becken's eyes remained blank. "I believe the SD is trying to infiltrate the Abwehr. Canaris insists on the Wehrmacht's autonomy from SS control. Heydrich did not comply, but now with this Dasch thing, the Abwehr has been further discredited by the SD. The SD insisted that Kaninchen be aborted. The Abwehr refused, stating that they had autonomy."

"Why was Heydrich killed, Frank?"

"It was to send a message to Himmler."

"What are you talking about?"

"I could be wrong. But I think it has something to do with the camps."

"Concentration camps?"

Becken's eyes now watched Maxwell beneath the thin glasses.

"You know that I have connections with I.G. Farben, the German chemical company. They and their affiliates were very much hurt by the Rohm purge. They supported Rohm. With things as they are now, they had no choice but to get in bed with Himmler. My friend in Munich, Gustave Brempt, contacted me about some of their product development, through a pharmaceutical subsidiary--a gas called T-4."

At this Becken's voice temporarily broke.

"There are rumors coming out of Russia. Rumors about SS units, coming in behind the Wehrmacht, enacting what is being called 'extreme measures.' The orders came from Heydrich, which means ultimately from Himmler. He has been charged with a horrific task. Extermination. Not random acts. Systematic policy. My contact tells me that Einsatzgrouppen units are shooting Jews by the thousands and that Heydrich sought more efficient means......gas vans.......he was not explicit....

anyway, he thinks Heydrich has organized the same measures in Europe."

Becken belched before continuing.

"Canaris is crushed. Brempt tells me that his whole manner has changed. He is unkempt, dejected, uncharacteristically cynical. He opposes the SS initiatives in Russia. He is an honorable man. He wants the same things we want--negotiations. And I am told he is working with all his powers to strike a bargain for peace with the Allies. With

Hitler's challenge to the world and Germany now faced with a two front war, he believes defeat to be inevitable."

"Are you telling us to back out?"

"I am telling you to trust no one. Follow orders, yes, but remember that you may come in contact with those who have an interest in you being seen as disloyal."

"Are we still under Abwehr orders?" Maxwell asked.

"Yes, but the SD is everywhere, in every organization.

Their game is infiltration and intimidation. Heydrich's main function through the SD has always been disinformation. That's how Rohm was over-thrown, that's how the Wehrmacht's generals lost control of the army to the Fuhrer principle. Heydrich and the SD are everywhere. Heydrich is dead, but his SD is alive and well, under Himmler."

"What have you gotten us into Frank?"

"Your eyes were open."

"Yeah, they're open now."

"My recommendation is still for you to go."

"Let me guess, we catch a trawler to Mexico."

"I must go now. You have been briefed."

"This stuff about the Jews, Frank," Maxwell said, touching his beer glass, "is it possible you're mistaken? It sounds like a lie."

"Anything is possible, Tommy. Good luck to both of you. I have to go."

June 27, 1942

At dusk a gray taxi cab pulled to the shoulder on Highway 4, south of Morgan City. Maxwell and Thibadeaux paid and began walking up the road to a faded red pickup truck, a half mile ahead. On both sides of the two lane the reeds and thick undergrowth reached out in long fingers towards the asphalt. The trees were laced with Spanish moss. The sky was overcast. Shadows were falling, punctuated by an occasional rattle of a cricket or call of an egret.

When Maxwell and Thibadeaux reached the truck, they threw

their bags into the back. Maxwell got in on the driver's side while Thibadeaux opened the glove compartment, which yielded keys and a crudely drawn map.

"According to this we travel west until we come to a dirt road, leading south," Thibadeaux said.

The pickup was the only vehicle on the road and rattled slightly from a loose hood latch. Finding the dirt road on the left, the two men turned and drove eleven miles further in.

"Look like gator country to me," Thibadeaux said. The road wound snake-like through the forbidding marsh country. They slowed only once for an armadillo which was eating its prey in the center of the cow trail.

Several miles in, the road ended abruptly as it yawned into a small clearing, containing a mud-stained shack with a rickety dock in the back, made of barrels and planks. A small fishing boat was tied behind the dock. The dark water of the swamp stretched like a black mirror through the trees, their trunks descending directly into the water, the moss barely allowing view of the sky. The headlights of the pickup stood out starkly against the shack, their illumination giving no sign of life, save for the swirling insects, frantically spinning in the twin beams.

Maxwell killed the lights.

"What we do now?" Thibadeaux asked.

"Wait."

Within minutes they heard another car, coming in behind them. The old two-tone Buick which drove into the clearing was badly in need of a muffler.

Maxwell and Thibadeaux got out and greeted a tall man in baggy overalls and a mechanic's hat.

"You be the one we suppose to meet," Thibadeaux said.

In the darkness Maxwell could barely make out the man's scraggly features. The man did not answer, only walked over to the shack and unlocked the padlocked door. The inside of the hut contained shelves full of supplies, a gas stove, four cots, a table, and three chairs.

The man went over to the table and lit a lantern. The light revealed a face full of gray whiskers with small eyes, which burned under dark eyebrows. When the man removed his cap and motioned towards the two chairs by the table, Maxwell could see deep crow's feet around his eyes. The man's head was completely bald.

The man got another chair and the three men sat at the table.

"How do you do," he said, thrusting his hand out vigorously and shaking both men's hands in turn. "My name is Douglas Nikelsen. I am your contact and responsible for your safe passage out."

"Tommy Maxwell."

"No need for introductions, Herr Maxwell. I hope you don't mind me using the German form; you'll need to get used to it. I'm quite familiar with both of you. I've been watching you for weeks."

"Funny," Thibadeaux said, looking suspiciously at the man, "I think I would remember you, babe."

The man laughed deeply. "I can look different."

While the three men made small talk, Maxwell lit a cigarette.

Weather-beaten, a small brown splotch on one cheek, Nikelson looked every bit the part of a local fisherman. He was as much a part of the terrain and landscape as the moss that hung from the trees outside or the wind-driven palm trees by the sea. And yet it was obvious by his chosen vernacular that he had spent time in Germany or perhaps had been a citizen. When Maxwell broached the subject, Nikelson laughed aloud and with an upturned palm said, "I decline to answer anything about my origins. It is my job to know everything about you. Not the other way around."

"How much you know about us?" Richard asked, pparently offended.

Nikelson bristled. "Refrain from subjects that detract from the immediate purpose. Future training will teach you more discipline."

Maxwell and Thibadeaux laughed.

Nikelson frowned at the laughter. "Damn," he said.

"Americans find humor in the oddest things. What is funny?"

"Life is funny, pal," Maxwell said, looking Nikelson directly in the eyes. "It's a regular riot, especially when your ass is in a sling like ours."

Nikelson shrugged. "I know English well enough. But you will have to translate the slang."

"Forget it," Maxwell said. "Brief us. What the hell are we doing here?"

"Mexico," Thibadeaux said, as he lit a cigarette and looked at Nikelson with half-closed eyes.

The man leaned back and laughed in his deep tone. "Not quite, I'm afraid."

"So what's the story," Maxwell said, growing impatient.

"You two are anxious to leave," Nikelson said. "I do not blame you after what happened."

"It's our ass if we don't," Thibadeaux said.

"Dasch is a pig," Nikelson spat. "A jellyfish who....."

"Get to the point," Maxwell said, who lit Richard's cigarette from his. "I'd like to know what's going on. The F.B.I. proved pretty efficient in the last week."

"That's untrue," Nikelson said. "You've been reading

the newspapers too much. Dasch called the bureau three times before he could get anyone to believe him. The F.B.I. did nothing. They spent their time bickering with Naval Intelligence over jurisdiction. They would have known nothing had it not been for that spineless traitor."

"Whatever," Maxwell said, stubbing out his cigarette on the table and leaning forward. "It doesn't really matter, does it? The spies are now awaiting execution, that's what matters to me, god dammit. Now what's the scoop?"

Nikelson folded his hands together on the table.

"Midnight tomorrow you will rendezvous with a German U boat. The U boat is now submerged twenty miles off shore, awaiting her mission. You'll receive her passengers, help them stow their gear, then I'll carry them by boat back here to this safe house. They will embark from here to their assignments. Once your job is done on the beach, you will board a skiff and be taken aboard the U boat. You will remain aboard her until you arrive at the submarine base in Lorient, France."

Maxwell paled.

"You're joking," he said.

"Hardly."

"Us? On a submarine? I can't even swim, me," Thibadeaux said with a nervous smile.

The man's fist pounded on the table. "Be serious," he shouted. "I envy you greatly. It's time you confront reality.

This is no adventure you read about in the funny papers. The war out there is real, as you shall soon see."

"But France," Maxwell said, tossing his hair off his forehead. "Why France?"

"I don't know. I would assume it's for further training."

"Right," Thibadeaux said. "Frank mentioned that."

"His code name is Seawolf," Nikelson shot. "As I'm sure you have been told. Use it from now on."

"No need to get touchy," Richard said.

"That's where you're wrong," Nikelson said. "When you greeted me, you said, 'I guess you're the one we're supposed to meet.' A very stupid thing to say. At the risk of repeating myself, let me emphasize, that you cannot be too careful. You are obviously special in some way. It's time you started acting like it."

June 28, 1942

Late the next night the three men started out in the small fishing boat. Never starting the motor, they paddled in silence. Maxwell kneeled in the front of the boat and occasionally turned on the flashlight when stumps threatened their path. With one hand he held the flashlight and in the other a Colt 45 pistol. He fended off the low limbs as Nikelson sat at the back of the boat, steering the small craft through the gloom.

Thibadeaux, who sat in the middle, was assigned the task of paddling and watching both sides of the boat.

The night was dark in the swamp, and for the life of him, Maxwell could not fathom how Nikelson navigated. He made several turns and wherever they went, the stagnant black water, the moss hanging from the low, overhanging trees like old, tattered curtains, and worst of all, long vines draping into the water continually impeded their progress.

The slow movement of the boat in the blind swamp gave the impression that the boat was perpetually still with eerie black facades rotating around it. If Maxwell had been left alone now, he would have been helplessly lost.

"Keep a sharp lookout, Thibadeaux," Nikelson said from beneath his fishing cap. "Pan both sides of the boat constantly. Gators are known for charging fishing boats broadside. They like to sun in the day and feed at night."

"Swell," Maxwell said.

After over an hour of paddling, they ran out of swamp as the land gave a slight rise two miles from the sea.

Nikelson steered the boat into a pocket of branches. The two men climbed onto the land while Nikelson tied the boat on both ends. After both men had secured small back packs, checked their lights and pistols, Nikelson produced a long piece of rope from a metal box. Each man allowed a six foot interval between the other as they tied the twenty foot rope around their waists. Holstering their pistols, the men each took a stick from the boat in order to probe the ground for quicksand beds.

"Feel your way carefully," Nikelson said. "If you should step into a quicksand bed, immediately lie down. Don't try to stand up, you'll sink. Lie down so you'll float on top where I can pull you out."

"I can't tell you when I've had so much fun," Maxwell said.

Thibadeaux laughed. "Sort of like escaping the slammer huh?"

"What in hell are you two talking about?" Nikelson spat.

"You know your way around here, Nikelson," Maxwell said.

"Can't you tell us where the beds are?"

"It's always different at night."

A cool breeze blew in from the south.

"Feels good out," Thibadeaux said.

"Think I'll leave it out," Maxwell said.

Both men laughed at Nikelson, who shook his head in disgust at the joke.

The three men wound through the dark shadows.

It was close to 11:00 p.m. when they made the beach.

For an hour they remained hidden among reeds on a dune overlooking the beach and ocean. Maxwell and Thibadeaux spent their time converting the contents of their backpacks to seaman's bags, which they had packed in.

The night was moonless and there was no sign of life on the horizon. Not even the lights of freighters could be seen, only the occasional rush of a wave, breaking in a white line on the beach.

The breaking sea, the shrill, far-away cry of egrets, the black horizon of water which touched the dark sky--all these things threw Maxwell into a feeling of both nostalgia and anticipation.

He thought of his occasional perusals of the coastline, where he found great slicks of oil from a sunken tanker, debris washed on the shore; the only touches that America got of the war at sea.

Now it would be different. All the speculation was to end. The war would come in from the horizon to claim him in the form of a German inflatable raft.

He looked over the dunes and was mesmerized by the sea.

It was the same hypnotic effect one has while looking at a fire, forever changing and forever the same.

"How about a cigarette?" Maxwell said.

"No smoking," Nikelson said. "We sit and wait."

The three men maintained a silent vigil. Orders from the Abwehr, the intelligence arm of the Wehrmacht, had instructed them to meet a German landing party no later than midnight.

Thibadeaux's black mole was visible even in the dark.

"Okay, Nikelson, I thought the damn Germans least would be on time," Thibadeaux said. "It time right now."

Nikelson did not answer, only glared briefly at Thibadeaux and continued looking at the sea.

"I just wish I had a cigarette," Maxwell said.

Twenty minutes later they spotted what appeared to be a tiny dot on the sea. Gradually the dot grew little tentacles which felt the water. Soon it could be seen that the tiny dot was an inflatable rubber skiff with seven men rowing towards the shore.

Nikelson's eyes widened. "They're here, only minutes off time," he said.

When the skiff was within fifty yards of the beach, Maxwell could see that four of the men were shirtless and wore bathing suits. When they neared the shore, the seven men jumped from the skiff and ushered it over the breaking waves. When the inflatable was safely ashore, Maxwell, Nikelson, and Thibadeaux emerged from their positions. The men in bathing suits were removing large cartons onto the beach and were busied dragging them up the sand. The two men accompanied by Nikelson approached three German seamen, dressed in dark naval blues.

Nikelson spoke in German to the first officer. The two seamen were ordered over to the inflatable. Nikelson approached the four men in swim suits and began rattling German to them and pointing towards the dune. All but one kept to their task of unloading the crates while one raised up and listened. He had blonde hair and a thick moustache.

"Wie spat ist es?" he asked Maxwell.

Maxwell only looked at him.

"Sonst noch etwas?" Nikelson replied.

"Nein."

He motioned for Maxwell and Thibadeaux to accompany him down to the inflatable. The two German navy men, dressed in their blues, looked at Maxwell.

"Kaninchen," one of the Germans said.

"Ja," Thibadeaux said.

Maxwell laughed. "Didn't know you spoke such good German, Richard."

"Kiss my ass."

"Wer ist das?" the other man said to Nikelson.

"Das ist Herr Tommy Maxwell und Richard Thibadeaux."

The four men shook hands. The two Germans were seamen Mueller and Zimmerman. The four men in bathing suits dragged another carton to the brush beyond the beach.

"Bury them just over those dunes," shouted Nikelson.

"We'll retrieve them tomorrow night."

The shirtless, blonde German nodded and motioned to the others. With little difficulty they dragged the crate over the dune and returned for another.

"After the crates are concealed, you men can be underway,"

Nikelson said to the first officer, who was tall and bearded. "Maxwell, Thibadeaux....First Officer Danet."

The man that stood before them was taller than the rest with dark features. When Maxwell looked him in the eye, he noticed that the officer's eyes only met his for an instant, dancing and twitching to other objects even as he spoke, as if not able to focus on only one thing, hungrily searching for ore. The officer spoke with a slight, nervous stutter, as if his tongue was forever just a click behind his rapid thoughts.

"Pleased," Maxwell said on shaking hands.

"Stow your gear," Danet said, motioning to the raft.

Manipulating small shovels that they had packed in, the shirtless Germans dug into the sand in a great hurry. Quickly and without speaking, they finished burying the crates and rearranging the sand above the burial sites.

While all this occurred, the First Officer Danet and Nikelson spoke rapid German in low voices.

As Maxwell stowed his gear, he thought he heard Danet mention his name to Nikelson. As he walked up the beach, Maxwell saw Nikelson point at Thibadeaux and himself as he talked.

"He telling him to fix you grits in the morning,"

Thibadeaux said, nudging Maxwell with his elbow.

"Shutup, horseface," Maxwell said.

The tall German officer glared at the Americans as Nikelson again approached them.

The skiff was back in the tide now. Just before the Americans waded into the surf, Nikelson shook their hands and clasped their shoulders.

"You both are very lucky," he said. "You will be part of the greatest empire the world has ever known. Auf Wiedersehen and good luck."

"Thanks for everything."

"Heil Hitler," Nikelson said.

"Right," Maxwell said. From the moment he had met Nikelson, he was repulsed by his stiff behavior.

Maxwell and Thibadeaux moved to the rubber skiff. The blue-clad sailors joined them and soon they were up to their chests in the teeming surf before boarding the craft. The rowing was tough at first until they were out of the undertow. They rowed for an hour. No one spoke. Five miles up the coast to the west, beyond the swamp lands, the shore twinkled in the distance. Americans had not yet learned the trick of extinguishing lights on the coast at nights. Soon the land appeared as a long, gray finger. The breeze was constant, the waves gentle.

It was after 2 o'clock when Maxwell spotted a long, dark shape ahead. A tower jutted up from the shape. As they neared the boat, Maxwell could make out the depiction on the conning tower. It was that of the dragon's head of a Norse ship, its gaping mouth and wild eyes cast skyward.

When the skiff pulled alongside, the Americans were ushered on deck and down the conning hatch.

Soon there were no forms to be seen on the long, black shape. The sound of diesel engines interrupted the calm moan of the breeze off the sea. The boat began to cut through the gentle waves.

The sound of the U-boat's diesels like the diesels of a train--at night, their sound the portent of the great steel snake that rips through the velvet darkness--the land vibrating in great plains out the window--and always in the diesels images.

The tunnel swallows us in a funnel of darkness--blind, only now the rush and echo of the great wheels, the crash, the diesels.

CHAPTER 5

THE ACTION

Even as Maxwell was hustled down the conning hatch by Zimmerman, he could hear the bustle of activity behind him while two German seamen cursed as they deflated the skiff.

The gentle breeze of the night was transformed immediately as the two men descended the ladder into a red-tinted dungeon, which gave off the most disgusting stench.

"Show them around," said First Officer Danet. "Mueller, go with them, I'm going forward."

When Zimmerman and Mueller threw off their hats, Maxwell noticed how much they looked like all the rest of the crew, every man bearded heavily in the red-tinted darkness and smell. They had entered the control room, and people were scooting down the ladder from the tower compartment.

"Prepare to get underway," said a balding man with a black beard and white hair.

"This is Captain Schuller," Zimmerman said.

"Save the introductions for later, Zimmerman," Schuller said. "Take them aft."

"Jawohl, mein Kapitan."

A loud clanking sounded above as three men slid down the ladder with the remaining paraphernalia from the skiff. A loud, churning noise vibrated the boat as Maxwell and Thibadeaux ducked their heads, exiting the control room.

Men were busied on the two walls behind them, turning red wheels on the walls.

"30 degrees left and all ahead full," came the command behind them.

As they progressed through the boat, the scene completely changed every few feet. The only constants were the bearded faces of the men, the narrowness of the passage, and the smell.

"This is the galley and washroom area," said the smiling face of Zimmerman. "Too bad we have no fresh water to bathe with, right Mueller?"

Mueller laughed and pointed forward."Holger Duggan, these are our two guests, Maxwell and Thibadeaux....Americans."

"Be friendly with him, he is our cook," Zimmerman said with a smile. "And believe me, he is not beyond poisoning his enemies."

"Ja, welcome aboard," said the corpulent man who grunted as the ship turned sharply left and he dropped his paring knife in the sink.

"Kartoffeln again," Mueller said.

"Idiot," Duggan said.

Mueller and Zimmerman laughed.

Mueller hopped around in a comical, mimicking jig.

"Shutup and get out of my way," Duggan said amid the four men's laughter.

"Oh, yes, back here is the Petty officers' quarters. This is where you will bunk. Twelve men sleep in this little huddle, six bunks in shifts of two. This is Chief Petty Officer Hagermeister."

A stout man with a brown beard turned and shook both men's hands. He wore a customary seaman's undershirt around his hairy frame, the shirt in the pattern of black and white horizontal stripes.

"Wo wohnt sie?" said the burly man.

"Speak English, idiot," Mueller said.

Maxwell tensed as the officer turned, but the spark of mirth in the merry eyes, as he spoke stern German, caused the two seamen to laugh.

Hagermeister was apparently the type of officer that could remain on terms of familiarity with his men and still command respect.

"He asked where you are from," Zimmerman said.

"North Carolina," Maxwell replied.

"Ich ben aus Nord Caroline."

"I heard him, idiot," said the chief petty officer. "Here," he said as he grabbed from a side compartment under a bunk two neatly folded sets of rubber clothing and two orange life preservers. "Stow these under the two bunks. You two are lucky, you get your own beds....guests and all....let's hope we don't have to use these."

"Thanks." They stowed their gear.

The sound of the diesels grew as they proceeded aft. The submarine was still running from the coast and was yet to dive.

The hatch opened in front of the Americans. They ducked into a long room, full of sweaty, shirtless men, huge, churning pistons on both walls, and a deafening noise.

"We get to sleep next to this," Maxwell said smiling.

"This is the diesel room," Mueller said. "This is Officer Olmsbruck, Peter."

The shirtless man who stood in the middle of the aisle with officer's hat cocked to the side did not bother to speak, but merely smiled and waved at the two other men.

"It is not a pleasant sound on first hearing it," Mueller said, who put a cigarette into his mouth. "But you will grow to love it."

"It sounds like we're heading home," added Zimmerman.

Officer Olmsbruck smiled and shrugged his shoulders.

"Let's go."

The three men headed forward, through the galley and head areas, through the petty officers' area where four men amazingly slept against the walls amid the noise, into the control room which was bustling with activity as Schuller followed the periscope up, after giving the "Periscope level" command, while the men on the walls turned the red wheels madly. Men were monitoring the maze of yellow dials on the walls, two men worked over a chart while plotting coordinates, and men were running back and forth through the compartment.

"Prepare to dive."

Now the red wheels turning furiously as U-168 slipped gently under the water. Officer Danet reported the depth over the dial that read Teisenmeiser.

"Take her to fifty meters and proceed on course," the Captain ordered.

As he headed forward, Maxwell was reminded of the feeling which had assaulted him on first entering the U boat. It was a feeling mixed with the repugnance of the air coupled with a sense of claustrophobia. In the dank confines of the interior of U-168, the Americans felt as if they were in a close, poorly ventilated cave. Although at first Maxwell thought he would vomit from the stench, it was not long, he realized, before his own body would have the same smell. As Zimmerman explained, due to prolonged periods of being submerged and a shortage of fresh water, the men could not bathe for weeks.

"This is the radio room," Zimmerman said, lifting the earphones, and saying, "This is Hans."

The man with the weasel-like face, wearing glasses, smiled thinly and waved. Maxwell could hear the whine and crack of the radio with the voice amid the high-pitched whir, speaking in English.

"Got anything on that?" Thibadeaux asked.

"One of your eyes off New Orleans behind us has spotted an English freighter."

"Let's go get her," Mueller said.

"Can't.......orders," Hans said, who seemed relieved to return to his hydrophones.

Every inch of space was utilized to store supplies. Potatoes, pots and pans, and chains hung from the ceiling. The walls were a maze of pipings, wheels, and dials.

They walked into a cozy huddle with a map table between bunks. Two men slept here. A small radio sat on the table.

"These are officers' quarters, come on, I'll show you the toughest job on the boat.....this is the torpedo room."

Again Maxwell was amazed that the four men who slept in the bunks on the floor could sleep so soundly while men further on in the room labored over the huge torpedoes. Four shirtless men were moving torpedoes with a wheel apparatus on the floor. The end of the room was a maze of tubes, pipes, hatches, valves, and wheels.

"The aft torpedo room is behind the diesel room, which is the only place you haven't been. Oh yes, and this is the shitter," Zimmerman said as he pounded on the closed metal door. Someone cursed inside. "Usually it is full of provisions when we start, so we all have to use the aft one."

"Everyone seems to be in good spirits," Maxwell said.

"We've had good hunting off New Orleans......two sinkings, besides, some of us got to go ashore in Cuba too. Mickey even got a damned tree. Come, I'll show you. But the main thing is that we are heading home."

"You say hunting is good?" Maxwell asked.

"Magnificent," Zimmerman replied. "The American coast is still lit up at nights like a Christmas tree, silhouetting our targets."

"Ja," Mueller added with a yawn. "And the tankers are good enough to radio each other quite frequently. They give away their positions. We are returning heroes, and ah, here is Mickey and Rhinehardt."

These were two gunners who sat and smoked on their bunks. After the usual introductions, again the good-natured kidding between crewmen commenced.

"Mickey has a tree there from Cuba," Mueller said, who pointed to a pathetic little dried-up twig inside a small pot.

"Ja, you like it," said the blonde seaman, who with his Hitleresque moustache and knotty, high forehead, along with an eye that was obviously made of glass, had a distinctive appearance.

"Makes you realize how desperate we are for the good earth," laughed the huge man, Rhinehardt, at whom Mickey glanced with annoyance. "Shutup and give me a cigarette," Mickey said.

Maxwell and Thibadeaux had a brief word with the Captain and spent the remainder of their first day aboard in their bunks, where they slept for several hours like the dead.

Life aboard a U- boat was far from what Maxwell imagined it to be. From his first moments aboard the craft, he experienced that silent desperation, which was etched to one degree or another on each bearded face. Scores of shirtless men lived practically on top of each other. The machinery encroached from all sides. Tubes, valves, wheels, pipings coated the walls. Many places in the boat were dark. One could barely move in the corridors without brushing against another shirtless body, and the stench of the diesel fuel was prevalent during surface running. The noise and distraction to the nerves were constant. Maxwell and Thibadeaux soon became part of the daze that was to affect each crew member. They were a full day and a half at sea before they were summoned to the Captain's nook for a briefing. They found the Captain, sitting before a radio which played a Mozart concerto. Schuller was in his undershirt, yet still wore his captain's hat, white with the scrambled eggs on the bill. From his black beard protruded a brown pipe, whose every puff he seemed to relish. He smelled of lemon cologne, the same concoction that crew members used to wipe the salt water from their faces.

"Sit down, gentlemen. I hope you have been as comfortable as possible," the Captain said.

The Americans looked at each other. They could not help laughing.

"Ah, yes, I see you have not gotten over your culture shock yet," Schuller said, removing the pipe from his mouth. "Not from being around Germans, as much as being aboard our little floating casket here."

"That's......not funny," Maxwell said with a twist of his eyebrows. "Not funny at all."

"All right, and Herr Thibadeaux?" the Captain said.

"I do all right here, sir," Thibadeaux said. "I was in prison for a time, you know."

The three men laughed again.

"It is refreshing to have someone with a sense of humor along. The analogy quite fits, by the way, Herr Thibadeaux."

The affable smile disappeared from his face, followed by a thoughtful, then stern look.

"As for your briefing," the Captain said, "obviously, you gentlemen are involved in intelligence. What your mission is, or the nature of what you will encounter once ashore is none of my business. Personally, I would rather stick to the task at hand of sinking enemy shipping, rather than get mixed up in these intrigues. Nevertheless, I follow orders like everyone else."

"Are there any duties you would have us do while on board?" Maxwell asked.

"Right," Thibadeaux said. "Anything to pass the time."

"Sorry, regulations forbid you to do anything truly constructive. But since you have two weeks with us and probably at least that much coming back, you might as well afford yourself the opportunity of learning passable German. Chief Petty Officer Hagermeister can be most helpful. In fact, I will assign him the task."

"We don't want to put anyone out," Maxwell said.

"He is the type that enjoys such things," replied Schuller.

After asking permission, Maxwell and Thibadeaux lit up cigarettes.

"Now as for your briefing," continued the Captain, "as you can see, the biggest problem we have here is exercise. The crew rotates in groups of four for bridge time where you can help hold watch and get an hour or two of fresh air. Enjoy it while it lasts. It goes without saying that you are to discuss no part of your operation with anyone on board. When we arrive in Lorient, you will be well advised to stay close to your quarters. Bars and restaurants are full of British eyes and ears. It would not take a genius to spot you as Americans."

"A good reason for learning German," Thibadeaux said.

"Precisely, now," began the Captain, and then he broke off and rubbed one of his gray temples. "Now as for one other matter..." and again he broke off his speech and began knocking his pipe out.

"What is it, Captain?" Maxwell asked.

"Never mind," Schuller said. "I was going to alert you to one other factor, but there is no sense in anticipating trouble. Sometimes it is best to leave things alone."

"What you talking about?" Thibadeaux asked.

"It's nothing. Do you have any questions?"

"No sir."

"Chief Petty Officer Hagermeister will see that you are assigned bridge schedule. Now if there is nothing else, I have work to do."

Over the next three days Maxwell plunged into impromptu German lessons with Hagermeister. Thibadeaux made a feeble attempt, but quickly became bored. He spent the majority of his time teaching the boys in the engine room the game of poker. Within days, he had relieved several of them of a month's wages. Maxwell was fond of Hagermeister. His jolly cheeks and eyes, his husky, corpulent frame, reminded Maxwell of Frank Becken.

They spent most of their time talking of home. The German officer shared pictures of his wife and family, who lived in a small town called Bad Orb, and he seemed to take to the task of teacher and did his best to tell the American about life in Germany. He did not take offense that Maxwell declined to comment about his mission.

It was during their first turn on bridge, on their fifth day at sea that Maxwell and Thibadeaux became aware of the existence of Fritz Rosenberg and Hans Steinhoff.

The sea was calm, the sky without a cloud. U-168 was clipping along at 16 knots, her red and black colors flying at the top of the conning tower, the unfurled flag with the swastika in the middle, flanked by a depiction of the iron cross. The air flowed through Maxwell like a heady elixir. Hagermeister, Thibadeaux, and Maxwell stood on the bridge while two seamen accompanied by Officer Danet labored first on a radio aerial, damaged by a strong wind and then on one of the 3.5 deck guns. One of the men hung parallel over the deck on the cable, that ran from the bridge as Danet and a man with glasses shouted instructions to him.

Thibadeaux smoked and stared at the clear horizon, while Hagermeister drilled Maxwell on his German to pass the time.

"Are you ready?" Hagermeister asked, as he removed his hat, letting the breeze hit his forehead.

"Sure," Maxwell said, who knitted up his eyebrows. "I'll bet you a pack of cigarettes I get them all right."

"Only one pack, huh?"

"You want to make it more?"

Hagermeister laughed in his expansive way.

"Ja, let's make it two. You can't cheat now."

"No cheating." Maxwell noticed that Danet was now watching the bridge.

"Entschuldigen Sie, bitte."

"Excuse me please, is that right?"

"Ja, okay, Gehen Sie geradeaux und dann."

"Go straight ahead and then."

Hagermeister laughed. "And then, what?"

"That's all you said." Danet had walked to the foot of the bridge, staring up at the conversation above him.

"Danke gleichfalls."

"Thanks, same to you."

"Es tut mir leid."

"I'm sorry."

"Now say, 'Are you a teacher?'"

"Sind Sie Lehrer? Ja, ich bin Lehrer," Maxwell replied.

"Good, but I did not tell you to answer the question. I ought to charge you two packs of cigarettes for refusing to follow instructions," Hagermeister said.

"Vorne," Hagermeister continued.

"Up front."

"Hinten."

"In the rear."

"In der mitte."

"In the middle."

"Are you sure?" Hagermeister asked, raising his eyebrows and rubbing his stomach.

"Hell yes, I'm sure."

By this time Danet, his eyes dancing nervously back and forth, mounted the bridge, a large wrench in his hand.

"Ah," Hagermeister said, pointing a finger at Danet, "Mechanikerin."

Maxwell understood this to mean, "Mechanic." Danet flushed, his eyes danced madly. He spoke in heated German.

"Warum sind sie hier?"

"Die freizeit, mein oberleutnant," barked Hagermeister.

Danet stiffened and spoke in slow English. Maxwell noticed, as he spoke, that the two seamen were heading for the bridge with a black bag of tools.

"You seem quite interested in our repair work, Herr Maxwell," Danet said.

"Not really, first officer, I have no idea what you are doing."

"I am merely drilling him on his German," Hagermeister said.

Thibadeaux turned and grimaced as he flipped his cigarette away. "What you driving at, Danet?" he said.

Danet spoke in heated German at Hagermeister, the chief petty officer responding in kind.

"What's the problem?" Maxwell asked.

"You should know," Danet answered. "Since you sprechen sie Deutsh so well."

"He does not feel we are obligated to teach you German," Hagermeister said. "And I explained we are acting under Captain's orders."

Danet visibly shuddered. By this time Maxwell could see the faces of the two seamen, who had climbed onto the conning bridge and now stood shoulder to shoulder with Danet and seemed involved with the conversation. The shorter one was Fritz Rosenberg, as he was introduced by Hagermeister. He stood at five foot ten and had a well-muscled, compact torso. His eyes were set deep inside extremely pale skin, the nose above the beard, wide and flared like the snout of a boar hog; his moustache was in the style of Hindenburg and hid most of his ugly, down-turned mouth. He stood with his feet slightly spread, his arms folded across his wide chest, his neck stiff; he looked ready for a physical attack.

The other man was introduced as Hans Steinhoff. Much taller than his counterpart, Steinhoff had sandy hair, and wore wire rimmed spectacles over cold, clinical eyes, which contained a hint of laughter mixed with cold scrutiny. His face was thinner as was his mouth, and again inexplicably, he stood in the exact stance as Rosenberg, as if they had synchronized their every move in anticipation of this moment.

Thibadeaux sensed the situation and took a step back.

"Sprechen Sie English?" Maxwell asked Rosenberg.

"Nein."

And before Maxwell could say anything to Steinhoff, he answered in kind, "Nein."

Hagermeister's expression widened. "We are acting under orders, Herr Oberleutnant and if you are finished, we would like to continue."

Danet stood tall and peered down at Maxwell. "Continue what?" he said.

"Mindliche Ubung," Maxwell answered, meaning Oral Exercise.

"Mindliche Ubung," Steinhoff said, laughing and pointing down at his crotch. "Ja, Uben sie das, American."

Understanding the gesture, Thibadeaux tensed and raised his hands.

Rosenberg stared through him and spat just past his shoulder. Danet intervened.

"Let's go below."

"Jawohl, mein oberleutnant," Rosenberg screamed, all the time staring at Thibadeaux.

The three men went below.

"What was that all about?" Maxwell asked.

"Who are they?" Thibadeaux asked.

"You will find out soon enough," Hagermeister said.

Maxwell took a deep breath. Even ten minutes later as he stared at the edge of the horizon, where the azure sky met the sea, his stomach still tensed at the thought of the cold feeling that had run down his spine when Steinhoff had looked at him and pointed at his crotch. It was inexplicable, the feeling he had, as if in the gazes of the two seamen, there had been a conjured emotion, as regimented as their stiff gaits, a murderous look.

For the remainder of the bridge time, Hagermeister was jumpy and nervous. When queried again as to the identities of the two seamen, again he refused to discuss the matter.

The sea became choppy as black clouds emerged like a great black hood on the horizon.

"Yes, Yankee," Hagermeister said after Thibadeaux had gone below. "When you see Germany, you will see the world's most beautiful place. After the war you should become a citizen."

"Looks like a storm coming," Maxwell said.

"Ja."

Maxwell lit a cigarette. The great hood of black cloud crept over them. The sea below tossed U-168 in larger swells. A gray veil hung over the sea ahead.

"See there," Hagermeister said. "It's raining. A real storm in the damned Atlantic."

"One more time," Maxwell said. "Who were those two with Danet? What do you think?"

"I have learned long ago not to do that. If you are smart, you will do the same."

"Quit speaking in riddles," Maxwell said. "What's the dope?"

"I will not discuss what I think. I am a seaman, not a politician. I will discuss only what I see."

Maxwell shivered from the stiff breeze, blowing in from the storm.

"What do you see?"

"I see two seamen, Rosenberg and Steinhoff, who have joined our crew for this voyage. Supposedly experienced U boat mariners. I see them constantly doing special exercises on their own, never speaking to any of the crew, and staying exclusively in the circle with each other and Danet. They eat together, and only speak to each other....they are....."

"Yes?"

"I've told you what I see."

"And your conclusions."

Hagermeister took a deep breath as he gazed at the churning sky ahead.

"I have told you what I see. And now I see that we better get below."

"Die treppe hinunter," Maxwell said.

Hagermeister smiled. "Ja, die treppe hinunter."

The next two days were miserable for the Americans and many of the most experienced U boat mariners. U-168 headed due east into a terrific storm, which tossed the boat violently.

The Americans joined several other crew members, including Waisenhoffer, Mickey, and Rhinehardt in sharing a bucket for vomiting. During a particularly bad three hour spell, the boat constantly swayed and shifted. Maxwell continually focused on the little swinging lamp as it swayed over the middle of the aisle in the petty officer's quarters.

"If this boat be still for one second, I think I be okay, me," Thibadeaux said, his face a sickly pale color.

"Why don't the son of a bitch dive?" Maxwell said.

"Guess he making time and charging his batteries."

The next day Thibadeaux provided the crew with a touch of humor. He had ventured over to Schnegel, the steersman, who wore a beret and a foul weather coat. Thibadeaux had tried to start a conversation with the steersman, but the bearded face barely acknowledged the fresh American, so intent were his attentions both to the orders from the bridge and the various dials and mechanisms around him. He seemed hardened, yet at the same time, exasperated by the constant splash of waves, which came through the open hatch on top of him.

Thibadeaux had walked over and lit a cigarette when a great shoot of water shot down through the hatch, drenching him and leaving the soggy cigarette broken in two in his mouth. But in three hours both Americans had retired to their bunks for the duration of the storm.

Two men passed Maxwell in slick oil skins. They were speaking in rapid German and Maxwell made out that one of them was afraid of being washed overboard.

Schuller kept to the surface five hours into the second day before diving. Finally, the waves had become unbearable. Men were tossed from one side of the cabin to the other. Once a closet door had opened and a seaman buried in an avalanche of potatoes.

"At least we're safe in a U boat," Maxwell said. "Don't have worry about sinking."

"I feel better dead," Thibadeaux said, who managed a smile before his turn with the bucket.

Eight hours later when Schuller again surfaced, the sea still tossed U-168 like a tiny stick. It was not until 5:14, nearly dawn, on their twelfth day at sea that they came out of the gale.

The cool air flowed through the boat. Breakfast was served--sausages and hot, cooked vegetables--the mood of the crew was lively.

Mickey and Rhinehardt were joking at the young Stephan, whose girlfriend was French.

"She has this gap in her teeth," Rhinehardt said, as he swaggered and laughed. "How did she get that?"

Stephan, the boy with the brown lock of hair over one eye, was long past answering.

"She probably sounds like this," Mickey said, who made a wheezing noise with his teeth as if he were in the middle of the sex act.

Everyone laughed.

"Stop it," Hagermeister said. "Leave the kid alone. What's wrong with being in love."

"Nothing," answered Mickey, "but the damned whistling....."

Again he whistled rhythmically through his teeth to the accompaniment of laughter.

The sound of the diesels and the chain hanging from the ceiling to my bed and the sound of coughing always the u boat cough in the mornings--a sound so normal, so prevalent that I almost cease to notice it. Rosenberg is SD, I know he is. And Richard with his constant card games, poker under the yellow halo of the light down on my wool blanket. Steinhoff is SD.

It was early afternoon when Chief Petty Officer Hagermeister came by Maxwell's bunk. Listlessly staring up at the gray piping, Maxwell had not even looked Hagermeister's way, thinking him just another seaman passing through. Hagermeister tugged on Tommy's ankle.

Maxwell sat up.

"Did you know we've changed course?"

Maxwell rubbed his eyes and yawned. "Changed course? Why?"

Thibadeaux, in the lower bunk, sat up to listen.

"Intelligence has spotted a convoy. We are to form a wolf pack with three more U boats to the west and attack." Hagermeister smiled.

Maxwell stretched and hopped out of the bunk. "What is everyone doing?"

Hagermeister slapped Maxwell on the shoulder. "Getting ready, what else? Don't worry. You two can continue your nap if you want."

Hagermeister waved and headed aft.

Maxwell sat down beside Thibadeaux, who pounded a pack of cigarettes and offered one to Tommy. "Oooowee," Richard said, a nervous smile running across his face, "looks like we finally get to see the war."

Maxwell accepted the cigarette and lit it.

"Doesn't the Captain know we're just along for the ride?"

Thibadeaux shrugged. "Hope these U boats are good as we heard."

In their stroll through the boat, they noticed the change that had come over the crew. An alertness had seized everyone.

Men were laboring over torpedo detonators, while others manned the diesels, or helped monitor gauges. With the announcement the crew was to see action, an air of happiness and efficiency permeated the mood of the boat.

Maxwell almost understood the emotion. Even the threat of death was better than the boredom of the last four days. Schuller roamed theboat shouting orders, as did Hagermeister and Danet. When Danet saw the Americans in the control room, he ordered them to their bunks to keep them out of the way.

Two hours later an announcement came over the loudspeaker:

"English freighter sighted at 46 degrees."

"Prepare to dive," the Captain ordered.

Men leapt from the side bunks and filled the aisles in a steady stream of motion. The madness of the men frantically turning the red wheels, the full sprints of the crew as they entered the control room by swinging through the hatch, grabbing the handles above the opening--everything soared past the bewildered Americans.

"Take her up to periscope level."

Maxwell and Thibadeaux proceeded to their bunks as ordered. It had happened that Hans had picked up on his radio coded signals from three other U boats that convoy F-511 was eastbound, not thirty miles south of U-168's position. U-301, U-415, and U-227 had positioned themselves at right angles to the convoy's course, approximately forty miles east of U-168's position. The plan, as coordinated from Lorient, France by radio, was for U-168 to make contact first, at a point of convergence thirty miles southwest. This was a most dangerous task, since escort destroyers would devote full attention to the first boat that attacked. While the escorts were on the hunt, the wolf pack would position themselves in the lanes of the oncoming convoy, each boat free to roam and sink the most valuable vessels.

Maxwell and Thibadeaux had been so disoriented from their sea sickness, that they had not noticed the change in course. Contact was made at 5:34, just before dusk.

U-168 followed the newly spotted convoy for two hours. At 2100 Captain Schuller gave the order to surface.

Above, on the bridge, Schuller, Danet, and Hagermeister monitored the choppy horizon with binoculars.

Finally, after having spent two hours in their bunks, watching the eerie flashlights move past in the dark corridor, Maxwell and Thibadeaux could stand it no longer. They swung themselves silently into the red-tinted control room. Maxwell craned his neck upwards towards the conning hatch and yelled, "Permission to come up."

After a slight pause, they heard Schuller's voice. "Permission granted."

By this time the wind had died down. The sea was calm. Above, the cool night air, the sound of the sea against the hull and the churn of the diesels assaulted Maxwell at once.

He could see nothing but a stretch of calm, moonlit sea, and fog on the horizon.

"Take a look," Schuller said, nudging Maxwell and handing him the binoculars. "See what it feels like to be on the hunt."

With the binoculars in place Maxwell could make out the thin gray fingers against the fog. The ships looked remarkably peaceful on the moonlit sea, and it seemed impossible that anything could disturb their stately serenity.

"Strange," Schuller said, "no escorts in sight...she is outbound; looks like three columns."

Danet laughed. "We've got them, sir. They haven't a chance."

"Not so fast. Let's have a look first." Maxwell returned the glasses to Schuller.

Schuller took a look at the convoy, then at the moon, then at his watch.

"Come left to 150."

"Steady on course 150, sir," came the reply.

"Your recommendation, Danet."

"Attack sir."

"Prepare tubes one through four for surface firing," Schuller muttered to Zimmerman, who stood on the bridge and relayed orders down the hatch.

"Tubes one through four flooded, sir."

"Clear the bridge."

The men scooted down the ladder, Maxwell and Thibadeaux to their bunks, the other men to their duties.

"All ahead full, left full rudder, come to 106, standby to attack."

Below, the men in the diesel room scrambled about amid the deafening noise.

Danet, Schuller, Zimmerman, and Hagermeister stayed topside.

As U-168 plodded through the waves, cutting them like a knife, she centered on a large ship, that appeared to be an oil tanker. Below, the men were poised and professional, each going about their duties in a mechanical fashion. Mickey and Rhinehardt prepared the machine gun belt and checked the large machine gun in case of a surface attack. The men in the torpedo room obsessively re-checked the torpedo detonators.

Hans gave reports to Schuller every one hundred meters of the U boat's approach, as Danet manned the periscope.

At their bunks Maxwell and Thibadeaux found it impossible to relax. Tommy Maxwell was experiencing several conflicting thoughts. Doubts about his own survival, inexplicably, were intermingled with a rush of excitement and anticipation unlike any he could remember. His heart pounded. He had no idea what to expect.

"Bow angle 060."

"Range 3200 meters."

"Check."

"Targets in sight and overlapping, sir."

"New angle 064."

"Lock in tubes one and three."

"One and three, standby to fire."

With a motion of the hand, Schuller communicated to Zimmerman his orders, all the time keeping the binoculars glued just below his white officer's cap.

"Right full rudder, swing her around for torpedo angle."

"Jawohl."

The crew swayed below as U-168 made a quick turn to the right, then steadied and lined up for attack.

"Fire one," Zimmerman said.

Below, the seaman pulled the red lever down once.

"Fire three."

"One and three fired and running."

"Two ready."

"Two ready."

"Two fire."

"Two fire."

"Four ready."

"Four ready."

"Four fire."

"Four fire."

Danet and Schuller came below, the bridge hatch closed. Danet held a stop watch in his palm, the Captain looking over his shoulder. The ticking of the watch not audible in the control room as the crew held its breath.

Presently Danet spoke. "One is a miss," he said in a low voice.

The clock kept ticking, "three is a miss."

"Damn," Schuller said, jerking his hat around and putting his eye to the periscope. "How many seconds for two?"

"Ten seconds, sir."

The crew in the control room glared upwards at the maze of piping in the red-tinted darkness.

Then came the low boom of the explosion. Torpedo number two had hit. Everyone in the boat cheered as Schuller turned from the periscope and raised a fist in the air. Putting his eye back to the periscope, he said, "Got her broadside, by the flames she is belching, she looks to be a tanker."

Amid the cheers of the crew, Schuller turned back to the periscope and paused, his face turning into a scowl. "Shit," he said.

"Destroyer ahead. Prepare to dive."

Seconds later, U-168 dove with a wing of white spray. The destroyer, at full speed, fired her deck gun. The sea splashed thirty feet behind where the U-boat had disappeared.

The men ran to the front of the boat as ordered and huddled in the forward torpedo room.

"Move, move, hurry, hurry," screamed Danet.

Then the glaring faces upwards in the red lights, straining as if the mazes of pipes held a vital message.

They heard the sound of the creaking and wailing of metal as the bulwarks of the ship gave way, the sound at first frightening Maxwell since it sounded as if their own boat were groaning, squeaking, grating against itself.

"The bulkheads have collapsed," said the bearded, smiling face of Rhinehardt.

Maxwell stood beside Mueller, watching his bearded face straining upwards.

At the sound of approaching propellers overhead, Maxwell felt his first pang of fear. Several of the crew stripped out of their shirts and shoes. As Maxwell quickly did the same, he realized that at any moment the green sea might be rushing into an exploded breach in the boat. He swallowed. A claustrophobic panic began to spread infectiously among the men. Nothing was spoken, but every man of the crew felt it. The Germans called it Blechkoller.

"Destroyer approaching," the sound man announced. "Standby for depth charge attack."

"Depth charges dropped."

Maxwell heard two clicking sounds. Suddenly they were inundated in a terrific explosion which sounded as if it had gone off inside the U-boat, and another, another tremendous vibration and shaking as men were thrown in all directions in the sudden darkness as light bulbs burst. The swooning avenues of the frantic flashlight beams twitched before the third explosion, a fourth, and a fifth.

During the explosions, Maxwell was hurled onto the deck plates and to his horror, he discovered that he had lost control of his bladder.

He felt the hot sensation of urination in his crotch and immediately was afraid that another crewman would notice the expanding stain on the front of his pants.

Sounds of clanking metal, breaking glass, the screams of the crew.

"All ahead full....take her to 150 meters, get auxiliary fuses."

The vibration of one of the explosions had been so dramatic that the helmsman's hand was jerked off the wheel.

And suddenly the vibrations stopped and there were only the faces, red-tinted, eyeballs strained upwards, silence, the sound of heavy breathing, the twitching flashlight beams in the blue darkness, and then the sound shrill and hideous coming in the form of an innocent and high-pitched ping.

Ping, ping.

"Jesus," Mueller said, who rested on one arm on the floor. "It's Asidic."

Even Maxwell knew what this was.

Asidic was the single most valuable aid to a destroyer's U-boat detection. It worked on the same principle as that of a bat's radar system. A radar signal was transmitted from the ship and when that signal found an object under water, the signal bounced back to the receiver. The time it took for the signal to get back to the receiver indicated the range of the detected object.

Ping.....ping.....ping.

"Those bastards," muttered the strained face of Thibadeaux.

Danet tiptoed through the compartment. He gestured with his palms downwards.

"Quiet boys, not a word," he said.

Ping, ping.

When Danet shined his light into the back torpedo room, the sight was like that of a mass grave. Bodies heaped onto one another in a collage of arms, legs, and faces.

"Quiet now, silence."

Ping, ping, ping.

Maxwell heard water dripping. The pings grew steadily louder, closer, followed by the roar of the engine overhead as the destroyer headed straight over them. The red faces.

Again the deafening explosion, the cruel vibrations, Maxwell tossed to the left. The young lad whom the crew had joked about his girlfriend was thrown into the wall. He writhed on the floor.

"My arm is broken," he yelled.

"All ahead full." Another explosion, and another.

The wailing and the screaming of the men as panic ensued,

Followed by the miraculous ceasing of the vibration, silence, and the sound of coughing.

"Deeper, chief, silent speed."

The faces in the haze.

"What's her bearing?"

"065 sir."

As U-168 went deeper, the hull began to react to the pressure of the quick dive. Loud popping sounds came from all around the men, as the rivets strained with the pressure of the water. Maxwell froze.

With every pop from the hull he felt as if a bullet were entering his body. He looked over at Thibadeaux, who lay on the floor beside him.

Richard merely shook his head and gazed upwards. The thought that he might die in this small compartment at the bottom of the sea was impossible for Maxwell to digest. He broke into a cold sweat.

He only wished that if he had to die, it would be on the surface.

Anything to get into the air.

Then there was a low rumble of yet another explosion farther away.

"Sir," the weasel-like face of the hydrophone man reported, "she's moving out of range, sir."

Everyone cheered frantically to which Danet screamed in protest, "Quiet, silence, you idiots."

The pops of the hull continued. At any second Maxwell expected the rivets to begin shooting like bullets throughout the compartment.

"The wolf pack must have made contact," whispered Schuller to the helmsman. "Take her deeper."

"Sir?"

"You heard me."

They stayed down for thirty more minutes, before there was another explosion detected in the hydrophones. Schuller gave the order for a slow ascent. The crew headed aft to their various stations. Moving through the dark corridor was a tremendous relief for Maxwell as he and Thibadeaux stopped in the control room.

On walking behind Thibadeaux, Maxwell noticed Richard's pants sagging in the back; then the awful smell.

"Tommy," Richard said, turning to Maxwell and speaking loud enough for Hagermeister, who was in front of the two Americans, to hear, "Ashamed to admit it, but I so goddamned scared, I filled my pants, me."

Hagermeister turned, a look of pity on his face. "It is nothing to be ashamed of, believe me, everyone does it their first time, sometimes I do it even now, and believe me, I have been in plenty of attacks. Do not be ashamed. We have plenty of changes in the laundry, and I can promise you, that you won't be the only ones of the crew, who will need a change of pants. It's just a part of combat that no one tells you about."

The Tensenmieser showed a rapid ascent. "Hold her at periscope level," Schuller commanded. As soon as Maxwell had seen Schuller, following the periscope up out of the well, the Captain's hat turned around, he felt safe again.

The Captain threw the levers of the periscope down, turned his hat around and gave the command, "Surface." The men began furiously turning the red wheels on the walls.

"Permission to come up," Maxwell said to Schuller.

"Very well, but stay clear and out of the way."

Maxwell and Thibadeaux waited their turn as the men lined up to go out on deck. Rosenberg and Steinhoff were right in front of Thibadeaux. They carried shells for the large deck gun which would be loaded for surface firing.

When Maxwell felt the cool salty air, he experienced a surge of elation unlike any he could remember. What he saw above gave further exhilaration.

As Mickey and Rhinehardt brushed past him with the deck machine gun, Maxwell and Thibadeaux leaned over the forward rail.

Only three miles away was the conflagration. A great fire from the sinking ship rose up in a huge, black pillar of smoke. The flame was burning from the stern of the tanker, which was now standing on end, and other flames were burning in various islands of fire where the oil burned on the water. Above the flames three flares burned, casting a flicking green light down onto the sea, sparks dripping down in the night sky over the conflagration.

In the foreground of the islands of fire, Maxwell could make out a small lifeboat on which several survivors huddled. He could hear wails of pain and screams, bouncing off the acoustics of the sea. It was at this time that Steinhoff wandered from his position at the deck gun and approached Captain Schuller.

"Permission to take aboard prisoners," he said.

"Permission denied," Schuller said.

By this time Maxwell had moved close enough to hear the tail end of the conversation.

"Much can be learned from prisoners," Steinhoff insisted.

"Enough," Schuller shouted, "return to your post immediately."

Steinhoff saluted and obeyed.

As Maxwell returned to his forward position, he could hear further explosions coming low and resounding from the west. Small twinkles of flares could be seen over the western horizon. The battle was still raging inside the convoy.

Schuller ascertained his orders from Lorient. U-168 was to proceed on course to France. A total of four ships had been sunk without a single U boat lost, but the escorts had forced the wolf pack momentarily down.

As Schuller gave the order to proceed, Maxwell went below.

The battle left a lasting impression. Tommy had seen his first action of the war, and he was puzzled. Alone in his bunk that night, listening to the sounds of the churning diesels, he tried to dissect the origins of his exhilaration on seeing the burning tanker. Men had been suffering, some no doubt drowned or burned alive amid the islands of fire. Although Maxwell had seen this, there had been no sense of loss for the death that U-168 had caused, only a sense of elation at sight of the great mass of flames, inundating the horizon.

Not much like a pacifist, Maxwell thought. He shrugged the thought off, attributing the elation to the happiness of merely being able to survive. But the raging flames appeared again in his dreams.

Exhausted, he had fallen into an uneasy sleep.

Within two days of France U-168 made good time, running steadily on the surface by night and submerged by day. The heat of the battle had taken its toll on the men's nerves, but each moment the ship neared France, the morale became increasingly better. The men listened to a French girl sing on the radio and often sang along as they performed their duties. Pennants signaling the amount of tonnage sunk were being prepared, and Captain Schuller, feeling the need for entertainment, announced that on the eve of their arrival, the crew would be allowed to break out the lager.

the celebration for the crew was held in the compartment aft of the control room. It started in typical German fashion--plenty of music, sausages, and beer, served both cold and hot.

Lyons, one of the torpedo men, who had a thick beard on his chin and sideburns, began the festivities with his accordion. The tunes he played were pleasing to Maxwell, soft and somber. Several of the group swayed to the tune and sang along.

Rosenberg was drinking lager on the other side of the compartment.

He was speaking to Hagermeister. Maxwell saw the wide back of Hagermeister shaking with laughter, then saw Rosenberg smile with his widely spaced teeth. Hagermeister was the ship's jokester. Danet and Steinhoff huddled in the corner, speaking in low tones, each nursing their lager.

Soon Lyons was replaced by a livelier tune on French radio. As the music picked up, the crew came to life. The thin boy, who had broken his arm, swung from an overhead pipe with one hand like a monkey. Then the men played "bobsled." They drew straws, and two men proceeded to pull Mickey belly-down up the aisle, while everyone threw beer and fruit at him. Two of the oranges, which were rolling in the aisle after this activity, were put to good use. Waisenhoffer stuffed two of the largest oranges into his undershirt, grabbed a set of dress grays and improvised a skirt, and began dancing to yet more accordion music, bouncing his homemade breasts to the cheers of the crowd.

After over an hour of this, two of the crew headed aft, already sick from drinking. The party settled into a series of humorous conversations throughout the compartment. Each conversation had a common thread-
-women.

Maxwell and Thibadeaux became part of the largest circle, which included Duggan, Waissenhoffer, and Schnegel. In the middle of a burst of laughter at one of Thibadeaux's jokes, Maxwell noticed Rosenberg. He sat across the aisle from Maxwell and appeared to be in a drunken stupor. Apparently a mean drunk, he began glaring at both the Americans. Steinhoff, who was standing at the end of the room, began watching Rosenberg.

"Now this girl is young, oh, I'd say seventeen," Waissenhoffer said loudly. "But ah," and with this he raised his mug in toast and sloshed half his beer out, "the girl has a certain experience, if you know what I mean."

Duggan spoke over the laughter. "Yeah, and you'll end up like Ulrich on U-406. You know him, don't you? He's got some girl in Lorient pregnant."

"I wouldn't be spreading that around," Schnegel said.

"Oh, is it catching?" Duggan retorted to laughter.

Schnegel, who was the oldest seaman on board with the exception of Schuller, took his pipe out of his mouth. "If the French underground hears of it, they will kill her."

The instant of silence was quickly interrupted by Waissenhoffer.

"All in a little fun, Schnegel," he said, slapping the older man on the shoulder. "You need to loosen up a bit, old man, why don't you come with me to Mimi's, I'll get that serious look off your face."

Schnegel smiled and drew on his pipe. "No, I'm going home to my wife and two boys," he said beaming. "In my last letter, they said we had a new dog."

"Not me," said Mickey, who was staggering through the circle aft.

"I'm glad I don't have a family while I'm out here on this God forsaken sea."

Rhinehardt, Mickey's partner, laughed in his swaggering fashion.

"Family, you haven't figured out how to get one pregnant, you beggar."

Thibadeaux then began talking in a low tone to himself in French; there was a pause, then the whole crew began laughing.

"Where did you get all that?" asked Waissenhoffer. "I thought Americans were only English speakers."

"I know German," chimed in Maxwell.

"Like hell you do," yelled Hagermeister from the end of the compartment as he raised his glass in salute. Maxwell returned the gesture with raised glass and a gulp of beer.

Danet knitted his brow and made eye contact with Steinhoff.

"I don't speak English so good," Thibadeaux said. "I Cajun, from Louisiana, speak French pooty good, I be tryin' out Cajun style French on dese Paris bitches, bet they go for it, what you think?"

As the crew laughed with Thibadeaux, Maxwell again glanced at Rosenberg. He still sat in the same manner, glaring at Maxwell with unrestrained hatred.

Growing more uneasy, Maxwell began to get the idea that Thibadeaux, who sat next to him, was becoming aware of the situation.

Steinhoff, as well, sat across the aisle and stared at Richard. The taller German maintained his singular demeanor. His wide mouth, sandy blonde hair, and scholarly gaze beneath his spectacles gave the impression of a cynical, depraved intellectual, and while more pleasant than his cohort, produced an overall impression that was equally as malignant.

Suddenly the singing died off. The crew began watching the interchange of gazes across the compartment.

"Yeah," said Thibadeaux to Mickey. "We had this whore in Jersey and this girl had three titties. A nipple right there. They called her 'three booby Ruby.'"

Waissenhoffer laughed.

"What are you laughing at?" inquired Danet, whose eyes jumped under the exceedingly bushy eyebrows.

"What is a booby?"

"A breast....one of these," Thibadeaux said, and with his tongue in his long cheek, he gestured with his hand.

Maxwell broke up with laughter.

"Americans have a certain preference for breasts," interrupted Danet. "It must have something to do with imperialistic tendencies."

Maxwell looked sideways at Danet.

"Hey American," Danet said, his eyes twitching madly, "what is your definition of imperialism? You are a school teacher.

See what you can teach us."

A short stutter of laughter escaped Steinhoff.

"Do you think Germany is imperialist?" Danet asked.

"'Imperialism' is another word for thievery," Maxwell said, who immediately flushed, feeling he had stepped into a trap.

"So Germany is the great thief," Danet pressed.

"The United States is the biggest thief in the world," Maxwell answered. "They are less honest about it."

"You gentlemen will be setting off for training," interrupted Danet. Rosenberg visibly stiffened across the aisle.

Maxwell felt his face scald. "You are testing us," he said, knitting his eyebrows as he spoke. "You know we are not allowed to discuss our mission. I have no idea....."

"Ja, training," popped Danet. "The other Americans were trained," his eyes now jumping, "the ones now in prison."

"Yeah," Maxwell said, knowing that Danet was referring to the Dasch case. "And what else?"

"I asked you once," Danet said. "Do you approve of Germany's imperialism?" He had directed the question to both Maxwell and Thibadeaux.

"What does it matter to you what I think?" Maxwell said, who by now had correctly read the first officer's tone.

"It matters. It matters quite a bit."

"I am here to follow orders," Maxwell said. "Nothing else."

"Ja, Yankee, everyone is following orders, even the English. It all depends on whose orders you are following."

"Look Danet," Maxwell said. "You got something to say, say it."

"I will say it," Danet said, as Rosenberg rose from his seat and glared over the conversation. "In the last operation of this sort, all the German agents were captured in a matter of days. They were betrayed by their American comrades. I am sure you see it as a coincidence that the Americans received lighter sentences."

"You be sniffing us since we hopped this boat," Thibadeaux said.

"What you want?"

"Just come out and say it if you got the guts," Maxwell said.

"Guts.....what's guts?"

"Courage," Maxwell said, looking Danet directly in the eyes.

At this Steinhoff took off his seaman's coat, wearing only a black and white undershirt. He continued to stare at Thibadeaux.

Sensing trouble, Duggan, the corpulent cook swung through the hatch into the control room. He was going to get the Captain.

"Yes, Yankee," Danet said. "I will say it."

Maxwell waited.

"Verrater. Traitor. Ja, you are nothing but Yankee traitors."

"There is no reason for you to say that," Waissenhoffer said.

"No basis," said Schnegel who had backed up from the conversation. He sensed trouble and put down his pipe.

"I have given you my reasons," Danet said.

"Listen," said Maxwell, who again looked Danet squarely in the eye. "I am not interested in your opinions. We're going to France to obtain and carry out orders, orders that, I'm sure, will come from higher authority than the likes of you. So you see, Danet, your opinion has no bearing on my mission. You have a right to it, but you have stated it, and that's that."

"He talks like a Freemason," said Steinhoff, pointing his little finger at Thibadeaux.

"That's enough," said Captain Schuller who swung through the hatch. "Stop this now, you two," he said, pointing to Maxwell and Thibadeaux. "Come with me."

His voice had the tone of a reprimand. Everyone stared in silence.

The crew had become immobilized by the entrance of Rosenberg and Steinhoff into the conversation.

The Captain and the two Americans went topside.

The cool breeze coming off the sea revived Maxwell from the mood he had felt below. The three men stood for the longest time, smoking and looking at the darkness and the sea. No stars were visible.

Schuller dismissed the watch. Whereas the Americans had felt that they were going to be reprimanded when coming up the hatch, when they arrived topside, the atmosphere changed. Schuller seemed to enjoy silence, was mesmerized by the gently rolling waves. As Maxwell watched the thin line of smoke whirl furiously after the soft orange glow of the old pipe, next to Schuller's whiskered face, he was reminded of his father.

The diesels churned like a locomotive.

"I love the sea," Schuller said softly.

"How long you served?" Thibadeaux asked.

"Five years," Schuller said. No one spoke for nearly two minutes more. Finally, Schuller got to the point.

"I'm afraid I must bore you with some advice," he said.

"This is not easy for me, but if I did not fill you in, I would be doing you and my country a great disservice. Rosenberg and Steinhoff."

Maxwell saw that the Captain's face had again changed into a most grim expression.

The Captain took three puffs on his pipe before continuing.

Stay away from these men," he said. "Do not speak to them and by no means must you challenge them."

"Look," interrupted Maxwell. "I'm not afraid of either one of them."

Schuller held up a hand. "I'm not talking about being afraid of them. I tell you to stay away from them. If you are not afraid, Herr Maxwell, it is not entirely a tribute to your courage, as it is to your ignorance. Now please," he said, holding his hand up, indicating silence, "again I ask both of you only to listen."

"What you must understand," he continued, "is that the nature of your mission may entail your being watched by forces with which you may not be familiar. Let me fill you in on these men."

"Our mission," Maxwell said, "what do you know about that?"

"Both are fanatical Nazis and both are killers. Rosenberg was at one time in the SA and was transferred to the SD. Rosenberg's main goal, as I have heard, was to become part of Germany's military elite, that is, a member of the sacred order of the Death's Head, the SS. He failed the physical, probably the height requirement.

He subsided after this failure into the SD."

"From what I have heard, his comrade Steinhoff is less fanatical and more of the classic SD material. He is more the intellectual and yet quite dangerous."

Schuller paused. The breeze had died down. As Schuller re-lit his pipe, the smoke rose furiously.

"A Captain in my position does not make it a practice to get involved in the personal disagreements among his crew. This isn't my usual procedure, believe me. If you were German, I would assume that you understood all these things without my telling. Here is the thing."

He folded his hands and leaned over the bridge railing.

"As you know, in the last mission of this sort, the Americans betrayed the Abwehr. You must understand that the SD and Abwehr's areas of jurisdiction oftentimes cross lines. It is not always apparent which agency is responsible for certain areas of covert activity. There is a power struggle within the ranks here. It is vital that you understand this. The last Abwehr mission of this sort failed miserably, and the SD is poised to take advantage of it. The SD has come out in direct confrontation to the Abwehr's handling of this mission. I believe that Rosenberg and Steinhoff are connected with the SD. It would not surprise me if they were put aboard to observe you two very closely. Do not be caught sleeping. Do not talk to these men, and do not tell anyone what has been said here."

Maxwell and Thibadeaux were silent.

"We arrive in Lorient tomorrow. I am due a promotion to the Gibraltar fleet and I want no undue trouble to get in my way. I would prefer that the cruise pass without further incident, any questions?"

"Yeah, I've got a question," Maxwell said.

Schuller nodded.

"You are a U boat captain. How do you know so much about your men?

Do files of your crew contain political profiles?"

"A very intelligent question, Herr Maxwell," Schuller said with a smile. "Let's just say that I am more 'informed' than most U boat Captains."

"What do you mean 'informed'?" Maxwell asked.

Schuller again smiled as if he had been found out.

"Remember, this conversation never occurred," he said. "Let me say this much. I am an old friend of Wilhelm Canaris. Do I need to say more?"

"Why are you doing this for us?" Maxwell asked.

"Do I have to explain everything?" Schuller snapped, as he snatched the pipe from his mouth. "You have enough information to go on without having all, as you say, spelled out. As for me, there are Germans and there are Germans. I am a patriot and a sailor."

Schuller frowned and shook his head. "This is as much as I'm going to say. I will no longer be the Captain of this boat on your return to America. But I will bet my pension that Rosenberg and Steinhoff will be on board."

Later, below in their bunks, both men agreed to give Danet, Rosenberg, and Steinhoff a wide berth for the duration of the cruise.

July 16, 1942

The next day dawned with an azure sky. U-168 ran submerged in her approach to Lorient. Finally, having made radio contact with the minesweeper, she surfaced.

The order to surface brought loud cheers throughout the boat. Soon crewmen streamed out onto the bridge, hanging off the bridge railing, while others were busied putting up their pennants, displaying the tonnage sunk. The pennants, totaling seven, were hung vertically on the periscope extension.

On the approach to Lorient, U-168 had been in radio contact with other boats heading to quay, and whereas the crew had much to be proud of, theirs had only been an average amount of tonnage sunk. It was obvious from the other boats' reports that if the war continued in this manner, Britain would soon be starved and must fall.

At 1100 every hand that could be spared was on deck, leaning over the rail, straining for a glimpse of the French coast. Maxwell, on hearing a crewman shout to his right, strained his eyes to see a gray line, which with the rocking of the boat, gradually grew out of the horizon. The sight, which seemed to materialize as if by magic out of the gray distance, brought a loud cheer from the crew on deck. The sun burned off the haze and revealed the Brittany coast. Soon green ribbons of vegetation could be seen; then white houses, sitting high over the water on the sea cliffs, their roofs of various colors.

U-168 churned around a peninsula and past an ancient fort on a crag. This was Port Louis, which marked the entrance to Lorient harbor and the Bay of Biscay.

All hands were dressed in their clean grays. Maxwell and Thibadeaux had been given a full issue of seaman's uniform for their shore leave.

"Look," Hagermeister said, as he combed his full beard again.

"They're waiting for us."

Seeing the welcoming party ahead, bathed in light, Maxwell felt a feeling of release and hopeful expectation. Five miles away were the brown canals and bunkers. He saw amid a crowd on the dock a small band, dressed in blue. The band struck up a marching tune.

On either side of the canal were cranes and construction debris, piles of scrap metal and workers waving at the U boat, running alongside the canal and dodging the debris on the sides of the bank.

As U-168 headed into her quay towards a great concrete bunker, which shielded its contents from British bombers, Maxwell could make out faces among a file of saluting officers.

On seeing the officers, each crew member immediately snapped to attention and saluted.

Just before entering the bunker, U-168 swung to the side dock, threw out her lines, and as the gang plank fell, the men in their grays streamed off the boat. The blue-clad officers saluted and two women threw bundles of white flowers. As each sailor stepped off the boat, a nurse greeted him with a kiss and a flower.

The Commandant of the Second U-boat Flotilla, adorned in double breasted dress blues, greeted Captain Schuller with a salute and a handshake.

While the crew hurried off to the halls of the French Naval prefecture, where they would be treated to a dinner of lobster and champagne, the Americans were greeted by a sergeant in a Wehrmacht uniform of olive green. He introduced himself as Lancer and announced he would show them to their quarters.

In 1942 Lorient was a teeming, French, seaside village. The economy thrived from its quaint shops full of vegetable and flower displays on the sidewalks and its famous establishments, which specialized in night entertainment. Everywhere one went, the atmosphere of security and frivolity prevailed. Military personnel meandered the streets during their leave time. The natives of Lorient were generally in good spirits and seemed to enjoy the prosperity the war brought them.

As they walked down the avenue, lined with acacias and palm trees, Maxwell and Thibadeaux smiled at the street marketeers, who shouted the virtues of their wares in the French tongue. Three women passed and smiled. These women were beautifully dressed in the long skirts, colorfully embroidered blouses and white head coverings of their native Brittany.

The Americans were assigned quarters in the Beausejour, the nicest hotel in town, which was generally reserved for German officers. The hotel overlooked a broad courtyard in the middle of which was a large gazebo. The courtyard was outlined with shops and taverns and was the hub of the town's pedestrian traffic.

The two Americans spent the entire day in their room at the Beausejour. The room was handsomely decorated in the style of old German houses and, according to the proprietor, had been previously occupied by a German officer of high standing, who was on a two day leave.

The large brass bed was flanked by shelves, which contained an impressive collection of German steins. The carpet was crimson and the walls a soft gray. The room was brightened by a large window, which overlooked the courtyard and gazebo below. The window had both French blinds and French shutters. Fresh flowers had been placed on the sill.

On the wall were three large portraits, apparently sent from the Rhineland. One was the famous portrait of Otto von Bismark, by Franz von Lenbach, another of the red-bearded Barbarossa and another of the corpulent Hermann Goering.

Maxwell and Thibadeaux's first thoughts were of a bath, and they argued who was to go first. Maxwell won the coin toss and was the first to bathe. Constantly harassed to hurry, Maxwell lay in the porcelain tub for an hour.

It was among the most pleasurable experiences of his life. The U boat's stench and confining atmosphere demanded at least an hour of soaking, and shaving was almost as good. After they were both bathed and shaven, their thoughts turned to their stomachs.

Thibadeaux, who insisted that his Cajun origins made him more qualified, called room service for breakfast. He chose croissants, fresh cheese, and fruit accompanied by a dry, white wine which went to both men's heads.

They napped better than three hours before being awakened by a sharp knock at the door.

Maxwell struggled into his shirt and rubbed his eyes as he opened the door. He made out the face of Sgt. Lancer.

"I trust your stay has been satisfactory," he said, tucking his double chin next to his chest and green Wehrmacht blouse.

"So far," mumbled Maxwell, who never was at his best after waking up.

"You are wise in not leaving the room. Your lack of German might tip you off immediately as Americans. The Resistance is everywhere, despite the cheery appearance of the town."

Maxwell snorted. "What can we do for you, Sergeant. We're trying to catch some shut-eye."

Lancer's tone turned abrupt. "Take breakfast at 0800. At 0900 a staff car will be waiting to accompany you to the Lorient Bahnhoff."

"What's a Bahnhoff?"

"A train station," he said as the chin poked up, un-doubling. "You are to be transported to Paris where you are to report to the office of Naval intelligence promptly July 20 at 0900."

Lancer handed a sealed envelope to Maxwell. "You are lucky men. You get to meet the Lion himself."

"The Lion?"

"Admiral Karl Doenitz seeks an audience with you," Lancer said, again tucking in his chin. "Be on your best......nevermind, enjoy your nap."

CHAPTER 6

July 19

The next morning the Americans rose at eight, took breakfast as ordered, and dressed in clean seaman's grays, brought by the girl who had been sent up to do yesterday's wash.

Lancer picked them up in front of the hotel in a staff Mercedes convertible. They took the road overlooking the harbor. The sunshine was brilliant, the day clear and warm, a perfect summer's day on the sea. Below, close to where U-168 had landed the day before, a ceremony was taking place. Two full U boat crews were assembled in their blues. The men were all clean shaven and newly bathed. A great deal of activity was taking place, speeches made, medals awarded, and by the smiling faces of the men, all were enjoying themselves. The U boat bulldogs were being treated as heroes.

The summer of 1942 became known as the second "happy time" for the U boat fleet. Their successes had been enormous. In 1942, they were to sink over 4 million tons of Allied shipping.

Maxwell strained to see anyone he knew. He made the face of Duggan, the cook, and looked at the commanding officer whom he did not recognize.

The train station was small, but bustling with activity. Most of the passengers leaving Lorient were soldiers on leave.

Maxwell and Thibadeaux rode in the general quarters car. They spoke to no one on the way, amusing themselves by listening to a group of Wehrmacht soldiers singing towards the back of the car.

The French countryside was green and sleepy in the sun. Peasants tended a great field far away, and Maxwell observed a winding country road beyond the field.

The landscape seemed untouched by war, although Maxwell could remember the newsreels only months back of those same French roads, choked with refugees as Paris panicked with news of the successful German Blitzkrieg.

The plight of the refugees had often been disastrous; many slaughtered by the Luftwaffe bombers.

Maxwell finally drifted to sleep.

The train made one stop at mid-afternoon when reaching the demarcation line, crossing from unoccupied to occupied France.

Squeaking to a halt at a checkpoint, the train was boarded by German border guards, who ordered all non-uniformed passengers off the train. Their papers routinely checked, the small amount of non-uniformed passengers were admitted for the last leg of their journey.

The train arrived at Barbees Metro Station in Paris at 5:19.

By this time Maxwell and Thibadeaux were awake from their naps and looking forward to Paris. They got in behind the Wehrmacht regulars and filed off the train.

Their orders stipulated that they make contact with a Sergeant Hoffman, whom they found by an abandoned baggage cart at the end of the track under the large depot veranda. The steam from the train's brakes hissed as Maxwell and Thibadeaux blended into the traffic on the walkway.

Hoffman escorted them to a staff car, bound for the hotel Bon Maison, a small establishment on one of Paris's back streets.

Paris was not what Maxwell had imagined. Having always seen pictures of the Champs-Elysees, fraught with traffic under the Arc de Triomphe, Maxwell was surprised that, but for three German motorbikes with sidecars, their staff car was the only automobile on the road. The Champs d' Elysees was full of pedestrian traffic--bicycles, people walking, and makeshift taxis, fashioned from ox carts, which industrious young Frenchmen pulled along like horses. They passed beneath the Arc de Triomphe as Maxwell craned his neck behind him to get a second look at the great structure. The sun shined brightly on the Champs-Ellipses with its two files of well-pruned green trees, ruffling in the afternoon breeze. The sidewalks were choked with people in front of the shops and cafes. Hoffman explained that the presence of the large number of German military personnel was due to weekend leaves. Men from all over Europe were being transported in to enjoy Paris. Maxwell even noticed women Wehrmacht, arm in arm with their German boyfriends, looking at shoes in a display window.

As Hoffman drove through the back streets towards the Bon Maison, Maxwell asked him to slow down.

"I've never been to Paris, you know," he said with a smile. "Want to catch all we can."

It was impossible for Maxwell to ignore the beauty of the last two days. The open air and sunshine were a balm to him. He drank it all in, always in the back of his mind remembering the confining darkness of the U boat.

Despite the dirtiness of the back streets, Paris was as beautiful as Maxwell had imagined. As he had heard, its architecture and character were completely unique.

When they entered a particular section, Maxwell noticed that the streets were absent of the normal pedestrian traffic. Flowers, either in bunches or single stems, adorned the front doors or stoops of many of the small shops and residences along the way. But the flowers were not merely in trellises or pots, but were pinned on doors, or dropped haphazardly in front of a mail box. When Maxwell saw, at the end of one of the streets, a German detachment pulling the flowers off the doors, his curiosity got the best of him

"What's going on here, Hoffman," he asked. "What are they doing?"

Hoffman laughed nervously. "Oh, you mean the flowers. They are left every night by the Resistance. And every day the Gestapo picks them up."

"I don't understand," Thibadeaux said.

Again Hoffman's laugh was shrill and nervous. "Oh, that's right, you missed all the excitement. It's been three days since the purge."

"The purge?"

"Ja, the purge of the Jews on July 16," Hoffman shrugged. "The Gestapo came through and gathered about 12,000 Jews."

"Where did they go?"

"They were taken to the Velodrome d'Hiver, the sports stadium. From there, who knows? Re-settled I guess."

Maxwell sat on the edge of the back seat and stared out the windows. Signs on several of the shops read: "Judisches Geschaft" or "Enterprise Juive."

The room at the Bon Maison was more modest than their lodgings in Lorient. The room contained two roll away beds, yellowing wallpaper, and wash basins beside each bed. By the time they settled in, night had fallen. They passed the time enjoying the gentle breeze, which blew through the window, carrying with it the faint rhythms of the city.

July 20

The next day the Americans had their breakfast of tea and fresh fruit and were on time in front of their hotel in meeting Hoffman.

They were driven to a large courtyard, which sat before a great stone government building. Squads of Wehrmacht units were being put through their morning paces in the courtyard. One file went through a manual of arms drill while another double-timed by.

Hoffman led the Americans past the steps and the wary guards at either side of the large wooden doors.

They walked into an echoing hallway with a shiny, hardwood floor.

As they passed several checkpoints in the hallway, they were surrounded by a sense of brisque efficiency. The building was heavily guarded every few feet by green clad German soldiers; the quarters overstaffed to the hilt with office personnel and military. At each checkpoint they were caught up in the spirit of the place, each officer, after receiving the sergeant's clearance and efficiently stamping the papers, then standing, clicking his heels, saluting, to which the sergeant and the Americans responded in kind.

At the outside of Admiral Doenitz's office Hoffman introduced them to staff officer Osterman, a German with slicked-back hair, who checked with the confines of the office before exiting, clicking his heels by the door and shouting, "The Admiral will see you now."

When the Americans entered the large office, they saw a man, standing next to a large, bay window overlooking the city. He stared out at the Eiffel Tower and at a column of goose-stepping troops below. He seemed barely aware of the Americans, as if he were in deep thought. His dark blue, military blouse flashed its gold decorations as he turned.

They walked to within four steps of his desk, and saluted. The Admiral, a man in his early forties with salt and pepper hair and a slightly turned-down mouth, returned the salute and commanded them to stand at ease. They relaxed.

"Would you like some coffee or tea?"

They declined.

"Please, have a seat."

As the Admiral talked, Maxwell picked up first the high-pitched tone of his voice. This was not an unpleasant sound. In fact, the twinkling gray eyes above the hawkish nose, whose tip nearly touched the down-turned mouth--the interplay of these features at once, gave the impression of a quiet, confident strength.

The Americans sat in two plush, leather chairs while the Admiral sat at his desk. He reached for the file folders, the dossiers of the two Americans. He knitted his black eyebrows as he scanned the folders quickly, glancing at first one, then the other of the two men as he read.

Finally, he closed the folders, looked across the desk and spoke.

"Do you gentlemen have any idea why you have been called here?"

"No sir," they answered nearly in unison.

"Your dossiers show you have been outstanding in your training as agents and also in sabotage and demolition."

"Thank you, sir," Maxwell answered.

The Admiral leaned back and folded his hands on his stomach before continuing.

"As you may or may not know, the agents which were put ashore in New York and Florida have now been neutralized. On return to your country, you will assume the duties they were sent to do. As Americans, you will be able to freely move about without suspicion to obtain the necessary information you will need to carry out your assignments."

"Furthermore," the Admiral added. "We would prefer you to concentrate on the aircraft and shipping contractors. These two industries will be our first concern. Without ships and aircraft, the Americans cannot deliver the supplies necessary to the British. Our U boats alone have almost neutralized the American shipping and with internal strife, the friction and propaganda we intend to use, along with your efforts, we can achieve victory. You two will work alone or together, whichever is convenient for you, but it is for victory you must always be thinking. If we lose this war, the British have made it plain, Germany will be destroyed forever. You will be sent to Berlin for further specific training, given the necessary equipment and funds, and then returned to the United States with your assignments. Do you have any questions at this time?"

"When do we leave for Berlin, sir?" Maxwell asked.

"As soon as we can get your orders made out. If you should have any difficulty, do not hesitate to use my name, or get in touch with me. This is my plan, and I would not like to see it bypassed by some of those fat generals in Berlin. I want you to concentrate on your training, ask questions, do what you are told, and do it until you have it perfect."

"One more question, sir," Maxwell said. "If we should run into difficulty when we return to the States, will we have communications with anyone that could help us get out before capture, or before we are neutralized?"

"I will try to arrange something while you are in Berlin. But I hope you will not be disappointed if I cannot. When you have finished your training, you will be sent back here. I will see you before you depart for America."

"Thank you, sir," Maxwell answered.

"You may return to your quarters, pack your things, for you will probably be leaving by midnight. Good luck."

The Admiral dismissed them, and before leaving for the Bon Maison, they were issued five hundred Reichmarks and two changes of U boat blues, which they were to wear in transit to Berlin.

The sounds of metal on metal, startling crashes--you get used to them--and every time you feel the jolt, you check the window for motion--and finally discerned, the motion takes you after the crash into the clattering night with its rockings and twists of iron sinews, the throbbing of the diesels, the wail of the train's wheels on iron--you could be anywhere if you close your eyes--even in America--or under the sea--or in France bound for Germany.

They arrived at the Berlin station at 1:14, precisely thirteen minutes ahead of schedule.

The Berlin train station was vast and jammed with people, mostly soldiers returning from the war on leave. It so happened that at this time Hitler had called for unprecedented numbers of leaves on both the Eastern and Western fronts. Everywhere soldiers could be seen being hugged and greeted by wives and children. At times during an impassioned embrace official military dress hats fell harmlessly onto the soiled concrete in the shadow of the great partition.

When Maxwell saw this mass of unchecked emotion, he was touched.

Even though he hated war in the intellectual sense, he freely admitted that compared to any other form of human endeavor, war produced the greatest of all dramatic spectacles. This contradiction bothered Maxwell as they entered a taxi, bound for the Naisenhoff hotel, as ordered by the Abwehr.

The driver drove past the great East West Axis, which Hitler's architect Albert Speer had presented his Fuhrer for his fiftieth birthday. They went past Olympic Stadium, took a short tour of the Tiergarten with its beautifully manicured gardens and trees; and finally, the Chancellery at Wilhelmstrasse. Beside the Grunewald and Havel lakes people were gaily roaming the great grass parkways. Everything was bathed in sunshine. The city was a beehive of activity.

The beerhalls were full of beautiful girls in their full dresses. Maxwell noticed one girl carrying three pitchers of beer to a group of soldiers, one of which had his heavy blouse unbuttoned, a beer in one hand, a girl at the other.

Many of the most distinctive buildings had fountains in front, with people around the water. The sidewalks were flanked by stylish lamps. The sunlight streamed down upon the gently roaming mass of people on the walks. On Havelstrasse Maxwell saw a small boy with shorts, knickers, and a black hat with a white feather. The child was chasing his little sister.

Except for the abundance of uniforms among the people, one would never have guessed that Germany was virtually at war with the world.

After checking into a modest room, Maxwell and Thibadeaux visited the beer gardens all down the Kurfuerstenndamm. They spoke to no one, except to order a drink, which with Maxwell's command of the language, limited their menu considerably.

Construction and the atmosphere of a thriving economy were everywhere. Hitler had intended that Berlin be a showcase for the world, and as far as Maxwell was concerned, he had succeeded.

That night, with incessant energy, the two Americans went to an open air garden, enclosed by four buildings. A throng danced and sang to a fiddle band until the small hours of the morning. No lamps or candles were lit in the square, according to security regulations.

The entire night passed without the bomb sirens going off. Up to this point in the war, the raids of the British Tommies had been only token ones. German air defense had been excellent. It was generally held that Britain was on her knees, due to the constant onslaught at night by the Luftwaffe.

Sufficiently drunk, the Americans returned to their room by three o'clock.

At 10:00 a.m. the following morning the Americans reported as ordered to the headquarters of the Abwehr in central Berlin. The headquarters was located in a six story concrete building with the flag of the OKW, the high command of the armed forces, at its top. The building's departments included: espionage, counterespionage, false documentation, and sabotage. Officials in this building supervised a network of 13,000 workers worldwide.

The Americans moved past the guard in front of the large building where a huge poster hung--a battle ship beneath a red flag and swastika and iron cross. The inscription read: "Einsatz Der Kriegsmarine." When Maxwell translated that the poster literally said, "Join the Navy," Thibadeaux broke into laughter.

"Hell, babe, we done that."

They cleared the various checkpoints and reported to an Officer Hohl's office.

Once admitted, the Americans assumed demeanors appropriate for soldiering. Hohl, a tall, lean German, spoke abruptly.

"You will be sent to a special training school for sabotage which is near Hanau, a little east of Frankfurt. There you will be taught the necessary skills to carry on with the war effort."

He paused for a reaction and when he got none, continued.

"Your training will take six weeks, and at the end of that time, you will return to America to implement the training you have received here. Now, if you will report to Captain Braun downstairs, you will be on your way."

He stood and threw a stiff arm to the ceiling.

"Heil Hitler."

"Heil Hitler," the Americans replied.

Captain Braun was waiting with their orders. They would be leaving immediately.

The two men slept on the train.

They were met at the Frankfurt Bahnhoff at 2:00 a.m. by a tall, German officer twenty years of age.

An hour later the Americans were asleep at the training center just east of Hanau.

The training center was on the edge of town and over four acres in size. The building complex was surrounded by a ten foot stone wall. The buildings inside were three stories high and built in a U shape, with classrooms on the second and third floors and all the offices on the first floor. The classroom buildings as well as the training officers' quarters were white stucco with brown trim.

Outside the buildings were compact, well-pruned trees, painted white five feet up their trunks. The bushes, near the brown, Roman arch doorways were trimmed into perfect squares.

After a shave and a haircut at a room in the officer training center, Maxwell and Thibadeaux reported to the courtyard where several long tables had been set out. Here, the candidates were issued uniforms-- two changes of classroom pants, shirts, ties, and regular Wehrmacht issue boots, blouse, belt, pants, and helmet for training and inspection.

The training was rigorous. Awakened at four by a sergeant's whistle before a three mile morning run, the men assembled in the mess hall for breakfast, which preceded three hours of classroom training, two hours of concentrated German, followed by a period of military drill and lessons in hand to hand combat.

Their instructor was Hans Heller, whose fastidious military bearing matched his personality. In his early fifties and wearing a monocle, Heller constantly paced the classroom as he talked, gesturing with a riding crop in his right hand, which he wielded at desks and students alike. He gave no quarter for dawdling or inattention and demanded from his students nothing short of perfection.

Candidates were permitted no free time, were forbidden to discuss among themselves either their origins or their missions and were maintained on a diet heavy in carbohydrates but purposely low in protein.

I'll get through it--back to Paris--I'll get through--I'll be in Paris again--I can do anything, get through anything.

Despite the almost irresistible nature of the propaganda, his mind took paths contrary to what the conscious self envisioned as being "good" for the completion of the task at hand. His mind--while treating the outward stimuli such as the dismantling of a rifle, the placement of explosives, or the proper kill points on the human body--ran in veins contrary to its conscious purpose, as perhaps like a flying fish, even as it soars only inches over the emerald waves of the sea, at the same time contemplates the velvet blackness of the deep.

So in this fashion while Maxwell was sitting over his German texts did his mind swoon downwards, treating with a quick scanning of his past a series of reeling images.

The image of his father spiraled up at the most unlikely times.

He remembered, as if it were a dream, being led by the hand in an old neighborhood, his earliest memory, in the time when his parents were young, before they decided to farm, and being led on a ridge overlooking the quaint, white houses and seeing and hearing the freight train on another ridge across the way. And his father saying and the boy feeling the words in his own fingers within the huge, strong hand: "That's grandpa's train." His mother's father had worked for the Carolina Central Railroad. His father's face young and although still wearing glasses, shining with enthusiasm, his limp from his stiff leg a sign of vitality now, rather than in its later decrepit manifestation.

The diesels take us to a factory. Heller talks as we walk through, pointing out areas vulnerable to sabotage--but the guards in the aisles and the faces of the workers --the accusing eyes--Richard, these workers aren't German, they're Slavic, look at their faces, they're not German, Richard.

Or later, as they marched on the field in Hanau, his Wehrmacht helmet over his ears, his rifle heavy on his shoulder, the drumbeat from the band, making the time and announcing the marching cadence, each foot responding to that drum beat, regimented, the dust splashing with the intrusive feet that respond to the phrase of the drum beat, the drum beat inspired, the unit moving as one--as they marched, the image of his father came forth, as if the mind must automatically move to a field beyond the regimentation, to origins unspoken and generally unpondered--his father's face porous as he leaned over the bright lamp that shown on Tommy's homework, the geometry, the problem that his father, in helping his son, over explained, made him do over, and the tears of rage and frustration in the boy as he had to continue on, continue to not understand, continue to listen when there was a radio show coming on, but the feeling in memory like love when pondered, like love until he thought of those sermons.

It was as if his mind had to escape the classes, the zeal, the rigor of ceremony, the constant monitoring--the class, some four hundred strong standing in the assembly hall, forced to listen to the words of Adolf Hitler from the film of a Nuremberg rally as he spoke to the

Hitler Youth, part of the German lessons, the students writing down the translation of the speech, Maxwell doing his best:

"You are my sons. You are the youth of Germany. You are the strength of my strength, the blood of my blood. You are lucky not to have to face the struggles of your fathers. You are lucky now to have pride in yourselves and your country. You are my boys. Part of me. You are the hope of this nation and the hope of Mankind. Someday, you will rule the world."

And Maxwell feeling his legs stiffen and his hands sting as he rose with his class as one and felt the vibration of the standing ovation, the instructor staring through his monocle now, on the stage.

Is it not a father that they seek? Maxwell thought, his mind irresistibly conjuring the face of his father. Is that not what the German nation wanted, a father for the Fatherland, and the image of his own father in the sheriff's office, that bright light shining down on the boy like the sun, also capturing in that radiance the cherub-like face of Dr. Hough the town reverend, his face as calm and rapt as if he were praying over the congregation: "You was caught Tommy, there's nothing else I could do." And until after that day neither the sermons nor the limp bothered him that much. His father in the front seat of the car, receiving his mother's harshness, her pretty face scowling, her green eyes hard, "Landsakes roll down the window." And it never being the things she said, only the tone which captured all the unhappiness, all the frustration of her person, the young boy cringing at the violence of her words and the passivity of his father, that same father who, as if in fear of silence continually played the radio sermons, oftentimes sitting up late on the divan, the radio buzzing and crackling as he searched the dial for yet another voice of assurance, of godlike authority, speaking in that hated singsong of the Trinity, the Virgin birth, the Dissension into Hell, as if the sermons contained some affirmation of his father's hopelessness, as if they battled within him some awful void of silence, a silence as fearful as the deepest recesses of a cave under the sea, immense and threatening in its void.

The scream of iron, the sound of the train horn through your guts, the vibration of the diesels in history--a German immigrant family I knew--the girl, an American, married into the family--she and her German husband to have a baby--the objections of the boy's father--no, you can't name the child Joshua, not Joshua, for God's sake, have you lost your mind?

And in my dream the feel of the train's horn and the diesels--another train, freight cars, the silent, naked arms, limp, sticking out tiny air windows, the sunlight pale on the naked arms.

"Months after the war began, the American Navy operated essentially without standards of procedure either for destroyer skippers or radio operators. But recently the British have begun transferring corvettes to the U.S. and this alone has updated American training......"

And his monocle holds me. Look at his monocle and he will not see my thoughts.

Indeed amid that drum beat, on the marching field, his mind now ran to the sea, swooned in the pleasant memory of the French coast, bathed in sunshine, the sea ever changing--one day its emerald waves sprouting white tops, like foaming milk, churning and tossing in their fluctuations, never uniform, ever rhythmic, the floating birds as white apparitions above those waves, seeking sustenance from the generous ocean, hovering dreamlike above the tossing waves, and on occasion swirling upwards, tucking their wings, and diving headlong into the white foam, content to nibble the gifts from the sea, until it finally claimed them.

On Sept. 9, after a big breakfast, at 0645 all candidates reported to their classrooms. Maxwell and Thibadeaux carried their seaman's bags, since all students were to be ready to embark upon receiving their scores and being granted graduation.

Herr Frankel was dressed with full dress greens. The morning sun streamed in the window, as Frankel read each student's score publicly. Maxwell and Thibadeaux had received two of the highest marks in the class.

Frankel paced the room as he talked.

"Some of you will leave with certain doubts," he said. "All men have had them, especially in your lines of work. Keep in mind, that while lonely, your assignments are just as vital to our war effort as if you were on the front lines."

As Frankel spoke, Maxwell reviewed in his mind the last three weeks.

The training had concentrated on sabotage techniques of aircraft and shipping manufacturers. The men were made to memorize the necessary ingredients, which were easily available, to make explosives, how to make transformers for the disruption of telephones, in general, ways to create general havoc inside Allied countries.

The last two days had been devoted to hand to hand combat techniques.

"Hesitation to kill in wartime situations is synonymous with death," Frankel had said. "You must learn to train your most natural instinct, which is for survival and self-preservation into the immediate destruction of your enemy, without the slightest trace of hesitation."

"Be pitiless, be perfect, be disciplined. Remember, there are no innocent bystanders and there are no neutrals. My thoughts shall always be with you. Heil Hitler."

The class then filed by Frankel. The informal diploma was a handshake and a final wish of good luck.

The men left the classrooms and reported to the officers' building for their orders.

Maxwell and Thibadeaux were to return the way they had come. At 1400 that afternoon, they caught the train bound for Paris via Berlin at the Frankfurt Am Main Bahnhoff. They were to report in Paris on Sept. 11 at 0800 to the Office of Naval Intelligence where Admiral Doenitz would give them further orders.

September 11, 1942

"Good, gentlemen, well done," Admiral Doenitz said, his turned-down mouth curling into a wide smile. He sat before the same large picture window, overlooking Paris, as when the Americans had first met him.

"Reports on your training have been excellent," he said. "And what did you think of our Herr Frankel?" He leaned back laughing, as if to answer his own question.

When the usual pleasantries were exchanged, Doenitz got down to business. "Your orders have already been made out for return to your country. You will return in the same boat that you came in, the U-168, now under the command of Captain Karlheinz Frick, a very capable man. You are to be put on shore off the coast of Florida."

There was a pause. Maxwell noticed Thibadeaux shifting in his seat.

The Admiral continued, "Before you arrived in Lorient, I believe you expressed the desire to have necessary funds to adequately cover your expenses. Upon arrival in the United States, Captain Frick has been instructed to give you an attaché case containing 150,000 dollars in American currency."

Thibadeaux could not suppress the smile that played briefly over his face.

"How you work is completely up to you," continued Doenitz, who ran his right hand through his hair. "Whatever is best. You can work together or alone. We will expect a report on the progress of your first sabotage mission within two weeks of your arrival in the United States. Your contact will be Seawolf."

Doenitz cleared his throat before continuing.

"Unfortunately, there has been a delay in your departure. U-168 is undergoing new re-fitting orders. This is unavoidable. You will not be departing until October 8."

Maxwell crossed his legs. "What are we to do in the mean time?" he asked. "That's nearly four weeks."

The Admiral pulled two forms out of his desk drawer. He scribbled on the forms as he talked.

"Did you turn in your uniforms?"

"Yes sir, we thought we were supposed to."

"Each of you will be re-issued German sea uniforms while you are here in France. You are to wear them at all times. I trust your French and German are sufficient to get you by until you leave."

"Yes sir," Maxwell answered.

"Still," continued Doenitz, "the less contact you have with the townspeople in Lorient, the better. That is why I have made arrangements for you here in Paris. You have a room for two weeks at the Hotel Jacob. You can enjoy yourselves here before your journey. You are to embark by train to Lorient on October 4. Your room in Lorient will be again at the Beausejour. I'm sorry for the delay but it cannot be helped. I must be brief. I'm off to Kerneval," he said, as if thinking out loud. "You may pick up your uniforms and expense money downstairs in room 10."

Doenitz stood up. The two Americans saluted and shook his hand.

"Are there any further questions?"

"No sir."

"Your mission is a vital one for the Third Reich," he said as he handed each man his sealed orders. "Report to room 10 for your uniforms. Good luck."

September 15

Burning red over the black sea, the wind slanting the flames, the sea pitching under the green flares, the iron hull half-sunk amid the islands of fiery oil, and the screams from the faceless men--Maxwell awoke in a cold sweat.

He rose naked out of his bed--the sheets sticking to his skin before he tossed them off. Hearing Thibadeaux snoring in the next bed, he staggered over to the blinds where thin lines of gray light filtered into the dingy room. He lifted one blind.

The street vendors, selling flowers and cheese were already setting up their sidewalk displays across the way. Maxwell put his right hand up onto one of his throbbing temples. On his third night in Paris he had gotten blind drunk, just as he had on the previous two nights. He cursed under his breath.

Walking as quietly as he could, so as not to awaken Richard, he dressed in his tight-fitting U-boat blues with the white sailor's hat. He would go it alone today. He had had months of Thibadeaux's company and that was enough.

Even as he shoved Richard's shoulder roughly and told him he was going out, his mind was elsewhere. He heard Thibadeaux grunt his approval and headed for the door.

Maxwell would not return to the room until night.

He walked down the narrow stairway, through the lobby and out into the gray light of the street. The first order of business was breakfast, which he could take at the Cafe de Flore.

Still feeling drunk, he managed to stagger three city blocks to the sidewalk cafe where he ordered coffee, bread, and a bowl of fruit. As he drank the coffee, he broke into a sweat, as if coming out of a fever. The dream bothered him.

That makes three times, he thought, three times dreaming of that, to hell with it, I'm just hungover.

He ordered more coffee and forced down three aspirin. The last time he had gotten that drunk had been in Morgan City, just before he had accepted his mission.

The sun began to burn brightly, melting the early fog and bathing the street in golden color. Maxwell lit a cigarette, paid his bill, and walked down the avenue.

Paris teemed in the mornings. The city's spirit was irrepressible. For the last three days Maxwell and Thibadeaux had roamed these streets, never seeing any sign of the war, except for an occasional parade or review of German troops, or the uniforms among the crowded streets.

Then Maxwell remembered the poster he had seen yesterday on the Rue Delambre. Adorned with a red swastika, the poster had been written in French in bold print. It announced the execution of one

Henri Moulin at Rue de Temps for the murder of a German officer at the metro train station. The poster had warned that any further acts of sedition would be severely punished by the German authorities.

Maxwell headed instinctively for Rue Delambre.

Paris expressed herself in every mode imaginable. The streets bustled with life. He passed a fish market, where the fishermen laid out their wares, rows of gray fish, caught from the Seine, lying gape-mouthed along the walk. He could not walk a city block without seeing a statue of one sort or another. Sweet smells of freshly baked bread and cheese wafted through the air as he passed the bakery shops. An artist with an easel, set up under a partition, painted a portrait of a German officer and his girlfriend--the artist with his beret cocked, and his eccentric, Frenchman's scowl never leaving his face.

As Maxwell walked past a baker's stand filled with baquettes, he decided that the charm of the Parisians lay in a complete lack of pretension. The German army personnel could be seen sitting next to the French in the bars or the sidewalk cafes. No doubt many of the Germans had French girl friends, and the prostitutes were not starving. But in general, the relationship between the French and the Germans was strained. Underlying the sullen faces of the French was a cold sarcasm towards the German occupation force. Next to the French, the Germans appeared stiff, pale, and affected in their shiny boots and brass buttons.

Maxwell's ideas were reinforced on the Rue Delambre. Next to a sidewalk display of an artichoke stand, he found the poster. He broke into laughter. It was the first time in days that he had laughed.

Only posted yesterday, the bill, announcing the execution of Moulin was now coated with pinned-on flowers. Just below where a purple violet had been placed were the words, scrawled in crayon:

Defense d'Afficher.

A chill ran down Maxwell's spine. So this was the way the Parisians fought their war, in silent protests of beauty and tribute.

Maxwell stared at the poster. A strange sensation was coming over him. He breathed in deeply. For the first time in weeks, he felt alive again.

As he reached up and plucked the purple violet from the poster, he saw her.

She was a street walker. She had long, flowing black hair to her shoulders and lovely dark eyes. She wore a white straw hat, cocked elegantly on the back of her head. Beads dangled from her long, elegant neck, and the white summer dress she wore just barely covered the nipples of her generous breasts. As she twisted past, Maxwell impulsively handed her the violet.

"Pour vous," he said.

The woman took the violet with light fingertips, raised it to her nose, and seeing Maxwell's German blues, scowled as she dropped the flower onto the sidewalk.

"Sprechen sie Deutsch?" Maxwell said.

"Non," she said, and as she started to walk away, Maxwell gently grabbed her elbow.

"Je ne parle pas Francais," he said, smiling reassuringly. "How about English?"

The woman was beautiful, but she did not melt. She looked suspiciously down at her elbow until Maxwell removed his hand, then squarely faced him.

"Yes, I speak English," she said. "What do you want?"

Maxwell pointed to the words scrawled in crayon on the poster-- Defense d'Afficher.

"What does that mean?" he asked.

For the first time she smiled, only with her eyes. "It says, 'Post No Bills.'"

Maxwell laughed.

"Is that all you want, German?" she said as she started to walk away.

Maxwell quickly reached into his pocket and produced a ten franc note.

"I want you," he said.

She took the note and thrust it into her purse, finally admitting a smile which showed even, white teeth. "Of course you do," she said.

"Come with me. My room is only a block away."

"No," Maxwell said, again touching her elbow, and pulling another twenty francs out of his pocket. "I don't want that. Not now anyway.

I only want you to walk with me today, be my guide and companion. We won't talk German or French--only English, that way we won't think about the war."

She laughed and quickly took the money. "Very well, German," she said. "If speaking English makes you forget about the war, then we speak English." She stepped back slightly and watched Maxwell.

"You have paid for a day," she said coldly. "I will be your guide, but if you want my body, you pay more."

Maxwell smiled. He enjoyed directness in women. It reminded him of Julie. He crooked his arm and felt her light fingers, and they started on their way.

They walked for a time before catching an ox-cart taxi. They were taken to the Luxembourg Gardens on Rue Guynemer. Inside the spiked iron fence was the garden with its stately trees and flat, green stretches. Bare wooden chairs were placed in various parts of the garden. Maxwell found two chairs under a shade tree.

The whore sat down primly, crossed her legs, and shook her hair.

Despite the oddity of his approach, she appeared comfortable with Maxwell.

"Want a cigarette?" Maxwell asked.

"No, I have my own."

"Good, then I'll try one of yours."

When he lit up and grimaced, again she smiled. "Is it that bad?"

"These French cigarettes are all the same," he said.

She raised an eyebrow slightly. "They were better before the war."

"What is your name?" he asked.

She inhaled the cigarette, letting the smoke go out into her small nostrils before answering.

"Evette," she said.

Maxwell paused to see if she would ask his name, and when she did not, he said, "Call me Tommy."

"Tommy? That's not a German name."

"A nickname," he said. "Do you hate all Germans?"

She looked at him sideways as a woman strolled by with a baby carriage. "Germans are men," she answered. "No more, no less."

"Then you hate all men."

Again she faced him squarely. "I thought we were going for a walk," she said.

When they finished their cigarettes, she entwined her fingers in his, and they set about seeing Paris.

They made their way to the Place d'Observatoire where they sat by the huge fountain, which was lined with the stone statues of the upper torsos of horses. They strolled by a street violinist, who played in front of bookstalls, and passed two statues with long, flowing robes.

The sunshine, the warm touch of her hand, the variety of Paris, its unbridled beauty and life--all this purged Maxwell. The weeks of tension in Louisiana, when he thought he might be arrested for sedition, then the tense confinement of the U-168, the six weeks at the Hanau training camp--all these events had followed one another as rapidly as cars on a speeding freight train. The training had made him think like a soldier. He no longer weighed events or emotions as before. Instead, his thoughts had been unclouded by the purity of military goals.

They took lunch in the Dingo Restaurant, where they sat at an elegant table with stiff napkins, folded in pyramids beside wine glasses--the centerpiece, a simple jar with water and purple flowers.

They both had fish with white wine sauce and boiled potatoes.

The girl ate ravenously, cheering up slightly after the meal.

"You seem satisfied," Maxwell said, leaning back.

She smiled and reached across the table, touching his fingers. "We don't eat as well since the occupation," she said. "At first the Germans came in with soup kitchens to feed us. They were quite kind, but now with the Reichsmark and the Vichy government, no one has enough money."

"Were you a whore before the war?"

She answered directly, apparently not offended. "Oui, it is a living."

"Then you should do better now than ever."

She stared off, then scrunched up her shoulders. "I have known a lot of Germans," she said. "And a few sailors too. You spend money like an officer. Are you rich?"

Maxwell leaned back and laughed. "Would you like more wine?"

"Non, you didn't answer my question."

"No, I am not rich. So how do I compare to the other Germans you have had?"

She shrugged. "I have not had you yet. Like I said before, I don't mind men. The only Germans I hate are the SS."

She watched his face turn. The boyish spark in his eyes hardening.

"And why do you hate SS?" he muttered as if the question had significance.

"The last one I was with ordered me about. And he would clap his hands at me when he wanted me to move," she said, shaking her head and hunching up her shoulders as if cold. "And he wore his gloves the whole time. It was very strange. I hate to have hands clapped at me. It reminds me of my father."

"Something tells me I shouldn't ask you about your father."

She laughed.

He drained the glass of white wine, leaned back, and stretched.

"I enjoy your company," he said. "It's fun to forget about the war. That's all anyone in Paris is doing. Living and trying to forget."

She shrugged and put on her hat. "Are you ready to go?" she said.

They bought a liter of white wine and spent the remainder of the day on the Seine. On a large grass embankment they lay, drinking wine from paper cups and kissing. Below, the sun twinkled off the green water. From their vantage point they could see four bridges criss-crossing the river. Old men sat just below them with long cane poles stretched out over the water. Fishing was good. Maxwell watched one old man with a crinkled hat fill a straw basket with large, gray fish. Barges moved slowly past, the small tug boats churning the water behind them.

The sky turned violet as the sun got low behind clouds on the horizon. Evette and Maxwell walked arm-in-arm towards her room. On the way when Maxwell saw the sign Rue de Temps, he insisted they walk down the street.

"What do you find so interesting about Moulin?" she asked.

As Maxwell turned towards Rue de Temps, he smiled and cocked his cap lower over his eyes.

"I don't know. Just curious, I guess."

She frowned with disgust. "You're like a tourist."

He laughed. "Funny you should say that."

"Why?"

"It just is," he said with a smirk. "You speak of Moulin as if you knew him. Did you?"

"Of course not," she said defensively. "He is Resistance, that is all. They all have one thing in common."

"What's that?"

"They all die. They are already dead and they don't even know it."

"The Gestapo is that efficient?"

She pulled her hand from his. "You're German, at least you say you are. You should know."

As they headed down Rue de Temps, he grabbed her hand again.

"I'm sorry, just humor me this one time, and I promise we won't talk about the war again."

The dusk light filtered gray down on the modest street, lined with shops and small apartments.

Until he reached the middle of the block under the statue of a gargoyle, Maxwell saw nothing special.

The couple stopped.

Underneath the gargoyle lay a pile of long-stemmed flowers of all colors. The pile was ankle-high and long. On the other side of the pile of flowers two children stood staring, a boy and a girl. Maxwell looked at the little boy's eyes, huge and full of wonder.

"This is the place where Moulin was executed," Evette said sarcastically. "Pretty aren't they?"

"Flowers," Maxwell muttered with a strange smile. "Always flowers."

Evette tugged on his arm. "Come on, German, we have a long way to go."

Maxwell turned and looked her in the eye. "I'm not German. I'm an American."

"An American....."

"Don't ask me to explain, because I won't," he said, then grabbing her hand. "Come on, let's go."

His grip was firmer now and he walked with such long and determined steps, that she had to run with little steps to catch up.

As Maxwell walked, the words echoed in his soul. I'm an American. Why had he risked everything, even his life in telling her?

It was because he had felt an overwhelming urge to tell her. That was all. And in those words he felt the admission that everything he had felt initially at Hanau was false.

They arrived at her room, in a decrepit section off Champs d' Elysee. After climbing the steps and arriving at a small door, she stopped and faced him.

"If you want to come inside, you owe me another fifteen francs."

He jerked off his hat comically. "Fifteen. It was ten this morning."

She smiled. "I forgot to figure the Vichy tax," she said.

For the next eight days they were lovers, as much as a whore and her customer could be. He insisted on paying for every minute of her time, and she never refused a franc.

He made love to her without the involvement of past relationships.

The sex was good in itself. He only sought human contact, and ultimately, an escape from his situation, and himself.

When the day came for him to leave for Lorient, he asked her to come with him.

"I will pay you," he said. "It can be a holiday for you. We'll have three days before I set off."

She had been in bed next to him when he asked her. She rose to an elbow, not answering, only regarding him with her dark eyes.

"We can have a room by the sea. What do you say? Can you get travel papers?"

She smiled and kissed him on the mouth. "I can get papers," she said.

They traveled separately on the train, and met in front of the Gazebo in Lorient.

The next three days were as good as Maxwell had hoped. They never spoke about his departure or why he was an American in a German uniform. They stayed in a decrepit little hotel on the beach.

At nights after she was asleep, he would wander over to the window, looking at the breakers, lining white in the darkness, the moon reflecting a lane of light off the sea, touching the horizon.

He was a long way from home. Despite his doubts he still maintained that he would go through with his mission. The war was bigger than any one person now, but he continued to tell himself that his own part in this "huge sarcasm" was a just one. Or was he merely rationalizing a mission that had long ago lost any real meaning to him? The answer lay over that horizon. He would carry on, but until he reached America, he did not know what he would do.

October 6, 1942

Tommy Maxwell sat before a window, the morning light streaming in with the breeze from the sea. Maxwell drew on his cigarette and watched the waves break lazily on the beach below. A white laced curtain blew by his still face.

He heard her shift in the bed behind him. He turned his chair around. Her right breast rose and fell with her long sigh, the sheet just revealing the pink top of her aureola. She opened her eyes which were as deeply brown as her hair. She leaned up on one elbow, the sheet falling from her breasts.

"Want a cigarette?" Maxwell asked, as he got up from the chair. He wore only his blue navy issue pants and an undershirt with white straps.

"Non," she said.

He went over to the sink by the wall and dipped his shaving brush, panning the lather in its familiar pattern over his face.

"So when do you go to sea?" she asked in English.

"Day after tomorrow," he said. When he finished shaving, he returned to the side of the bed. He watched her face in the gray light.

"Are you sad to leave me?" she asked with an ironic smile. "Don't lie."

He put his hand over one of her breasts and kissed her.

"I knew another woman as blunt as you once," he said.

She helped him on with his seaman's shirt. "Where?" she asked. "In America?"

He watched her face. He had never trusted a woman this much.

"Yeah, that's right," he said.

He walked over to the window again. Thibadeaux was now standing on the beach. He was ten minutes early.

"Close that window, will you?" she said. "I want to sleep." He closed the window and the latch and pulled the curtains together.

She sat up for a final kiss. She embraced his neck as he kissed her. He stood up and pulled out his cigarettes, placing one in her mouth, despite her earlier refusal.

"Merci," she said sarcastically, and then after lighting it and taking her first drag, "you don't have to pay me this time. Call it your going away gift."

He laughed and reached inside his pocket. "Have you ever been in the middle of something," he asked, "and before you're halfway through, you look up and don't know who you are?"

"I don't understand the question," she said, tilting her head so that one eye was hidden by her hair.

He pulled out the remaining money in his pocket and folded it under a half-empty pack of cigarettes on the bedside table.

"I don't know," he said. "Before the war, Hitler preached peace, Churchill preached peace, Roosevelt....."

He stopped when he heard her giggle.

"I am not a deep-thinking person like you," she said, tossing her hair back from her face.

She looked down at the money on the table.

"I told you. You don't have to pay."

"None of us have to do anything," he said, and blowing her a kiss, he walked out the door.

Moments later he was walking towards Lorient with Thibadeaux. Thibadeaux was expansive. He was happy to be heading home.

"Shit, cheri, it's been fun and all," he said, walking in long strides, "but I seen enough of France and Germany. What's eating you?"

Maxwell shrugged. "I don't know," he said. "Guess I'm just itching to get to sea."

"Sea hell," Thibadeaux said. "You ain't been in a decent mood since Doenitz said he was paying us the dough. Come on. It's true, ain't it?"

"It's not the money that bothers me."

"Yes, it is," continued Thibadeaux in his boisterous voice. "Well, it don't bother me for a second. I never hid my 'tentions. One of these days you going to wake up. You the typical idea man, grits.

Nuts, Tommy, just face the fact. You being paid to do a job. Big deal." He laughed and slapped Maxwell on the shoulder. "How do it feel to be a second story man?" he asked.

Maxwell smiled. As he walked, he figured that he was mostly bored. They had one more day to kill. Tomorrow they were to report to an officer's suite on the third floor of the Beausejour where they were to meet with Kapitan Karlheinz Frick, newly appointed Captain of U-168.

Captain Karlheinz Frick, age 38, was married and had a son. He was a capable officer, who had petitioned both Admiral Raeder and Admiral Doenitz for sea duty in the U boat arm. He had been transferred to the submarine training base where he underwent his initial studies. He had gone to sea for two cruises on the U-47 as Executive Officer under the command of the Reich's top U boat commander, Gunther Prien.

Entering Frick's suite at the Beausejour, the Americans saw a thin man, dressed in his dark blue Captain's dress blouse with gold braids and a chest full of decorations. He sat behind a broad desk in a handsome parlor, the desk before a large bay window, overlooking the courtyard.

As the two men approached, the Captain rubbed his chin as he read from a dossier. The Americans snapped to attention as the Captain rose and saluted. The Americans returned the salute and relaxed as Frick pointed to two chairs in front of his desk.

Frick possessed medium height, with dark, thin features. On his desk were a framed photograph of his wife and son and a model of the Bismarck.

Frick looked up from the dossiers and made eye contact. He rubbed his chin as he spoke.

"Captain Schuller has fully briefed me on your mission," he said, knitting his eyebrows seriously. "I trust your stay in Lorient has been pleasant."

"Quite pleasant, sir," Maxwell said. "But we are anxious to get on with our mission."

"Excellent," the Captain replied, his frame coming to attention in his chair. "I really don't have much to say. All hands are to report today at 2200 hours. As you know, stragglers are to pay penalties. In your case I will make an exception."

Maxwell shifted uneasily.

Frick looked from one man to another and relaxed in his chair. He took a deep breath and sighed, his brow smoothing, as if distracted.

"You are to report tomorrow morning at 0600. There is no need in your coming aboard any sooner. The crew will be getting ready for sea and supplying the boat today and tonight. You would only be in the way."

"Sir," Thibadeaux said, "we glad to lend a hand. We want to do our part."

"Regulations forbid it," Frick answered with a polite nod of the head. "I appreciate your attitude. As you might already guess, I am a seaman, and like Captain Schuller, I am only interested in getting to my assigned post off the United States, laying my mines, and sinking Allied shipping. Frankly, having you two aboard complicates my task. British patrol planes are spotting U boats and giving their positions to destroyers. American coastal defenses are constantly improving. I quite simply want to deliver my passengers, lay my mines, sink all available Allied shipping and come home."

A look of dejection ran briefly across his dark features, replaced by a firm resolve.

"The challenge for our nation grows greater every day. We are fighting a two front war........." his words broke off, his brow again smoothing out. "My hope is that myself and my crew can survive. Any questions?"

When the Americans said nothing, Frick closed the dossier in front of him. He leaned forward and folded his hands on the desk, gazing deeply into both men's eyes, as if to make a strong point.

"Captain Schuller reported to me an incident concerning yourselves and two seamen on board. I want no repetition of this. Is that understood?"

"Jawohl, mein Kapitan," both men replied.

Frick leaned back. "That is all."

The Americans spent most of the next day packing and drinking.

Tradition held that U boat crews throw a drunk the night before shoving off, and by 2100 the Americans had located a few of their crewmates, whom they chose to view from a distance at Mimi's.

There were only five mates from U-168 down by the piano and they were completely oblivious to anyone's presence, save for the pretty French girl in a purple dress. Although they were hard to recognize with their clean-shaven faces, Maxwell and Thibadeaux finally succeeded in identifying them as boys from the engine room. The men raised their glasses to the girl on the stage, who sang their every request. At one point Lyons jumped onto the stage, unbuttoned his seaman's blouse, and danced with the girl. When the song ended, the girl gave him a hug and a kiss on the cheek; Lyons swooned and fell off the stage onto a table, occupied by three other sailors from another craft. A short fight broke out, which was not stopped until Lyons was spitting blood and being led staggering to the washroom to vomit.

Thibadeaux laughed and took a long drink of lager. "Amazing what a fool a man become over a piece of ass."

Maxwell put down his beer and leaned forward. "I have a confession to make," he said. "I mentioned to Evette in Paris that I was an American."

Thibadeaux was in mid-swallow and spit lager over his shirt. "You what?"

Maxwell shrugged and folded his arms. "I know it was a fool thing to do..."

"Stupid ass," Thibadeaux shouted. "You goddamned right it was. I ought to kick your ass. What you trying to do? Get us killed? I guess then you and you fucking conscience will be satisfied. What come over you?"

"What can I say? You're right. I had no right to jeopardize your safety."

Thibadeaux's fist pounded the table. "You safety too, babe, shit.

You done forgot our briefing about talking to whores?"

"She was no spy," Maxwell said. "And don't ask me to explain why I did it? I've been asking myself the same question for days. Maybe for once I just wanted to disobey a German's orders."

Thibadeaux scooted his chair back and crossed his legs, looking at Maxwell as if he were a strange, unidentified creature. "You take the cake. You know that? This ain't no game. What else you tell her?"

"Nothing, nothing," Maxwell said, holding up his hand. "Look, I told you I was stupid. That's enough said. And by the way, fuck you."

Thibadeaux sighed and lit a cigarette. "I just hope you ain't cooked our asses, that's all. I be glad to get to sea."

The two men drank the rest of their beer in silence. The only hint of remaining levity was the site of the four engine room boys hoisting Lyons out the door at 2145, carrying him like a sack of flour to his duty.

CHAPTER 7

At 0530 on October 8 Maxwell and Thibadeaux wore their dress grays as they entered the great brown bunker at the Lorient harbor. The inside of the huge bunker was frantic with activity. Construction workers were everywhere. They moved past the flashing lights of welders--guards with their rifles in sling over their shoulders, a puff of white smoke here, crews being inspected, men hanging in the air over the various U boat berths where cranes were loading provisions. Great lights hung down from long wire. Rows of men rushed by, carrying tubing. Huge torpedoes were rolled down the aisles on rails.

U-168 sat in an outside berth in the morning light. The crew, dressed in gray, was scurrying over the deck, hoisting in supplies from the bridge hatch, as the supplies were lowered from an overhead crane. Others of the crew were manning hoses, washing down U-168's flanks and decks. Maxwell saw Rosenberg at the forward end of the boat, working with the large deck gun. Rosenberg was the object of laughter once, as a stiff breeze blew his hat off into the water.

Hagermester and Danet were inspecting a new portable aerial setup that had been mounted near the bridge hatch.

By the time Maxwell and Thibadeaux had gone aboard and stowed their gear, Captain Frick had called for inspection formation topside. The time was 0740 when the last supplies were lowered and U-168 was pronounced ready for sea.

The crew had labored all night for last minute preparations. Once at sea, half the crew would be relieved for sleep, while the unlucky ones would have to wait until 1400 to rest.

When Maxwell and Thibadeaux reached the deck, they hardly recognized the crew since all were clean-shaven and getting in formation in their clean grays.

As the brief inspection was carried out by Frick and Danet, a crowd had gathered next to the quay. Friends of the departing sailors, French women, waving to their boyfriends, and bystanders from the town of Lorient buzzed behind a railing overlooking U-168.

As Frick and Danet passed him, Maxwell felt a nudge on his arm.

"Look up there to the right," Thibadeaux whispered nervously. "It's that damned bimbo."

Evette stood in the back of the crowd, behind two sailors who were jumping up and down, waving their arms. When she met Maxwell's gaze, she crooked the thin fingers of her hand into a wave. She wore the same dress as when Maxwell had first met her.

Immediately Maxwell knew that he was safe and that she had told nothing. He regretted nothing.

When the inspection ended, Frick gave the order to get underway. The crowd gave a loud cheer as the diesels began to churn and the lines were cast off. The sea wolves quickly dispersed, some going below to assume their duties, the others hanging off the bridge, waving to friends and well-wishers.

The Americans had intended to stay topside as long as possible until Danet approached them on the bridge. His face scowled and his dark eyes twitched back and forth. "Get below and get out of those uniforms," he ordered.

Maxwell felt his stomach tighten with anger.

He snapped to attention, clicking his heels and saluting. "Jawohl, mein Oberleutnant," he shouted sarcastically.

By the time the Americans were in their civilian clothes and had turned their neatly folded grays and blues in to Hagermeister, the U-168 had cleared the fortress at the mouth of the harbor. When Maxwell kept his golden U boat garland as a souvenir, Hagermeister pretended not to notice.

"Say, Hagermeister," Maxwell said, tucking in his shirt, "I noticed Rosenberg and Steinhoff today twirling these gold watches today, on a chain. They looked like railroad watches."

Hagermeister blushed and shrugged. He reached into his right pants pocket and pulled out a gold watch, just as Maxwell had described. "Like this one?" he said, blushing.

The chief petty officer showed the Americans a handsome gold watch, encased in gold with ornate Roman numerals on the face.

"Everybody got one, all the sea wolves," Hagermeister said, as he tucked his chin in as if suppressing a belch. "They're all gold and all different. Frick let us pick the ones we wanted from a big box when we reported to duty. He said thousands of the watches are being given out and only to the Waffen SS units in Russia and the U-boat sea wolves. He says we are considered elite fighters. Rosenberg got two watches. He said the gift was from the SS, as ordered by Himmler."

Maxwell leveled his gaze at Hagermeister, who dropped his eyes to the deck plates.

"Where did the watches come from, chief petty officer....in your opinion? Where would Reichsfuhrer Himmler get so many watches? And all a different kind? Does he own a jewelry manufacturer?"

Hagermeister jerked his body as if suddenly awakened from a nap.

"It's none of my business. If I were you, I would not make an issue."

The morning of October 8 was heavily overcast, with reports of heavy rains due west of Lorient, extending over three hundred miles westward.

U-168 followed the pilot boat out of the harbor. The wind was blowing from the southwest, and waves were cresting at three feet. U-168 experienced no difficulty with these slightly rough seas, the waves breaking white off her flanks.

Once clear of the harbor, the pilot boat turned, waved, and slipped back into Lorient. U-168 set a course of 250 degrees. This course would take her to a rendezvous with the sub-tender, where she could take on more fuel and any other provisions she needed to extend her cruise. The rendezvous was just north of the Bahama islands. She should make contact with the tender in ten days. Frick had instructed his radio operator to monitor all weather broadcasts while listening to the various frequencies used by Allied shipping. With luck, he might learn how the weather was shaping up west of the rain storm now at sea. He would prefer to stay on the surface and make all the time he could. Submerged, his speed would be reduced twenty-five percent or more.

As they moved southwest, Frick studied his charts. The shipping lanes were clearly marked and his grid square had been designated just southeast of the Florida straights. This section had proved fruitful for the U boats with ships coming through the straights from the U.S. Gulf coast, headed for New York and the convoys for Britain.

As they moved west, the rains increased; the waves had now reached six feet. The waves would increase as they moved into the storm. U-168 held her course at 250 degrees.

Meanwhile, back in Lorient Evette walked slowly towards the gazebo.

As she strolled, she noticed several sailors watch her. They would be easy marks, and there would be plenty of time for others.

She yawned.

She was to meet Marcel in one hour at the L'Orange Tavern. She knew he would be angry at the sparseness of her report. Why she had failed to contact him about U-168's departure time she could not say.

She could expect a beating for that.

But she would make up for it.

In those long hours in bed, she had gathered enough trivial information--she surmised--to determine U-168's probable course. Small facts, such as Mickey's twig from Cuba, a comment about New Orleans' food, and a tale about a certain storm at sea would be enough for British intelligence to profile U-168's course. Small facts such as these had sunk many a U boat previously, she told herself.

She stopped to buy a flower for her dress. From an old street vendor she was given a single purple violet, pinning it over her left breast.

She knew immediately what she would not tell Marcel. Perhaps it was the most important detail of all. This "Tommy" who had been her lover, was American.

With light fingers, she touched the purple violet over her breast. Her eyes welled with tears.

No, she thought, I will not tell him that.

She knew that the detail of Tommy being an American was an important one, but she rationalized that they had the usual profile--enough possibly to kill everyone on board U-168.

Besides, she thought, he was different. Kind of sad, and very kind.

She shook her head as she walked. She scolded herself. It was ridiculous these days to fall in love.

Below decks, the Americans were reading training manuals in the morning hours. After lunch they would wander around the sub, talking to the crew, asking questions concerning the various operations.

They examined the torpedo rooms, the detonators, and timing mechanisms.

Inside, the boat was more cramped than ever, since far more provisions hung from the ceilings.

All of Maxwell's friends were aboard--Hagermeister--the chief petty officer whose face looked much fatter with the absence of the beard, Mickey and Rhinehardt, the blonde gunner with the glass eye and his large-sized counterpart, his beard now manicured into a well-trimmed rectangle. Duggan, the cook, always preparing a meal in the galley; Danet, who had barely spoken to the Americans, was expansive. Rosenberg and Steinhoff seemed constantly aware of the Americans, but for now, were keeping their distance. Waissenhoffer, the burly red head with the loud mouth was aboard, and but for the new officer in the diesel room and the Captain, the crew was the same.

In the next four days U-168 made good time. The weather was rough, but the storm was not as bad as the Americans had experienced enroute to Europe. Morale was high. The radio was tuned to Germany, and quite often the entire boat would break into song if one of their favorites was played. The singing seemed to enhance the Germans' abilities to work.

Particularly interesting to Maxwell was what the German radio stations did every night at midnight. Different elements of the German fronts would call in, giving their greetings to the German people. The

North African front, the Eastern front at Stalingrad, the U boat front in the Atlantic, the troops in Greece, Paris, Holland, Norway and the rest--all acknowledged.

By night the U boats talked incessantly on the buzzing radio waves, discussing dispositions of convoys and weather conditions.

Coincidentally the summer of 1942 brought about a number of new developments in the Battle of the Atlantic. In June the British had scored enormous successes against German U boats.

The U boats had always been aided chiefly by three things--the early breaking of the British code and superior intelligence early in the war, their surface speed, which was much faster than any convoy afloat, and their low silhouettes, which made them practically impossible to spot at night.

In June of 1942 this last advantage had disappeared with the advent of the Leigh searchlight, suitable for mounting on British patrol planes. The summer had been highlighted by unprecedented U boat sinkings. The Leigh light, used in unison with new British radar aboard patrol aircraft, led to the sinkings of U-502, U-705, and U-751, all put out of action as they had set out on various missions.

These new Allied successes had caused the delay in U-168's departure from Europe. German sea command held emergency meetings in Kerneval. Admiral Doenitz came to the inevitable conclusion that the British had developed airborne radar. It was the only explanation to these surprise attacks. The meetings were held in Paris, where the German technical experts came up with a counter to the new radar developments.

U-168, as well as any other U-boats set for embarkation, was equipped with new search receivers. These receivers could pick up enemy radar long before U boats came into range, where the signal was strong enough to reflect back to the aircraft. The device needed was found in the French Meto set. Aerials were hastily improvised. A length of wire was wrapped round a plain wooden frame known as a "Biscay Cross."

By August all U boats were equipped with these Biscay Crosses and by October all surprise attacks of boats leaving their bays had halted.

A stalemate ensued. When the aircraft were detected, the U boat dove, hence, temporarily out of operation for attack.

However, the greatest aid to the German hopes in the Atlantic was the limited range of Allied search planes. Not until 1944 were planes able to cover the entire span of ocean. Britain, Greenland, and America were the major bases for search planes. Their ranges were not sufficient to cover the four hundred mile stretch in the mid-Atlantic known as the Atlantic Gap.

October 13

On their fifth day at sea Maxwell and Thibadeaux rose at 0800, took a small breakfast in the galley, and went topside to take the air. Schnegel had just taken over the day watch, and he waved to the Americans as they moved past him to the forward deck.

The sea was still choppy, but the worst of the storm's winds were over. The sky was clearing and the sun was already beating down on the blue sea. As had become their habit in the mornings at Hanau, Maxwell and Thibadeaux went through a routine of exercises on deck.

It was not long before two more men appeared on the bridge.

Maxwell was in the process of doing sit-ups when he saw the dim figures against the glaring light. Rosenberg and Steinhoff moved past the colors of the flag bearing the swastika. Before this, only these two Germans had carried out their private exercise routine while at sea.

The two Germans stood over the Americans while they finished their sit ups.

"Up early for pleasure passengers," Rosenberg said, grinning against the sun.

"Working on their tans," quipped Steinhoff, who was wearing his black and white striped undershirt, his shoulders shining white in the light.

Maxwell and Thibadeaux assumed push up positions. "Can't let you two get ahead of us," Maxwell said, as he dipped down for his first pushup.

"That right," Thibadeaux said. "I so damned tall, I spend all day stooping around inside. Give me back problems."

"Too bad," Steinhoff said, "such a very sad story."

Rosenberg started to speak when Maxwell interrupted. "Yeah, Steinhoff, that's kind of funny. You're nearly as tall as him," he said, tilting his head to indicate Thibadeaux. "You and Danet both." Maxwell continued to pump off pushups as he talked, "but I didn't think they let tall guys like you and Danet into the submarine service." He pumped off ten more, his back glistening with sweat. "That's very strange," Maxwell continued. "Suppose the Kriegsmarine just ignored your height. You guys must have other special requirements."

Rosenberg flushed and took a step forward. Steinhoff intervened, grabbing his cohort by the forearm.

"Come on, Fritz," he said, "let's go aft."

Maxwell and Thibadeaux continued to pump off the pushups, keeping their heads up and watching Rosenberg and Steinhoff as they moved aft.

"Taking a bit of a chance, ain't you?" Thibadeaux said. "You remember what Frick said."

Maxwell smiled mischievously. "Yeah, that's right," he said. "I just want those two to know where we stand. We're on to their little surveillance game, and I want them to know it."

"Those two tough sons of bitches, Tommy."

Maxwell laughed. "I refuse to be scared of trash like that," he said. He stopped his pushups and began stretching out his legs, "besides," he added, "I figured you could handle them."

Thibadeaux stood up and smiled. "Oooweee, you is definitely touched, the ride, that's all this boy is handling. I ain't out to prove nothing, me."

"Good," Maxwell said, "because you ain't proved a damned thing to me."

Thibadeaux stretched. "That's right, go ahead and give the shit. I can take any amount of shit gumbo for a cool seventy-five thousand."

Maxwell laughed and continued stretching.

By now six other members of the crew were topside, taking the air.

Maxwell and Thibadeaux entertained themselves watching Waisenhoffer, troll fishing off the side.

For the next three days Maxwell did everything possible to cope with the sea wolf's worst enemy--boredom. Time lost all meaning aboard a submarine. When the three hours allowed for daily exercise were used up, the Americans were forced at close quarters with little to do but hang around and watch the rest of the crew carry out their duties. The Captain's refusal to let them have any duties at all only contributed to their tension.

Thibadeaux attacked his boredom by trying to sleep twelve hours, but Maxwell had never been a big sleeper.

With a deck of cards he had bought in Lorient, Maxwell played every game imaginable, including spending hours tossing cards at a hat.

Drills for the crew were the highlight of the day. Frick took the crew through the daily pace of diving drills, constantly testing their reactions to his orders and monitoring the ship's ability to withstand pressure.

The crew began to look forward to the meeting with the sub-tender on October 16. Although they would be hard at work re-supplying the ship, at least the rendezvous with the "milch cow" offered them comradery--a reminder that they were not the only collection of lost souls on the lonely Atlantic.

For Maxwell not even the tender offered to break up the journey, since he and Thibadeaux were to stay below for security reasons.

Neither were any of the crew to mention the Americans to anyone aboard the tender. The only thing the sub-tender meant to Maxwell was that it marked the two-thirds milestone of the trip.

When Maxwell finally ran out of things to do, he found himself mesmerized by his surroundings. The sway of the light in the aisle, the churn of the diesels, the belch of a sailor in the top bunk, he lived within these sights and sounds, as if, just like a man gone blind, with the deprivation of seeing the daylight, other senses are heightened.

In the time just prior to U-168's meeting with the sub-tender, the overall morale was low. Crew members' faces had begun to take that haggard look that Maxwell had first seen when boarding U-168 off the Louisiana coast. The beards were now thick, and the bodies had begun to stink, permeating the boat with one dank, collective odor.

Sailors spent most of their time writing letters, which they would give to an officer on the sub-tender. And whereas they had little hope that the letters would arrive home before they would, the exercise of writing was therapeutic.

October 16

The weather remained perfect, and the seas were as smooth as glass. As the Captain kept to the surface both day and night, U-168 was on the proper schedule for rendezvous with the sub-tender.

At 0350 Frick occupied a grid square designated to meet U-459, the sub-tender. U-168 cruised on the surface at maximum speed. Frick was unconcerned with the possibility of being spotted by aircraft, since this grid was still in the area known as the Atlantic Gap.

At 0359, U-459, a huge 1700 ton "milch cow" surfaced to loud cheers aboard U-168. Both crafts stopped all power as the respective crews tied the crafts together with rope and gas lines. U-168 took on fuel, lubricating oil, replacement parts, and food. Those of the crew, who were not involved in the fueling or re-supplying of the boat were the first to go through what the Americans referred to as "short arm inspection." This done, several of the crew went overboard for a swim, while others merely fraternized. The entire operation took three hours, and at 0702, U-168 had cast off and headed for the United States, setting her course at 250 degrees.

Frick maintained they would arrive at the U.S. in four days, barring any delays.

As darkness fell the crew took turns coming out on deck in two's and three's. The sky was a bright canopy of stars. All hands were in a state of high morale.

Once out of sight of the sub-tender, Frick ordered lookouts on the conning tower to be changed every two hours until further notice.

The Captain spent most of his time in his nook, studying his charts.

U-168 cruised on the surface until the next day. The lookouts reported nothing. It was as if she were the only ship in the Atlantic. The weather remained perfect and indications were that it would remain so for several days.

Maxwell and Thibadeaux spent the night playing cards and talking with Hagermeister at the chief petty officer's bunk. By now they were within seven hundred miles of the American coastline.

As Maxwell stared at the cigarette smoke, curling up into the gently rocking ceiling light, the crackling radio picked up a country music station.

"Always did hate country music," Maxwell said. "Makes me want to fuck livestock."

Hagermeister laughed.

"Give me three," Thibadeaux said, slapping down three cards on the bunk.

The men continued to joke, and the music station continued to twang out its rhythm against the night. Despite his earlier joke, the music was affecting Maxwell. Inexplicably, the sleepy music produced within him a feeling of warmth. Perhaps this warmth came from the fact that it was the first thing American he had heard in weeks. He felt he had been away for years.

"Beats me," Thibadeaux said.

"Not me," Hagermeister said, as he laughed with his belly.

"How do you like that?" Maxwell said as he stretched. "Teach him poker and he smears me. Ain't that swell?"

"Right," Thibadeaux said, winking at Maxwell. "He a natural."

"It all comes out equal," Hagermeister replied. "I teach him German and now he speaks better than me."

Thibadeaux farted and the three men laughed.

"That's it," Hagermeister said. "I will instruct Duggan that neither of you are to have onions again."

"But he fixes them special for us," Maxwell said with a comic shrug.

The men continued to chat. The peace and solitude of the night gave no hint of the violence that awaited them the following day.

Later, Maxwell slept like a baby, the sound of the diesels reminding him of a train.

October 17, 1942

The next day the temperature was soon in the eighties. The crew had changed into their short pants since it was so warm inside the sub. Those not on duty spent their time on deck, sunning. Every night there had been a new batch of bodies to be treated for sunburn.

Maxwell and Thibadeaux had eaten a leisurely lunch and were lying on the deck when they heard the lookout yell, "Ship, two points off the starboard bow."

Just before Maxwell and Thibadeaux scooted down the bridge hatch ladder, Maxwell took a quick look over his shoulder.

A tiny gray speck could be seen on the horizon, starboard bow. The glare of the sun off the waves was so great, and the ship appearing so small in the distance, Maxwell wondered how she had been spotted so soon.

He slid down the ladder in the seaman's manner, mounting his knees around the outside rungs of the ladder and leaping down when he was within five feet of the deck below.

Captain Frick was in the control room. "Do you hear anything?" he asked the soundman. The weasel-like face of the soundman strained.

"No sir," he replied. "If she's there, she's not making way, sir."

"Lookout, what's the range?" yelled the Captain.

"About six kilometers, sir," answered the topside voice, "and it doesn't look like she's underway, sir."

"Prepare to dive," Frick commanded as the alarm sounded. At either end of the ship men rushed to get inside, for the boat was already going down. Men were frantically turning the red wheels and racing through the hatches and aisles.

"Battle stations," Executive Officer Danet ordered, his eyes jumping back and forth.

"Up periscope," Frick said, a half-smile lurking around his pleasant features. Even in times of crisis Frick's face appeared youthful, his eyes with a light of intelligence and clarity.

Danet put on the headphones. "Forward torpedo room," he commanded, "load all tubes, aft tubes load, confirm."

As the periscope came out of its well, the Captain was bending low, following it up.

"Take a look at this," he said to Danet, as the Captain turned to him and moved a step away from the periscope.

The Exec. took the periscope, looking into it, turned to the Captain and said, "Sir, she's lying still, not making any headway at all. Maybe she's making repairs."

Frick twisted his mouth. "Something's wrong," he said, then with a different tone of voice, "Hard right, bring her around to 340 degrees, take her down to three hundred feet, sound man, keep a sharp ear, this looks like a trap." When he turned to Danet, he stared into his eyes, as if searching for the answer. "Down periscope," he said.

The U boat's nose turned down and the Teisenmeiser started going up, indicating a fast dive.

The Captain turned to the soundman, "I want to know if you hear a whisper there."

"Jawohl, mein Kapitan," the soundman replied as he started adjusting his instruments and phones to high volume.

Maxwell was standing by Schnegel, the helmsman, with Thibadeaux nearby. Neither spoke, but given the language barrier, they were both taking in the exchange as best they could.

Glancing at the compass, Maxwell saw that they were on 340 degrees and holding, moving at eight knots.

Frick and Danet were at the navigation table. They leaned over the large chart, making their calculations.

"Got any idea what kind of trap he's talking about?" Maxwell asked Thibadeaux as he lit a cigarette.

"Hell no-- building or warehouse, I smell a trap, me."

Maxwell laughed. "Yeah, well Frank told me you got your biscuits burned pretty good with one of your second story jobs."

"Ain't sayin', I can't go around bragging about my work after I do it. These boys go out, blow up a ship and get a medal from the big man. I do it and they want to give me life. How bout them apples?"

The Captain looked at them, and they stopped talking.

U-168 kept on her course.

"Anything yet?" Danet asked the soundman, who was preoccupied with his phones.

"No sir."

Captain Frick leaned against the chart table and stared at the piping on the trim panel. Suddenly he turned to Danet and said, "Stop all engines."

Danet repeated the order into his phones. The humming motors subsided, the movement of the boat ceased to be noticed, as it slowed to a stop.

"Hold her right there," the Captain said, "and pass the word, not a sound from anyone."

Danet repeated the order into his phones.

Silence permeated the boat. Even breathing was not audible. No one moved. Frick leaned against his chart table as Danet stood near the hatch with the phones on, motionless.

Maxwell leaned against the bulkhead. He was remembering the Asidic.

The soundman turned, signaled to the Captain, and handed him a piece of paper. Scribbled on the scrap of paper was one word--"Contact."

"Speak up," whispered the Captain, "but keep it low."

"She's getting underway, sir, she just started her engines."

"Are you sure?"

"Jawohl."

The Captain turned to the Exec. "She must have contacted us. Why else would she suddenly get underway?" Tiny beads of sweat could now be seen on Frick's forehead.

Danet looked at the Captain, but said nothing.

"Got a range on her yet?"

"Jawohl," the soundman reported, "fifty five hundred meters, sir."

"Which way is she moving?"

"Directly broadside, sir."

"Bring her up to periscope depth," Frick said, "and easy."

As a hum was heard, the boat did not appear to be moving, but a glance at the Teisenmeiser indicated she was slowly rising.

"Up periscope," Frick ordered.

The Captain followed the scope up and as it broke surface, was right on target.

"What's the range?"

"Fifty two hundred meters, sir."

"That's three hundred closer than before," Frick said, his voice cracking slightly. "She must be making a slow turn."

Danet's eyes jumped back and forth. "That doesn't make sense, sir," he said. "If she has spotted us, she'd be making a run for it."

"Bring her around to 300 degrees," Frick said sharply. "We'll go at her head on, silent running. Tell the engineer to be ready to give me full speed. Standby to blow the ballast tanks. I want that sharpshooter, Rosenberg, ready for the deck gun. We won't get but one chance at her. We've got to be successful. Tell him five shots is the most he'll have time for. We will play this little game also."

The boat slowly turned.

"On course 300 degrees, sir."

"All tubes, standby," the Captain said, taking off his hat.

Danet turned to the soundman. "Give me a range every two hundred meters."

"Jawohl."

"Range, forty-six hundred, sir."

U-168 moved slowly towards the target; every meter increased the chance of a hit. The Captain kept his eye to the periscope.

"You two," Frick said to the Americans when he pulled back from the periscope. "Go to the galley and stay there. I don't want you in the way with the crew passing through."

Frick returned to the periscope.

"Forward tubes, standby to fire one and three," he said to the Exec.

"Range, forty-four hundred, sir."

"Holding steady at 300 degrees, sir," answered the helmsman.

When Maxwell and Thibadeaux had reached the galley, Duggan, the corpulent, balding cook seated them at a table. He brought them both a cup of ersatz coffee.

"The Captain will have this thing over in about fifteen minutes,"

Duggan said. "Then I can get dinner started. Got a special treat for you fellows tonight."

"You take sugar, don't you?" Thibadeaux said, shoving the bowl to Maxwell. "I agree with you, Duggan, the Captain a good man."

"Seems like it," Maxwell agreed as he sugared his ersatz coffee.

In the forward torpedo room, the lights shone off the pale skin of Fritz Rosenberg. His plump nose and deep-set eyes were pointed down in concentration. His loader, Alex Steinhoff, removed his wire-rimmed glasses momentarily to wipe sweat from his eyes and returned to the business of getting ready. Rosenberg was humming the Horst Wessel tune as he prepared for action.

"Must you incessantly hum?" Steinhoff protested.

In the control room Frick continued to search for an answer.

"Range, four thousand meters, sir."

Frick turned to Danet. "Down periscope," he muttered in a puzzled tone.

U-168 moved silently on.

"Range, thirty-eight hundred meters, sir."

"Have you identified her yet, sir," Danet asked as he nervously thrust both hands in his pockets.

"She looks like a tanker," Frick said with the same puzzled look, "but I tell you, something's wrong."

The Captain furrowed his brow. He turned to the identifying charts, flipping through them hurriedly. "Can't seem to find her," he said.

Danet watched Frick's face, searching for a sign of reassurance.

"Range, thirty-six hundred meters, sir."

"Is she still making that slow turn?" Frick asked.

"Jawohl."

"Let me know when we get within two thousand meters."

The Exec. repeated the order to the soundman.

Frick turned back to his book of silhouettes. "Damn," he said, "I can't find anything like her here." He turned page after page.

In the galley Maxwell asked Duggan, "How about turning on the speaker so we can hear what's going on."

"The Captain doesn't want it on during an attack approach," Duggan answered as he rolled out a ball of dough on his preparation bar.

"It only makes picking us up easier for them."

Duggan threw down his rolling pin, poured himself a cup of coffee, and sat down beside the Americans. The three men drank their coffee in silence.

In the forward torpedo room, the shirtless crew had completed loading all tubes and were leaning against the bulkhead, waiting to hear the familiar whoosh as the torpedoes were being fired. Sweat streamed from each torso. They waited patiently, making small talk. They were ready to change the firing order as soon as they heard the first two go. They had been through this maneuver many times and knew their job well and could execute it with ease, proficiency, and swiftness.

The U boat moved swiftly towards the target. No one moved inside U-168.

"What's her course now?" Frick queried.

"Course 300 degrees sir," Schnegel said.

Captain Frick kept ruminating about the slow turn the target was making.

"It just doesn't make sense," he said. "Surely she has spotted us by now. No Allied ship today is without listening gear that can pick up at this distance."

The Captain closed his book, put it back on its rack, turned and walked over to the periscope.

"Range, two thousand meters, sir."

"Close all bulkheads, forward torpedo tubes, standby, gun crew on the ready, standby to blow the ballast tanks, all hands, on alert, we're going in."

Rosenberg heard the orders in his phones, turned to Steinhoff and smiling with his widely spaced teeth, he said, "This is it."

Steinhoff made his squinted eyes smaller and looked sideways at his partner through his glasses, as if watching the behavior of a laboratory animal.

Back in the control room, Captain Frick turned to the Exec. "Up periscope."

The periscope started out of its well with Frick again bending low to get a look as it came up.

"Range, eighteen-hundred meters, sir."

The Captain stared into the periscope and said, "Bring her around to 345 degrees."

As the seconds passed, Frick pulled his face back from the scope to wipe his sweat-streamed face with his sleeve. His face dry, he thrust his eye back to the scope.

"345 degrees, sir."

"Standby to surface, forward torpedo tubes standby to fire one and three, engineer, standby for full speed, gun crew, prepare to hit the deck, standby with two and be ready to fire."

The Captain turned to Danet. "When we surface, the gun crew will fire at will."

The soundman turned quickly with a look of panic. "Sir, another engine has started up. I'm getting three distinct engine sounds now."

The Captain's cheeks blanched.

"Engineer, full speed ahead, standby to fire forward tubes."

The engineer put full power on the submarine's motors, and the crew could feel its lunge as it gained speed.

"Range, fourteen hundred meters, sir."

Frick's eye was on the periscope; his voice contained an edge of panic.

"Engines," he said, "impossible, where they coming from?"

"Range, twelve hundred meters, sir, and closing fast."

"Standby to fire," the Captain ordered, looking at his watch.

"Course 350, bring her around head on and hold."

"350 degrees, sir."

"Fire one," the Captain commanded. "Fire three."

As the Captain watched the torpedo trails heading for the target, he saw what he had dreaded most. "My God," he muttered.

"Blow the ballasts," he screamed. "Gun crew on deck, machine gun crew, hit the after deck. It's an attack."

Men ran frantically in all directions. A pan fell and danced in the aisle.

Maxwell and Thibadeaux heard the air release as the torpedoes left their tubes.

"What was that?" Maxwell asked.

"Just fired two fish," Duggan answered.

Before Captain Frick had finished giving his orders, the various crew hurried about to get to their hatches with their equipment.

Rosenberg was climbing the ladder up to the hatch in the forward torpedo room and unlocking the hatch and pushing it open. As U-168 broke surface, he forced open the hatch with sea water rushing in, and scrambled out on deck into the brilliant sunshine. He headed for the forward gun with Steinhoff right behind him, carrying the shells.

At the after hatch, the machine gun crew, Mickey and Rhinehardt, had emerged on deck and were mounting their machine gun. They loaded it and were standing by for orders. Danet stood atop the conning tower. He too saw why the ship had made no effort to escape.

"Surface torpedo run, fire two and four, reload and standby," the Captain ordered.

Frick turned to the radio operator. "Contact headquarters. Tell them we are attacking and are being attacked, give them our position, ask for help if there is any in the area. Keep me posted."

The radio operator got busy with his equipment. U-168 was now at full speed and heading straight for the target. From around the bow and stern of the ship, two small boats came roaring straight for the sub, leaping over the waves with two trails of white spray behind them. Meanwhile, the huge, gray tanker continued its slow turn.

"PT boats," Executive Officer Danet moaned, his bushy eyebrows slanting upwards. He spoke into the phones.

The Captain had already seen them. "Damn," he muttered under his breath. "I hope the gun crews can get them, if they don't, we're finished."

Rosenberg was already aiming at one of the PT boats. He took careful aim, making sure of his elevation, and fired.

The shell hit a hundred meters aft of the PT boat.

"I got you now, bastard," Rosenberg spat out. He muttered again under his breath, took more time in aiming, and fired.

The PT boat was only two hundred meters away when it exploded with debris flying in all directions.

"Got him," Rosenberg screamed. "Now the other one."

Mickey and Rhinehardt were now firing the big machinegun.

Rhinehardt's large frame jerked as Mickey fed the ammunition belt.

Water splashed happily up where the bullets were hitting, but none touched the PT. It roared straight at them.

Lieutenant Charles Sorrick was six feet four and had brown hair.

He was from Ohio and had left a wife and a baby son to join the United States Navy. He had been on the bridge of the specially modified Q ship when contact had been made with U-168. He had been one of the original pilots of the PT boats and volunteered along with Lieutenant Leroy Ferguson when Captain Holmes had briefed him about the experiment.

The Q ships were designed to look like standard tankers, but were modified to carry four PT boats which could be lowered in a specially designed cavity inside the outer hull by winches. The side of the tanker appeared standard, whereas the other side contained doors on the hull, where a facade was lifted and the PT boats released.

Sorrick and the other PT commanders had practiced this maneuver in Long Island Sound, where they had successfully attacked their targets and theoretically sunk each one.

Sorrick was convinced the ploy would work equally as well in actual combat.

He knew that in most battles, surprise was one of the largest factors, and he was sure that surprise was in his favor. This type of U boat defense was completely new, and only a few men were aware of its existence.

Captain Holmes had ordered all commanders of the PT boats to their stations to prepare for the attack. Now Sorrick and Ferguson stood watching as the winches picked up the PT boats, one at a time, and lowered them through the open cargo doors on the side of the old tanker into the water. He checked everything, his depth charge load, the Y guns to spit the charges over the target, the four torpedoes mounted on the side, two port and two starboard. He checked the fuel tanks of the two 1200 HP Chrysler diesel engines and the gasoline tanks of the aircraft engine. Everything was aboard and in its place. He and his crew of six jumped aboard as the PT boat touched the sea. Each man wore a helmet and life jacket.

Two more PT boats were now being winched up to be put into the water. Sorrick stood by awaiting the order to start engines for the attack. The order was not long in coming. Only his and Ferguson's boat were in the water when the order to start engines came down.

"Warm 'em fast," Sorrick said to his pilot. "I want full speed when we move out. We'll have about five or six hundred yards to do this in and I don't want any foul ups. All hands on station the moment we move."

Two minutes later the attack order came. The PT boats roared down the side of the ship, one heading for the stern, one for the bow.

The moment had come.

As Sorrick's PT boat rounded the stern, he could see the U-168 coming to the surface with men pouring onto the decks. He knew they were going to open fire with their deck gun. He yelled to his crew:

"Hang on, we're taking a zig zag course." The PT boat was gaining speed as she sliced through the water.

Lieutenant Sorrick could see the gun crew loading and aiming. Then he saw the smoke and three seconds later knew they had missed. He was closing in and would make his turn in a few more seconds to get his torpedoes off. The last thing he saw was the white puff of smoke of the deck gun firing; then darkness closed around him--a direct hit.

On the other side Lt. Ferguson saw the same gun firing and knew he was not the target. He saw Sorrick's PT go up in a belch of orange flame and debris.

"Can't get us both," he yelled. "They won't have time to get a bearing."

He turned the boat hard right, straightened out for a few seconds and then turned back a hard left. The PT boat danced over the waves. He was lining up on the submarine.

Rosenberg lost no time in swinging his gun around to the other PT boat. By the time he had aimed, Steinhoff had it loaded, and he fired. The shell fell short with a splash. He knew he only had time for one more shot. Rosenberg took a deep breath, and his close-set eyes narrowed even further. Steinhoff did his loading in silence. He knew Rosenberg would start yelling the minute he made a hit. Steinhoff was staring absently at a piece of dirt on the side of the gun as he went about his business. He thought it was the last thing he would ever see. Steinhoff quickly reloaded, closed the breach and stepped back. Rosenberg fired. The deafening firing of the gun. The white smoke. The shell hit the PT boat and went right through it. It did not explode, but the boat stopped at 300 meters away. The PT boat started down. Men in life jackets began jumping overboard and swimming away from the stunned craft.

Captain Holmes was on the bridge of the Q ship and could see the two torpedoes coming at him, cutting the sea in an aqua green line.

"Hard right, bring her around and head for a ram," he ordered, but knew he would never make it.

The ship had just started to turn when the explosion forward of the bridge occurred. The second torpedo hit directly under the bridge. Holmes was knocked down by the explosion and never saw the fate of Sorrick's PT boat. His ship slowed and started sinking and rolling over at the same time. He spoke into his phones, "Abandon ship, all hands."

The explosion had knocked over the two additional PT boats which had just been put into the water. The other two inside were demolished. The four crewmen working the winch apparatus were blown into pieces. Only one of the PT commanders managed to escape. He dived overboard and started swimming away from the ship. He did not want to get caught in the suction the tanker would make when she went down. Shouts of rage, screams of agony, moans of pain amid desperate pleas for help.

On the upper deck of the tanker, seamen were trying to lower the life boats. The explosions had jammed the winches, and the men could not get the boats down. One by one, each jumped into the sea.

Rosenberg was jumping up and down, yelling, "I will get the Iron Cross for this. Maybe from the Fuhrer himself." He slapped a smiling Steinhoff on the back and continued to jump around.

Suddenly he stopped, the spark of mirth fading from his close-set eyes. He looked out over the water at the seamen, swimming around, looking for anything to hold onto. He raced for the rear of the sub.

In the galley when Rosenberg had fired his first shell, Maxwell and Thibadeaux had looked at each other. Maxwell spoke.

"We're surfacing and they're having a shootout. Let's go up and see what's happening."

"Hell no," Thibadeaux protested, grabbing Maxwell by the sleeve, "the Captain....."

"Look," Maxwell said, jerking his arm free, "if this boat goes down, it won't matter if we're down here or up there, our chances are about the same."

Maxwell darted for the hatch. Thibadeaux followed. Duggan yelled behind them. Maxwell stopped and looked back.

"Don't go up there," Duggan said, holding a greasy knife in one hand. "You'll just get in the way."

Maxwell heard Rosenberg's second shot. "To hell with it," he shouted. "If the Captain wants us below, let him order us below."

He started up the hatch. As he climbed, he could hear the machine gun chattering. He reached the top, saw the machine gun crew, as Rosenberg's third shot went off. Maxwell turned to see the target. A PT boat was coming gray in the sunlight right at them.

"Goddamn," Maxwell said aloud. "Today isn't my day."

Thibadeaux's knees buckled. "Holy Jesus" he said, "that son of a bitch..........." and his words fell off, his gaze fixed.

Thibadeaux was looking straight at the PT boat when Rosenberg's fourth shell hit and it started to sink.

"I don't believe it," Maxwell yelled with joy, and he threw two fists into the air as words failed him.

"Dead in the water," Thibadeaux yelled. "And the speed it was coming."

"That guy on the deck gun must be a wizard with that thing," Maxwell exclaimed.

Maxwell stood up and started walking towards the bow to see who had been doing the shooting. As he rounded the conning tower, he could see Rosenberg waving his arms and yelling.

Maxwell turned around and walked towards the rear where the machine gun was. Mickey and Rhinehardt had stopped firing, had put on a new ammunition belt and were standing on the bridge, watching the PT boat sink and the seamen floundering in the marbled water. All hands on the U boat were laughing and animated. Maxwell stood near the base of the conning tower, Thibadeaux over near the machinegun.

Rosenberg looked up at the conning tower and yelled to the Captain, "Sir, we should put a boat over the side and take prisoners."

"Permission granted," the Captain answered.

Rosenberg went charging towards the rear of U-168 with Steinhoff right behind him, heading for the skiff which was anchored to the deck.

The Q ship beyond burned in a sea of oil and started down.

As Rosenberg raced blindly for the rear of the boat, he collided headlong into Maxwell and almost knocked him overboard.

"Get hell out of the way," Rosenberg roared. Maxwell had bitten his lip and could taste the blood in his mouth. He regained his balance and looked at Rosenberg.

The German appeared to be staring right through him as if wanting a confrontation. He saw Maxwell's fear and laughed, showing his widely spaced teeth.

He raced past Maxwell, and he and Steinhoff began unhooking the inflatable skiff and paid no more attention to anyone.

Within two minutes they had the skiff over the side, fully inflated, and each grabbed a paddle and began digging into the sea.

They were rowing towards the sinking PT boat which was almost completely under.

The Captain yelled from the conning tower, "No more than four prisoners. We are cramped for space as it is."

"Jawohl, mein Kapitan."

They rowed hard, straight for a group of seamen and were soon near enough to reach out and grab them. Rosenberg grabbed a seaman and with incredible strength pulled him aboard. The seaman had red hair and was in his twenties. While Steinhoff was guarding this prisoner, Rosenberg reached out to bring aboard another one.

The red head looked grateful to be aboard as he panted, his cheeks red in the sunshine. Steinhoff's mouth turned down, and he gazed clinically through his spectacles. "You English bastards," he said in English. "We ought to leave you here to drown."

"I'm not English, I'm American," the seaman answered.

"What's the difference? You're all pigs, anyway," Steinhoff said.

"Go fuck yourself."

"Shutup," Rosenberg spat at the American. "Open your mouth again and I'll kill you."

"Go to hell," the American said.

Maxwell and Thibadeaux were watching all this and could hear parts of the conversation. Suddenly they both stiffened.

They had watched Rosenberg without apparent reason pull out his seaman's knife and thrust it into the prisoner's throat. The red head tried to yell as he went down, but Rosenberg grabbed a handful of red hair with one hand, while he gave the knife a vicious twist with the other. Blood shot like a fountain straight into the air. Another motion and the head fell to the side of the American's shoulder, only held on the torso by a brief twist of flesh on the right side.

Rosenberg took his foot and pushed him into the water.

"Kill them all," he roared. Steinhoff pulled his knife and slashed at the seaman near the boat.

His glasses reflecting two blinding glints in the sun, Steinhoff's face turned briefly skyward as with a scream he brought the knife down, almost falling into the water himself, as the knife with a white splash went to the hilt in the seaman's chest. Steinhoff caught himself on the side of the skiff, regaining his balance.

"Dammit," Steinhoff screamed. "Lost my knife."

The seaman screamed, his eyes cast upwards to the sky, his arms raised up, as if pulled stiffly upwards by a puppeteer, he suddenly flipped over, face down into the sea, floating and bobbing amid a bloody spot, which grew larger.

"Schweinhunts, stop it," cried the Captain. "Leave the survivors and return to the boat immediately."

By now Maxwell had lost his lunch and coffee. But when the nausea was gone, his eyes widened, and he felt his chest filling up. He turned to Thibadeaux and said: "That was murder. Those two nuts have just murdered two unarmed men. They'll be hanged for that, for sure. That's one way to get rid of idiots like that."

"The Captain probably only reprimand them, Tommy.

This is war, babe, crazy things happen."

Maxwell watched Rosenberg rowing in.

When he said it, he could feel his face flush; he said it without even thinking. "If the Captain doesn't do something, I damned sure will."

"What can you do?" Thibadeaux asked.

"You just watch. If the Captain doesn't put them in chains, I'll personally fix their wagons."

"Jesus...."

"Shutup," Maxwell whispered viciously. "Don't tell me nothing."

He grabbed Richard's arm and faced him. "Don't you see that we will be next?" he said. "That was murder, and there is no excuse for murdering unarmed men. I will not accept it, no matter who says I should."

Rosenberg and Steinhoff had by this time returned to the U-168 and were climbing aboard, with others of the crew helping to get the skiff back on deck. As Rosenberg walked past Maxwell, a smile still lurked in the close-set eyes. He looked pleased with himself. Steinhoff, as always, looked neither pleased nor displeased, merely clinical, analytical.

"They're a pair of psychopathic killers," Maxwell reiterated while running a hand through his hair. "Let's go below and see what happens over this thing."

As Thibadeaux followed Maxwell, they could see Frick speaking to Danet before he came below.

Maxwell went down the hatch with Thibadeaux following.

Richard was anxiously watching Maxwell. Maxwell turned right and headed for the control room. As he passed the galley, Duggan glanced at him, but Maxwell did not even look at him. He was walking straight ahead with a determined gait, his sun-tanned face and nose remarkably white. He marched into the control room and stood near the hatch. As he passed through the aft battery, Mickey and Rhinehardt, the machine gun crew had put their gun on the work bench and were taking off their side arms, which they also laid on the bench. Maxwell appeared not to notice. He stood in the control room, waiting with Thibadeaux, leaning against the opposite bulkhead.

The Captain was talking to the Executive Officer.

"Rosenberg was far out of line," Frick said in rapid German.

"It could cause us a lot of trouble."

"What about Steinhoff?" asked Danet.

"We'll have to take disciplinary action, just what, I am not sure."

Maxwell was surprised to hear Danet's answer. "You will have to do better than that," Danet said. "I think Rosenberg and Steinhoff both should be put in chains and when we return, recommended for court martial."

"If I order a court martial and they are convicted, they will shoot them," Frick said, deep lines now appearing on his forehead. "Those types are everywhere now. They can make trouble for us both."

Danet frowned. "Do you think he is tied in with SD?" Danet said, his eyes moving to and fro, unaware that Maxwell understood any of the German he was rattling, "or is he just SS at heart and cannot control himself?"

"I don't know," the Captain answered, rubbing his chin, "but we must act in some way."

"Jawohl," Danet answered. "At least we will have to make a report of the incident to headquarters."

Frick stared off. "None of the crew seem to be upset by it.

Maybe we had best forget it, like it never happened."

Again Danet's answer surprised Maxwell. "Sir. If we do that and one of the crew mentions it, you will be in a lot of trouble.

Sooner or later it is bound to come out. It will go on your record and your career will be finished."

"It's quite a dilemma, Danet," Frick said, suddenly looking quite old. "It will be a bad mark on me any way I go. Captain Frick, the U boat commander who cannot control his men. At the least, I will lose my command, at the worst, court martial."

"You are the Captain, sir. What are you going to do?"

Maxwell, while not able to hear or understand all of this, was taking in as much as he could and getting the general gist.

"Bring Rosenberg and Steinhoff in here, now," the Captain ordered.

"Jawohl, mein Kapitan."

"Tell the engineer to get underway, unload the tubes, get back on course. We will get out of here before any stray Allied ships or planes come along. Post a double lookout for now."

"Jawohl," Danet replied and turned to his phones and repeated the orders he had just been given.

Minutes later, Rosenberg and Steinhoff came into the control room. The boat was well underway; the lookouts posted topside, and the U-168 was back on course, heading for the Florida coastline.

Rosenberg and Steinhoff entered the control room, stopped, clicked their heels, and saluted.

"Seaman Rosenberg reporting as ordered, sir." Tiny brown flecks of dried blood were still on his greasy seaman's shirt.

"Seaman Steinhoff reporting as ordered, sir."

Both men stood at attention.

Frick rubbed his chin, his brow knitted severely. "At ease," he said.

He paced the length of the compartment twice before stopping to speak.

"Rosenberg, you and Steinhoff have just committed what could be called 'murder,' the execution of unarmed survivors. Can you give me an explanation as to why you did it?"

Rosenberg looked straight at the Captain. "Sir, they were the enemy, that is all that is necessary."

"What do you say, Steinhoff?"

"I feel the same way, sir," he answered. "They are the enemy and it is our duty to kill them at every opportunity."

"Killing men in combat and murdering unarmed survivors are two different things," Frick said. "Can you actually justify your act on the grounds that they are the enemy?"

"With all due respect," Steinhoff said, his eyes growing smaller under his glasses. "If Herr Rosenberg were not so proficient at killing the enemy, we would probably be at the bottom of the sea at this moment."

Frick's voice rose as he spoke. "I will repeat the question.

Do you feel justified in what you did?"

"Jawohl," they replied in unison.

"I do not believe there is a German alive, who would not have done the same," Rosenberg continued.

"You and Steinhoff have made it rather difficult for all of us," Frick said, "and there has to be disciplinary action taken.

You will not like it."

Maxwell's full attention was now centered on the Captain, who apparently was so absorbed in Rosenberg and Steinhoff that he ignored anyone else.

"Report back to me at 2100 hours," Captain Frick said, "and I will give you my decision."

"Jawohl."

The two men snapped to attention, saluted, turned, and left the control room.

Maxwell looked agitated. Thibadeaux watched him. He felt he could read Tommy's every mood by now, and he had never before seen him so disgusted.

The Captain told Danet he was going to his nook to make out a report of the incident and for him to question the members of the crew who had been on deck at the time and to report to him what he had found.

The Captain then left the control room and went to his quarters.

Maxwell walked towards the galley. "I'm going to have a cup of coffee," he said, his mouth turning into a sneer and his nose wrinkling.

As the Americans entered the galley and asked Duggan for the coffee, Richard was still watching the face of Maxwell.

They sat at the table.

"What you think he gonna do about it?" Thibadeaux asked.

"He's going to figure a way to whitewash the whole thing,"

Maxwell said as he stared past Thibadeaux.

Maxwell did not know what was happening to him. The reaction to what he had seen created an uncontrollable sensation. He was not afraid, yet there was a rage growing greater inside him every moment.

All of the ideologies, all of the training, all of these years spent reconciling his ideas--everything shrank to insignificance compared to the spectacle of what he had just seen.

He sipped his ersatz coffee, hot and bitter, mixed with the stench of diesel fumes, which wafted through the boat.

Thibadeaux leaned back in his chair and crossed his legs.

"So you think Frick will whitewash it."

"And he ain't gonna get away with it," Maxwell repeated, surprising himself at the easiness of the words, yet not totally believing them himself.

"What can you do?"

"I don't know yet."

"Things like this happen, you know," Thibadeaux insisted, leaning back forward. "This is war."

"I know. I've heard about the stuff that goes on during wars, but I never saw it before. I suppose it gets back to what the instructor said. There are no innocent bystanders. But just suppose it was you or me, or someone we knew, what would you do?"

"I don't know."

Maxwell leaned close to Thibadeaux, looking him in the eyes. He spoke in a low voice so Duggan could not hear.

"Don't you see that if they get away with this, they can do anything? We could be next, partner. Yeah, that'd be the next thing."

Thibadeaux lit a cigarette and listened with interest.

"What if I had taken a swing at him on deck," Maxwell continued in the same voice. "Yeah, that could have been me. Dammit, don't you see?"

Thibadeaux pulled back. "As you say, these red-blooded American hypocrites be doing the same thing," Thibadeaux said, hoping that by using one of Maxwell's own expressions, he could sway him.

"That doesn't make it right," Maxwell replied, staring off with a fixed look. "I wonder if it's true what we've been hearing about the Gestapo and SS?"

"When we were in Hanau, we heard plenty stories about what the

Americans and British were doing to prisoners, and in the U.S. we get what the Germans and Japs do."

"Probably both sides are doing it," Maxwell answered, trying to make a decision on an idea he could not quite accept. "Anyway, we'll know at 2100 hours what the Captain intends to do. I hope he makes the right decision."

Thibadeaux sipped his coffee and watched Maxwell's face.

"Right now, I'm going up on deck for some air. Want to come along?"

"Sure."

They put their cups in the wash basin, thanked Duggan and headed for the rear hatch.

It was two more hours before they could receive permission to go topside.

Once on deck, both men's spirits heightened. It was the beginning of another radiant summer's night on the Atlantic. The first stars were winking over the endless, gentle waves. The two lookouts carried on a friendly banter as they scanned the open sea. The Americans walked forward on the cat walk to the bow and sat in silence, drinking in the open air and the solitude. One by one, various members of the crew took the air and chatted in low tones.

At 1900 Duggan announced that supper was ready. The Americans fetched their meals and brought them back topside. The cook had done a fine job. He had prepared pork chops, with baked potatoes, plenty of onions which he knew the Americans liked, and lemonade.

When Maxwell finished with his plate, he looked at his watch--1945.

He motioned to Thibadeaux to follow him below. They put their plates in the wash basin and walked towards the control room, for they did not want to miss the Captain's decision.

As they proceeded forward, they passed again through the aft battery compartment. Mickey and Rhinehardt were still there, their gun lying where they had previously had it; alongside lay their side arms in their holsters. Unconcerned about hurrying to put the guns away, the two gunners leisurely talked while they slowly coated the various parts of the gun with oil.

Maxwell took note of the clean shine of oil on the guns, watched them wipe the oil off, and noticed that the extra clips to the side arms lay in the pouches attached to the belt.

"Mind if I look at it?" he said, pointing to the machinegun.

"Go ahead," Mickey answered, his glass eye trained downward and his brown moustache knitting in concentration.

Maxwell walked over to the table where the gun lay, picked it up and examined it. It was heavy, but he knew it had been made to be mounted rather than carried. It could be fired without the mounting but would not be very accurate.

"Open breach?" Maxwell asked.

"Ja," Rhinehardt replied.

Thibadeaux had walked over to the table and was looking at the two hand guns. "Those ain't regulation issue, are they?" he asked.

"No, they are our personal weapons," Rhinehardt said, who swaggered his large frame slightly as he talked. "Picked them up in Belgium a few months back. They're real beauties, aren't they?"

"Sure are," Thibadeaux answered. "What kind is they? I never see any like that before, me."

"They're P-38's," Mickey said. "They can be fired like a revolver and will automatically reload like a semi-automatic.

Shoots 9 millimeter and is a very hard-hitting gun. Mind if I try one of your cigarettes?"

"No, not at all," Maxwell said, pounding the pack of cigarettes and handing them to Mickey.

When Mickey lit the cigarette, he closed his good eye and had the momentary appearance of being a one-eyed corpse, as his bad eye shone empty.

"I didn't know you have your own weapons," Thibadeaux said as he gripped the handle of one of the pistols.

"We're not supposed to have them," Rhinehardt answered, "but the commander looks the other way. A lot of men have their own. They all use the same ammunition and we captured a lot of these in Belgium and France, along with millions of rounds of ammunition. We've been getting in a lot of practice."

Rhinehardt ducked his head as he got up and walked to where Thibadeaux was looking at the pistols and proceeded to show him how they worked.

Mickey did the same with Maxwell with the machine gun.

"One man can use this thing, if he does not try to take too much ammunition at one time. The belt comes loose at various intervals so the belt can be shortened. With these long belts, it takes two, one to fire the gun, the other to feed the belt and make a rapid reloading."

"I noticed on deck that you didn't hit the boat coming at you," Maxwell said.

Mickey sucked on the cigarette and exhaled. "It was too far out," he answered. "Sure, it's hard to hit at that distance, but sooner or later he would have run into a stream of steel. We were just getting the range."

Maxwell smiled. "It looks like it could raise havoc with anything it hit."

"I wouldn't want to be on the receiving end," Mickey said.

The clock ticked towards 2100.

Thibadeaux got into a lively discussion comparing the 9mm lugar with the Colt 45. From time to time, members of the crew would pass through going aft or forward.

Danet walked through, his eyebrows knitted and his eyes moving back and forth. He stopped, glancing nervously at the four men and the guns.

"At 2100 the Captain wants to see you four in the control room," he said nervously.

"Yeah, we heard," Maxwell said, looking hard at Danet. The first officer avoided the American's gaze and headed forward.

Outside, a few cumulus clouds drifted across the sky.

U-168 remained on the surface, her diesels churning and taking her west at 15 knots. At the rate they were moving, they would be off the Florida coast within 36 hours.

Maxwell raised an eyebrow at Mickey. "That gunner on the 3.5 deck gun really did a job, didn't he?" Maxwell asked.

If Mickey had any opinion as to what had happened with Rosenberg, neither his face nor manner betrayed his thoughts.

"Ja, Rosenberg is an expert shot with that thing," Mickey said. "He seldom misses at all. It surprised me when he missed those two shots out there." Mickey laughed nervously as he stubbed his cigarette out on the deck plates. "He got them, though, didn't he?"

"Yeah, so I noticed," Maxwell said, staring off.

Mickey's moustache twitched. He watched Maxwell's face as he spoke.

"We need more men like that," Mickey said. "Most of this crew could not hit a building from the inside, but Rosenberg, how do you say it, is very precise with his shooting."

Rhinehardt snorted.

Maxwell looked at his watch--2050. "Ten minutes to go," he said to Thibadeaux.

Mickey looked at Maxwell and shrugged. It was obvious that he knew what Maxwell was awaiting.

Maxwell motioned for Thibadeaux, got up, and started forward to the control room.

"Hey, wait for me, what's the hurry," Thibadeaux said, an edge of fear in his voice.

"No hurry," Maxwell said, "besides, how far can I get ahead of you?"

They went forward with Mickey and Rhinehardt following them into the control room and standing near the hatch. Maxwell and Thibadeaux leaned on the after bulkhead. The Captain was standing near the chart table, leaning over his map, Danet near the ballast tank control levers on the trim panel.

Frick jerked up from the chart and said, "Bring them in here and let's get this over with." Frick rubbed his chin and grimaced.

Danet stepped over the hatch and called for Rosenberg and Steinhoff.

Steinhoff entered first with Rosenberg right behind him. They stepped inside the control room and stood at attention. Both were wearing clean, newly pressed clothes and both looked as if they had recently washed.

This fresh appearance made them look even more hideous to Maxwell.

The Captain jerked his upper body, as if snapping out of a trance.

He began looking at first Mickey, then Rhinehardt. "Since you two were out on deck this afternoon, take the helm. Helmsman, you and Mikel, go forward into the torpedo room and stay there until I call for you."

The two gunners moved towards the helm, the helmsman and his partner through the forward hatch.

"Close both hatches, no need for the whole crew to hear this," the Captain ordered. The Exec. closed the hatch nearest him.

Maxwell turned and closed the after hatch.

Captain Frick turned to Rosenberg and Steinhoff.

"You men have placed us in a rather precarious position," he said, his eyebrows knitting in concentration. "One that will be hard to explain, especially to the Admiral, whom I am sure would recommend a court martial, and you know what that means. Now the only people, according to what the Exec. says, that saw what happened, are here now, so I am going to try to resolve this thing for the benefit of all."

Maxwell blushed.

Rosenberg and Steinhoff did not flinch. They remained at attention, statuesque and undaunted.

"I have filled out a complete report on the incident this afternoon," Frick continued. "The incident involving the two American survivors."

As Frick paused, apparently for the lack of proper words, Maxwell noticed two lines of sweat running down his cheek.

Rosenberg, noticing Frick's nervousness, shot a quick look at Danet.

"The details and the brutality of the deaths of these two survivors have been fully outlined in my report."

Frick continued, as he began pacing slowly and looking at his feet. "However, I did include in my report certain.....well, what I consider to be extenuating circumstances."

Frick stopped again and surveyed the room. Mickey and Rhinehardt were at the helm, their expressions showing only boredom. Thibadeaux leaned against a bulkhead in the same attitude. Maxwell's eyes were on Frick, while Rosenberg and Steinhoff continued to stare ahead. Danet shifted his feet nervously.

Frick paced over to the two accused seamen and looked first at one, then at the other as he spoke.

"It must be understood that in no way do these extenuating circumstances excuse what you did, what we all witnessed this afternoon. Your actions go beyond all excuses."

Frick paused and cleared his throat.

"The circumstances that I did not include in my report are obvious to all, that is, the crew has been under a considerable strain, no branch of the service has to put up with the stress of confinement known to men in the U boat arm. Furthermore, during the action this afternoon, it goes without saying that all hands were in a high state of anxiety, and given the odds, had every reason to believe that they would be killed or captured within seconds."

Frick now leveled his gaze at Rosenberg, whose eyes darted to Danet before meeting Frick's stare.

The Captain continued.

"It has been noted in my report that seaman Rosenberg's shooting with the deck gun saved the boat and the crew."

A smile flickered in Rosenberg's eyes. "Thank you sir," he said.

"Shutup," Frick yelled, his reddened face inches from Rosenberg's. "You will not speak without permission, is that understood?"

"Jawohl."

"I am not here to decorate you; you will remain at attention and you will remain silent until you have been permitted to speak. Is that understood?"

"Jawohl, mein Kapitan," Rosenberg shouted with Steinhoff remaining silent and at attention.

Frick continued.

"Admiral Doenitz issued a directive, dated January 1942. It stated that in the taking of enemy prisoners, a U boat seaman has every right to defend himself, if necessary. However, this by no means advocated the senseless slaughter of prisoners. All military law forbids this. If a court martial convicts a seaman of murder, that is, the unlicensed killing of unarmed survivors, the penalty is death by firing squad."

Frick paused. Both Steinhoff and Rosenberg watched his face now.

The diesels of U-168 churned like a locomotive. Danet rubbed his fingers over the overhead piping and surveyed the oil on his fingertips.

"If I had included in my report that the deaths of the two American survivors was unwarranted," Frick's voice rose, "if I had said that it was nothing short of murder, then my report would be tantamount to a sentence of death. Do you understand, seaman Rosenberg?"

"Jawohl, mein Kapitan."

"Seaman Steinhoff."

"Jawohl."

Frick turned from the two men, took off his white hat and put it back on. He paced more rapidly now, talking as if to himself.

"The idea, the unrestrained gall, the complete lack of any sense of honor and decorum. More than that, the blatant disobedience to all canons of military code is...." he shook his head violently, trying to find the right word, "is totally irresponsible, you both lack discipline and have no regard for anyone but yourselves. Who in hell do you think you are?"

Rosenberg looked at Danet, but before he could speak, Frick pointed his finger at him, shouting, "Silence."

"Fortunately, for both of you, we still have a long patrol ahead of us, mines to lay, and many more torpedoes to fire. We need every hand available. Fortunately, for both of you, I have the crew to think about.

Their survival is foremost in my mind. Having two men in chains for the duration of the cruise would not only lower morale, but, in my judgement would lessen our chances for survival."

Frick paused again, looked past the two seamen, then back down again.

Relief already manifested itself on both Rosenberg and Steinhoff's faces.

The Captain continued speaking as Maxwell was deep in thought.

"I have filled out my report that you two acted in self defense," Frick continued. "And you both will do well to remember that and forget it ever happened. For the next two months, you are restricted. You will forfeit two months' pay and promotions will be withheld for six months.

Meanwhile, you two will not be handling the gun anymore.

I intend to replace you. You have been relieved from the gun crew and will be placed in the engine room until further notice.

Have you anything to say?"

"Sir," Rosenberg began in German, then thought better of it and said, "No sir."

"Steinhoff?"

"No sir."

"Then the matter is ended," Frick said.

Maxwell spoke very deliberately, releasing his words slowly.

"Not quite, Captain," he said, stepping forward. "The matter is not ended at all."

Rosenberg turned at Maxwell. The Captain was livid.

"Mr. Maxwell, Mr. Thibadeaux," the Captain shouted. "You are guests aboard my boat. I am in command here and what I say will be obeyed. You are under orders from Naval Operations, of which I have no control, but while you are under my command, you will take orders, just like the rest of the crew, and I have made it a part of the record. The incident is closed. There is nothing you can do about it. Now go to your quarters and remain there until I put you ashore, which should be within the next forty hours. Good night, gentlemen."

"Good night, hell," Maxwell said, his neck craning slightly forward. "These two psycho's just murdered two unarmed men. I saw it. He saw it," pointing to Thibadeaux, "you saw it, the Exec. saw it, and you're making it look like they were justified. I won't take it, Captain, not now, tomorrow, or any other time. As soon as I get ashore, I'm notifying Naval Operations about what happened, and I hope to hell they hang you." Unlike the first words, these rushed from him.

The Captain jerked his hat from his head and rapidly put it back on. He was beside himself with anger. Danet had taken two aggressive steps towards Maxwell and was trembling, on the verge of attacking him.

The Captain glared at Maxwell as he spoke. "Mr. Maxwell, you will do no such thing. All this will be covered in my report, even your hallucinations about it. Now go to your quarters. That is a direct order, otherwise, I will have to have you put in chains. Is that clear?"

At that instant Thibadeaux thought Maxwell would strike the Captain.

Maxwell shuffled his feet around and started, his face red with anger. He glared at the Captain as he spoke. "Yes sir," he said.

"Dismissed," the Captain said.

Rosenberg and Steinhoff stood triumphantly. They had not moved from where they were.

Maxwell turned, opened the hatch door, and stepped through it with Thibadeaux close behind him. They closed the hatch after Rhinehardt and Mickey were relieved and out of the control room. They started aft towards their quarters.

"Guess I got a little excited," Maxwell said to Mickey as he slapped the thin man on the back and smiled. "Haven't had enough sleep, you know."

Mickey smiled and seemed relieved. "No use getting involved," he said.

Maxwell shrugged as they passed into the aft battery compartment again. "I guess it's no secret that I don't like Rosenberg or Steinhoff, but anyway, that's that."

He pulled out a cigarette and offered Mickey another. Mickey accepted and closed one eye as he lit it.

The guns were still lying on the table. Rhinehardt yawned, sat in a chair and began pulling off his boots.

Maxwell smiled at Rhinehardt. "By the way, would you show me and him how to load that thing? Someday, I may need to know how."

Mickey looked sideways at Maxwell and took another drag of the cigarette.

"Sure," Rhinehardt replied, standing in his sock feet and rubbing his eyes with his fists. He moved to the table with the guns. "It's quite easy," he said. "Here's how you do it."

The gunner instructed Maxwell. Maxwell went through the routine himself. He loaded it, put it on ready and swung it around the compartment.

Mickey threw his cigarette down. "Be careful with that thing," he said. "If it goes off, it will wreck this boat." Mickey shot an angry look at Rhinehardt. "Put that down," he added.

Maxwell unloaded the gun and laid it on the table and picked up one of the P-38's lying there, inserted the clip, injected a shell and made like he was shooting an imaginary target.

"Want to do some trading?" Maxwell asked.

Rhinehardt laughed in his swaggering fashion. "Not a chance," he said.

"Come on, there'll be plenty more of these when you get back to Lorient. I'd really like to have one of these babies."

Rhinehardt grinned, as if he had gotten the best of the American.

"What have you got to trade?" he asked.

Maxwell twisted the gun in the air, balancing it in different positions in his hand.

"In my bag I got a 45 ACP which I can get plenty of in the States. How about that?"

Rhinehardt snorted. "You'll have to do better."

"Like how?"

"Got any money?"

"How much money we talking about?"

"Twenty-five dollars American."

Maxwell raised the pistol into the air and straightened his arm, holding it out stiffly as he looked through the sights.

"You're way off base," he said. "How about ten?"

"Twenty."

"Fifteen is my best offer," Maxwell said as he saw the acceptance in Rhinehardt's eyes. He put the gun temporarily down.

"It's a deal."

"Done," Maxwell said, with a thin smile. "Give me the gun and I'll go back and get the 45 ACP and the clips and bring them here. Be back in a minute."

Maxwell picked up the gun and turned to go for his bag when Danet entered the hatch from the forward section.

He saw Maxwell holding the gun.

"What's going on here?" he asked, his eyes jumping. "Put that thing in the gun room and report to the Captain immediately for disciplinary action; you know those should have been stowed away when you came down from the deck."

Maxwell could see the fear in Danet's eyes, and it struck him immediately what he was going to do.

"Mr. Danet, sit down right there," Maxwell said, pointing the P-38 at his chest. "I have something I want you to do."

The Executive Officer did not move to sit down, but stood glaring at Maxwell.

"Have you lost your mind?" he said, appearing to grow taller as he spoke. "Threatening an officer with a gun, that's mutiny."

"Mr. Danet," Maxwell said calmly, "please sit down before I blow your goddamned head off."

The Exec. sat down at the end of the table. Rhinehardt and Mickey backed up from the table.

Maxwell looked at Thibadeaux and said, "Are you with me?"

"We come this far together." shrugged Richard, who looked remarkably undaunted. "What you want me to do?"

At that instant Maxwell felt both extreme admiration for Thibadeaux, who appeared much less scared than he himself was, and at the same time, shame for ever doubting Richard's loyalty.

"Just cover my back, that's all," Maxwell said, as if his mouth were moving independently of his body. "From here on in, it's going to be touchy. One mistake and we're dead."

He felt his nerves tense and with that feeling, extreme alertness, which struck him suddenly like a splash of cold water.

"What you going to do?" Thibadeaux asked.

Maxwell was looking straight at Danet when he answered. "We're taking over this boat and we're going back to Lorient. I may get us both hanged, but I won't be a party to murder."

Mickey and Rhinehardt sat staring, not believing what they saw or heard, but they made no move to interfere.

Maxwell spoke. "Mr. Danet, please step to the hatch and ask the Captain to come in here, use whatever you need to get him here." And as he said these words and watched the dancing eyes, glowering with hatred at him, he remembered Danet calling him, "Verrater."

"I will not do it," Danet said, leaning forward on the table, his eyes still with determination.

And Maxwell acted before he thought. With a quick step forward, he swung his arm and the heel of the P-38 directly at Danet's face. The gun struck the first officer between the eyes, his tall frame going to the deck. Maxwell kicked Danet viciously in the head, and Danet's full length lay on the floor. When he started to stir, Maxwell kicked him again, temporarily unconscious.

During all this the two gunners sat as if mesmerized.

Maxwell's chest rose and fell as he panted. "Richard, open the hatch, call the Captain in here, tell him the Exec. has had an accident and is hurt."

Thibadeaux opened the hatch which was already ajar. He could see the Captain standing in front of Rosenberg and Steinhoff, just as they had been when the Americans had left. He called out, "Captain, come in here, please, the Exec. he done fallen. He hurt and we need some help."

Frick slapped at his chin, disgusted at the interruption as he nodded, dismissed the two men and turned to enter the open hatch.

Maxwell had stepped back, put the P-38 in his belt, moved over to the table where the machinegun lay, picked it up, inserted a partial belt and moved to one side, making it difficult for anyone entering to immediately see him.

Thibadeaux stood by the hatch.

"Close it when he comes in," Maxwell said, again wondering where the words were coming from and thinking, what in hell am I doing?

As the Captain entered, Thibadeaux slammed the hatch and threw the latches on it.

The Captain looked at Thibadeaux, then turned to face Maxwell.

"What is the meaning of this?"

"I prefer to do this in a peaceful manner, Captain," Maxwell began, his voice again cool and deliberate, "but I am prepared to take direct action against anyone opposing me." Again that innate sense of alertness seizing him.

"We're taking over this boat," Maxwell said, "and we're going back to Lorient. Rosenberg and Steinhoff will stand trial for murder. We may have to stand trial for mutiny, but we're going back. Do you have any ideas to the contrary?"

Richard blanched.

"At the moment, no," the Captain answered, at once impressing Maxwell with his coolness. "But I would like to attend to my Exec. What did you do to him?"

"He wouldn't do what I told him so I hit him. He's not hurt bad. He'll live."

"What do you want me to do?" Frick asked.

"Just give the order to turn the boat around and head for Lorient, that's all. We'll all go to the control room while you give the order. Is that clear, Captain?"

"Tommy," Richard said, starting to protest.

"Shutup," Maxwell shouted.

There was a pause. "O.K., Richard, open the hatch."

Thibadeaux threw the latches to the open position, opened the hatch, and stepped into the control room. He could see Rosenberg and Steinhoff in the next compartment.

As they entered the control room, Rosenberg saw Richard with his hands in his pockets, but could not see Maxwell.

Rosenberg motioned to Steinhoff and they stepped through the forward hatch, heading forward. He heard the Captain give the order.

"Bring us around to 140 degrees and hold it there."

Rosenberg stopped. "What's he doing?" he said.

The helmsman also wondered about the course change, but proceeded to obey the order and turned the helm to bring her about.

"Captain," Maxwell said loudly, pulling the P-38 from his belt. "You as good as told me where we were when you ordered us back to our quarters. Remember, we're about forty hours from Florida. We won't get back to Lorient by going southeast, bring her around to the right course, how about 60 degrees, and please don't try that again. I'm a decent navigator and don't forget it."

Frick looked at Maxwell and twisted his mouth.

"And while we're at it, Captain," Maxwell said, nodding his head once. "I want to look at that report you made out."

Rosenberg and Steinhoff were half way through the forward compartment when they heard Maxwell telling the Captain to come around to 60 degrees. Rosenberg's eyes lit up. He turned to Steinhoff.

"Did you hear that? Maxwell is ordering the Captain to turn the boat around and go to France. Why?"

Steinhoff looked over his spectacles. "Maybe those two can give the Captain orders if they like," he said sarcastically.

Rosenberg tilted his head quickly. "It didn't sound that way when the Captain told us about our suspension; he ordered them back to their quarters, and they went. Do you think they have the Captain under restraint, or maybe some kind of threat?"

"I don't know."

"You just don't give ship Captains orders unless you are higher rank or holding him under some kind of threat."

"What are we going to do?" Steinhoff asked, adjusting his glasses.

"Find out if the Captain is under threat or not. If he isn't, he will just give us a reprimand. If he is, he will thank us for it, maybe even lift the suspension. What have we to lose?"

Steinhoff did not answer.

"Follow me," Rosenberg said, his stout frame moving forwards towards the torpedo compartment.

Maxwell's face streamed sweat. He turned to Thibadeaux, "Close that forward hatch and lock it."

He was wondering if Rosenberg could have heard him. He was beginning to feel confused and desperate. He cursed himself for being too quick to chastise the Captain about the course change.

He kept his distance from the Captain and his hand near the pistol.

He backed up to the bulkhead where he had placed the machinegun, picked it up, looked at it, and held it in the cradle of his arm.

In his haste to have the Captain turn the boat around, Maxwell had not attended to Mickey and Rhinehardt. They had not come into the control room.

"Richard," Maxwell said, "go back there and get the rest of this ammo belt for me, will you?"

Thibadeaux moved towards the rear compartment.

And now alone with his prisoners, Maxwell felt the gravity of what was happening. Things had been moving too fast for him. Danet had voluntarily walked in and was sitting on the chart table. Thibadeaux came back into the control room.

I must be a total fool, Maxwell thought, but one thing is certain. There is no backing out now.

And the knowledge that his hand had been played and that there was but one way out, created an edge of alertness and resolve within him that he had long been without.

What the hell, he thought, no one lives forever.

Strange as it may seem, the furthest thing from his mind was the massacre of the two prisoners, only thoughts of his own survival. He was totally enveloped in the action, as if this preposterous situation had always existed.

Rosenberg had arrived with his cohort in the forward torpedo room. The torpedo man was sitting on a stool and reading a book.

Rosenberg strode up and grabbed the phones. "Let me use your head phones for a minute," he said. "I think we have a problem and I can't talk to the Captain."

Waisenhoffer moved aside as Rosenberg put the phones on and began speaking.

Maxwell was leaning against the bulkhead when the speaker blared, "Captain, this is Rosenberg, we have a problem, can I speak with you?"

As Maxwell leapt up, the first officer raised his hand as if to fend off an attack. Maxwell's features had twisted, his nose wrinkling and eyes widening with rage.

"Close that conning hatch now, damn it," he yelled.

Thibadeaux rushed to close the hatch.

"Captain, tell him to mind his own business," Maxwell said, his eyes burning with hatred and fear.

Frick looked sideways before he spoke. "Rosenberg, whatever your problem is, it will have to wait. I'm busy right now."

Rosenberg answered back without hesitation. "Captain, are you under any threats? I heard Herr Maxwell giving orders. If that is the situation, then we will come in and take care of him and his friend immediately."

Maxwell stiffened.

"I just told you. There is nothing wrong," the Captain said, looking now as desperate as Maxwell.

Rosenberg again continued, "Captain, if there is nothing wrong, may we enter the control room to discuss our problem?"

The Captain started to speak when Maxwell violently ripped away the phones.

"Rosenberg, mind your own business," he cried, "and stay out of this control room." He instantly regretted it. His entire body seemed to burst forth with a cold sweat as his shirt, in a matter of seconds, was drenched. Not only did Rosenberg know that the Captain was under his command, but the whole crew as well.

Rosenberg put the phones up and turned to Steinhoff and the torpedo man. "You heard it yourself," he said with a strange smile. "The Captain is under a threat from our two guests. I am going in there to take care of those two. Anyone with me?"

Steinhoff bumped Walsenhoffer aside. "Do you think they are holding a gun on the Captain?" he asked. "But why would they do that?"

"There are many questions I would like to have the answers to," Rosenberg said. "We won't get them here. Let's go."

"Go where?"

"Aft to the ordinance room. We are going to need a gun."

They climbed the hatch out onto the deck and made their way aft, heading to the ammo and gun storage room compartment.

As they walked down the deck, they noticed the night was clear, the moon shining.

No one was in the storage compartment when they entered.

"Go forward and see if you can locate the gunner's mate and get him back here," Rosenberg said, a sneer running across his face. "Tell them to get back here and open this damn storage compartment."

Steinhoff found Mickey and Rhinehardt back at the table talking about the run of events.

"Get back to the gun room," Steinhoff said angrily. "The Captain's under a gun we think, and we're going in after him."

"We know," Mickey said with a drawn look. "We saw it happen, what's going on anyway?"

The U-168 cruised on smooth seas at 14 knots. The lookouts made no reports and were still unaware of the situation going on below them. They had merely looked at each other, shrugged their shoulders when the control room hatch had suddenly closed.

Maxwell spoke to Thibadeaux, "Put on those phones, and see if you hear anything."

After listening for a while, Thibadeaux said, "I don't hear nothing."

"Keep listening," Maxwell said as he began to regain control of himself.

Mickey hesitated when Rosenberg told him to open the gun cabinet.

Rosenberg swelled up, his eyes narrowing and his eyebrows knitted. "Open the damn door," he screamed, "or I take the keys and do it myself."

The gun doors opened, Rosenberg took out two submachine guns, inserted the clips, put two extra in his pocket, and turned to the men around him.

"You," he pointed to Mickey, "go up and guard the conning tower hatch and don't let anyone out."

He turned to the other gunner. "You go forward, Rhinehardt, and stay by the aft hatch to the control room. Steinhoff and I are going back forward and try to get into the control room from there. If there is any shooting, be careful. We don't want to kill our own men."

With that, Rosenberg and Steinhoff climbed out of the hatch onto the deck and made their way back forward to the torpedo room. They went down and then aft towards the control room. When they reached the control hatch, they noted it was closed and the latches in place.

"Damn," Rosenberg said. He sat down and pulled at his Hindenburg beard, trying to figure a way to storm the control room. Five minutes later, he had reached his decision.

While Rosenberg had been getting the gun compartment opened, Maxwell was thinking of his next move.

"We'll never make it back to Lorient," he said. "Not with that psychopath on the loose. The only chance we got is to head for the Florida coast and hope we can hold him off long enough to get ashore."

Frick wiped his forehead with his hat.

"Fat chance, huh?" Maxwell said to the puzzled Captain.

"Bring her around to 250 degrees, Captain. We'll be heading for the coast, the better chance for all of us."

The Captain gave the order.

Rosenberg felt the boat sway as it started to turn. He got up and rushed forward to the hatch, climbed out onto the deck and noted the boat was turning around towards the west.

As he raced along the catwalk aft, U-168 straightened to 250 degrees.

Rosenberg sprinted into the engine room. The noise of the diesels was deafening as the huge pistons churned up and down on each wall, monitored by the shirtless men on duty. The engineer was leaning over one of the pistons, talking in a crewman's ear when Rosenberg approached.

Seeing that Rosenberg was agitated, the engineer tapped the crewman on the shoulder and accompanied Rosenberg forward into the next compartment.

"What's wrong?" the engineer asked when facing Rosenberg.

"Shut down your engines," Rosenberg said.

"What are you talking about?" the engineer responded with a half-laugh on his face, apparently thinking Rosenberg was joking.

"I said to shut down the engines."

"You know I can't do that."

Rosenberg seized the engineer's sweaty shirt and lifted him off the deck plates. "I won't ask you again," he said, putting him down roughly. "The Captain is under restraint. It's mutiny. The Americans have taken over the control room. Now do as I say."

Maxwell suddenly became aware that the engines had stopped. U-168 was riding dead in the sea.

"Tommy, they shut down the engines," Thibadeaux said. "What we do now?"

The Exec. looked sick. He was ordered to sit on the deck in the corner. "If there is a gunfight aboard this boat," Danet began as he sat down.

"Shutup," Maxwell yelled. "Captain, get on those phones. Tell the engineer to get underway right now, or I am going to shoot Mr. Danet."

Danet looked up, his arms curled around his knees.

"If you don't get it done," Maxwell continued, his eyes growing wider with every word, "that idiot Rosenberg is going to get us all killed, and for what? He's crazy, Captain, and you know it."

Frick habitually rubbed his chin. "I think you're all crazy," he said, but he gave the order into the phones.

"Chief engineer, get underway immediately."

Rosenberg's voice boomed back at them. "Nein, Captain, you're giving orders under a gun. I am giving them from behind one. This boat does not move unless I say so, and I say we stay right here until those two come out and surrender."

The Captain sat down. The helmsman was watching Maxwell.

"What a mess," Maxwell said aloud, his face streaming sweat. "Someone is going to be killed or hurt."

"Give it up, Maxwell," Frick said. "No one can win this way."

"Shutup and let me think," Maxwell said. "Now what can this nut do?" He started contemplating all the moves that Rosenberg could make and came down to the same decision that Rosenberg had made. He had only one choice; he had to storm the control room.

Rosenberg and Steinhoff had returned to the forward hatch of the control room. They sat down. The torpedo man was leaning against the bulkhead, waiting for Rosenberg to make his move. This was the same seaman, Hillman, who had months ago picked up the two Americans in Louisiana.

"You," Rosenberg said to Hillman, "go back to the ordinance room and get some smoke grenades, about six should do it and take half of them up to Mickey at the control room hatch, bring the rest down here."

Suddenly Steinhoff lost his clinical look, his small eyes got larger and he quickly pinched his nose. He looked bewildered.

Rosenberg began fidgeting around the room. "We've got to get some smoke grenades in that control room," he explained. "Either through this hatch, the rear hatch, or the control room hatch. Once we've got them in, the smoke will blind everybody in there and we can rush in and take them. That way, no one will get seriously hurt--except for those Yankee bastards."

"Good," Steinhoff said, returning to his old demeanor.

Maxwell looked at Thibadeaux. "I don't hear nothing," Thibadeaux said.

"Richard, keep your eyes on those two hatches and watch that conning tower hatch too. If anyone makes an effort to open them, let me know, and I'll try to discourage them," he said, indicating the machine gun cradled in his arm.

"Captain," Maxwell said, "you better try talking that psycho out of what he's planning, and you should know what it is, or do you?"

"There is only one thing he can do," Frick replied, with a stern look. "He has to break in here, and that means shooting, and shooting in here can be just as dangerous for you as for anyone else. You can understand what Rosenberg is trying to do, and I doubt if he would listen to me anyway, so why even try? If he succeeds, I will have to reward him, and if he fails, probably none of us will be around to tell what happened. But I tell you this," he said, tilting his hat back so Maxwell could see his wrinkled brow and small, dark eyes, "if you knock out Rosenberg, the rest of the crew will take orders from me."

Frick's brow smoothed out.

Danet looked up, still with his arms curled around his knees.

"What did you say, Captain?" Danet asked.

Maxwell wheeled on him. "Shutup Danet," he shouted.

But the first officer ignored Maxwell and looked with steady, accusing eyes at his Captain.

"Did I hear you right, Frick?" Danet said, struggling to his feet. "You're offering amnesty to these two traitors if they hand you the heads of two men?"

"I said shutup," Maxwell cried.

"What are you going to do?" Danet said, taking a step forward. "Hit me again, kill me?"

"That right," Thibadeaux said.

Danet turned again to Frick. "You are conspiring to kill two of your own men, Captain, is that correct?"

Frick turned away in frustration. "Stay out of this, Danet," he mumbled.

"You're as responsible as anyone, Danet," Maxwell said, leveling the machine gun at the first officer's chest. "You've been itching to see this happen ever since we boarded this boat."

"Why are you angry at me?" Danet said with a strange smile. "I labeled you as a cowardly traitor from the beginning, and now you have proved me correct."

Maxwell's face went livid, his hands on the gun trembling with rage.

Frick walked quickly between them. "Danet, sit down and stay out of this. You are only complicating matters," he said.

Danet pointed his finger at the Captain. "No, mein Kapitan, I am complicating nothing. I am merely clarifying your position."

Frick slapped at the pointed finger.

"Don't point your finger at me. You've been operating behind my back and behind Schuller's back for months. Don't bother to deny it. I don't know who you're working for, but I have some advice for you. Sit down and be silent. I am still Captain of this boat...."

"Wrong Captain," Danet raised his voice, seeming to grow taller, as Maxwell felt like firing. "This American pig is the Captain and you are acting as his first mate."

"That's enough," Maxwell said in a strangely calm voice.

"Step aside now Frick."

The Captain turned and gave way to a slowly advancing Maxwell, the gun pointed directly at Danet's chest.

"Everyone has to kill for the first time," Maxwell said in a chilled tone. "I'm told that it is very easy. This will only take a second."

At that moment both Frick and Thibadeaux panicked, both convinced that Maxwell was going to shoot.

Thibadeaux started up behind Maxwell, and Frick leapt between the gun and Danet, holding his arms out to the side.

"Are you mad?" the Captain said. "Stop it. Stop it now."

Maxwell stopped, watching Frick. Frick then turned around and stood face to face with Danet.

"I am ordering you to sit," the Captain said.

Slowly the first officer, still watching Frick's eyes, backed into his corner and slid into a sitting position.

Frick turned to Maxwell, holding his hands up. "Now tell us what you want us to do?"

Maxwell's eyes bulged wide, his mouth tight with tension.

"Calm down, now," Frick said. "Do we have a deal?"

"Deal?" Maxwell said, raising an eyebrow, forgetting himself. "It's Rosenberg or me. And if I get him...."

"I will drop you off on the coast," the Captain said.

"But I will not give you your equipment. That will be up to Naval Operations to get that to you."

"If I get Rosenberg and Steinhoff, you put us ashore, and go about your business."

"Correct," the Captain replied.

"Your word of honor, Captain."

"My word," Frick replied.

"You got a deal, Captain. Rosenberg is dead."

The words seemed to solidify a resolve within Maxwell, seemed to make possible what before had seemed absolutely impossible, the fact that he, Tommy Maxwell, would actually fire this gun with the intention of killing a man. He remembered when as a child, home alone, at nights, once he had seized a butcher knife when he heard a creak in the house.

Through an over-active imagination, he had convinced himself a prowler was in the house. Deep down, he knew there was no prowler, and that had one showed up, he would not have attacked him. The present situation was equally fantastic, yet it was happening.

He pursed his lips. He had reached a resolve. He knew that Rosenberg had killed before--and he, Tommy Maxwell, was still a virgin. He remembered the words of Frankel, "hesitation is synonymous with death."

He felt suddenly that his head was clear; the clouds had drifted away. It was as if he were within the throes of a fever and extremely muddled thoughts were followed by those of extreme clarity.

He looked around the control room.

"What are you looking for?" the Captain asked.

"A rope, a piece of cable or something like that."

At this time on the catwalk above, the two lookouts watched Mickey creep up the forward hatch, and, half-crouched and walking on his toes, move to the bridge hatch where he laid aside what looked to be a smoke grenade and gingerly began opening the hatch.

Mickey was plagued by several thoughts at once. He knew he had to act since Maxwell had his gun. He himself might face court-martial.

The water rocked the boat. They had rarely sat dead in the water and the sensation was different. The sky above was brilliant with stars.

A brief moment of rage struck Mickey. He began opening the hatch. As much as anyone else on board, he had been a friend to the Americans. He found it impossible to believe that Maxwell would actually fire on him.

He shot a quick glance at the smoke grenade, smelled the air, and twisted the hatch.

Thibadeaux started. "Tommy, somebody opening the conning hatch."

With that new clarity of mind, Maxwell walked deliberately under the hatch, aimed the machine gun directly up. The hatch opened. Maxwell let off a burst. Mickey's face jerked out of sight. When the echo of the burst faded, simultaneously there was a scream above, then a moan could be heard drifting away, as someone was being moved away from the hatch.

Maxwell stood mesmerized as did all the others.

Finally, it is done, he thought. He felt an immense sense of relief. Now that he had done it once, he could do it again.

He felt his adrenaline flowing and his heart pounding.

"Get up there and tighten that thing as good as you can," he said to Thibadeaux, "but keep your eye on it just the same."

Thibadeaux climbed the ladder and sealed the hatch, then came back down and stood where he was.

The two lookouts had not budged as Mickey climbed onto deck, put his finger to his mouth and had begun creeping towards the hatch. They watched him take out a smoke grenade and with the sea wind blowing his shirt into ruffles, they saw him lay the grenade to the side and begin to open the hatch.

They heard the burst of firing, quickly muted by the sea wind, saw and heard Mickey screaming and writhing about on top of the hatch.

Schnegel rushed to the hatch, grabbed one of Mickey's pants legs and pulled him away. Within minutes Mickey was delirious, his speech garbled. He had been hit twice in the chest and once in the throat.

Schnegel, ignoring the blood, which spurted warm on his own chin, got over Mickey and tried to blow air into his mouth, but each time he blew into his mouth, the air along with a small fountain of blood spurted up through the huge hole in Mickey's neck.

Suddenly repulsed, Schnegel moved his face back up. "No good," he yelled with tiny droplets of blood cascading through his beard.

Schnegel held Mickey for a time in his arms, but soon dropped him as he realized during the last throes that there was nothing he could do. Mickey's good eye now looked as blank as the glass one. Schnegel had felt a sudden repulsion for the dying man and stepped back a few paces as Mickey began his death rattle, shook, and died.

"There should be some rope at the top of that ladder," Frick said, whose fixed gaze indicated that he had begun to fear seriously for his life. "There on the platform," he added.

Maxwell climbed up to see, found the rope dangling there and came back down with it. He took out his knife while Thibadeaux covered the others and cut off a twelve foot piece. Then he walked over to the forward hatch, made a loop around the hatch handle, and drew it tight enough and tied the other ends to the pipes on the bulkhead. If he had tried to open the door, it would have opened only about ten inches. Anyone on the other side trying to jerk the hatch open would fail; the rope would hold it shut.

"That hatch opens into the forward compartment," Maxwell said." I know Rosenberg is in there. He'll be standing by the open side of the hatch. That is the only way he can get through that hatch in a hurry, if and when he comes through. What we are going to do is give him a surprise, like we are going out after him. I'm hoping the surprise will delay him for a couple of seconds, that's all we need."

Maxwell tried to settle himself down, but the excitement was mounting. If something did not happen quickly, it seemed he might burst.

This has got to work, he thought, or we're dead.

All in the control room stood, as if hypnotized, as they watched

Maxwell. It was apparent to all observers that like a newly caged animal, Maxwell was in an extreme state of agitation and in this state, very dangerous.

Maxwell moved around until he was at what he thought was the right angle. He motioned for Thibadeaux to come over to where he stood.

Maxwell whispered in his ear. "There's six latches on that hatch door. I want you to go over and take them off, one at a time, leaving the bottom one for last. When you pull off the bottom latch, be sure you fall to the floor, knock the hatch open with your foot and hold it. If he's out there he's going to get a dose of steel. You won't get hit. I'm aiming right through that crack when the hatch opens. Understand?"

Maxwell stared at Thibadeaux's black mole.

"Yeah," Thibadeaux said, "but make sure you don't spray me with that thing."

Thibadeaux moved to the hatch and started undoing the latches.

Maxwell braced the machinegun against his hip. He was ready. First one latch came undone, then another, each very slowly.

Rosenberg opened his mouth and grimaced, his separated teeth showing briefly. He saw the second latch complete its turn and watched with fascination as the third one started turning.

"Someone in there is opening the hatch for us," he whispered to Steinhoff.

Steinhoff gazed at the latches, slowly turning, one by one, and stiffened.

"It has to be the Captain or the Exec. one. Here Hans, give me the smoke grenade. When that last hatch opens, jerk it open. I'll toss this in, and that will force them out."

Thibadeaux laid down and with his left foot, kicked the bottom latch open, and simultaneously jammed his right foot against the hatch. It flew open over a foot and a half.

Rosenberg was raising his arm to throw the smoke grenade when Maxwell fired the machine gun. Rosenberg took every shot in the chest and stomach, and Steinhoff caught two from the ricocheting. Rosenberg was dead before he hit the deck plates, Steinhoff dying, slowly bleeding to death from two neat holes in his side. The pair of wire rimmed glasses lay next to his face.

Rosenberg had dropped his smoke grenade, and it started spinning, spewing out and filling up the compartment as Maxwell yelled to Thibadeaux, "Close that hatch and lock it," the echo of the shots still ringing in his ears.

Rosenberg's smoke grenade was still burning as Waisenhoffer quickly entered, then exited the compartment. He rushed to the forward torpedo room hatch, climbed through and closed the hatch. He slowly climbed the ladder up the forward hatch towards the deck. At the top, he paused, listened, then peered out on deck. By now Hagermeister and Rhinehardt were standing with the two lookouts over Mickey.

In the control room Danet sat on the floor with his hands curled around his knees. He was pale except for a greenish color his face had taken on the left side where Maxwell had kicked him. He stared blankly, in disbelief.

"Did you get them both?" Captain Frick asked, the edge of panic back in his voice.

"I know I got Rosenberg," Maxwell said, his face still sheened with sweat. "I don't know about Steinhoff."

The Captain got on the phones. "Steinhoff.....Steinhoff, are you there?"

No answer.

Maxwell lit a cigarette and looked up. A flurry of footsteps could be heard topside.

U-168 still lay dead in the water.

"Steinhoff.....Steinhoff, answer, are you out there," the Captain called.

Hagermeister, Rhinehardt, and Waisenhoffer stood over Mickey as the lookout told them what had happened.

"They're traitors," Schnegel shouted. "They're going to kill us all and take this boat to America for a war prize."

"Rosenberg and Steinhoff are dead," Waisenhoffer said, turning to Hagermeister with burning eyes. "Schnegel is right. If we don't do something, there won't be any of us left alive to say what really took place. Your friends," he said, shoving Hagermeister, "have made a nice mess of things."

Hagermeister stepped back and raised his fists. "You shutup and keep your hands off me," he snapped.

"Settle down, both of you," Rhinehardt said, tugging at his beard. "We've got to stay calm."

"What are we going to do?" Waisenhoffer said. "We don't even know if the Captain or the Exec. are alive or not. We have to do something before we are all shot."

"You're the one who let them have a damned gun," Hagermeister said to Rhinehardt, who had been trying to conceal just that fact.

"Shutup, fat boy," Rhinehardt shouted, swelling up.

Now Waisenhoffer stepped between these two saying, "Come on, we have to observe rank." He nodded to the Chief Petty Officer. "Take command."

"Waisenhoffer is right," Hagermeister said, the tone of command returning to his voice. "We have to do something. Let's go back and talk to the engineer and see if he can come up with anything. We can't just stay here on the surface and not move. Someone is going to come along and then we won't have a chance. The gunner is dead. The loader is dead, we can't fire the deck gun. Those guys below have the machinegun and all we got is smoke grenades and hand guns. All I know is we've got to think of a way to out-think them. They have killed three of us already and probably plan on killing the rest of us."

Hagermeister, Waisenhoffer, and Schnegel headed for the engine room.

The Captain had plugged in the forward torpedo room, calling for anyone to answer. No one did. He called again, still no answer.

The Captain turned to Maxwell. "If there's anyone forward, they're not answering, but then that burst could have hit a speaker cable so they can't hear us."

"Keep calling aft and see if you can raise anyone," Maxwell answered.

Hagermeister in the aft compartment had moved into the galley and along with Duggan, the cook, had proceeded to the engine room.

Waisenhoffer and Schnegel had been a few seconds behind him as they came down the hatch.

The Captain called the aft compartment twice and received no answer. He went through the same routine with the galley. No response.

When he called the engine room, the engineer answered.

The engineer hesitated as Waisenhoffer motioned him to be silent.

Waisenhoffer moved close to the engineer and whispered, "Tell him it's o.k. and find out what he wants us to do."

"Everything is fine here," the engineer said into the phones. "What are your orders, Captain?"

The Captain spoke again. "Lay down your arms and get this boat underway as soon as you can. We've got some repairs to make before we can submerge. It will be daylight soon, and we can't afford to get caught out in the open."

"Jawohl, I'll tell the men to get back to their stations," the engineer said. "And what repairs, sir?"

"Get the bridge hatch repaired, check the forward compartment and see what needs to be done. Get moving."

"Jawohl, mein Kapitan," the engineer replied.

The engineer turned to the men present and said, "Get back to the machine shop, get what you need, fix that hatch, check that compartment forward. I want this boat down by daylight."

Hagermeister handed Duggan his gun. "Hide this somewhere in the galley. If anyone checks the gun room, we'll all say it fell overboard when the gunner was shot. Keep it hidden until we find out if the Captain is back in command. The Exec. is sure to check."

"Alright," Duggan said, "but only till we find out for sure."

Crewmen went to the various parts of the boat, checking for damage.

"We might as well have sea burials," Hagermeister commanded.

"Since there is no way we can transport those bodies back, unless the Captain wants to empty the refrigerator, which I doubt."

Duggan waddled back to the galley to hide the gun and get back to his kitchen duties. Hagermeister and Waisenhoffer headed forward. No one made an issue of the fact that the control room hatches were still closed. The lookouts went back to the bridge.

A more relaxed attitude prevailed in the control room. The engineer had put the boat underway. The churn of the diesels was comforting to all. The course was still 250 degrees which would take them to the Florida coast.

Maxwell guessed they would see land just above Jacksonville, along about St. Mary's, on the edge of the Okeefenokee swamp. Once ashore, they would work their way north along the edge of the swamp. The chances of encountering anyone in that area were slim. He hoped to come out at Waycross, Ga. and from there get a bus north.

He had only one problem. He knew the Captain had the funds given to him by Admiral Doenitz in Lorient. He planned on taking the money with him.

Maxwell turned to the Captain.

"Get the Exec. to check and see if all the guns those guys had are back under lock and key. I don't want any of them to start this thing all over again. Thibadeaux and I will stay here until we make land. Then we'll get out of your life, Captain, we don't want any more trouble."

Hagermeister was thinking in other terms. If and when he got the chance, he intended to avenge Mickey, Rosenberg, and Steinhoff's deaths. He felt especially betrayed by Maxwell.

Almost immediately after Rosenberg had been shot and dropped his smoke grenade, the main induction had been closed off to prevent smoke from being blown all through the boat. When Schnegel opened the hatch, the room was still saturated with smoke. He couldn't see anything. He closed the hatch and told one of the crew to go after the portable air pump.

They would have to pump out both compartments before they could enter where the two bodies were. They had to hurry, for daylight was less than three hours away. U-168 moved easily through the gentle sea.

The Captain ordered the sea burials to take place at dawn, after which U-168 would submerge.

As the orange, elongated needles of the sun shown over the eastern horizon, the crew began preparing for the burials and the swift execution of the Captain's orders.

Occasionally when the members of the crew moved topside, they observed flying fish, disturbed by the boat, shooting over the troughs of the emerald waves, and once just before four of the crew made their way topside with three large, wrapped bundles over which words were said and the bundles dropped overboard into the green waves, several of the crew observed two dolphin, their shining, wet, gray flanks reflecting infinitesimal dazzles of the sun, like diamonds, as they leapt just feet ahead of where U-168 cut the waves in a burst of white spray--the dolphin playing with the bow of the boat, with happy, yet powerful leaps and swift undulations, they swam just below the surface, in and out of vision.

"I'll take the guns, now," Captain Frick said.

"Not a chance," Maxwell replied with a thin smile. "Which brings us around to one more thing. You have something we're supposed to take with us and you might as well have it sent to us now." Maxwell turned to Thibadeaux. "Get back to our quarters and bring our bags up here. We'll be staying right here till we sight land. Then we'll go ashore. We came here to do a job, Captain, and we intend to do it if Naval Operations gives us the word after we report in, but we're not going ashore broke."

Frick evened his eyes at Maxwell. "When I make my report," he said, "you won't need to worry about anything but staying alive. You know there will be someone coming after you."

"Captain," Maxwell answered, "I would prefer not to make any recriminations, nor do I want to hear any threats. For my part, this thing is over, and I hope it stays that way."

"You'll never make it," the Captain said, "but I know you're going to try, and I have no intentions of interfering. I have enough trouble as it is, trying to explain all this."

"You gave your word, Captain, and I expect you to honor it."

"What do you want?" Frick answered with disgust.

"Get the equipment and other stuff you're holding. You know what I'm talking about."

Frick's eyes narrowed. "That wasn't part of the arrangement."

The P-38 had been aimed at the floor. Maxwell raised it to the level of Frick's stomach. "It's part of the deal now," he said.

"Take it or leave it. I'm not going to discuss it further. Now send for it immediately."

After Danet finished with the charts, Frick instructed him both to fetch the Americans' suitcase from Admiral Doenitz and to check the gun compartment, to make sure all firearms were stowed.

Five minutes later, the Exec. returned with a small suitcase, which he set on the deck.

Maxwell picked it up, laid it on the chart table, and opened it. He smelled the money. He did not bother to count the stacks of American currency which would add up to one hundred and fifty thousand dollars.

"How bout them apples," Thibadeaux said with a wide smile.

"Good enough," Maxwell muttered as he re-sealed the suitcase.

When Danet explained that he had not yet checked for weapons, the Captain ordered him to go aft and check the gun room, to see what was missing, lock up everything, and bring the keys back to him.

"I don't want any of the crew to start a vendetta," the Captain said.

Just after daybreak, the Captain gave the order to "prepare to dive." The crew went about their appointed tasks.

Deck hatches could be heard closing, the nose of U-168 pointed downwards, and the Teinsenmeiser showed they were rapidly submerging.

"Take us down two hundred meters and hold her there. Tell the Chief to give me all she's got."

Minutes later U-168 was riding level at two hundred feet.

Maxwell and Thibadeaux remained in the control room. The control room hatches still closed, Thibadeaux took the opportunity to sleep. Using his shirt as a pillow, he curled just beneath the trim panel and only five or six feet from Schnegel, the helmsman.

"Officer Danet here," a voice said outside the aft hatch.

"Let him in," Maxwell said, again removing the P-38 from his belt and watching both the hatch and the machine gun on the chart table. The Captain opened the hatch as Danet ducked his head and entered the control room. He held his arms up, offering for Maxwell to search him.

"All weapons have been stowed and accounted for," Danet reported to the Captain, "except for one."

"Go on," Maxwell said.

Danet never looked at Maxwell, but continued speaking to the Captain, as if Maxwell were not in the room.

"The lugar, that Mickey had topside, fell overboard when he was shot."

Danet now turned his eyes to Maxwell and seeing his reaction, added, "No, I am not lying. Both Hagermeister and Waisenhoffer saw it."

Maxwell's stomach fell. In seconds his face was again streaming sweat.

He pointed the P-38 at Danet.

"Now you go back there and find that gun and stow it," he said.

"Mr. Maxwell," Danet replied. "I want no more trouble. I have checked everywhere for the gun. If it is on board, it is being hidden from me. I will not take orders from you. I take orders from the Captain."

Frick's eyes met Danet's, and the latter nodded in a gesture of respect. Danet sighed, ran his hand through his hair, and sat down in his corner, removing his shirt.

"If the Captain has no objections, I am now going to sleep," he said. "My head hurts and I am tired."

"Permission granted," Frick said.

The Captain had barely spoken before Danet had curled into the corner asleep.

Maxwell put the gun in his belt and sat on the chart table beside the machine gun. He lit a cigarette and inhaled. Dejected and tired, he fixed his gaze on the trim panel.

"Captain, I'll ask you again, what are you going to do?

You don't believe that gun fell overboard any more than I do."

Frick wiped his brow with his sleeve.

"With the hatches closed in here I would appreciate it if you wouldn't smoke," Frick said.

"If you can breathe these damned diesel fumes all day, you sure as hell can breathe a cigarette. I've got one if you want one.....Schnegel?"

The helmsman shook his head.

"Want one?"

"No," said the Captain, who stared blankly at the deck plates.

"You look as tired as I feel," Maxwell said, ignoring the harsh look Schnegel fired at him.

Frick smiled thinly and walked over close to Maxwell. The latter took a step back.

"Don't worry," Frick said. "I won't try to take your gun."

"I wasn't worried about that," Maxwell said, inexplicably blushing.

"No use lying now, is there?" Frick said, looking Maxwell in the eyes. "No point hiding anything for decorum's sake."

Maxwell smiled. "No, guess not. Answer my question."

Frick stared off, distracted. He spoke as if to the pipings on the wall.

"I'll tell you the same thing I told you before. The crew is under my orders not to offer resistance. If they do, it will be insubordination. What else can I do? I could make an announcement to that effect, but what would it accomplish?"

"Who were Rosenberg and Steinhoff's friends on board?" Maxwell asked.

Frick's eyes blazed. "You know better than I," he snapped. "These men were your crewmates before I took command."

"If the crew is planning a vendetta, I promise you," Maxwell said, placing his hand on the machine gun. "We'll take more than one of them with us. Neither one of us can afford that."

"Listen, Maxwell, I cannot guarantee anything. I have done everything I can. I know nothing about Rosenberg and Steinhoff's friends, but I do know this. My crew are good seamen and good Germans. Mickey had plenty of friends. You can bet that the crew would like nothing better than to see you dead."

"You feel the same way, right, Captain?" Maxwell said with a strange smile.

Again Frick stared off, lost in thought. Finally, he muttered his answer.

"Personally, I don't care one way or another. Maybe I'm too tired to care. It would be better for me if you pulled that trigger."

"Killed you?"

Frick shrugged. "I'll have to answer for what has happened. That is for sure. After Danet finishes talking, who knows, at the least, I will lose my command, perhaps face a firing squad."

Maxwell threw his cigarette on the deck plates and stepped on it.

"You need some sleep, Captain, that's all."

Frick looked at Maxwell. "You cannot fathom a man who no longer cares to live, can you?"

"You want to die?"

"What do you think?"

"I think you want to live."

"What in hell do you know about me? Why don't you just shut your mouth."

"Your life is none of my business. Just trying to be friendly, that's all," Maxwell said.

"Trying to make the best of the situation," Frick said sarcastically. "You have committed mutiny, killed three of my crew, and probably destroyed me in the process. So why can't we have a friendly conversation? Act like nothing has happened."

Maxwell shrugged, looking off. "World's going to hell in a hand basket anyway. This is war, you know. And as far as your crew goes, I don't think you can blame me for defending myself."

Frick stared down at his hands. "What does it matter anyway?" he said. "We must all do our duties."

Frick now looked quite old.

Maxwell smiled. "How many kids you got?"

Frick's brow smoothed. "Two boys, twelve and fourteen."

"I'd like to have kids some day."

Frick only shook his head. "Don't wish for such a thing."

"Why not?"

"Who knows? You may live to see them grow old enough to be sacrificed for a government, but I doubt it."

"Why do you doubt it?"

Frick shifted his feet. "You may get off this boat," he said, "but I assure you, neither you nor your friend there will survive this episode."

"You will make sure of that, right?"

Frick's eyes did not waver. "I will have nothing to do with it. I will make my report."

"You do what you have to do," Maxwell said. "I'll do the same." Both men were silent for a time. By all indications, everything sounded normal. As Maxwell reflected about the past twenty-four hours, it all seemed so senseless.

U-168 moved silently through the deep, maintaining two hundred meters.

The crew went about their duties, changed shifts regularly, and by all indications appeared relaxed.

Thibadeaux yawned, remained motionless. He seemed to be concentrating on listening and staying awake. Maxwell wondered how many times Thibadeaux had waited this way when on one of his night excursions. Nothing seemed to bother him. Over the last few hours Maxwell had formed a new respect for Richard. His partner had shown courage in opening the hatch with Rosenberg and Steinhoff on the other side. He had proved he could act swiftly and decisively when needed.

The soundman sat at his equipment, listened, but said nothing. The helmsman watched his gauges and his compass. He kept it steady on course. By the time daylight was breaking, Maxwell had thought out his plan to get ashore without any more problems.

Frick watched Maxwell and knew he was devising a plan to get ashore.

His only hope was that they did not have to go in too far past the one hundred fathom bank. U-boats were vulnerable that close and two had been caught and sunk only recently. He did not want to become another missing submarine, that ridiculous phrase headquarters used, that silly presumption so carelessly tossed, "presumed to be lost." He winced at the thought.

Frick had been well-briefed that the Allied anti-submarine tactics had improved and were proving to be very efficient in combating boats working alone. The one thing that kept coming into his mind was the story of the missing gun.

Maxwell watched the Captain. The room was closing in on him--the white, illumined faces, the pipings around the hatch, and the smell, always the smell, the whir of the motors, the swaying overhead light, all came down upon him from all sides--that same feeling of "cabin fever" so well-known among U-boat mariners possessed him--"Blechkoller," the Germans called it.

He was beginning to get nauseous, and he broke out in a cold sweat. He imagined the bright sunshine above the surface, just as a man in prison imagines endless rolling fields.

He had to get out. Try as he would to rationalize his feeling, it would not go away. It was as if there was an entity in this dank, moaning crate that was slowly swallowing him. He did not know what to do. And the thought suddenly occurred to him that perhaps he had committed mutiny, merely as a result of this prolonged confinement, not as a result of morality, as he had originally told himself, but rather in response to Blechkoller. It was the smell that had made him do it.

His thoughts became muddled in his fatigue. He felt feverish, verging upon delirium.

A gun, he thought, a gun out there for me. And look at their faces, Danet and Frick, so white and clammy. Jesus, why don't I just kill them all.

And the thought frightened Maxwell and at once startled him as his frame shook, as if coming out of a seizure.

Frick was watching Maxwell, but his thoughts were entirely with his boat. He knew daylight would be fading soon, and if there was nothing around, he planned to surface and run as long as he could to charge his batteries. He would need them if he had to go close to shore.

The Allied shipping had been traveling very close to this spot in the past. He knew that these cruises had been easy since the beginning of summer, but now he could find himself, under the circumstances, under attack, in shallow water, with no place to go.

Nightfall was only two hours away. He waited.

"Let's go up and look around," he finally said to the Exec.

"Bring us up to periscope depth." The Exec. passed the order.

U-168 slowly rose.

Thibadeaux had sat down and was dozing. Maxwell screwed up his eyes as the boat started to rise. No one made a move towards him and no one spoke.

"Periscope depth," the helmsman said.

"Up periscope."

As the periscope rose from its well, the Captain followed it up, looking into it as it broke surface. He panned the horizon in a slow circle. He turned to the hydrophone man with the huge, white frontal lobes.

"Hear anything?"

"No sir."

"Surface," the Captain ordered. The Exec. passed the order.

The U-168 slowly broke surface, hatches were opened, the main induction system was opened, and fresh air began to circulate throughout the boat.

Maxwell reeled with the smell of the air and came out of his daze.

The motors were stopped and the diesels started. U-168 picked up speed to fifteen knots. The seas were smooth, the weather clear.

The bridge hatch was opened. The Captain invited Maxwell topside.

"Maybe later," Maxwell said.

"Better take it while you can," Frick replied with a sly glint in his eyes. "We may have to dive at any minute. We're getting close to the coast. We're not much over two hundred miles out, should make landfall early tonight."

"Maybe later," Maxwell repeated.

With the boat on the surface, most of the crew could go topside and get the sun. Even the engineer would go up for short periods of time.

Hagermeister took the opportunity to go topside. He strolled and spoke to several members of the crew, then worked his way aft towards the engine room, and forward to the galley. Duggan saw him coming.

"Preparing you fellows something special for tonight," Duggan said, his yellow teeth smiling through his beard. "Schnitzel, probably the last chance we get before going on patrol."

"Good," Hagermeister answered, scratching in his own beard. "But I came back here to get the pistol. I have discovered a way to get those two. I hated Rosenberg, but he was one of us. The Americans will never make it ashore."

Duggan turned and opened a cabinet, producing the pistol.

"They will chop you to pieces," he said grimly. "You must be as crazy as Rosenberg."

Hagermeister put out his hand. "Hand it over."

Duggan thrust the pistol into the chief petty officer's hand. "Just leave it alone," the cook said. "You'll end up like Mickey. If anything is to be done, let someone higher up do it."

Hagermeister put the gun under his shirt, did not speak, looked questioningly at the cook, turned and went for the hatch.

Maxwell kept going over his plan. Was the gun really missing? And if not, which of the crew had it? He was unconcerned about Frick or Danet. There was the engineer, but he never came out of the engine room. The cook? Waisenhoffer? The three men in the control room took their orders from the Captain. The radio operator had made no effort to make distress calls. Who were Rosenberg and Steinhoff's friends? Perhaps even Hager-meister had turned against him now. He could put nothing together. But he did know that since the shooting, everything had been going too smoothly.

Thibadeaux was still sleeping.

The U-168 diesels kept their steady churn.

Strange, Maxwell thought, none of the crew has attempted to come into the control room, or is that so strange? He sighed to himself, feeling incredible fatigue.

Frick had been standing on the bridge, his face already red from the sun.

Maxwell felt he could read the Captain's thoughts.

Frick was also thinking that all was going too smoothly. It was unnatural that the crew was not complaining, and especially about the recent confrontation. All he wanted to do was get the two Americans ashore without incident, get to his grid square, and sink Allied shipping, for he was certain that once his report had been received, the two Americans would be just two more war casualties.

But Frick was feeling a strange resignation. He had lost his animosity for the Americans' acts. His resignation arose from thoughts prompted by fatigue, a tired fear about his own future career, and a muddled despair about the entire war effort in general.

He was also aware that he should not be on the surface in broad daylight, but he wanted to get his batteries charged to the limit, for once inside the hundred mile zone, he may have to go down and stay submerged for a prolonged period of time.

Frick had told the radio operator not to make any effort to use the radio. He was sure Maxwell and Thibadeaux would destroy it if he did. There would be time enough.

He wondered if Headquarters had been trying to contact him. He was certain they had, but as soon as he got rid of his unwanted guests, he would report.

It was past 1300. Frick decided to take a bearing.

When he had finished his calculations back in the control room, he confirmed his thoughts. They were now within 100 miles of the American coast.

The cook called for dinner, and one by one, the men filtered to the galley for their meal.

Maxwell instructed Thibadeaux to bring back all the meals for the control room, making sure all the plates were the same.

Maxwell was afraid they might be poisoned.

Hagermeister was so shocked at seeing Thibadeaux in the galley that he had not acted at all. He saw the bulge under Thibadeaux's undershirt and knew he was armed. He felt the gun under his own shirt but did not make a move. There were too many men around. He could not get the drop on him.

Things were too cramped, too unpredictable. A shootout in close quarters like these was unthinkable.

So in that murky darkness of the galley, Thibadeaux and Hagermeister actually brushed shoulders as they passed. And try as he may, Hagermeister again could not suppress the glance of hatred and betrayal as he looked into Thibadeaux's dark features.

Richard returned and those in the control room ate their meals in silence.

At 1400 the Captain ordered the helmsman relieved.

"Get some sleep," Frick said. "You'll be needing it later when we leave the coast."

The helmsman left and went aft to his quarters.

The weather remained fair, the seas smooth, with a few cumulous clouds drifting around. Four of the crew were lying on the deck, taking the sun.

Maxwell turned to Thibadeaux and said: "I'm going to take a short nap. Wake me if you even think something's wrong. Keep an eye on everything and everybody. We should be ashore by midnight. The Captain will be diving soon. He has taken a chance staying up this long, but he will stay as long as he can. We're taking him in real close to shore. That's the only safety factor we got. There are a couple of other things he won't like either, but we have no choice."

Thibadeaux nodded. It did not occur to him once what Maxwell had planned. So far Maxwell had shown presence of mind in his planning, and Richard was not about to interfere.

U-168 maintained her speed at fifteen knots. The day passed without incident.

The sun went down slowly and shone red off the sea.

Maxwell stirred on the cold deck plates of the control room. He sat up and rubbed his eyes. He looked at Thibadeaux, who was wide awake and watching.

"I'm going back up on the bridge, be back in a few minutes," Maxwell said.

Maxwell cautiously climbed up the ladder and upon emerging topside, felt his eyes sting at the sudden change in light. The sun was low and sending red dazzles across the face of the calming waters.

Maxwell went back below. He looked at Thibadeaux and nodded his head. Richard shrugged.

Dusk sifted down over the ocean. U-168 remained on the surface, cruising at full speed. The Florida coast grew nearer.

The closer the American coast, the more alert Maxwell became.

By 2130 darkness was complete. The moon was not yet up, and the Captain was in the control room.

"Prepare to dive," he ordered.

Danet, whose face was still green on the right side where Maxwell had kicked him, passed the order.

U-168 slipped under the water. All that could be heard was the hum of the motors.

"Take us down to periscope depth and hold her there," the Captain ordered, then scratching beside his eye, he turned to Maxwell. "How far do you intend to go in?"

Maxwell twisted his mouth and looked squarely into Frick's eyes. "To about five miles, Captain."

Frick threw off his hat. "You are endangering my boat," he yelled.

"I know," Maxwell answered calmly, "but we've got to do it."

"If I'm attacked that close in, we don't have a chance."

"Captain," Maxwell replied in that same even tone. "I'm not the least bit concerned about it. We're going in, and the reason is that one of your crew has a gun. You and I both know it. So let's quit playing games. Something is being planned. I feel it. I have other plans. I don't intend to be shot. Now take us in," he said, again gently removing the P-38 from under his belt and pointing it to the deck plates.

Frick stared hard at Maxwell, picked up his hat, turned it around backwards on his head and said to Danet, "Up periscope."

He followed the periscope up, took a look around the entire circle, saw nothing and said so.

"Hear anything?" he asked the hydrophone man.

"No sir," replied the white face with the large frontal lobes.

"Mr. Danet," Frick said, "take the periscope and let me know when you sight land. We should be just above St. Mary's."

"Jawohl, mein Kapitan."

With that he walked over and took over the periscope. As the Captain was leaving to go forward, he said, "Half speed from here to the coast. Listen sharp for anything."

With that he left.

U-168 slowed down. Every few minutes Danet looked into the periscope. The Captain soon returned.

"Nothing yet," Danet reported.

"You will see land within the hour, Mr. Danet," Frick said.

The American people had finally gotten the message about keeping the lights on along the shore. Too many of the Captains of the merchant marine had been complaining that they were silhouetted against the shore lights for the U-boats to see. All along the shore there was darkness now. There would be no guiding lights to aid the enemy.

"Land sir," reported the Exec. taking his eyes from the periscope, "about seven miles."

"Steady as she goes then," Frick said, alertness returning to his voice. "We'll surface in close. We cannot take more than fifteen minutes. I want to get back into deep water. Here we stand no chance."

"Stand by to surface," Frick added.

U-168, still running at half speed, slowly rose to the surface.

Maxwell picked up the machine gun.

"Captain," Maxwell said, his brow knitted severely, "the only hatch I want opened is the one on the bridge. If I see any other hatches open, I'm turning this baby loose on them. Order your men to keep hatches closed, and stay below. Under no circumstances are they to go topside."

Maxwell stuffed the P-38 in his belt.

"What are you going to do?" Frick asked.

"You and Danet, Thibadeaux and myself are going topside," Maxwell said. "We're going to take the inflatable and some supplies, and we're all going ashore. When you get there, you can bring the skiff back. You and the Exec. If all goes well, and I hope for your sake it does, you will be back here in an hour or so."

Frick took a deep breath and released it. "You are taking us ashore as hostages," he said. "Suppose we are caught."

"I don't think that's likely," Maxwell said. "Not in this neck of the woods. This is about as deserted as you can get. You're going, Captain and so is he," Maxwell said in a stern tone, "or this boat will not be able to submerge until you get back to Lorient. You get the picture? And if I have to go to that much trouble, I won't give a damn if you make it or not. Just between you and me, I'm still going through with my end of the bargain. I spent all this time learning. I intend to give back in return what I was sent here to do."

This time it was Frick who spoke in a calm, even tone. "I cannot understand you at all," he said, taking off his cap, "Do you realize what you have done, Maxwell? You killed three of my men, and you are still working for our side. You nearly make me laugh. Personally, I think you are crazy. Like I told you, they will be coming after you and your friend here. They will not be asking for explanations."

Maxwell interrupted. "Frick, I may be nuts or crazy but I made my choice, and until they make their move to do what you think, I intend to carry out my mission. Can you understand that?"

"Nein, I cannot. You are a traitor to the Third Reich, and you are a traitor to the United States."

Maxwell broke this off.

"Shutup and move it. Topside now," Maxwell said.

The Captain got on the horn and issued the order that all hands were to stay below and that the forward and aft hatches were to remain closed.

While Maxwell guarded the prisoners in the control room, Thibadeaux carried their gear topside.

Thibadeaux had taken their seaman bags, the suitcase, a compass, canteens and four days rations. Maxwell then sent the machine gun up with Richard. This done, he brandished the pistol and motioned to the ladder.

Danet climbed the ladder, and moved out onto the bridge. The Captain followed, then Maxwell. Thibadeaux was waiting on the bridge with the machine gun, which he handed to Maxwell.

"Richard," Maxwell said, "you and the Exec. go down and get the inflatable out, get it ready, and we'll join you. Don't take all night."

As the two men complied, Maxwell and the Captain stood in silence, Maxwell watching first the forward hatch, then the aft. The boat rocked gently.

When the boat had been taken to the surface, Hagermeister, wearing only a sweat-soaked undershirt and shorts, started making his way aft.

With the faint red light shining in his face, he had crept to the control room hatch and heard the entire conversation when Maxwell explained his plans to get ashore.

Not only had Maxwell's plan thrown him off, but the Captain had also passed the order that no one was to go topside. If he tried rushing the control room, there was no certainty that he could successfully get the two Americans without creating a dangerous situation for the Captain. When the shooting started, he knew that more than one of the crew would get in the line of fire. He stood motionless, pondering his dilemma. His original plan had been to wait until they were in the inflatable, then let them get some distance from the boat, and shoot a hole in the raft.

Since there was no way the Americans could hold onto the machinegun and stay afloat, he could easily dispatch them.

Now what could he do? If he went topside, it would be insubordination, and he wanted no part of that. He would have to wait and see if a chance presented itself. As soon as he heard the four men climb the ladder, he stepped into the control room. The crew looked at him, all the stunned faces in the red light, but no one spoke. He waited until he heard the four men climb down from the bridge. The pistol in hand, he slowly started climbing the ladder. When he reached the top, he could hear them getting into the boat. He lay flat and looked out of the drain holes of the bridge. They were entering the boat, getting ready to cast off.

He could not take a chance as long as the Captain and the Exec. were with the Americans. He lay there, watching helplessly. The inflatable moved away and headed for shore.

Danet and Frick were ordered to start rowing.

Maxwell kept his eye on U-168. He saw nothing that aroused his suspicion.

U-168 in the darkness, sitting lean and black in the gently rocking water, looked the same as when he had first seen her that night off the Louisiana coast. As they rowed, the boat's silhouette got lower, and soon she was only a vague line in the darkness.

He could not help but wonder what would happen to the crew, if any would survive the war.

They headed for the beach, which by their calculations was five miles away. The night was moonless, and the only light were the stars. Behind the beach was the thick wood of tall, thin pines.

The Captain and Danet did not speak. Maxwell and Thibadeaux had the pistols trained on them as they rowed. Within two hours they saw the white lines of waves, breaking on the beach.

The inflatable ran aground just a few feet from shore. Maxwell and Thibadeaux jumped into the water. The machine gun was heavy as Maxwell held it over his head. He walked ahead while Thibadeaux pulled the boat onto the beach.

It took Maxwell a short time to get rid of his sea legs. Thibadeaux grabbed the suitcase.

At the feel of land under his feet, Maxwell felt elated, suddenly energetic. It was nearly over.

"You two get out," Maxwell said in a stern voice. "We're going for a little walk up the beach."

The Captain and Danet hesitated, looked at each other, then finally climbed out of the skiff.

"Start walking this way, Captain," Maxwell said, pointing the gun north.

Maxwell grabbed the rest of the supplies with one hand.

They began walking in the giving sand. The sea roared to their right.

Thibadeaux was behind the two Germans with Maxwell behind him.

"Where are we going?" the Captain asked, his voice slightly atremble.

"Up the beach a ways," Maxwell said.

To the left the woods were a silent, black wall. After a few minutes of walking, Maxwell said, "Let's stop here. Both of you turn around."

Danet's knees buckled as he turned.

"Captain, we leave you here," Maxwell said. "Go back to your boat. As ridiculous as this might sound, I hope there is no animosity between us." Maxwell felt foolish even as he said this.

The Captain's eyes twitched back and forth, then leveled at Maxwell. He spoke with authority.

"You know I have to report this," he said.

"Yes."

"I will try to make them understand," Frick continued, "but they will not, I promise you."

"Maybe, maybe not," Maxwell said. "Anyway, what's done can't be undone. Captain, Mr. Danet, I hope you get out safely. And give my regards to the Admiral. I suppose he'll think we're a disappointment. We still intend to do what we trained for. Just tell them to watch for something along the Gulf coast."

"Ja, good luck," said Frick, who suddenly felt an unexplainable empathy.

"Good luck."

With that, Maxwell and Thibadeaux headed inland. The Captain and the Exec. turned and started trotting back to the inflatable.

Within minutes the Captain and the Exec. were in the skiff and on their way back to U-168. Soon they were aboard.

"Turn this boat around and head out fast," Frick said to the startled helmsman. "Our luck cannot hold all night."

The engineer responded, and the U-168 was soon headed for deep water.

Frick sent for the report and scribbled an addendum, reporting what had happened on the beach. Hans, the radio man, stood by and watched the Captain until he finished writing.

"As soon as we get past the bank," Frick ordered, "get in touch with headquarters and give them this report."

Frick was solemn as he handed Hans the written message. Their luck had held. U-168 was heading for safe waters. Everyone relaxed.

Within two hours the radio operator had made the report. Headquarters acknowledged, with no comment.

When Frick heard the acknowledgement of the report and the silence that followed, he could see it all. He felt a sudden pity for the Americans. Knowing what the silence meant, he already saw the bureaucratic wheels turning. He knew that bureaucrats only were capable of certain mechanistic responses; no emotion involved, only the proper and correct response. It would take a little time for the wheels to grind out the inevitable result, but Frick knew they had started with their characteristic and implacable efficiency.

As Maxwell and Thibadeaux walked inland, they did not speak. For hours they moved cautiously through the pines, through the reeds and patches of stagnant water. It was dawn when they reached U.S. 301.

The morning had that subtle, gray quality as the first light filtered in, and Maxwell felt a brief chill. They walked north. Each time a car came along, they would leave the road until it passed, then resume their trek north.

Just after they had left the beach area, Maxwell had hidden the machine gun at the bottom of a pool of water. He put the P-38 under his shirt. Thibadeaux kept the 45 ACP while Maxwell carried the suitcase.

They saw few houses as they walked, and no one approached them or paid any attention to them.

Close to noon they came into Nahunta, a small, sleepy Georgia town.

They turned west and headed for Waycross, arriving before dark.

They had a meal of fried chicken, mashed potatoes, lima beans, biscuits, gravy, and coffee. Each man bought two full meals.

The sight of the pretty blonde waitress in her white apron, the warmth of the coffee, the sound of the radio as it cranked out the country music--all this appeared fantastic to Maxwell. The meal nearly put both men asleep right at the table, but they managed to force themselves on.

They made their way to the bus station, catching the bus to Atlanta. They slept most of the way. None of the passengers took any particular notice of these two men, except for one fat, old woman, who had the seat directly across the aisle. She could not help but notice the smell.

CHAPTER 8

November 1, 1942

One hundred and twenty miles south of Berlin, in a bare forest, sat an old, gray-stoned castle. With gables and spires on the front gate, the castle served as a country manor. Once past the frozen moat and on the interior of the inner building's great wooden door, all signs of the Middle Ages disappeared, as the interior had been refurbished, according to modern fashion.

A man sat in the study.

The fire still burned invitingly near the large schrank. The man finished tidying up around the room, took the last drag from a cigarette, smashed the butt in the ash tray, then emptied the tray in a nearby waist basket. He picked up the basket and met Rolf, his chief house servant, at the study door. Only he and Rolf had keys to the study as no one else was allowed admittance.

"You know the staff car is waiting, sir," Rolf said, a graying old gentleman from lower Saxony.

"Of course, thank you," the man said as he handed Rolf the waste basket. "Here, dump this for me, will you? And don't bother to put it back. I am locking up."

"Very well, sir," Rolf said without surprise, for he knew the master would never allow even the smallest bit of cleaning in his study while he was gone. "Your baggage and coat are in the parlor," Rolf said.

"Thank you."

The master surveyed the study, which he had just tidied up. He had hardly been back from his last assignment long enough to mess the room up properly, he told himself. Oh well, he shrugged, a month is more than most get.

He glanced casually at the large painting as he locked the door. He had painted the picture himself and was quite proud of it. The picture would not have elicited such a casual glance from most, since it had a striking effect. And as the door of the study closed, the flames in the fireplace ran up the walls in orange scales and bathed the painting in flickering color.

The painting had a dark blue background. The central figure of the picture was a single skull, viewed from the side, and smiling with its hollow eyes and clenched teeth. In the top of the skull, piercing what would have been the brain, was a dagger. On the dagger were the twin lightning symbols, engraved in gold, displayed on both the very top and sides of the handle. Above the entire visage and dagger were larger twin lightning symbols in brilliant red. Below the skull were the words, which the artist had rendered crimson, in the effect of blood: "Ein Mitglied die Gruppe Erschossen."

The man walked into the large parlor, threw his coat over his arm, put on his hat, and grabbed his suitcase.

"Here, allow me," said a uniformed German near the door. This was the driver of the staff car, who apparently had taken it upon himself to wait out of the cold. The driver was dressed in a military blouse and trousers of heavy wool, in the olive green issue of the Wehrmacht.

"Thank you," said the master, as out of habit he removed his hat again in order to put on his overcoat. The master yelled across the parlor at a young girl in a black and white maid's uniform.

"Louka, yes, you girl, you will attend to the terrace properly from now on. Did Rolf tell you?"

"Yes sir, I'm sorry, sir," said the young girl with an edge of flirtation in her voice. She knew the master was a stickler for cleanliness, and she took no offense.

"See you soon," the master said.

As the driver approached to get the suitcase, he got a full view of the master, Otto Koler. He was thirty-three, stood approximately six feet two inches, and weighed one hundred and seventy pounds. His combed-back blonde hair, which looked nearly white in the morning light, set off his tight facial features. His handsome mouth was full below a stern nose and brilliant blue eyes. The man had at once the look of intelligence, yet there was a different look, that added to the overall impression. Perhaps it was the way the jaw muscles worked slightly, tightening the sinews on his face. He was dressed in a black uniform, which fit tightly over his prominent muscles. But most of all, the driver decided, the main impression came from one of the master's eyes. So alert was the gaze from those eyes at all that they touched, that the left eye was opened slightly wider all the time than seemed necessary.

The driver had seen these kind before. The handsome face etched an impression, which vacillated between a look of refined taste to that of controlled rage. On the master's collar were the twin lightning symbols of the SS.

The man put on his overcoat and hat. "Are you ready, driver?"

"Jawohl, herr Obersturmfuhrer."

"We will not stand on formalities."

The master said his farewells to his household, and the two men stepped out into the cold. The car motor was still running, and but for a thin layer of snow which had just fallen, the road seemed clear. They drove over the frozen moat and through the huge, iron gate to the black-spiked wall, which surrounded the manor.

"Be careful," Koler said to the driver. "This is probably the most dangerous leg of our journey right here."

He was referring to the narrow road, which ran along a twelve foot bank with the bare forest below on both sides of them. Once they crossed the little stone bridge and got to a normal level, Koler would feel better. He took one last look at home, straining his eyes to see the snow-swept vineyards, which he longed to work in the Spring.

Koler arrived in Berlin and secured a room at the Hotel Fuerstenhof, the city's most celebrated establishment. The day was cold and icy, and the night dark, since the burning of excessive night lights had been forbidden. The token raids of the British Tommies filled the air with the sound of screaming sirens and, in general, played havoc on Berlin's once famous night life. The Kurfuerstendamm, where Koler liked to dine, was not the same. He retired early to his room and spent a restless night in his hotel. His appointment was the next morning at 0900.

November 2, 1942

At the office of Obergruppenfuhrer Barbie von Heine in RSHA headquarters, Amt 6, which was the SD's division of foreign intelligence, Otto Koler reported promptly at 0900. Heine, a plump, unassuming sort, nodded as Koler entered and threw his arm to the ceiling. Heine, his eyes half-open, duplicated the gesture with equal flair before both men relaxed in the two leather chairs on either side of the desk.

"Congratulations on your last assignment Herr Koler," Heine said, as he pulled out a cigarette. "How did you like Greece?"

"It was fine," Koler said, whose widened eye and half smile, that lurked constantly around his mouth, gave him a look of arrogance. "The weather is a bit more favorable than here."

"Ja, you fellows are lucky in that respect, but I'm afraid you must go to a bit of a colder climate this time."

"Colder than here?" Koler said, already picturing Russia.

"Nein, nein, not at all," Heine laughed. "Here are the dossiers." As Koler flipped through the dossiers, Heine studied his face.

Otto Koler was a confirmed Nazi. He had been in the SD and was promoted to the SS as an Obersturmfuhrer before his transfer to Amt 6. During the six years since he had received his dagger of Blood and Honor, he had been trained thoroughly in the art of killing. He had become one of the elite men of Der Gruppen Erschossen. Unlike many of what he called the butchers of the concentration camps, he viewed his job as one of much more finesse and style. His brand of killing was cleaner and required the skills of an artisan, rather than a hatchet man. Der Gruppen Erschossen had been especially trained to do one job. They were to execute enemies of the Third Reich.

Heine watched the man. Koler, in his early thirties, was strong, mentally alert, and fast. He was a crack shot, a skilled knife man, and knew many methods of poisoning. Over the last few months he had disposed of two double agents in Greece and one in North Africa. His earliest assignment went as far back as 1935, when a suspected traitor of Rohm's former SA had been found one evening, slumped in his favorite tavern with a bullet placed neatly through his temple.

Koler finished the dossiers, which contained names, photos, habits, descriptions, home addresses, and preferences of the two subjects. He had read rapidly, but could study them more thoroughly in the days to come. He tossed them back onto the desk.

Heine leaned forward. "You are to depart by plane in two days for Lisbon. From there you will be transported to Argentina, work your way north into Mexico, and slip across the border into the United States. With your fluent English, you can easily pass as an American. Here are the details of your orders," he said, tossing him another envelope. "Commit them to memory and destroy them before your departure in the usual manner. No weapons will be necessary in transport.

You can easily acquire whatever you need in the United States. All forms of weapons are available there. You will report to this office tomorrow to obtain the necessary funds and further briefing. Any questions?"

"Ja," Koler said, as he leaned back in his chair and smiled. "This looks like more of a job for say......Winetrop. How vital are these two subjects?"

Heine flushed. "Koler, I am surprised at you. We are now at the beginning of the thousand year Reich. These two men are security risks and......"

Koler looked quickly to the ceiling and back down in exasperation before interrupting his commander.

"Herr Obergruppenfuhrer, the Captain of the boat indicated they are still loyal."

"Koler," Heine shouted.

"Jawohl," Koler said briskly, as if snapping out of a trance.

"These two men have insulted the Reich, killed three of our men, two of which were SD agents. They forced one of our U boats into unsafe waters and forced the Captain and the Executive Officer ashore. They spit in our faces. They cannot walk away. And in case there has been any doubt in your mind as to the importance of this assignment, rest assured that the matter has even been called to the attention of the Reichsfuhrer. Apparently the Abwehr will not be allowed to bungle another operation of this sort in the future. The end of the road is near for those incompetents. So your mission has elements of political importance as well. Need I be more explicit?"

"Nein, mein Obergruppenfuhrer," Koler said briskly. "Have they made any contact?"

Heine relaxed. "Not as yet. It is all in the dossiers. The contact in New York, Seawolf, is your best bet at first. And there has been no sabotage attributed to them from any of our agents. They have disappeared. Your job as always is a simple one--execute the two men, then return to Berlin as soon as possible."

"Zu befehl," Koler shouted as he leapt to attention, saluted, and left the office.

He spent the next two days obtaining further briefing and materials. He made a quick trip to Switzerland to obtain personal funds and returned to Berlin on November 5. It was a routine assignment, and he had no doubts as to its outcome. The Americans knew nothing about him, yet by the time he reached Argentina, he would know everything about them. They would never know what hit them.

November 12, 1942

At 2:14 p.m. a hydroplane landed on an inland lake in Argentina. The plane taxied over to a dock where seven small boats were tied. A man, his face bathed in the bright sunshine and wearing a great Panama hat and sun glasses, greeted the pilot and passenger. The passenger was the first to exit the plane. His face appeared snow white in the bright sunlight. A Spaniard followed, carrying the blonde man's suitcase.

"Herr Koler," the man with the Panama hat said, opening his arms wide and revealing with the gesture a substantial paunch beneath his bright red and white shirt. "How was your trip?"

The passenger did not respond to the gesture, but with a cold gleam in his wide, alert, blue eyes, stiffly put his hand into the air in the attitude of a half-hearted salute.

"The trip was fine, but tiring as usual," he said. "I am anxious to be shown my quarters." Then with a superior nod of the head, he took the suitcase from the pilot and started towards the large, white house on the bank.

On reaching the house, the Spaniard was paid handsomely and the two men drove in a jeep to the neighboring village. They drove past the lazy fruit stands of the town. The host ventured only token conversation. They arrived at a shabby hotel across the street from a tavern.

Miffed at the stranger's cool attitude, the man in the Panama hat handed Koler his key and wished him a good night's rest. "I will meet you promptly at nine a.m. when you will fly out."

"Thank you," Koler said, as he exited the vehicle, at the same time bestowing upon his host a rare smile-- a smile disjointed from the placid, blue eyes. "Please do not be late."

"It is not my habit to be late, Herr Koler," the miffed driver said, and as soon as he said it and saw the white flicker in the blue eyes, he regretted his statement, felt a small pang of fear, and hurriedly drove off.

Koler walked through the shabby lobby and up the stairs to his hovel of a room. He locked the door, distastefully inhaled the stale smell of his quarters and threw his suitcase onto the bed.

He was dressed modestly, wearing gabardine pants and a white, short sleeved shirt. He took a deep breath, sighed, lit a cigarette, and opened his suitcase. The suitcase was not full. On top of neatly folded civilian clothes were the two dossiers which he had studied on the trip from Portugal. He would have plenty of time to study them further on his flight to Mexico tomorrow. He tossed the folders on a bedside table, along with a change of shirt and pants. He then took out the Bausch and Lombe rifle scope, which had been atop the stacks of American currency. The scope represented a mild disobedience, since he had been instructed to obtain all necessary weapons in America.

He was sentimentally attached to his scope since the early days. He told himself that it represented an easily explainable item, especially with the absence of an attendant gun, and he shrugged at the thought of this slight deviation from orders. He felt again that he was an artist and deserved his small indulgences. The Bausch and Lomb was the best scope in the world, and he was a man used to the finest accoutrements in all facets of his craft.

When he had changed his clothes, he looked at his watch, put his cigarettes in his pocket (he had already begun smoking American Lucky Strikes) and walked into the hall. From the lobby he called for a cab.

A taxi arrived an hour later and drove him to Peron, a town some thirty miles away. They pulled up in front of a small bank where Koler entered, and after a lengthy discussion with the president, whom he had contacted through an anonymous correspondence, made a deposit of 26,000 dollars cash, under the name of Simon Ballard.

Because the anonymous correspondence from Switzerland had contained a handsome stipend, the bank president was only too happy to open such an account, along with all the necessary guarantees of confidentiality.

After the drive back, Koler tipped the cab driver, climbed the steps to his room, and ignoring his hunger, took a short nap. His first thought, on waking, was his suitcase. He could not help but check and see if everything was intact. Relieved at finding all in order, he decided to wash up and have dinner in the tavern across the street.

As he again left his room, he felt a pang of guilt.

The Reich had given him everything, it was true, and he told himself that his allegiance to the great Fuhrer was still unquestionably intact. What he did with his private funds, he told himself, was his own business. But as he ordered his meal of enchiladas and beer, he knew that he was merely deceiving himself.

The deposit is easily explained, he thought, if there was ever a temporary setback, the Order must survive for the future. It is only a question of being thorough.

This was the way he rationalized the removal of an amount of currency from his Swiss account and his plan to open smaller accounts in places, where he might someday affect an escape.

He smiled at the waitress, a small, buxom girl with beautiful black hair and shining eyes. She had a full mouth and that easy beauty of so many Spanish girls. Her skin was the deep tan that looked to Koler like the woman he had had in Greece. There was something he had begun to relish in the deep, caramel tones of skin. He simply had not been able to help himself. And like in Africa where he had taken a Negress, he looked on these small indiscretions, at least in the Order's eyes, as small deviations from the norm, something which he richly deserved, and a mere part of his handsome collection of tasteful indulgences, much like the attachment to his Bausch and Lombe scope.

"Thank you very much, pretty lady," he said with a charming smile. The woman's smile lit him up as he spoke in broken Spanish to her and slipped five pesos under her tray. He intended to have her, and he was rarely disappointed.

As he ate, he continually wiped his mouth with his napkin. He never could stand the slightest trace of food on his face, no matter how ravenous his hunger. He sat for hours and watched the inhabitants come and go. He studied the girl and sampled the local rum.

As he sat, he thought grimly of his bank deposit and after weighing each detail, decided that he was right in his actions. After all, things were reaching crisis proportions in the East.

In trying to capture the oil fields near Rostov, Hitler had stripped the Sixth Army of all its reserves at Stalingrad.

Winter had come for the Wehrmacht. Infantry regulars were dying daily in the bombed-out city, and it was rumored that soon they might be eating horseflesh.

The Fuhrer will think of something, he thought automatically.

Koler, always unquestionably loyal, was also one of the most intelligent, elite, and cultivated beings on earth. So he had been taught from youth and so he believed. This belief carried with it an air of infallibility in his every thought and action. Besides, he knew for a fact that many of his comrades had already planned escape routes. He would fight to the end to preserve a better Germany, but there was no harm in taking precautions.

He shrugged the thought off and lit another cigarette.

The hours passed quickly as Koler relaxed and indulged himself several drinks. It was not his habit to drink in this manner, but he found himself taken with the girl. Her large flashing eyes and full body took different dimensions with every passing moment, and he soon convinced himself that she was a necessity. He thought little about his mission, and when his mind wandered to it, he thought of it only fleetingly, with the same detachment, that a man on holiday thinks of the mundane worries of his business.

The outcome would be the same as it always had been. It was merely a matter of time and planning. And since he was still far away from America, he felt with his third after-dinner rum as if he were on holiday.

He had begun to watch the girl now with a wide, boyish gaze, as if in his flickering eyes he were suppressing the most eloquent secret. A smile lurked around his handsome features every time she looked at him. It was a technique he had often used. And remarkably enough it had worked for him many times in the past, that is, the exercise of communicating with a woman one's desire, merely with a fixed, adoring gaze. There could be no mistake in his intentions, and he loved the exercise, seeing in it a beautiful assertion of the will.

By ten o'clock the tavern was half-full. Three men were singing to a guitar across the room.

The technique was working. Each time the girl waited on Koler's table, her features became more animated; so much so, that on one occasion Koler even boldly reached up, took her fingers with his own gentle touch, and with the attitude of a connoisseur, delicately taking a first sip of vintage wine, put her fingers to his lips in the manner of a Frenchman.

One of the men, a short man with a beard, who had been singing with the guitar, took offense, and spoke in rapid Spanish to his friends. Koler noticed him gazing now in obvious hatred at him, but he paid the little man no attention and continued to enjoy himself with his worshipful gaze.

Finally, the little Argentinean apparently could stand no more. Whether he was the girl's husband or boyfriend, Koler did not know, but with a drunken swagger, the little man strode up to Koler's table, followed by two of his friends.

When Koler rose to face the three men, he stood nearly a full head taller than the little man, who gazed balefully into his widened eyes.

The little man still held a drink in his hand as he spoke.

"You go back where you come from, gringo."

The little man's face was now only inches from Koler's chin. The little man saw the blue eyes lose their sparkle as a cold, murky look came over them, seeming vacant and deadly.

The talking in the tavern stopped. Koler looked as if in his tightening jaw muscles he would spit directly into the little man's face. The Argentinean felt a cold sensation when the "gringo" suddenly turned on his heels and walked out of the tavern.

As he hit the door, Koler felt liquid from a drink splash on his back.

"Run gringo," the little man shouted after him.

Koler paused briefly, started to turn, and then contemplating his discipline, strode evenly out of the tavern and across the street to his hotel.

He cursed himself for this ridiculous breech of discipline and vowed that such an occurrence would not happen again.

The next day he was taxied to an airfield near Peron where he boarded a twin engine plane. His host still wore the Panama hat and was more affable on Koler's departure. The pilot of the plane was a Brazilian in his mid-thirties, who had shoulder length hair and sported a proud, black beard. He insisted on making sure that Koler was unarmed before allowing him to board the plane.

The plane glided over the great grasslands of Argentina due north. Neither the pilot nor Koler spoke. Koler opened one of the two dossiers as he glanced briefly at the pilot.

At least this man is a professional, he thought, these mercenaries are all the same.

The plane stopped to refuel three times.

The hours passed slowly as they glided over the purple peaks in Bolivia, the southern, uninhabitable bush of Brazil, and night falling in its regal, deep blue velvet over southern Colombia. The darkness overcame the landscape before the sea at the coastal town of Buenaventura where they landed and spent the night.

Koler had passed the time during the flight in different ways. First, he amused himself by drawing sketches of his two victims in light pencil. Before getting down to business with the dossiers, he had taken advantage of the silence and scenery to mull over several conflicting thoughts he had suddenly acquired about his mission. Something inexplicably vague was gnawing at him from beneath the surface. Something which made Koler doubt himself.

This mission had a different flavor. It represented the first time the SD had finished an Abwehr operation. Koler's previous assignments had been confined to subjects which had been from the first to the last SD projects, usually involving purges of undesirable elements within the SD itself--as in the case of the double agents in both Africa and Greece. These men betrayed the Order herself. Koler's assignments had been in the nature of a top secret purge within the SS, with specific instructions never to break the vow of silence, regarding these missions, to anyone outside the Order.

The unprecedented nature of this mission was precisely what puzzled Koler, and whereas he understood intellectually why he had been chosen for this mission, he could not accept it emotionally. The men he had hunted in the past had been killers of sorts, and while not as skilled as himself, familiar with the ways of the sacred Order--traitors not so much to the Reich as to the SS. Koler told himself that anyone could have been chosen for this mission. It was simply too easy. Militarily, it could not in any way be viewed as vital, and given the recent Allied invasion of North Africa and the increasingly critical situation in the East, Koler knew instinctually that his talents could have been more aptly used. This was what annoyed him. He knew he was the best among the best of Die Grouppen Erschossen, and the fact that his superiors had chosen him strictly as an instrument to insure a victory in a political infight, bothered him.

Since their inception as intelligence organizations, the Abwehr and the SD had been at quiet odds for the forefront of power in the Third Reich. The SD had acquired information in early 1941 that the Abwehr was making overtures for peace through the Vatican. Since that revelation, the SD slowly infiltrated every facet of the Abwehr, although the assassination of Heydrich had temporarily slowed the process.

But by the fall of 1942, only a matter of days prior to Koler's assignment, further discredit fell on the Abwehr. RSHA headquarters found that Abwehr agents in Czechoslovakia were being paid with counterfeit money. Further tracings of the money led to Wilhelm Canaris and further confirmed that Canaris was trying to negotiate covertly for peace with the Allies.

For some time now the Abwehr had been resisting unification with the SD under the new RSHA. With the recent assassination of Heydrich by Allied agents, it had appeared that the Abwehr could maintain its integrity. But the Czechoslovakian scandal proved to be the beginning of the end. It would finally lead to the disintegration of the Abwehr entirely, and the Wehrmacht would be the only army in the world without its own military intelligence organization.

The U-168 incident along with the Abwehr's failures regarding the Amagansett arrests were only further feathers in the SD's caps. Although originally conceived by Admiral Doenitz, Canaris had tried repeatedly to take credit for the Kaninchen operations. But the SD had kept its agents poised to monitor the performance of the Abwehr in these operations. Fritz Rosenberg and Hans Steinhoff had been two such agents. Their mission had been to report to SD headquarters the status of Abwehr performance.

As Koler read through the dossiers further, he had begun to articulate his doubts regarding his personal involvement in these matters. For years he had viewed his job as the most desirable among any in the sacred Order. He was the purger, the reckoning force within the entire organization. In many ways he was the most feared member in the bureau. His missions were carried out in the privacy of the various reaches of the world and without anyone looking directly over his shoulder. But given the nature of his recent financial activities, especially the deposit he had made in Peron, he began to analyze his own actions, and for the first time since he could remember, he began to doubt, however silently, the correctness of his mission and his Order.

The activities of the Abwehr and the Vatican disturbed him deeply. He knew the Generals of the Wehrmacht had always been men of impeccable honor, and he had always freely stated this to any of his brothers in the Order of the Death's Head, no matter how vehemently they disagreed. Koler, like so many others in the German hierarchy, seriously doubted the wisdom in allowing Hitler to head the decision-making of the Wehrmacht. Whereas Germany had been successful enough so far, the concept of a two front war seemed to be pointing to fatal ends. Everything hung in the balance in Russia. Stalingrad was being contested in thousands of lives in a fight, which had reached staggering proportions.

Koler had silently harbored doubts as to the wisdom of the Resettlement Program regarding the Jews, which had been turned to the activities of Einsatzgrouppen. And even more ominous were the Anti-slavic policies in Russia, which had declared the Slavs as sub humans. Like so many others, Koler believed that if the Germans had recruited Russians to fight against the Communist regime, that victory in the East would be assured. But the advent of the extermination camps and the untermenschen program put forth by Himmler had inflamed the Russian people. The Russians were fighting with fury and aided by the icy landscape, were mounting a formidable defense which could amount to a complete German disaster.

Koler snorted. And with all this at stake, he thought, I am to be the silent instrument of some petty, internal squabble.

It hurt Koler to think in these terms. Like all of the members of the Order, the blind obedience to Adolf Hitler, "the greatest brain of all time" was the first and last rule. How beautiful had been the abandonment of the earliest days to that great sense of historical paganism, of biological theory and of the great campaign of justice and salvation of the Fatherland. Where had such a great dream stumbled?

Koler shivered and with the resolve that no matter what, his Fuhrer's orders would be honored, turned his attention to his two "subjects." In the cold enactment of his lonely craft, Otto Koler would find his solace. He was not like the butchers at Dacchau and Riga. His was the job of a cleanly skilled crafts-man. He plunged himself into his job with blind joy and the beautiful abandonment of obedience.

The next day dawned clear over Buenaventura. Koler rose, ate a breakfast of bananas and oranges, with coconut sprinkled over them, and sat on a terrace overlooking the sea. He wore sun glasses and a casual shirt and light weight pants. Even from the brief morning exposure to the sun his skin had already acquired a reddish tint. He finished the coffee, tipped the pretty waitress and met the Brazilian mercenary in the lobby. As always, the dark-haired man went through the formalities of searching Koler on the abandoned airfield, spoke only tersely, and to the admiration of the passenger, concerned himself with a Spartan duty to the intricacies of the machinery.

The plane glided over the deep blue sea, enroute to Mexico. Soon all land had disappeared and the illusion of stillness took over. Koler felt somehow relieved, rid of all the previously confusing thoughts concerning the constant fluctuations of inner-party politics, and turned his thoughts to the purity of his two subjects--two men who would be insignificant casualties to the vast maze of political machinery, in which every man on earth had become a part.

He opened the first dossier.

With typical German efficiency the various details of both men's lives had been compiled through the contact in New York with amazing clarity. His first subject, Richard Thibadeaux, was typical of many of Koler's previous assignments. A gullible fool, Koler thought. Born in the Cajun sections of New Orleans, he had moved with his family to New Jersey when he was 16 years old. In Newark Thibadeaux's history had been one of a street kid, who after the death of his father in a union dispute, had become a typical, big city thug. He had been jailed twice on minor assault and battery charges before discovering, after a construction job, a propensity for explosives. A number of arson plots had been credited to him, according to Seawolf, the last of which failed due to a breach in security with one of his accomplices. While in jail, his employers, either out of fear or a sense of duty, attended to his material needs and even managed to arrange a type of pension for him after his release. Thibadeaux had served three years with early probation for good behavior. He had been married once and divorced. His favorite hobbies were gambling on horses and an occasional trip to his neighborhood brothel. One thing, which was obviously lacking in his dossier, was any list of current friends or local habits. He had come out of prison and begun immediately his activities as a sabotage trainee for the German American Bund. Thus, the only contacts he had were with Maxwell and Seawolf, otherwise known as Frank Becken. Koler felt that if Thibadeaux were apart from Maxwell now, which he doubted, he would be difficult to find, but it would merely take time. Either he would eventually visit his mother in Newark or begin gambling again. Thibadeaux seemed a self-destructive creature of habit, like so many of the thugs Koler had liquidated in the past. These thugs were entirely predictable in their gullibility, in their insistence on remaining on the bottom rungs of society.

During all the time he studied Thibadeaux's file, Koler's expression had not changed. Etched on his face was the expression of bored professionalism, like that of an examining physician.

But when he turned to the dossier of Tommy Maxwell, his eyes took a sparkle of keen interest.

Unlike Thibadeaux, Koler had been surprised to find that Tommy Maxwell not only was an educator, but was entirely middle class, and prior to his petty bookmaking business in 1939, he was without a criminal record. In fact, nothing in his dossier pointed towards anything other than typical American naivete. Although the family was rural, his father had been an educated man, had graduated with high marks from high school and was middle class. His mother was an alienated sort, but no more than many middle class women, who bore their silent resignation to staying married to one man and raising a family during the Depression. The Depression had touched them, as it had everyone, but given their farm as an economic base, it had not damaged them as much as most. Tommy's siblings had typical histories. His habits of hunting and partaking in sports--especially collegiate wrestling and tennis proved him a man of renaissance interests. Details concerning a sort of religious rebellion were mentioned only vaguely. And Koler found Maxwell's sudden leave-taking of the teaching profession and his appearance in the Bund extraordinary. Perhaps due to a romantic, suppressed notion of drifting, he had suddenly acted in this manner. Americans were the drifting sort. And the charge of moral turpitude by the Murphy principal, which Seawolf had mentioned, did not satisfy Koler's curiosity. The man was a student of history.

Could he have been approached by the FBI to penetrate the Bund? All evidence pointed to the contrary. Amazingly enough, even after the daring and successful mutiny, which this young crusader had pulled off, he had told the Captain that he was still loyal. Was it possible that this man had seen in Adolf Hitler the same great vision that Koler had seen? Certainly with the differences in their nationalities, Maxwell's zeal for the German dream could not have been as strong or taken the same force.

Koler decided that Maxwell was simply an idealist, a romantic idiot, who through the naivete of so many Americans in thinking they can save the world, had acted here, there, forever drifting and searching, and when confronted with Steinhoff and Rosenberg, had moved both out of paranoia and a muddled sense of morality. Above all, he had been very lucky.

An uneasy feeling in Koler's chest fluttered each time he read the Captain's report of Maxwell's actions aboard the U-168. Koler knew that the men of the SS were the most vicious collection of killers in the world. Although the death of the gunner's mate was almost accidental, Maxwell had later shown presence of mind and an unhesitating instinct for killing.

At last Koler began to sum up Tommy Maxwell. His pacifism was like that of so many men, merely an avoidance from their real natures. Maxwell's propensity for hunting and his activities as a wrestling coach had been the expressions of a subliminal instinct which Koler believed existed in all men-- the instinct of animal survival and the love of the taste of blood. The Germans were great believers in instinct.

The details concerning the whereabouts of Maxwell's former fiancée, Elaine Cory, and his live-in companion Julie Miller were complete enough. Unlike Thibadeaux, Koler felt less disinterested about Maxwell. He was glad the element of surprise was on his side. As always, he would take no chances and would be ruthless.

As he closed the dossiers and looked over the sea, he wondered about many things. He mused over the possible fate of U-168, which was assigned to the waters near the Bahamas. He thought for a time how incredible it was that he was staring at the beautiful jewels of sunlight, which danced off the deep blue waves, while his brothers were busy on the Eastern front.

Probably hanging deserters or killing helpless Jews, he thought with a bitter expression, looking as he had at the tavern two nights before, as if he were going to spit.

As time passed, the rolling bush of Panama passed beneath him; yet another feeling intruded into the usually clinical mind of Otto Koler--the insult the two Americans had heaped on his country. They had killed three Germans, two of whom were brothers of the Order. Such an infraction would not be tolerated.

And yet as the plane made its way into the Mexican mainland, peaks here, deserts there, decrepit little towns every hundred miles or so with their tangles of fruit stands and the inevitable huts and of course, the central building of the Catholic church, Koler was besieged by more ambiguous thoughts about his mission. He was going to kill two Americans, who were still possibly working for Germany. The Reich needed all the help she could get; and what, besides revenge, was the use in such a mission?

A security risk, came the inevitable answer. But no matter how many times Koler thought this, still he was not convinced. There was not now, to speak of, any German espionage in America, and very little sabotage. Seawolf had many things to answer for. Why could the Americans not be spared and allowed time to carry out their mission?

Koler shrugged violently and lit a cigarette. He could not understand the reactions he was having. He had never been besieged by so many doubts. He silently cursed himself, chastised his leaning to interpret his orders, and with a renewed sense of obedience, decided that he would blindly carry out his assignment. He was convinced that the statement that Frick had reported: "watch for something on the Gulf Coast" had been a diversionary tactic by Maxwell. The Gulf was the last place they would be.

First, he would go to the heart of the matter. He would pay Frank Becken a visit. He told himself that the Americans not only deserved to die, they were already dead, as a matter of course, whether they deserved it or not.

Koler spent the rest of the flight, sketching in pencil the visage of Tommy Maxwell on a scratch pad. He drew mainly to pass the time, but like his Fuhrer, he had always dreamed of being an artist. He felt his painting exhibited talent. If only he had more time to work.

The plane landed at Saltillo, Mexico where Koler made contact with a Raoul, who provided him with an automobile with Texas tags. Koler spent the night in Saltillo, drove north into the next day through Monterey, Nuevo Loredo, and crossed the border into the United States at Loredo.

Before leaving Saltillo, Koler, who possessed a talent for mechanics, had managed to wire his Bausch and Lombe scope underneath the car.

The border guard had not even checked his baggage.

He spent the night in Houston, drove the next day to St. Louis, and arrived in New York city four days later.

At four o'clock on the afternoon of November 21. Koler drove through the Lincoln tunnel, heading into New York City. The bus passed a light blue Chevrolet heading the opposite way. In the car were two men--Tommy Maxwell and Richard Thibadeaux.

CHAPTER 9

I sick of Atlanta, Tommy, sick, babe. Let's go home, back to New York, Jersey. We can get jobs as tackers. We'll do one job, blow a ship, and disappear for good. Maybe Canada, babe.

And all the time he talks, I marvel that he still wants the mission. The mission is over. As I think this, I hear myself say okay, okay, one job, then Canada. Yeah, Canada is a good idea.

November 23, 1942

Over the last two years life had frowned on Frank Becken. He had been completely underground for much of 1941, something that not only had taken its physical toll in the form of ulcers, but had cost him his job, wife and family. In February Cheryl had filed for divorce, taken the children to Connecticut, and refused to even speak with him. Most of his friends in the Bund had become disillusioned or had joined the American war effort. As for Frank, he had soured to Germany's dream of a thousand year Reich with the first rumors of Jewish concentration camps. His views had changed one hundred and eighty degrees, and he only spoke of the way he had been, just before the war, in very hushed tones of shame. It was not that he despised his old views; he still agreed in principle with the way he had thought. His real source of shame came when he thought of his family and how through his stubbornness and intellectual pride, he had caused them such pain and lost them. His every thought and action was now geared toward reconciliation with his wife and children.

He had begun to pick up his life again. He had gotten a new job, selling appliances in Morley's Hardware, and he was now seeing his children as much as he ever had when he had been married. His recent medication had helped his ulcers and with a lessening of tension, he had gotten his appetite back and was gaining weight. His cheeks again had that rosy shine underneath his wire rim glasses and merry eyes.

Predictably, when after Pearl Harbor, Germany had declared war on the United States, Frank Becken had been asked politely to leave the Michaels and Associates stock brokerage. Despite the profits and the customers, that Becken had brought in, with his I.G. Farben and Krupp accounts, his supervising broker, Jack McCallie had seen no way that the firm could afford to keep Frank on. Although Frank had expected the move that McCallie made, he had not been prepared for the harm that his reference from the brokerage would cause him in getting on with another firm. With bankruptcy and divorce staring him in the face, Becken had been forced to accept a full time position at Morley's Hardware as a sales clerk.

And so on that Monday morning at 10:00 a.m. when the first customers had begun drifting into the store (it was usually exchanges and repairs this time of day), he had not given the tall, blonde man, who was standing next to the tool display and slowly smoking a cigarette, a second thought.

Frank, always reluctant to begin the day, sighed and headed over to the customer. The customer wore brown corduroy pants and a red plaid shirt. His hair was combed straight back, and there played around his handsome features a half smile. His jaw muscles were working, as if he could barely hold in his laughter.

"Is there anything I can help you find?" Becken asked as the stranger turned to him and smiled pleasantly.

"Why yes, yes, I think there is," the man replied in a cordial tone. "Help me find Tommy Maxwell."

Becken straightened and took the look of one who had been slapped in the face.

"Did you hear me?" the man in the red shirt said, smiling again.

"Can't you guys find anything better to do than bother me?" Becken replied heatedly. "Isn't it enough that my wife and….who are you and what the hell do you want?"

The man tilted his head back and laughed. "I see, yes, you think I am from the F.B.I. Is that it?"

"Look, buddy, I don't know no Tommy Maxwell. Now, if you haven't got any business here, I suggest you leave."

Becken had turned his back to leave when the tall stranger spoke again.

"I have another suggestion, Seawolf."

Becken stopped and turned stiffly around. He craned his neck forward as if to get a better look at the man.

"Who are you?" he said in a half whisper.

"My name is Simon Ballard," the man said with a warm smile and shaking the stunned salesman's hand as if only now recognizing a lost friend.

And with the pleasant smile, he added, "Maybe it would be more convenient to talk across the street in the diner. I'll buy you coffee and rolls."

Frank started to speak, but the smiling stranger held up a hand and said: "No, no, I insist. Think nothing of it. I'll see you there in five minutes." Then he casually walked out of the store.

When the waitress saw Frank enter the diner, she waved and smiled. She knew most of the local merchants, and Frank was one of her favorites. As she saw him sit in the booth across from the handsome blonde man, she brought the coffee and apple danish which the man had ordered upon the arrival of his "guest."

"Thanks Trudy," Frank said, forcing a smile.

"You got it, handsome," the woman said.

The smile disappeared from Frank's face and without even looking at his coffee or danish, he looked into the vacant, blue eyes across the table.

"Who are you and what do you want?"

"Aren't you going to eat your danish?" the man replied in the same cordial, mocking tone.

"Look," Becken said shortly. "I know you and your kind don't have to work very hard for a living, but I'm different. I have to get back, so if you will dispense with the preliminaries..."

"As for my kind as you put it," the stranger interrupted, "it was my understanding that you were very much in the same category for many years, Mr. Becken."

"It's over," Frank said with a note of finality. "I want nothing else to do with it. I don't know who you are or what you want but......."

"I've told you what I want."

Frank took a sip of coffee. He appeared to be pondering a thought.

"Okay, supposing I admit having known a Tommy Maxwell. Why are you so anxious to find him?"

The man raised one eyebrow. "I am a friend," he said. "I want to help him."

"In what capacity?"

"He'll need help with his operations here. I have been sent to give him aid."

Becken visibly flushed. "So you are not with the F.B.I. It doesn't matter. I'm going to say this once and then be done with it. I don't know where he is. The last I heard he was leaving the country. That is as specific as I can get."

"Why has he not reported?" the man said in a severe tone. "For that matter, why have you not reported in as instructed?"

Again Frank looked at this man, as if he were now someone completely different--the blonde hair, combed back in the manner that Europeans combed their hair, oftimes without a part, unlike an American's style. And the eyes, separate in their placid blue stare from the tight facial features and the tight sinews of the jaws.

"No, you're not an American, are you?" Frank said, as if speaking to himself. "What do you want with Maxwell?"

"I told you what I want. You have not answered my questions."

Frank felt his stomach tighten. There was an element about this stranger, which gave him a cold feeling. He felt his face flush as a chill ran up and down his spine.

"Look, I've told you what I know," he said. "If I run across Maxwell some day, I'll tell him. As for my activities, you tell whoever wants to know that I'm through with it all." He lost his fear as he talked, replaced with a sudden anger.

"You thugs are all the same. It doesn't matter what government you work for. You could just as well be in the F.B.I. or one of these local jokes, who pass for gangsters. It really doesn't matter. I've learned a lot in the past few years. I know now that the world can do without you and your kind. It doesn't matter what your superiors tell you to believe. Ideology has nothing to do with it. You do what you do because you are too stupid to do anything else. You enjoy it. The sooner the world is rid of trash like you, the better off everyone will be."

"Are you quite finished?"

Frank jerked off his glasses. "Yeah, buddy, and so are you. Now get the hell out of here before I call a cop."

The assassin looked up. Trudy was apparently in the back, and as far as he could see, none of the other customers had paid any attention to the fact that they had been arguing. He stood up, slipped a two dollar bill onto the table, and again smiled cordially.

"Thank you," he said, as he casually walked out.

Koler left the diner and got into his dark blue Ford. In no particular hurry, he drove over the Jersey bridge. The traffic was steady, and he blended into the flow.

When he arrived in a suburban area in Newark, he saw a parked telephone truck in front of a small grocery. The two telephone linemen were working on a pole in front of the store. One man was looking and smiling into the sunlight as his partner shinnied down the pole.

Koler had been in New Jersey only yesterday when he had checked out the address of Richard Thibadeaux, where he had discovered that Annette Thibadeaux had left months ago with no forwarding address.

He was bothered about Frank Becken. It had not been the insults, nor did he doubt that Becken was telling the truth. He had expected these things. It was something else. Some innate sense of regard had shown in Seawolf's eyes when he had heard the name "Maxwell" mentioned. Koler told himself that he could be wrong, but he had interpreted the look as that of friendship and loyalty. Apparently Maxwell had commanded a great deal of respect in this man. Had Becken appeared totally indifferent to what had happened to Maxwell, Koler would not have taken notice, but there was an element in his instinct which had stirred him.

"I don't care what you say," said one lineman to the other. "She's a fat bitch."

"Only chubby," the other one said, laughing as he spoke.

"Fat," the other said as both men piled their equipment into the back of the truck and walked into the grocery store.

Koler looked around. No one was watching. He strolled up to the back of the truck and grabbed the standard issue Linemen's Test Set, which was cradled in a brown belt. He quickly stuck the set under his coat and got in his car.

He took the linemen's set from under his coat and threw it on the front seat.

He had noticed before, that Morley's Hardware closed at 9 p.m. so he had time to kill.

He spent the morning hours driving around the city. He reviewed the great skyline, rode on the Staten Island Ferry, and drove by the shipyards in New Jersey. His impression, while driving through New York, had been much as it had been on his trip across country. The sheer scope of the land, the mass of natural resources, and the teeming efficiency of the various industries--all this awed Koler. The entire nation was working with a fury, which would choke Europe with steel. American steel would be on the white plains of Russia to the scorched streets of France. Koler began to realize, only now, how hopeless the entire war effort was becoming. It had been a tough pill to swallow. A great dream, a great and beautiful dream, but in the face of reality, nothing more. He saw no strategy for war against this isolated paradise. No matter how naive her people, there would be no fighting her. The only possible solution would be to negotiate peace, to stall the great industrial explosion America was creating.

Koler ate an Italian meal at Guiseppi's, saw a John Wayne movie on Time Square, and just before four o'clock, in a mood of utter depression, made a visit to the Chase Manhattan Bank, where he opened an account and deposited the greatest part of his personal currency under his assumed name.

The final bank deposit represented the last leg of the struggle he had waged within himself. The trip to America had purged the last illusions from him.

Security risks indeed, he thought to himself, when he bitterly remembered the conversation with Heine. It would take a lot more of a sabotage force, than the pittance Germany had employed, to stop this mammoth war effort. His mission must be seen as it is, one of political advantage and revenge.

He spent time walking in Central Park. He came to a large knoll which caught his eye. On the side of the knoll were several artists with their easels and brushes. The sight temporarily cheered him.

He wandered around the park for three hours, spending most of his time at the pond just below the knoll. At the edge of the pond was a boat house, where couples could rent a paddle boat and travel along the edges of the pond. Koler watched the various couples. One couple in particular had found a cozy place under the overhanging trees on the far shore.

Across from the pond, just below an observation deck and the knoll, was a fountain area. Beside the fountain wound a bridle path. Koler leisurely strolled along the path as he smoked Lucky Strikes. There were places on the path that were so surrounded by trees and greenery that one would not know he was in the city.

As the light began to fail, Koler again moved below the knoll. The artists were gathering their gear and departing.

Koler could not resist climbing to the observation deck which overlooked the knoll. The landscape was bathed in orange color as the sun set. The bare trees, the pond, the fountain, the winding bridle paths meandering in and out of gently rolling hills, all this took Koler by surprise. He tried to picture what the landscape looked like in the Spring. No wonder the artists gathered on the knoll. It would make a lovely landscape.

He knew that some day, probably after the war, he would return to New York. He was charmed by the city's immense diversity and particularly this spot. He longed to be one of the artists on the knoll, painting the landscape.

He finally left the park at approximately 7:30.

He found the same parking place across the street from the hardware store at eight that evening. With infinite patience he chain-smoked Lucky Strikes until he watched the various employees, leaving by the side entrance. He watched as Frank Becken got into his Buick and headed east towards Long Island. Koler remained several car lengths back. Since Becken seemed to be in no hurry, the assassin had no difficulty keeping up.

Becken made one stop on his way home--the service station on Childers Road in Long Island, just blocks from his house on Holsum Road. Koler pulled past the service station and parked on the shoulder. He saw in his rear view mirror that Becken had a brief conversation with the attendant. Five minutes later Becken pulled past him--Koler lying down in the seat-- and began the final leg home.

Holsum Road was a quiet little street with small, white houses, only recently built, in neat rows. The yards were of adequate size, the front porches with the normal two seat swings and the garages separate from the houses in the back.

Koler noted where Becken turned in. He drove cautiously by the house and circled the block, parking his car, as near as he could figure, in front of the house directly behind Becken's.

He had been lucky. He was one house off. The lot behind Becken's had not been built on yet, and there was a small patch of woods leading directly to the white fencing that marked his property line. Koler killed the engine, sat long enough to see if he had been noticed, and finally took his Linemen's Test Set and crept through the empty lot to the edge of Becken's back yard.

The night was cool.

A light was shining through the back porch from the kitchen, glancing off the chipped white paint of the garage, a self-contained wooden building, thirty yards from the back of the house. The air smelled of dust where Becken had driven his car in.

Koler was playing a hunch, and he hoped and counted on being lucky. He rummaged behind the fence for nearly five minutes when he found what he was looking for in the bushes.

At the bottom of a telephone pole lay a gray junction box where the phones of four houses tied in. Koler extracted from his coat a small flashlight and a pocket knife. Making sure that his body shielded the light's view from the house, he flipped the little light on with his left hand and deftly opened the junction box with the knife. The box creaked slightly as it opened. It took him only a couple of minutes to find the correct line. The test set was standard. It had a rubber handle, a dial, a receiver element, receiver cover, a transmitter with a 550 mh induction coil, a capacitor, varistor and connector clips. Koler tied into the line and hearing the steady buzz of the dial tone, he then flipped off his light and lay down in the high weeds. He flipped the test set switch to monitor. He might as well make himself comfortable, he thought, for he might be in for a long wait.

Three minutes later he heard the rude sound of the receiver coming off its cradle and the grinding sound of the dialing.

He bolted upright and with glaring eyes, stared at the light coming out of the kitchen.

"Operator," he heard the voice say, "I would like to make a long distance call to Murphy, North Carolina." Had there been a slight tremble to the voice? Koler laughed to himself. He was delighted that his instinct was still sharp. He had been right all along. Perhaps with a break or two he could finish this mission off in quick order and start for home.

"Would you like to make it person to person?" "No, thank you, would you please dial it for me? The number is Madison 2-1957."

A far away ring, sounding as if it were coming out of a muffled box. "Hello."

"Is this the Maxwell residence?"

"Yes it is."

"Mrs. Maxwell."

"Yes."

"You don't know me. My name is Frank Becken. I'm an old friend of your son, Tommy. I'm calling from New York, and I wondered if you could give me an idea of how to get in touch with Tommy."

"Oh yes, all right, I remember Tommy mentioning you, Mr. Becken. He spoke very highly of you."

"Thank you. I think a lot of him too. Can you tell me where he is?"

"No sir, not really. He called just two nights ago and said he was somewhere in New Jersey. I was so excited to hear from him, I didn't think to ask him where. I'm surprised he hasn't called you. Honestly, we've been at our wits' end worrying about him."

"It must have been a relief to hear from him."

"Oh, Mr. Becken, I can't begin to tell you. Why until he called, we hadn't heard from him in over a year. We were afraid something had happened to him. I must say I cried my eyes out over that boy. We're glad......Did you have anything to do with him being missing? Do you know...."

"No, ma'am, I'm sorry I can't talk about it, but let's just leave it this way," Becken said in a serious tone. "I'm worried about him too. He hasn't called me or even bothered to come by. If you hear from him, have him call me. It is very important. Here is the number."

"Just a minute. Let me get a pencil......all right."

"Elmherst 3-1411."

"Fine, Mr. Becken."

"Before I let you go," Becken said. "What did he say when he called?"

"Like I said, he's working some kind of job. He sounded just fine. I don't know if I will hear from him before Christmas, but he did promise he would be home for Christmas. He said he would be staying about a week. He's bringing some friend along, Robert, I think."

"Robert?"

"Yes. I think so, anyway, if I don't see him before Christmas, I'll have him call you in any case, Mr. Becken." "Thank you."

"It was nice of you to call. Why did you say you were worried about Tommy? Is there anything we should know? My husband nearly skinned me alive for letting him get off the phone the other night, but he seemed in a hurry....."

"I'm sure there is nothing to worry about, Mrs. Maxwell, especially since he called you. Like you said, none of us have heard from him, and I guess it's only natural to worry."

"Shall I give him a message when I see him?"

"Yes, just tell him that I called. In fact, perhaps I will try to call during Christmas."

"That would be just swell, Mr. Becken, I'm sure he would be happy to hear from you."

"Goodbye."

The click and the hum.

Suppressing a self-satisfied smile, Koler glared at the light. He had been right on two counts. Indeed Becken was loyal to Maxwell and was going to try to warn him, but warn him of what? This brought Koler to the second conclusion. Becken was smarter than he looked and somehow had determined that Maxwell was in trouble. The tone of his voice on the phone had been unmistakable. There had been an edge of panic, unlike the confident anger he had displayed in the diner. He had probably reviewed the conversation again at work where he had been impotent to do anything about it. He would never chance such inquiries at his place of business for fear of being overheard.

All this clarified Koler's next steps. He now knew that Maxwell was in the general area and probably still with Thibadeaux. Koler was convinced that this "Robert" was actually a "Richard." Becken would either make things much easier by tracking Maxwell down immediately, or he would make things much harder. In any case he was now a nuisance, who must be removed. The assassin could let him play a few strings to try and pull Maxwell in, but he did not want his subject warned. He would give Becken a little rope, but not too much. He would have to be exterminated very soon. Koler had already learned nearly all he wanted to know. He knew where Maxwell and Thibadeaux were, in general, but after seeing New York, he figured that they might as well be in Alaska. But he did know where they would be in one month, and as he thought it over, he decided immediately that it would be best to take them in North Carolina. They would be away from their old contacts. They would be relaxed and on holiday. And most important of all, the master would have plenty of time to prepare for them.

He heard the receiver lift again. The grind of the dials.

"Yeah," the voice on the other end said.

"Jerry, this is Frank Becken."

"Frankie, how's tricks, ain't seen your ass in a while."

"Yeah, I been busy. How you been?"

"About the same, still running a little bit. Want some of the action?"

"No thanks. I'm through with that shit. Hey, listen, you remember a young guy used to come over to the house on those Saturday nights? He was in the Bund......"

"Don't talk to me about no Bund," the other voice said in anger. "You know better."

"Don't worry, Jerry, I'm through with them too."

"That's swell. I didn't know at the time what assholes them Germans were......"

"Look, Jerry, you remember a kid named Maxwell. He used to be at the meetings."

"Sure. Hell yeah, the teacher man, right?"

"You seen him?"

"Hell no, I ain't seen him. I thought he was tight with you."

"Yeah, listen, Jerry, you remember that bimbo he used to live with. Julie Miller wasn't it? You knew her pretty well, didn't you?"

"Yeah, sure, I knew her."

"You got her phone number?"

The other man laughed. "Hey, Frankie, you're a married man. That broad will fog your glasses with those tits of hers."

"I'm divorced now, Jerry, ain't you heard?"

The man laughed even harder on the other line. "Right, right, and now you want some of Julie, you and every other horny bastard in town. I ain't got her number, but you won't find her home anyways. She works nights. Down at the Fuzzy Duck. I think it's on Second

Avenue. You ought to catch her there. She dances from midnight till three or so. A real class act."

"Thanks Jerry."

"Look, if I run across this Maxwell bird, I'll give you a buzz."

"Yeah, thanks."

Koler sat for another hour and listened to the monotonous hum. Finally, the light went out. He unhooked his connection and closed the box.

He made his way back to his car. Becken was going to bed and so was he. He had plenty of work ahead of him the next day.

Koler rose early the next morning and after checking out of his motel, he ate breakfast across the street at a breakfast house. As he glanced over the morning paper, an article caught his eye. On page E-7 at the bottom of the page, the caption read: "Man Killed In Park." The article made brief mention of a man, who had apparently been robbed and killed in Central Park the night before. Koler found it most interesting that a murder would attract so little attention. He smiled to himself. He finished his breakfast and was off for the day.

He made a token run by Morley's Hardware and after ascertaining that Frank Becken's car was there, he set about his shopping. Within the next four hours he had purchased a pair of black leather gloves, a dark tee shirt and toboggan, a large burlap sack, and at another hardware store a hunting knife. After lunching at a delicatessen, where he ate a delicious German sausage sandwich, he drove into New Jersey to the nearest gun shop. After looking carefully over the wide selection, he chose a Colt 45 automatic pistol and a box of shells. He drove south until he ran out of civilization and on finding a deserted patch of woods with a gravel road leading into the trees, he turned his Ford into the undergrowth. After a leisurely cigarette, he inspected the gun more carefully. It appeared to have excellent balance and fine workmanship. He loaded three shells from the box and stepped into the bright, cold air. He walked a few feet into the woods and picking out a knot hole on a tree forty feet away, he raised the gun, squinted, and squeezed off three shots. He was most impressed. As the plume of smoke drifted away, he saw where the three shots had gone directly into the knot hole in slightly different positions. Tiny fragments of freshly cut wood adhered in spots to the bark and lay in little flecks at the foot of the tree. Knowing that if he used the gun that night, it would be at close range anyway; he was completely satisfied and returned back to the car.

He did not plan on needing a gun, but it would come in handy later. For his purposes there could be only two methods of operation--poisoning with a skin contact poison or knifing. The latter seemed preferable, given what he planned to do with the body. It would be more messy than poisoning, but much more plausible. As he drove back towards the city, he entertained the idea of firing the Colt with a towel wrapped around the barrel as a makeshift silencer, but dismissed the idea. There simply would be no problem.

In order to kill the rest of the afternoon, Koler decided to drive around the city. He stopped at a service station and got a map.

"How much do I owe you, sir?" he said to the fat attendant with the cigar hanging out the side of his mouth.

"Free pal," the attendant said, as he read a sports page in a corner chair. "Goddamn Dodgers ain't gonna be worth shit next year."

"I'm sorry?"

"The Dodgers for Chrissakes. Where you from anyway?"

"North Carolina."

The attendant snorted without taking his eyes off his paper. "North Carolina, huh? No wonder you don't know nothing."

Koler unfolded the map as he looked for various interests around the city.

"What is this area? It's quite large--Harlem."

The attendant put his paper down, pinched his nose, snorted, then wiped his chin. "Yeah, Harlem, dey, you'll like it. A real nice residential section, real class. What you want to go there for?"

"I'm re-locating here. My wife and two sons will be coming up in a couple of weeks. I'm looking for a house."

"A house, well, Harlem has the nicest houses in the city dey, real class, give it a shot."

"Thank you, I will."

The throngs of huts on the sides of the road, children in the streets, a ball bouncing out from one of the postage stamp yards, three kids running in front of Koler's car, men leaning against store fronts, wearing all manner of hats, one black-brim with a red feather, endless games of jump rope and hopscotch by the little black girls in dirty dresses.

Koler stopped his car. A tall man eyed him as he leaned against the lamppost.

"Excuse me," Koler said, as he rolled down his window and leaned his head out. "Is this the area called Harlem?"

"Bigger than shit."

Aimless driving brought the world of tenements, asphalt, dilapidated buildings, scraps of discarded linoleum on the sidewalk, brick walls with painted slogans, women with ebony skin, large mouths, and full, beautiful white teeth--he remembered his African mistress, she had been an ambassador's maid, educated, short and thin, but gifted with those full lips and with that smooth elongation of muscle and flesh, which is the gift of black women--and her skin like silk in the darkness, her sighs, her body moving under his in eternal rhythm, much like the couple he saw dancing now on the sidewalk, in response to that inaudible orchestration of blood.

The music on the radio was a concerto by Beethoven and was wrong for this sight, for the tributaries of thought and remembrance into which Harlem plunged him, he the object of a joke, and yet in an area which nourished an irresistible splintering of his mind--it had happened before in his solitude--a fragmentation chaotic and foreign to his training and his culture--the true strength of life, the real vitality not in sameness, but in infinite variety, from that which was forged from ugliness, distortion, beauty, screams of struggle--but the music wrong, his fingers moving his radio knob, tracing the spectrum of American music and voice, from the big band sound, the news, and finally a jazz station, the Duke Ellington Band, the rhythms of the music evocative of the movement of the street, he drove entranced, now into a Puerto Rican section, now Jewish, Polish, and finally coming to a stop, checked his map and with the sun shooting long, orange splinters through the gaps of the great buildings, made his way back to Long Island, then to Central Park, where he again watched the painters on the knoll, overlooking the duckpond and the paddleboats.

Darkness having fallen, and great white clouds blowing in, creating a low sky, he decided he deserved a good dinner. In the act of eating, sitting before a table setting, presiding over the stiff, folded napkins, the shining silver, the goblets of wine, in hearing the violin, playing the soft strains conducive to conversation and digestion of a subtle delicacy, here the fragmentation would stop, his various atoms would be sucked in again, and he would be whole--bland, hard, consistent--one of the Order--himself.

After a full supper at the Tavern On the Green Restaurant in Central Park, Koler made a pass by Morley's Hardware and still seeing Frank Becken's car at 7 p.m. the master headed towards Long Island. He would precede his victim by a full two hours, plenty of time to make everything ready.

By eight o'clock he had arrived again at the deserted lot. Placing his gun in a shoulder holster, he dressed in his black tee shirt and toboggan. He placed the knife in a belt sheath and a white towel in the large burlap sack. He neatly folded the sack and stuffed it into the back of his pants.

It was cold as he crept through the abandoned lot. The wind was blowing in ominous clouds from the north. The night was moonless and dark. When reaching the white fence, he paused for a time to ascertain his movements. Then with the agility of a cat, he leapt over the fence and darted to the shadow behind the garage, paused, and proceeded in a half crouch to the back screen door.

The latch was hardly a problem once he had cut a neat little hole in the screen. The door opened with the slightest creak. He moved over an old push lawnmower and a pile of empty cans. How sloppy these Americans are, he thought.

The kitchen door took a bit longer as he burned his little flashlight on the keyhole, but using a pen knife, with patient skill, he turned the tumblers and eased the door open.

He entered the warm kitchen, silently closing and locking the door behind him. With his flashlight burning a white hole in the darkness, he searched the house. The kitchen led to a dining room on one side of the house and a long hallway going to what appeared to be bedrooms on the other side. The living room in the front of the house was sparsely furnished, containing only a single couch and a table with a large radio. He moved down the long hall and found the bedroom. After rummaging around for a time, he found in an old deal dresser what he was looking for. Under socks and underwear, was a small handgun. He removed the six shells and setting everything on the bed and using his flashlight, he extracted the firing pin. He re-loaded the gun and put it back in the dresser. He returned to the kitchen and making sure that he had re-locked both doors, he began stalking out a spot. In the back corner of the house he came to a room that appeared to be a study. There were disheveled books on a wall of shelves, a large bureau with various papers scattered over the top and on a small table near the window, an ashtray full of cigarette butts and a half-empty bottle of cognac with a smudged shot glass beside it.

He entertained for an instant sampling the cognac, but fought off the temptation. He never drank on a job, and he would remain impeccable. With the movement of a black cat who scratches his back on a wall, he placed his back on the wall next to the door and slid down to a sitting position. This was obviously the room where Becken liked to unwind, and here would be the perfect place. Remembering one other thing, Koler moved a chair to the middle of the room and loosened the bulb of the overhead light. He tried the switch. Nothing. Now his victim would have to walk across the room to turn on the light of the bureau. He would never make it. Koler lay the white towel in the center of the room where he calculated the body would fall, threw the burlap sack in the corner and resumed his position next to the door. He calculated that his vigil would be less than an hour now. He waited. He had learned patience. It was his best friend.

He began to live within the sounds of the house--the wind howling outside, the various creaks of the walls, a loose shutter tapping against the wall towards the front. His eyes adjusted to the darkness until he could see every feature of the room.

He had to wait longer than he anticipated, but at 10:16 a pair of headlights swam into the window and illuminated the gravel and dirt just outside the study window. The window brightened until the large black shape moved past it. Koler crawled over to the window and watched as the car entered the garage.

Finally, Becken emerged, wearing an overcoat and a hat with the brim turned down. He was walking stooped over, as if he were cold.

Only one thing concerned Koler. If as Becken unlocked the back screen door as anticipated, would he notice the small hole in the screen? If so, Koler knew what he must do. He would have to take the towel from the floor, wrap it around his Colt, and finish the job from a distance. It was not the way he wanted it. He was counting on Becken in the darkness and in his hurry to get out of the cold wind, to open the door as quickly as possible and get in the house. The hole had been cut so small, that in the darkness, one would have to be looking for it. He would know one way or another in a matter of seconds.

He heard the whine of the screen door, then the knob turning and the kitchen door opening. The sound of the door and Becken's footsteps were nearly deafening compared to the silence to which the assassin had accustomed himself.

Koler slid over to his place by the door, unsheathed his knife, and made ready.

Frank Becken shivered as he moved down the hallway to his bedroom. He turned on lights as he progressed from back to front to the living room. He moved into his bedroom, took off his coat and hat, throwing them on the bed.

The next order of business was to fix himself a meal. He had tried to get out of the habit of eating just before bed since he had been on his diet, but due to the odd hours he worked, he simply could not help it. He could not go to bed hungry.

He moved around several pans in the icebox until he found a pan of vegetable soup, which he hurriedly put on the stove. He then went to the bread box and slid two pieces of toast into the toaster. While the soup was cooking, he moved to the front porch, picked up the evening paper and spread it out on the kitchen table. He read of the Russian and Italian campaigns and finding all accounts muddled and vague, he turned to the Sports. He got his soup and ate as he read.

When he finished, he put the bowl in the sink, filled it with water, and moved the telephone from the counter over to the kitchen table. He began dialing the number.

"No, operator, that's fine." He heard the familiar voice of his wife.

"Cheryl, yeah, it's me....yes, I know it's late, but I just got home. How are you.......look, there is no reason to talk to me that way, you know how I feel.......the check is in the mail....no, I'm not angry....... have I ever failed to send it?......what are you arguing about.....it's a habit, we argue out of habit, it's not why I called......did it ever occur to you that I might just want to hear your voice?.........I have no reason to lie........I want to make things right.........how are my babies?........... no kidding, he lost the tooth......make sure the tooth fairy pays him a visit," and while his wife talked, Frank lowered his head and rubbed his eyes........"please, Cheryl........you know what I want......do you want me to beg?......just come back and you'll see........I promise......don't start that again........let me talk to the kids........so they're ready for bed, I want to speak to them." There was a long pause, and the next time he spoke, it was obvious he was speaking to a child.

"Hello pumpkin, how's my baby.......do you like your school......I'm just calling to see how you are.....you and your brother getting along? Are you helping mommy.....that's good......it's very important that you help her......you're a big girl now..........soon, very soon honey.........so tell me what Santa is going to bring you for Christmas.........I think so honey, I will talk to your mom about it......so tell me what you want..... uh huh..........yeah......all right, well, write your letter, get your bath and let me speak to your brother......I love you too."

He changed his voice again for his son. "Hey there, tiger...... yeah you........I'm gonna come knock a knot on that head of yours soon........you will?.........how's mommy?......that's good........tell daddy what you want for Christmas........I hear you lost another tooth.........a big one huh........put it under your pillow and maybe the tooth fairy will come........maybe a nickel.........maybe even a dime....where is the hole in your mouth this time?.........the front, huh? That's the one that was loose........I remember.....you know what they're going to call you pretty soon?........no, they will call you, Grandpaw Thipeethaw........I said Grandpaw Thipeethaw.....well, don't you and your sister fight..... because you shouldn't......your big sister loves you, just like mommy and daddy........I'm coming back soon.......tell momma that you want me back.......well, tell her again........you better get to bed now.......Your daddy loves you."

He spoke briefly to his wife.

"I'm telling you that I'm different now. You wouldn't even know me. Is there someone else......then there is no reason we can't be together...... let's make it for Christmas.....well, think about it.......honey, honey, don't please," his voice seemed to be pleading, "we won't get into it all again......now listen, I love you......all right......don't cry.....I don't expect you to say yes right now......no, just think about it.....all right, goodbye."

The conversation seemed to drain him of all remaining energy. He sighed, got up, and loped into the living room. He turned on the radio and sat on the couch.

As the music played, he sat for the better part of an hour, smoking and staring off. He was doing his best, putting his life back together. He had made mistakes, and he was just now getting back his confidence. It would take time, but he told himself that he had turned a corner with his family. He felt dead without his kids, simply dead. He mused for a time over his children's voices, re-lived the conversation with his wife, and tapped his foot in time to a song on the radio. He yawned and stretched. He decided he needed a drink. He got up and headed down the hallway towards the study. The music blared.

Let's have another cup of coffee

Let's have another piece of pie

He walked slowly down the hallway, the hard wood floor under the carpet creaking with his steps. He came to his study door and flicked on the light. Nothing.

"Damn," he muttered as he stepped inside.

Koler struck. In one swift motion he threw his left, gloved hand over Becken's mouth, while with the right hand he plunged the knife upwards between the fourth and fifth ribs in one vicious, deadly blow.

Let a smile be your umbrella on a rainy, rainy day Becken stiffened and shuddered. Koler gave the knife a final twist. He had plunged into the proper kill area, taking in one blow the liver, spleen, and heart. The final shudder as the body fell limp onto the white towel. Koler ripped the towel from beneath the corpse and wrapped it around the blade, which he pulled with some effort out of the body. He then pressed the towel down urgently to soak up the blood. He wanted as little mess as possible.

Trouble's just a bubble, there's a rainbow in the sky So let's have another cup of coffee, Let's have another piece of pie He went to the window and looked outside. There was nothing unusual in sight. Pulling the curtains, he turned on the bureau light. There was considerably more blood on the floor than he had seen in the darkness. Leaning over the body, Koler then extracted a small pen knife from his pocket, which he applied to Becken's teeth. The master removed a tiny piece of black leather from between Becken's front teeth, where his victim had bitten into the master's glove.

After several trips to the bathtub with more towels, he managed to do a thorough cleaning job. He took out Becken's billfold from his pants' pocket, inspected the contents and put it in his own pocket. He removed the spectacles from over the small eyes, whose glassy stare still revealed a look of sudden surprise. He then stretched the body out and began the task of stuffing the corpse into the burlap bag. The arms and legs were still flaccid and as Koler picked the bag up and shook it, the body slipped in.

He made a final trip to the bathtub, then removed the bloody towels, carrying them gingerly to the fireplace in the living room. On the back porch was a can of gasoline. He doused the wet towels with gas and threw a match into the fireplace. When the fire burned down, he made one last tour of the house. It had been a messy job, but it had turned out as neatly as possible. He then went to the bedroom, replaced the firing pin in the handgun, and putting on Becken's overcoat and hat, returned to the study and hoisted the burlap sack over his shoulder. The body was heavy, but Koler managed to navigate it out the back porch to the garage.

Since he wore Frank's coat and hat, a neighbor who might see would only see Frank Becken, carrying a large bag to his garage.

Koler had taken the keys to Becken's car. He placed the body behind the car while he opened the trunk, then placed the body inside the trunk and closed it. He returned to the house, turned out all the lights, and locked the back door.

He returned to the garage and started Becken's car. He pulled out onto Holsum Road at 12:13. It would take him almost an hour to get into the city, and since it was not late enough in his judgement to plant the body, he had time to kill.

He knew he would have to leave town by tomorrow, so he decided that he would waste no time in making further preparations. The odds of Maxwell's finding out about Becken's death were close to even. And if he did find out, he would never make the connection with what had actually happened. It was Koler's intention that the murder look like an ordinary mugging. He would leave town and get ready down south for his prime objectives. But before he disposed of the body, he had one last angle to play. If it worked out, if he was lucky, erhaps he could go ahead and take his subjects here. He doubted that it would work out that way, but he would give it a try.

He turned his car towards East 60th. When he reached East 60th, he hailed a cab driver, who had pulled beside him at a traffic light.

"Hey, excuse me, can you tell me where the Fuzzy Duck is?"

"Oh, that peel joint? Just follow me. I'm going right by there."

Julie Miller was like a lot of aspiring young actresses, who had come to New York to seek their fortunes. The Thirties and Forties were the movie industry's heyday, and the American dream of becoming one of the great idols, such as Vivian Leigh or Marlene Dietrich was the dream of any young girl, who had been told that she had as much as an inkling of acting talent.

Julie had grown up in normal enough environments. Raised in Richmond, Virginia with all the middle class virtues, she had been endowed not only with above average intelligence, but also with a superior body. She had been a high school cheerleader and one of the leaders of her dramatics club. Whereas her chestnut hair, her large brown eyes and beautiful figure had appeared at first a blessing, like many physically beautiful American girls, who are adored only for their looks for most of their adolescence and young womanhood, she also discovered that these virtues could be a curse. When she was eighteen, she lost her virginity to a boy with whom she had fallen in love. His name was Micheal Vincent, and although he was not of the physical constitution of most of her previous boyfriends, who had been athletes, he was kind and gentle, and even frail. His dark eyes and hair had not struck her at first as especially handsome, yet with time, love clouded all his defects. When she became pregnant, she naively and proudly told her parents. She knew Micheal would marry her, and she knew her parents would understand. She had been wrong on both counts. After bitter quarrels with her father, who was a deacon in the local church and constantly reminded her of his public humiliation, she found Micheal equally as bitter for different reasons. Following the advice of his parents, he begrudgingly offered to marry her. The wedding date had been set when she took the only way out she knew. There had been a local doctor, who performed certain "favors" for young girls in the community. It had been expensive in more ways than one. After the abortion, depression had set in, and Julie had been temporarily committed to a mental institution.

Upon her release, although the initial depression had lifted, she found there was an additional burden. She saw every fibre of her parents' life now as a lie. She began to hate her own body, its normal functions and developments. Finally, she took the advice of a cynical friend. "If I had your body, there would be nothing I wouldn't have. What do you want? Whatever it is, you can have it if you play your cards right. What's so bad about it? Men use us. Why can't we use them?"

Taking all her savings that she had accumulated from a summer job and without telling anyone, Julie packed off one day, hitchhiking to New York. She had determined she would be an actress. At first, everything her friend had told her had been true. She made significant inroads to several theatre groups and although it was never out in the open, she accomplished these progressions by giving herself to certain important men.

She enjoyed none of these relationships, but she told herself that it was business and that she would carry on. Then she met Tommy Maxwell. Just like when she had first met Micheal, this man seemed to have with her everything in common. He too was outcast, and when she finally gave herself to him, she found to her amazement that she actually enjoyed it again. But her skepticism and remembrance of the past was her main drive. She remained guarded with Tommy and made it clear from the beginning that theirs was only a physical arrangement. She was glad he had left without saying goodbye; it was chiefly because she had felt herself falling in love, something she had determined never to do again.

Over the last two years during the war, she again had fallen into different kinds of traps. Her jobs as an actress disappeared. She tried dancing, but was told her "tits are too big" and that she was slightly awkward. It had been through sheer economic necessity and a pride that she would never return to her parents that she had taken the job at the Fuzzy Duck.

Originally her job had been merely to dance for a dollar with certain lonely men, mostly sailors on leave, but she found the income paltry at best; she had not been able to resist the approach by the manager to become a "dancer." Between paid dances were the strip shows, and she found during her first act that it was not only easy, but almost enjoyable. She even got a sense of worth out of satisfying vicariously the pitiful old men or lonely sailors. And when the inevitable approaches came from customers for the even bigger money, she had, on several occasions, been unable to resist.

On the evening of November 24, at midnight, she began her act with the usual sway and flair. She wore a pink fur and silky, pink briefs, which she was not allowed to take off. As usual, when she danced and rubbed the fur around her various parts, she did not look at the audience. Her undulations finally led to the finale and to the response of the audience. She relinquished her fur and laughingly shook her breasts to the darkness. When she finished, she returned to the back, put on her hose, panties, bra, and red dress and went out for the paid dances. As her manager had told her, the paid dances were much more lucrative just after a strip show, as customers would often bid among each other for the dance.

Such was the case when she stepped to the head of the line, next to the booth and the sign that read:"Dance-One Dollar."

Three drunk sailors offered her money.

"Hey, baby, here's ten for you."

"Make it eleven."

"Twenty baby."

"You asshole, what you running it up for?"

It was a typical reverie, and with Spartan indulgence she hesitated and waited for the bids to go up. Customers found that even though the sign said one dollar, the more they privately paid, the longer the dance and the greater the chance for further arrangements.

The sailors had come to an agreement when a blonde man with a very alert and handsome gaze stepped in front of them.

"Please, gentlemen, treat the lady with respect," he said, a fifty dollar bill flashing at the end of his fingertips. The gentleman walked evenly up to the booth, paid his dollar, and with a slight bow of the head, handed Julie his ticket as he slid the bill quietly beneath the upper folds of her dress.

"Hey, asshole, how would you like the shit knocked out of you?"

The bouncer, a tall Irishman, walked up and showed the sailors the way out.

The music started, the slow saxophone swaying the crowd as one.

She felt a sudden rush of pleasure as the man held her gently in his obviously very strong arms. His hand was gentle on her back. This might be one of those circumstances for which she would make an arrangement. The man was obviously rich, and as Julie made eye contact with Anne, the girl at the booth, she knew that she might be late for the rest of her stage dances. Anne would get her ten dollar cut, but hopefully, there would be more than enough incentive left over.

The music and the blue lights played over her. "I know you," the man whispered to her. She felt a pleasant chill go up and down her neck.

She pulled back from him. He stared down with laughing, blue eyes.

"Yeah, sure, buddy," she said. "You and everyone else knows me."

"No, I really do," he said. "You were pointed out to me once by a friend."

"Right," she said, again smiling wryly and scrunching up her shoulder as she felt his hand massage her right breast outside the dress. "Lots of people do that too."

"No really," he insisted, his face flushing with excitement. "It was Tommy Maxwell that pointed you out. It was one day, just a couple of years back on the street."

She stiffened and pulled back. The mention of Tommy's name had somehow embarrassed her. She felt ashamed.

"You knew Tommy. Where did you know Tommy?"

Koler noted the shock on the girl's face. He studied her every gesture, watched for any flicker of a lie that would come out of the soft brown eyes.

"I met him in New York. At the pool hall."

"Oh," she said, and put her head gingerly back to his shoulder.

"I haven't seen him lately," he said, this time pulling back to view her face. "Is he still in town?"

"I don't know," she said. "I haven't seen Tommy in over a year." And suddenly she flushed. The mention of Tommy's name, from her own mouth, at this place, made her doubly ashamed. Koler noticed the flush and narrowed his eyes, studying with all his will for the correct interpretation. Then his eyes took a glossy, distant, vacant look. For an inexplicable reason, Julie became afraid.

"Are you sure?" the man said. "Why are you flushing?"

"What do you mean, 'am I sure?'" she said. "Why would I lie to you?"

He watched her again. Her eyes were half-closed now, seeming casual, almost bored.

Koler felt weak and as had happened in the Argentine cafe, hardly able to contain himself.

"I have another fifty dollars," he said. "Could you adjourn for a few minutes to a place of more privacy?"

But Julie's mood had changed now. She reached inside her blouse and for reasons she could not even explain to herself, handed Koler his fifty dollar bill.

"Listen, you helped me out of a jam back there.

Those sailors would have left finger marks all over me if it hadn't been for you. This dance is on the house. And as for the other......" she blushed and looked up imploringly at the empty eyes that resembled blue pools. "It is generous," she continued, "more than generous, but not with one of Tommy's friends, no. He was kind of special see, and if you can see your way clear, do me a favor. Don't tell him I work here. By the time you run into him, I'll be gone from here surely. Just tell him to give me a ring. My number is in the book."

Suddenly the man stiffened and with an effortless shove pushed her back.

His eyes were aflame, and a cruel sneer came across his mouth, his jaw muscles working. As he spoke, his left eye bulged.

"And what is so great about him?" he said, as if personally insulted. "Why is he so special?"

And just as suddenly as his rage had appeared, his face again softened into a cultivated, distant gentility.

"Forgive me," he said with a slight bow. "I've forgotten myself. You're so beautiful......it's frustrating."

And with half-opened mouth, she watched the man turn and walk evenly into the darkness.

It began to snow.

Koler drove into Central Park for a look. He had seen one pair of derelicts hunched against the driving snow and beckoning for him to stop the car. There were no other signs of life. He reached a place where the trees encroached on the left side of the road. Seeing that there was a ditch on the other side of the cluster of bushes on up the road, Koler stopped the car. He left the motor running. Looking over the landscape several times before opening the trunk, he finally got started.

He threw open the trunk and grabbed the heavy bag. In a matter of seconds he had managed to close the trunk and drag the bag into the trees. There was a small path leading through the bushes. Everywhere was that cushioned silence and the slight tinkle of flakes which always accompanies heavy snowfalls. When he reached the ditch, he began dragging the bag along his side, helping move it with one leg. The corpse had stiffened and gotten much heavier. The bottom of the ditch was already covered with at least an inch of snow. He undid the string and released the body from the coarse cloth. The body lay black against the snow. Koler took out Becken's billfold, removed a ten dollar bill, then scattered the remaining contents over the body. He tossed the wallet just next to the fixed stare of the waxen face. He removed the spectacles from his pocket, and noticing that the left lens had a slight crack, tossed them into the ditch. He was still wearing Frank's overcoat and hat, so he took off the coat and forced one of the stiff arms into the coat. He threw the hat into the ditch, took one last look at the body, then the landscape, and headed back towards the sound of the running car.

He drove the car back the way he had come for two minutes, then stopped and parked it. The burlap bag still had crusty patches of blood on it, so on Koler's long walk back to the body, he hunched down in a patch of trees and managed to burn the bag. This took longer than he anticipated because of the wind, but a quick examination of the ashes with his little flashlight proved satisfactory. When he finally reached the ditch again, he placed the car keys in the right overcoat pocket. The snow had already lightly coated his victim's face.

Then a sound startled him. From beneath the body came the moan of a long, gaseous fart.

He re-traced his steps towards the exit of the park, passing the abandoned car and, an hour later, finally reached the exit of the park.

He paused at the park's entrance and looked back at the stretches of peaceful white. He thought back to the day he had first seen the grassy knoll with the artists perched on its side, painting in the bright sunlight. He liked this place.

He hailed a cab and promised the driver a handsome tip to take him to Holsum Road in Long Island.

Everything had gone according to plan. Koler could see it all-- from the routine investigation by the authorities to the small article in the paper. It might be days before the body would be discovered if the snow continued to fall. And even though the murder might attract attention, since it had been the second in only a few days, Koler was sure there would be only token interest. After all, these Americans had a rather casual view of violent crime. Besides, what was a simple mugging? There was a war on. No one would care.

The cab reached Holsum Road at approximately 4 a.m. The assassin found his car where he had left it, completely covered with snow, and undisturbed. After clearing the windows and starting the motor, Koler took one last look at the house on the other side of the vacant lot. Through the trees he could just make out the outline of the garage and the house. Everything looked normal.

The next morning Otto Koler packed, checked out of his hotel, and left New York, driving south. His destination was Chattanooga, Tennessee.

CHAPTER 10

December 3, 1942

It was unseasonably warm in Chattanooga, Tennessee. When the morning chill burned off, the temperature on Broad Street would be in the fifties.

Joel Rosenthal, a squat, balding man of sixty-one years, sat in the shoe shine chair and watched the red-coated black man finish his buff.

"That's plenty good, Norman," he said as he hopped down and gave the man a quarter tip.

"Thank you, Mr. Joel."

The sun drenched the side of Lookout Mountain, which overlooked the city from the northwest.

It was a short walk from the shine booth to Joel Rosenthal's store--the Continental Cleaning Service. He was feeling good from his breakfast at the Alamo Restaurant. He waved at a car that honked to his left and turned to notice the tall man standing in front of his shop.

"Good morning," Rosenthal said. He opened the door and heard the little bell tinkle. The man behind him carried the sign, which had been taped to the front door--Help Wanted-Route Driver.

Rosenthal walked directly into the back before returning to the counter. He always opened the store fifteen minutes before any of his help arrived. It was his superstition.

"So, young man, I take it you are interested in the advertised job."

"Yes sir, I am."

The man stood well over six feet and was blonde. His hair was combed straight back. His square jaw was cleanly shaven and redolent of shaving lotion. His blue eyes twinkled with intelligence, one eye slightly larger than the other. He wore a blue plaid shirt and gray corduroy pants.

"Simon Ballard," he said smiling and already nodding his head slightly.

"Joel Rosenthal," said the puzzled old man as he extended his hand. The stranger's handshake was like a vice.

"So young man, would you like a cup of coffee?"

"No, thank you," the young man said abruptly. "How do I apply for the position?"

The old man started to walk away from the stranger, and in his friendly waddle, fetch the coffee. He turned and looked the man quickly up and down.

"After an application, I may hire you today," he said.

"Fine," said the tall man.

"Where are you from?"

"Murphy, North Carolina."

The old man frowned slightly and tilted his head.

"We service Murphy," he said with a suspicious look. "In fact the route will include Murphy and Cleveland."

The young stranger appeared to immediately sense the old man's suspicion at such a coincidence. He laughed and slapped the old man on the shoulder in a friendly way.

"Listen, that was my understanding when I talked to Judi, I think it was, on the phone yesterday. It's perfect for me," the stranger said, conjuring up as much youthful naivete as he could muster. "I no longer have a family there, but I still know quite a few people."

"Know old Pete Wisentrop?"

"No," the stranger said shortly, with a cooler tone.

"It's been years since I was a resident."

"Peter's lived there for twenty years."

"Probably one of those names and faces one never attaches a name to," the stranger said, permitting another smile. "You know how it is."

The old man frowned slightly. "Most people in Murphy know everyone."

"As I say, it's been a number of years."

"What have you been doing the last year or so?"

The tall man's eyes twinkled. "I have been at school at Vanderbilt, studying pre-law. I ran out of money and needed a change of scenery."

Rosenthal rubbed his bald head. "A change of scenery you say."

"My sweetheart lives down here," the stranger added. "We hope to marry soon."

The old man sighed. He again rubbed his head. "You don't mind my asking, but none of the branches of the armed forces have......." and the old man raised his right hand and gestured in small circles, as if to suggest the last words of the sentence.

"The services will not take me," the stranger said, feigning with his agitation, that he was being forced to speak of a personal embarrassment. "I have an extremely bad knee and I'm diabetic."

The blonde man smiled winningly.

The old man returned the smile. "The job will require lifting," the old man said in a dismissing tone. "But nothing way out of line. Most of it is driving and servicing the various customers in outlying towns. You do have a social security card, don't you?"

"Of course."

As the old man described the job, Koler discreetly examined the shop. The sun cut through the blinds in the most charming fashion, making parallel lines of shadow on the wooden floor. The shop smelled of starch and crisp linen. The curtains were bright yellow.

Rosenthal described the pay scale to which Koler agreed.

Finally, Rosenthal covered the schedule and the hours required.

"Unfortunately," Rosenthal said with a sly smile, "we're on a staggered work week. Four days on, one off," he waved his hand in the air in a friendly way, "another on, another off."

The young man in front of him rubbed his chin and looked puzzled for the first time.

"'Off,'" Koler said in a low tone, "what do you mean by 'off.'"

Again the old man frowned and rubbed his head. He scanned the stranger up and down once more.

"'Off' is when you don't work."

"Of course," Koler said flushing, "just joking."

The old man shook his head and smiled. "Fill out the application," he said, handing the stranger a form and walking away.

December 4, 1942

Just after dawn Otto Koler made his first run into Murphy, North Carolina. He had become used to the gears on the truck by now, and as he headed north out of Chattanooga on Highway 65, the air was cold and the sun was bright. There was not a cloud in the sky.

Cleveland was typical of many of the towns that Koler visited-- merely a neat square of storefronts surrounding the city hall, which invariably was a brick building with a high clock of Roman numerals.

Koler made his scheduled stops, delivered his linen, picked up the clothing to be cleaned, and by noon headed north to Murphy.

The road ran along the banks of the Ocoee River. He passed two blanket stores, which sold Cherokee Indian paraphernalia. Soon he could see the faint, blue outline of the Smoky Mountains in the distance.

Thirty miles south of Murphy, the road avoided the trees and streams, yawning into the great farm fields on both sides, punctuated by the barns and country houses of all variety--huts with rusted cars in the front yards to aristocratic structures, with homespun simplicity, mostly painted white with deep, green roofs and bordered by freshly painted, white picket fences.

He passed a sign which advertised live bear.

As the clouds now came over the fields, intermittently covering half with shadow, half with moving patches of light, Koler felt a sudden chill. He rolled up his window.

A sign passed. Murphy ten miles.

On highway 65 Murphy was nestled amid the first mountains of the Smoky Mountain chain. The little village lay between great purple walls of mountains on three sides. Again, the town was organized in the traditional fashion of a town square with all the outlying farms and houses proceeding out from the square.

Koler's deliveries only took a couple of hours. While speaking to the various wives in the area, he had been tempted to ask the whereabouts of the Maxwell farm, but since it would be well-known that the farm was not on his delivery route, he was afraid it would arouse suspicion.

It was after four o'clock when he entered the town square and The Murphy Drug Store.

A bell tinkled as he entered the establishment. The room smelled of old wood and hair tonic. It was a typical country drug store. The shelves were well-stocked with the usual wares found in such stores from toilet water to Epsom salt. The regulars all gathered around the fountain, counter, and tables where the old Greek counterman Mr. Walters had orchestrated conversations for years.

Walters was a stout man, bald, with a huge nose and wide mouth. He was shouting at a farmer with a straw hat, one of the men sitting at the tables.

"Ruth is too old," the old man shouted with smiling eyes. "Anyone can see that."

"Cup of coffee, please," Koler said, sliding a dime across the counter to Walters.

"Baseball--you want to talk--but don't talk baseball wid me, "the old man continued as he poured the coffee for the stranger seated at the counter.

Redneck men, of all description, sat over their coffee and stared, amused at Walters' tirade.

"Break up the goddamn Yankees," Walters said, in his loud manner. "Ain't got no time for 'em."

"Who pays you no nevermind," the well-built man with a cropped hair cut said. "The Red Sox are better."

"Right, Hank, and-a you just keep you wallet handy--like last year," Walters shouted, reaching for a rag. An old farmer seemed offended, as he spit tobacco contemptuously into a paper cup. Everyone else laughed.

Koler listened for a full hour before saying anything himself. How incredible the entire conversation had been. Twice he had to restrain himself from bursting into laughter. Was it possible that these Americans could talk about baseball for hours on end?

Four of the six men had gone before Koler finally spoke.

"Yeah, one more for the road," he said when Walters looked his way.

When the old man brought the coffee, Koler gently grabbed his wrist.

"By the way, I wonder if you could help me," he said, removing his hand from the wrist.

Walters pulled his hand back and crossed his arms. "Shoo," he said, "what you need?"

Koler folded his hands and leaned forward. "I went to school about eight years ago with a guy named Tommy Maxwell," Koler said. "He said he was from around here. Have you ever heard of him?"

Walters uncrossed his arms and began wiping off the counter. "Shoo," he said, "I known him and his family for years."

"What ever happened to him? Is he still around?"

Walters glanced sidelong at the man. "Yeah, we see him every now and den."

"Ain't been in town for over a year now, I know," said the man with the straw hat, who looked straight ahead as if he were speaking to the empty booth across from him.

"Used to teach at the high school," the man added. "Damn good history teacher, too, the kids say."

Old man Walters slowly brushed his moustache down with his finger. He looked suspiciously at the stranger.

"Where did you say you knew him?" he asked in a quiet voice.

Koler's tone was exuberant. "Knew him in college," he said. "Chapel Hill. He's a good Joe. I haven't seen him in years, and since I get into town every now and then, I thought I might look him up."

Walters lit a cigarette and leaned on the counter. "Yeah, and what brings you to town?"

"I'm your cleaning man," he said with a smile. "I deliver linen here for Continental. It's my first time here."

Koler paused, watching Walters' face.

"Are his folks still in town?" Koler finally asked. "Maybe I could leave a message for him there."

Again the old man with the straw hat spoke without looking at anyone.

"Yep, the Maxwell's live out east highway. Can't miss it. It's the only farmhouse two miles east towards Hayesville."

"Thanks a lot," Koler said, standing up and stretching. "Don't guess I'll get there today. It's too late. Next time I'll stop for lunch."

"All right, now," Walters said, watching the man intently until he reached the door. "Come back."

December 24

On a winding road ascending Signal Mountain, just north of Chattanooga, a brown laundry truck lumbered up the grade. The road at times flirted with a sheer bluff on the left, which was made more threatening by a thin mist of rain. From the bluff Otto Koler could see the vast point of Lookout Mountain across the valley and the city of Chattanooga in the distance. The city was situated on the southeast side of the river, that curved gently like a brown ribbon at the mountain's feet.

The laundry truck approached a clearing on the left and slowed.

The little clearing in the woods, no more than a wide spot in the road, contained a trailer. A small light burned in the trailer in these early morning hours. The machine shack was to the left of the trailer and down a slight grade towards the bluff.

Koler pulled the truck into the clearing and parked behind a blue pickup truck.

He got out of the truck and saw the door ajar to the machine shop and noticed the little man inside. As before, the machinist's thin frame was donned in blue jeans, the same repugnant, dark green shirt and a soiled, gray baseball hat, which he wore low over his eyes.

Koler saw the figure wave from the shack. As he emerged from the truck, a look of absolute hatred and resolve ran across Koler's face, but was transformed immediately into a look of serenity and friendliness.

The shop smelled of oil. The rifle lay motionless on the table amid a collection of greasy parts and tools. Koler picked up the piece, which he had bought, and balanced it in his hands.

The job had been done to perfection. The entire length of the Bausch and Lombe scope was mounted perfectly onto the Winchester Model 70.

The old machinist spit. "How you like it?"

Koler smiled. "Splendid, absolutely splendid."

"Hell, it ought to be," said the old man. "Since you talked to me, I ain't left the mountain." The old man kicked at the ground. He took two steps forward. "Worked on it solid," he said, standing his ground. "Never mounted anything that large before. Who did you say sent you?"

Koler turned on the little man. A strange look had again crossed his face. A dull sheen came over the eyes, one eye opening slightly larger than the other.

"The man from Tiftonia," he muttered.

"Yeah, right," the old man said, taking off his baseball cap and wiping his scraggly face. "Where did you say you got that scope?"

Koler started, then gathered himself. "My brother, he lived in Europe before the war," he said, the small blue eyes intent on the little man.

The little man stepped back one step and took a deep breath.

"Let's give it the test," Koler said in another attempt to change the subject. He smiled and opened the breach.

"First the money," the little man said, holding out his right hand.

Koler smiled, the dull sheen disappearing from the eyes. He reached inside his jacket and produced an envelope. The old man grabbed the envelope and began counting the bills.

"Where are the cartridges?" Koler said with authority.

"Here's the box," the man said without looking up.

"Do you mind if I shoot a tree or two outside?" Koler asked.

The man stopped counting. He looked up. Koler could tell the machinist was pleased with the generosity of the sum.

"Go ahead," the old man said.

Again as he walked out of the shack, Koler was on the verge of bursting into laughter.

The old man watched him for a time, through the mist outside and the dirty window. The man had been a strange one all right, and where did that scope come from? The story had been ridiculous. But the money had been right, and he could talk to people about it later.

The old man saw the tall blonde enter the treeline. He waited. He looked suspiciously to the left. Whur did I leave that pistol, he thought, and headed for a drawer on a work bench.

From the drawer the old man took a Colt 45, checked the bullets and casually put it in his pants, pulling his greasy shirt over the gun.

Once into the treeline, Koler removed his knife, picked out a tree, and made three large notches in the bark. He negotiated the slight incline until he felt he was ninety yards away. This was the approximate distance calculated from the treeline immediately to the rear of the Maxwell farmhouse in Murphy. He had not decided definitely on that spot. Events would dictate the spot. If he could get a beat on the two men from the top of the hollow at the back of the farmhouse, he felt the spot would be ideal. It was only a possibility.

As he checked the breach and nestled the rifle to his shoulder, he thought briefly of the old man. Should he kill him? No, it was too much trouble for nothing. The man appeared to be a complete recluse. If he told anyone about the unusual scope, it would be weeks. Besides, tomorrow was Christmas and Koler would already be gone from the area in a few days.

He had bought the rifle a week before, so he was now used to its firing. He watched the right notch amid the crosshairs and grid of the scope. He squeezed off the first round. He cursed under his breath. The gun was still firing high and slightly to the right with the next two shots. He fired again. He had missed the notch by a full three inches. He adjusted the sites, fired again, and adjusted again. He fired a total of eleven shots, crackling off the acoustics of the woods. Finally, he was satisfied. When he last looked through the scope, the knottiest were no longer visible, so accurate had been his shooting. Flecks of fresh wood lay at the bottom of the tree.

He rose and brushed the dirt off him.

The old man was standing at the treeline when Koler emerged.

"Couldn't wait to shoot it, huh?" the old man said as he spit.

He watched the blonde man stand over him. "I didn't want to drive all the way for nothing," Koler said sneeringly.

The old man stepped forward, his small, mad eyes looking fearlessly into Koler's. "Did I screw it up?" he shouted.

"No, it's fine," Koler said, finally smiling. "Thank you and Merry Christmas."

The old man watched as the brown Continental Cleaning Service truck drove down the mountain.

December 25

The Christmas night was relatively mild on the road to Murphy. A black pickup truck rolled up the highway, the mountains jutting down as great black masses on the right.

The headlights came around the curve. A man was in the road waving his arms. On the shoulder of the road sat a brown laundry truck, its left front tire flat.

"Looky here," Ralph Potter said to his brother. "He's got a problem."

Both men were in their middle thirties and were returning to their house for a late Christmas dinner.

"Let's give him a hand," Potter said. "Howdy stranger, what you need?"

The cab came to a stop. The man held a flashlight to his face as he approached the truck. His features were pale in the light. The blue eyes laughed as he talked.

"I'm heading to Knoxville. Got this far and realized my jack and everything are in Chattanooga."

"Man should always carry a jack with him, brother," Potter's brother Ted said.

"No problem," Ralph said, "we got everything."

Ralph looked at his brother and smiled. "Okay, buddy, let's see, how's about a thousand dollars? How does that sound?"

"I will gladly pay you something."

"Yep, it's plum blown through, Ralph."

The stranger was silent, looking over the stooped figures. Finally, Ralph broke into laughter.

"Hell, we're just funning you, we wouldn't take a man's money. That's not the way we do things in these parts."

"Thank you."

The stranger stood in silence over the two men and listened to the friendly banter as they manipulated the jack, and efficiently placed the spare tire on the rim, tightened down the lug nuts with the cross wrench, and jacked the car down.

"How about twenty dollars," the stranger said with a smile.

"Hell, no, buddy, but if I were you, I would get a new spare. Don't get in them mountains without a spare."

"I'll take your word for it," Koler said, losing patience. "Thanks again."

"Don't mention it."

"By the way, where's the next town?"

"It's Murphy. Not five miles up the road."

"Good. After this, I think I'll turn in for the night."

"I would. Might as well get you a good night's sleep before tackling them mountains. Nothing will be open tonight or tomorrow."

"Thank you and Merry Christmas," the stranger said.

Koler arrived in Murphy at nine thirty-five Christmas evening. He got a room at the Murphy Hotel, registering under his alias.

Tomorrow he would begin his hunt. Everything was ready.

December 26

At seven- thirty in the morning Norma and Bill's Restaurant was almost full. Koler heard the bell over the door ring as he entered. At once amid the sounds of kitchen noise, he could smell coffee and bacon. His waitress had blonde ringlets above friendly eyes. Her cheeks were pock-marked.

Koler was taken to a back booth. He sat with his back to the wall in order to see who came and went.

He ordered ham, eggs over easy, with a side of cottage fried potatoes, biscuits, gravy, and coffee.

A regular English breakfast, he thought with amusement, it is good, I have a hard day ahead.

The walls were decorated with game trophies. A full head of a buck was to Koler's right; a wildcat near the door on a pedestal. The rest of the room was decorated with mounted fish, mountain trout from the nearby lake.

As he ate, Koler watched every person that went in and out of the door. Almost every man was dressed in flannel shirts and work jeans. Since they came and went in droves, Koler figured there was a factory nearby. He watched an extremely tall youth with a baseball cap pay and leave at the counter. Of all the people he had seen, no one resembled the two men he was looking for.

He paid his bill, left a quarter tip and walked across the street to the Murphy Drug Store.

Again he heard the bell ring and smelled the old wood. The regulars were sitting by the counter. Everyone was drinking coffee and smoking. Walters leaned over a paper, spread on the counter. His large Greek nose wrinkled at the sight of Koler.

"Cup of coffee, like usual," Koler said.

"Right," Walters said, barely looking up from his paper. Finally, he waddled over and picked up the pot.

"In town kind of early, ain't you?" Walters asked as he poured the coffee.

"Yes. I have a lot to do."

"There you go," Walters said, setting the coffee down.

"Thank you."

"Didn't see your truck."

Koler raised one eyebrow. "It's around the corner," he said shrugging his shoulders.

Walters put the tiny cream pitcher next to the stranger's coffee and returned to his paper.

The regulars were discussing Christmas.

The old man with the straw hat was sitting across from the thin man with the huge black stain on his bottom teeth.

"Yeah, we got this plate, the South Dakota plate. It's a family joke. Ever' year somebody gets it and this year it was Kelly," the man in the hat said.

"What's so special about the plate?" the other asked.

"Hell, it's just one of those family jokes," said the farmer, as he reached for a cigarette. "Speaking of jokes, did you hear what happened to Norman Poole the other day?"

"Nope."

"Done some trading with Clarence," the farmer said as he grinned.

Everyone laughed, understanding the joke.

"Seems that Clarence sold that old bird dog to Norman, gave him a good price too, anyway the dog was fine, so Norman took him bird hunting. He scouted around Baker's Point a time until he come on a mess of doves."

Again the farmer was interrupted by unanimous laughter.

"One bird flies up," the farmer continued, looking at the ceiling fans and gesturing with his fingers. "Norman shoots, the dog don't move. Norman shoots again, the dog don't even flinch. Norman yells at the dog and he's looking like this."

The man in the straw hat craned his neck amid the laughter.

"Come the next day Norman had figured it out that the damn dog was stone deaf. Looks up Clarence."

The farmer paused. Everything was silent. He continued.

"How's it goin, Norman says. Say Clarence about that dog you sold me, how come you didn't tell me it was deaf?"

Again the room was silent.

"You never asked." The farmers roared. "That's what he said--'you never asked."

"Don't seem Christmas without snow," the one with the stained teeth said, after everyone had settled down.

"Word is, we'll get a blizzard tomorrow evening."

"Bullshit," Walters said in his expansive way. "No one can predict the weather around here."

"Weatherman's calling for it," said the man in the straw hat.

"Tis the season," said the other.

Koler motioned for a second cup of coffee.

"I swear that Clarence," said the man in the straw hat. "By the way, you ever gone fishing with Clarence?"

Everyone laughed again.

But when Koler turned to look at the speaker, the man with the straw hat stopped.

"Oh, by the way, mister," he said. "Your friend's in town, Tommy Maxwell."

Koler feigned a look of elation. "No kidding. When did he get in?"

"I saw Patrick Maxwell yesterday," the man in the straw hat said proudly. "Said Tommy and this friend of his been in from New York for three days now. They're staying on past the New Year."

"I didn't know Tommy was working in New York," said the man with the stained teeth.

Walters looked up from his paper and watched Koler.

"Listen," Koler said, gulping his coffee down. "I appreciate you telling me. I'll drop by his place. What a surprise that will be."

Koler slid a dime across the counter, nodded, and headed out the door.

He would go back to the hotel for a few hours. He would book his room for two more days. Since he intended to be out of the area before then, he hoped to delay the authorities, if it happened that they were after him. But for now, there was no hurry. He had found his prey. He purchased a morning paper, read it, and spent the rest of the morning reviewing his notes.

As always, his heart pounded slightly harder, now that his prey was in his sites. A fluttering sensation filled his chest. He felt secure and quite pleased with himself. So Maxwell had indeed returned home. And Thibadeaux was with him. What a stroke of luck! But Koler reviewed the entire U.S. trip and congratulated himself that this time he had not been lucky. He had put in his time finding Maxwell, in the true spirit of his Order.

Blood and Honor, the thought ran briefly through his mind.

His plan was to cruise past the house around dusk, seeing if anyone was home. He would then work his way to the back of the farmhouse, in the stretch of woods that overlooked the house. His only desire was to get a look at his prey. He doubted that he would take them while still in the house. Knowing that the house, like many homes in the area, was built in a hollow with two steep hills jutting down to the back of the house, the hollow served as excellent protection from the wind and an efficient place to build, due to energy conservation. The treeline of these hills stopped only fifty yards from the back of the house.

It would be the perfect place to approach.

If an opportunity properly presented itself, he would seize it. But the major thing was not to get in a rush. Time was on his side, and he would nurture every second until the right moment.

He decided to nap. He wanted to be extremely sharp by dusk. Even the nap was a calculated element of his art. He closed his eyes and pictured the streets of Munich, where he had first been sworn into the SS. He smiled. His Order had been good to him. His assignments had always been quite pleasant and compared to others, had a minimum of personal danger. This assignment was equally as pleasant, and he had no doubts as to its outcome.

Those infernal fucking diesels--darkness throbbing--reaching up and finding no pipes, the air--clear--it smells like a train--I am on the train--the diesels take me home--three months in New York--tackers--I love the things I'm supposed to destroy--Richard, start bringing the stuff in--shit, Tommy, you crazy--I thought we had an agreement--don't hear me wrong--I do it--but you still crazy--diesels, take me out of the throbbing night, the dark green faces of the passengers in the vibrating rain storm, the drops and pounding on the outside creating veins and splotches on the passengers' faces--everybody's dying, someone must stop it--don't be a hypocrite, you—I still say you crazy--were we right or wrong, Richard--I don't know and you don't neither, you talk too much, think too much you, and as for blowing up a bay at Federal, you crazy--we agreed to do a job--fuck the job, Tommy, our only job now is to stay alive--fuck it, come with me to momma's house--where does she live--right here in Kearney--the dilapidated tenements--the empty apartment behind the garbage-strewn yard, no Annette Thibadeaux, no forwarding address--the hard look in Richard's eyes--where you reckon she's gone?--shit, Cher how I'm gonna know--probly run off with the nearest Tom, Dick, or Harry, her--and the nights after work, alone, in Pat Dumpy's Rose Room, the interplay between the girls and sailors--the sleepy jazz--mirrors in red haze, blue veins of cigarette smoke marbling his face in the mirror--not the same, my face, different--like Richard's since his mom turned up missing--or maybe since then--since that fucking day or night--he's right--our sabotage is just a sick fantasy now--too late--we could blow a hundred ships and the fucking war will still survive--what a goddamned fool I've been--must get out of Jersey--this place is dying anyway--the air smells like burning rubber--dead--hey rich, how'd you like to come to North Carolina for Christmas--here's bettin' wecan get off--hey, down home grits and shit--yeah, right--wetalk to straw boss and get the time off--the diesels take me home.

December 26

She was living on Amber Way, a mountainous, winding country road. In Tommy's initial discussions with his parents, her name had inevitably come up. His mother had been the first to mention her.

"Elaine is married now," she said, without looking up from her crocheting. "Married Perry Watkins. She lives alone now out Amber Way."

"Perry's in the Pacific," his father added.

The first five days of Maxwell's stay had been most pleasant. There was little discussion of politics after the initial questioning. Thibadeaux had fit in well. It had become the joke of the vacation when Richard had cleaned half the turkey platter off at Christmas dinner, leaving only the dark meat. They intended to stay until after the New Year. Maxwell was even entertaining staying for good, although he had not mentioned it to his partner. They planned to get in some hunting and fishing in the next few days, but first there was Elaine.

It was still early morning when Maxwell arrived at her house. He mounted the front porch and knocked on the door. No one answered. He saw her car in the driveway, so he walked around back. Then he saw her.

She was standing at the edge of the yard which overlooked a hollow- -mountains jutting straight down at the far end of the hollow. She was stooping over a clothes basket. When she raised up to hang up a blouse on the line, a swift breeze caused the sheet she had hung up to balloon out towards her, at the same time her light blue dress flew up, exposing her legs in the sunlight and her sheer white panties. She continued to struggle with the clothes line and since she did not see Maxwell approach from the rear, she was unconcerned about her dress. The wind died down by the time he reached her.

"Same old Elaine," he said.

She wheeled around and uttered a slight scream, but on seeing him, she smiled, shuddered, then stooped over to pick up the basket. She knitted her eyebrows slightly before she spoke.

"When did you get in town?" she asked.

"Here, let me help you with that."

He began hurriedly hanging up the clothes with the brown wooden pins.

"I came in with a friend about five days ago," he said. "When I heard you had married, I started not to come."

She took a deep breath and seemed slightly annoyed. She hung her clothes now much more briskly. She took his pins and clothes quickly, like a woman will do when showing disgust.

"I'm sorry," he said. "Maybe I shouldn't have come."

She was doing her best to hide her face from him.

"I just wanted to drop by."

"Come on inside, I've got a pot of coffee going."

He followed her up the wooden steps into the tiny kitchen with a gas stove and yellow curtains with white fringe.

She fetched two china cups out of the cupboard and poured the steaming coffee into them.

"Coffee is precious these days," she said with a sigh, "the rationing and all."

"Yeah."

"You take sugar, don't you?" She reached high into the cabinet and got down a tin cup. It was obvious the sugar was reserved only for special occasions. Maxwell was distressed at the formal tone of their conversation.

"Thanks."

When she looked him in the face for the first time, he was stunned. Again her huge eyes with their long lashes held him, just as they had for years. Her cheeks were flushed most beautifully.

"So you married old Perry," he said, as he lit a cigarette. "He was on my wrestling team in high school. He's a great guy."

"Yeah, I know he was on the team. I was there. Remember?"

Her tone contained a note of bitterness. He knew immediately she was not happy.

"And you say he is stationed overseas?"

"I didn't say it. Your parents told you," she said in the same direct way.

"Elaine....."

"Don't please......" and suddenly, putting her thin fingers to her mouth, she darted lightly out of the room.

He sat and smoked. Presently she returned.

It was obvious she had been crying.

"Something smells good," he said, leaning back in his chair and stretching. "What is it?"

"Gingerbread," she said, pulling down a strand of hair.

"How's your family?"

"Fine."

"And did you have Christmas over there?" Maxwell asked, leaning forward to put out his cigarette.

"Yes."

"Do you still see my parents?" he asked.

"Not very often," she said. "I can't. Memories of you have not been pleasant, Tommy. Let's see, it was exactly three years ago, wasn't it?"

He tossed his head in his familiar manner, getting the

hair from his eyes. "Most of the things I said," he began, "in those days.........were childish. I've tried to put the sarcastic side of me aside."

"You have changed," she said. "I can see it."

He frowned. "I hope I'm changing for good now," he said. "I hope it's over."

She looked at him, tilting her head to the side. "Go on," she said.

"My belief about the war," he stammered, then cutting his eyes to the floor, "not really......war....such a terrible thing."

"How do you know? You've never been." Her tone had a ring of accusation.

"I've seen things you'll never hear of, Elaine. Things I want to forget myself. I want to start over, go back to teaching, get married someday, maybe even settle here."

She laughed bitterly and tossed her head.

"I know what you're thinking," he said. "And I agree. If you're worried about me ever trying to complicate your life.....I wish you and Perry all the happiness....."

"That's enough," she said abruptly, running her finger around the rim of her cup.

"Are you unhappy?" he asked.

"What do you think?" He looked at the yellow curtains.

"I can see it," he said.

They sat in silence for a time. He was determined not to speak first.

"I got married just to say I had done it," she said, staring off.

"Just to say you had done it," he said, repeating her words and prompting her on.

"I don't know," she said, turning her head as if avoiding a fly. "I rushed everything. He said he loved me. I suppose I believed him....... but now.........I just don't know."

"You don't know what?"

She laughed bitterly.

"I don't know anything." Now her eyes glazed over. "When I was a little girl, I was taught that everything happens for a reason. And I believed that. Now I don't know. It seems that nothing happens any more except by blind luck. Things just happen."

"Things occur and that's it," Maxwell repeated, now annoyed at his own habit of repeating her words. "I don't know if I believe that or not." And his thoughts ran irresistibly to Julie and the night at the Breakers.

"Anyway, how have you been?" she said nervously. "If you're in town long enough, maybe Perry will be home on leave and you can get together........."

She stopped when she saw Maxwell smile.

"You're right," she said, understanding immediately and looking at him with caressing eyes. "A nightmare."

"You can still be happy," he said.

"I keep having premonitions about his death," she said. "I often dream about it. You were right about the war, Tommy."

"That's funny," he said, scooting his chair up. "I thought you were."

She laughed. "And now that we know that we're both right, where does that leave us?"

They both laughed. They talked of town gossip. Reeves Ferguson had been divorced from his wife and was reconciling. He had recently come under community pressure to resign his position. Word was that he would resign after this school year.

"You could have your teaching job back," she said. "People are always saying what a good teacher you were."

"It's funny," he said, leaning back and crossing his legs. "A week ago, all my options were closed, and now everything is opening up."

"Everything?" she said, smiling coyly.

She blushed. "I've missed you," she said. "I didn't even realize it until you came walking up."

He laughed. "I didn't realize it either until that breeze," he said.

She slapped at his arm across the table. She was blushing.

"Same old Tommy."

"That's right." And then a different look on her face, one of remembrance and adoration. She put the china cup to her lips and put the cup into the saucer with a note of finality. She gazed directly across into his eyes. The look was unmistakable.

"I'm sorry," she said, gathering herself. "If I had known you were coming........."

"It wouldn't have been any different," he said, his blonde hair hanging over his forehead as he leaned forward. "Believe it or not, it's hard for me too."

Her head turned quickly to the side as she grabbed a cigarette.

"Didn't know you smoked."

"Every now and then," she said.

Maxwell laughed. "You look real tough with that hanging out the corner of your mouth."

She laughed with him and dropped the cigarette on the table.

"You see what you made me do."

The laughter cut the tension between them. They laughed and joked for a time in the same manner as they had done as teenagers.

"You were right about something else, Tommy."

"What?"

"It would never have worked between you and me.........with the war and all."

Maxwell took a deep breath. "Times are hard for everyone," he said. "I've thought of you a lot in the last couple of years."

"Perry and I had a honeymoon, and two weeks later he was gone, that was it. Oh, I'm working and making the house payment....and there are letters."

"But it's not the same, is it?"

"The same as what?" she asked.

"As really being married."

She stared off.

"Like I say, times are tough everywhere. There's lonely people everywhere," he said.

She looked him directly in the eyes. "You know the truly horrible part," she said.

"No."

"It's waiting for the letter that will tell you he's dead. He's in the Marines, you know. Landing forces," she said, now grabbing his wrist. "No, let me finish, the horrible part is that sometimes I can't help thinking that if it happened, it would be a relief. At least it would be over. Isn't that horrible? I know it's wrong, but I can't help it."

"It's natural," he said. "Don't worry."

"At times, I wish I were in the war," she said. "At least it's not as boring as this."

"Never wish that."

"What's wrong? You never went, did you?" she said, the same tone of accusation returning to her voice.

He hesitated for a long time. "No," he said, "I never went."

"Then why are you looking like that?"

"It's nothing," he said.

She put her other hand over his. "Tommy," she said, "you never could lie to me."

Her words stunned him.

"Let's just say I found out some things," he began slowly. "Things inside me that I never could have dreamed of. When a man is confronted with certain situations, he sees a side of himself that he never knew existed."

He uttered the last part of the sentence as if only to himself.

"Tell me what you're talking about," she said.

"I can't," he said, blinking rapidly. "Let's just say in the last two months, I've been very lonely."

"Something very bad must have happened."

"Let's change the subject," he said.

She rose from the table. His hands were still enfolded within hers. She sat in his lap, facing him, put her arms around his neck and kissed him full on the mouth. He grabbed her small waist. He had not come for this, but it was happening. Her mouth and frame were trembling when their lips parted and she looked into his eyes.

They stood together. She looked up. He kissed her long and hard.

"Tommy," she said, "let's have this one time........no wait.........and then, we must never do it again, please agree to that."

Without answering, he swept her off the floor, picking her up into his arms.

"No, this way," she giggled, pointing him to the bedroom and laughing as he nearly stumbled over the coffee table.

He lay her gently on a brass bed. She lay propped on her elbows, watching him take off his shirt.

"You didn't promise me," she said.

He looked down and smiled. "I agree," he said. "Wouldn't have it any other way."

He sat on the bed and they kissed.

He began undressing her. He kissed her on the neck as he unzipped her dress. When she pulled the dress over her head, she wore only a slip. She shrugged her shoulders. The small laced straps fell. He pulled the top down. Her breasts were small and pointed. He put his mouth on her breasts, first one, then the other, running his tongue in circles over her nipples. With his right hand he massaged her inner thigh, then over her panties as she slowly spread her legs.

After a time his fingers were beneath the silk. He placed a finger inside her. She was wet. He pushed the finger slowly in and out. She began to moan. He kissed her repeatedly on the mouth, breasts, stomach. He placed two fingers inside her. Her breathing began to change.

Finally he pulled her panties off and put his mouth between her legs. She began to rotate her hips.

"Oh Tommy......."

He raised up and kissed her all over her face. He felt her nimble fingers struggling with his belt. He reached down and helped her. Her fingers were on him now; he felt his zipper going down.

She reached inside his pants.

In another minute he was naked and on top of her.

Twenty minutes later he lay propped on one elbow in the bed next to her. He smoked a cigarette.

"Thank you, Tommy," she said as she sat up, the sheet covering only her waist.

He smiled. "For what?"

"You know what."

"Do you still want me to keep my promise?" he asked.

She smiled and nodded, then giggled. "Well... don't know. Are you going to stay in town a while?"

A look in her eyes as they gazed at one another caused them to burst into laughter. He rocked her in his arms as they laughed.

"Ooowee, I a damn city boy, hunting rabbits."

Maxwell walked in front of Thibadeaux, down the thin path through the woods and thickets bordering Ocoee Lake. They were nearing Baker's Point, a favorite local fishing hole. Gus, a black Labrador, was darting back and forth on both sides of the trail ahead of them, snorting, and turning to his two companions as if to say, Let's get on with it.

When Thibadeaux had spoken, Tommy nodded to indicate he had heard him, but he did not speak. While hunting, Tommy preferred silence.

"Remember when we went hunting with Frank?"

"Seems like a long time ago," Maxwell answered.

"You got quiet on us that day too. You really like it, don't you?"

Maxwell smiled, indicating his slight annoyance. "That's right," was all he said.

"We could shoot a deer," Maxwell said. "You ever had venison?"

Presently Gus came to a thicket on the right, his frame jumping up as he howled once, then in a frenzy of snorts, darted to the back of the thicket where they could hear him rustling about.

"Get ready," Maxwell said.

Two rabbits darted across the trail; two gunshots--Thibadeaux missing badly while Maxwell's shot found flesh, blowing a bloody hole in the hide of a fat rabbit. Maxwell picked the rabbit up by the back legs and placed it in the game bag.

"Five to my zero," Thibadeaux said.

"You'll get the hang of it. Lead him a bit next time."

They reached Baker's Point, where two ridges jutted down to a wide slew. Tommy's favorite fishing hole-- even as the two men ate their breakfast of sardines, crackers, and tobasco sauce, the fish were jumping, leaving concentric circles in the calm, green water.

"Is that bass?" Thibadeaux asked.

"Right."

"I like to catch some of that mountain trout."

"Maybe I can carry you up into the Smokies one day. Fresh trout over a camp fire is the greatest thing since sliced bread."

Tommy sat in silence, watching the sun glow over the lake. The sardines and tobasco sauce reminded him of his father.

Soon they started the hike out.

By late afternoon, they had killed eight rabbits between them. When they came back across Highway 19, they decided to drive towards Murphy. Thibadeaux had mentioned getting a Coke and taking a load off their feet before heading home.

As he drove, Maxwell was pondering the best time to tell Thibadeaux that he had decided not to return to New York. He was going to stay home and start over. He would apply for his old teaching job, and if that didn't pan out, he would try in the next county.

They entered Murphy and pulled in front of The Murphy Drug Store and went inside.

The drug store looked the same as when Maxwell had been a boy. The familiar creaks of the old wood and the smell of the hair tonic were prevalent. The old face of Mr. Walters lit up on seeing him. The deep wrinkles on the bald forehead smoothed out as the old Greek smiled and shook Maxwell's hand.

"Good to see you, Tommy."

"How have you been, Mr. Walters?"

"Good," he shrugged. "Can't complain."

"Mr. Walters, this is my friend, Richard Thibadeaux." He shook Thibadeaux's hand.

"Pleased to meet you. You like it here in Murphy?"

"Hell yes," Thibadeaux replied. "Never thought I like a small town, but having a ball."

"He just likes my mom's cooking," Maxwell said.

Walters laughed. "What you have?"

"Two cokes. Make them cherry cokes," Maxwell said with a grin. "I used to love those when I was a kid."

Walters brought the cokes.

"By the way," the old man said, "did your friend find you?"

"What friend?"

"A tall blonde man. He say he know you in college."

Maxwell shrugged. "No, he didn't come by. Did he leave a name?"

"He told me once but I forgot. He drives the laundry truck through here each week....." Suddenly the old man broke off, the old Greek nose wrinkled slightly. He seemed puzzled. He went into the kitchen with two dirty plates.

Maxwell and Thibadeaux were each into a magazine when Walters emerged. The old man leaned on the counter in front of Maxwell in order to speak softly.

"Hey, Tommy, you had any problems wid de law?" he asked.

Maxwell felt his stomach fall.

"No, not that I know of," Maxwell said, looking up. "Why do you ask?"

"Curious, I guess."

"Curious about what, you mean about my being gone so long and suddenly showing up?"

Walters leaned closer. "No, nothing like that, it's just that dis guy's been coming around asking questions....."

"You mean, this college buddy."

"Yeah," the old man said, pointing comically to his nose. "But you see dis? It can still smell a cop. He dresses like one anyway. Just comes by every week or so and noses, so I thought you might be having trouble. Thought I let you know."

Maxwell leaned back, looking out the front window at Gus, who was fidgeting in the back of the truck.

"When was this guy last in here?"

"Dis morning. Elmer told him the other day you in town and the stranger say he be sure to drop by."

Maxwell asked for a description. Walters obliged.

"Thanks," Maxwell said.

"Shoo, anytime, can't stand the sneaky bastards anyway," Walters snorted.

Maxwell turned to Thibadeaux. "We'd better be getting home. It'll be dark soon."

Maxwell drove rapidly home.

"What you think?" Thibadeaux asked, anxiously watching Maxwell's face.

"I'll tell you after I make a phone call."

The telephone at the Maxwell house was located in the kitchen, and Tommy waited almost a half hour until his mother had finished making her blueberry cobbler. When she finished and left the kitchen, Maxwell searched in his wallet for the phone number he used to know from memory.

He talked to the operator, who dialed the number. He heard the phone ring, sounding far away as if immersed in a well.

"Hello," a female voice on the other end said.

"Cheryl......Tommy Maxwell..........Merry Christmas."

She did not answer. The silence caused butterflies to swim in Tommy's stomach before continuing.

"I'd like to speak to Frank. Is he around?"

"You'd like to speak to Frank," Cheryl said angrily, suppressing a sob. "That will be a bit difficult, Tommy. You haven't heard?"

Maxwell flushed.

"Frank's dead."

"What?"

"Murdered about three weeks ago....."

"God, Cheryl, I'm sorry....."

But she wouldn't let him finish. When she spoke, her voice took an angry, accusing tone.

"That's right, Tommy. They found him murdered in Central Park. Stabbed. I'm here today working on the house. We've decided to auction it off."

Again she suppressed sobs.

"You know, he never went to the Park at nights," she said. "At least not while we were together."

"Maybe it's my fault," she managed to say.

"Come on, Cheryl, you know better...."

"No, if I had been here....."

"Cheryl, you can't blame yourself," Tommy said as his mind raced.

And then what she said caused Maxwell to break immediately into a cold sweat.

"There's something else," she said. "The police found traces of blood in his study. It looks like his body was moved."

"Moved to Central Park?"

"That's right. You wouldn't know anything about this, would you, Tommy?"

"So, do the police think a professional did it?" he said, purposefully ignoring her question.

"Professional?" she said sarcastically. "Yes, I believed they used that word, if you can call what happened to Frank 'professional.'"

"Jesus," Maxwell said, "I'm sorry, Cheryl, I've got to go."

He hung up the phone, feeling the handle slide from his sweaty palm. He promptly picked it back up and dialed another number.

"Who you calling now?" Thibadeaux asked. "What happened?"

"Our asses are in a sling, that's what."

As Tommy talked to a local moonshiner, Ernest Hammond, Thibadeaux felt his own stomach sink. He did not like the look on Tommy's face. He had seen that look once before.

Maxwell hung up the phone.

"Let's go."

"Where we going?"

"I'm going to teach you something about country ways. The way us mountain boys protect ourselves."

"Protect yourselves from what?"

"You didn't hear what Walters said?"

"You think......."

"I ain't about to think nothing. I got to know."

Maxwell grabbed the truck keys.

"I asked you where we going."

"We're going to Ernest Hammonds, an old moonshiner. Used to

teach his kid. I don't want any surprises. Hopefully, we can get finished with this before dark."

"What in hell you talking about?"

"Frank's dead, Richard."

"Christ."

"Murdered," Tommy said with a look of significance. "Three weeks ago. A professional hit."

"Holy shit."

"You're damned right 'holy shit.'"

"Goddamn, Tommy, if someone hunting us, we dead. We don't even know what he look like, us. Some guy walk up and pow, that's it."

"It won't happen that way," Maxwell said, his eyes fixed to the road.

"What you mean?"

"If he's hunting us, you got to think like him. The only place he knows we will be is at the house."

"So what difference does that make? All dis open country and the woods."

"What do you think we're doing now? We'll find out who he is and where he is."

"How's that?"

"We'll tie a bell on his ass."

Ernest Hammond was a thin man in his fifties. His hair was close-cropped with flecks of gray near his temples. His face was stubby from a three day beard, and he was missing one of his front teeth.

It was before four o'clock when he saw the blue truck pull in front of his house. His feet propped on the front porch rail, he rocked back in his rocking chair and bounced up to greet his guests. The old hillbilly's eyes squinted as he saw two men exit the car. The features of the weather-beaten face hardened for a second, then smoothed out. His smile revealed his brown, stained teeth.

"Tommy Maxwell, long time, no see."

"Howdy Ernest. How's everything?"

"Can't complain. Gray's not here now. He'd sure like to see you."

Tommy shifted his feet.

"I came to see you Ernest. I need a favor."

"Name it."

"Ernest, how'd you like to earn twenty-five dollars before nightfall?"

"I know you like a snort now and then," the old man said, smiling. "But twenty-five dollars worth will kill you."

"It's nothing like that."

The old hillbilly tossed a whittling stick aside and folded up his knife as he sauntered off the front porch.

"Tommy, you got my attention."

Arriving back at the Maxwell farm--after Tommy spent a few minutes explaining to his parents that he would be busy putting a "deer screen" behind the house-- the three men set to work. Maxwell's father appeared skeptical, but he only shrugged and went to work at the family well.

"Now I'm gonna show you this once, and I'll take my time, soz next time you can do it yourself," Ernest said as he squatted in the back yard. "The real trick is how you cut these notches in these pegs. No, not that way, Richard, whittle it in longer strokes."

Ernest taught the two men the old moonshiner's trick of putting a protective screen around major paths in the woods. Maxwell intended to protect the back of his house from an intruder.

He concentrated his efforts on the two descending paths in the woods at the back of the house. The edge of the woods overlooked the Maxwell's back, screened-in porch.

First they devised triggers made out of wooden pegs. In the pegs they cut a notch, just deep enough to fit around a nail, placed at a ninety degree angle. They drove a nail into a tree. The heads of the nail were bent with a pair of pliers. The notches of the triggers were fit against the nails and held up by the tension of the line which ran from the top of the peg. On one side of the trigger, they tied a number ten staging line to the top of a sapling near the paths in the woods. They pulled the string taut until the sapling was bent over. The line ran from the peg, across the trail, ankle-high, over a limb to the top of the bent sapling, then around the trunk of another tree, and down to the house to a counterweight. The task was easily accomplished. The longest part of the entire setup was, as Ernest had said, the cutting of the notches and the wearing down of the bark of the bigger trees, where the line ran down to the house. The latter was necessary so that the line would not become frayed with the constant tension created by the bent sapling.

Now if an intruder approached and hit the string enough to move the notched trigger off the nail, the trigger would fly up as the sapling on the other side of the trail straightened. All the tension would go out of the line and the weight in the house would fall. A total of four screens were set at two distances on both trails and attached to counterweights in the house.

When Tommy's father saw Ernest and Richard attaching the line to a clock in the house, he pulled his son aside.

"Now you want to tell me what in hell you're doing?"

"It's a bet I had with Richard, dad," Maxwell said as innocently as possible. "We're just passing the time. It's no big deal."

"Don't lie to me, son."

"Okay, dad, I'll tell you the truth," Tommy said, slapping his father on the shoulder. "Mom has always wanted a still in the kitchen and Ernest is helping us protect against law."

Maxwell's father suppressed a laugh, shook his head, and walked away.

The work completed, Maxwell ran Ernest back home.

"Easiest money I ever made," Hammond said, grinning widely and showing his dirty teeth. "I'll tell Gray you dropped by."

Maxwell shook his hand. "Thanks, Ernest."

Hammond got out of the truck and before Maxwell drove off, leaned in the window.

"Looky here, Tommy, I ain't one to meddle," he said, "but if you're having problems with anyone, I'll be glad to help."

"You already have, Ernest. Thanks. If the triggers will work, we can take it from here," Maxwell said as he threw the truck into gear. "Say hello to Gray for me."

That night Otto Koler took a light supper at Norma and Bill's and headed towards Hayesville and the Maxwell home.

He had spent the previous day scouting out the roads around the Maxwell house and determining various escape routes. Now all that was left was picking the time and spot. He was ready.

He drove out the Hayesville highway and parked a mile and a half past the Maxwell farm.

He was dressed completely in black with a black toboggan. He was armed with a knife, a Colt 45, and the Winchester 70, which he had strapped to his back.

He began a cross country hike, which would take him to the far end of the hill, which descended to the back of the Maxwell home. In the darkness it was difficult to tell exactly where he was, but in time, he surmised he had reached the correct area.

Stumbling constantly in the descending darkness, and twice having to take major detours around thickets of rhododendron, Koler managed to climb the ridge.

On reaching the top, he was pleased with what he saw. Just as he had calculated, he was on the top of the correct ridge. The wind from the mountains moaned through the hollow.

The Maxwell house lay at the bottom of the hollow. A small light shone out of the house--a spark of light against the deep, velvet color of the darkness.

As Koler slowly descended on the path to the back of the house, the light from the house window slowly increased in size, swimming in and out of his vision. Twice he slipped and fell when he hit small gullies, that in the darkness were impossible to see. He was in unfamiliar terrain.

After a considerable descent, he saw the orange, twinkling light of the house grow into a larger, well-lighted rectangle of a dining room window.

The wind whistled from the mountains behind him. The sky was clear and shining with bright stars. The half moon had yet to rise to its height.

The closer he got to the house, the more catlike he became. He stopped and panned around him periodically, his training taking over.

He was unconcerned about noise, since he knew the strong wind would cover the sounds of his steps.

He fended off limbs from his face. The light from the tiny rectangle below swayed up and down, shielded at times by approaching trees. The closer he got to the house, the more alert he became.

This should have been done days ago, he thought.

Thoughts of his slight procrastination over the last day bothered him. He blamed it on the newspapers.

Reports in the paper about Stalingrad had stunned him. The situation looked, from all accounts, hopeless.

On December 12, encircled German forces had launched an attack aimed at breaking out of the Stalingrad encirclement. The force of three infantry, three tank and two calvalry divisions had in a few days succeeded in pressing back the Russians and developing an encirclement of their own. But the Russian flanks held with as much tenacity as the defenders inside the bombed-out city had held in September.

Koler snorted at how the Western newspapers were portraying the Red Army as heroes. Yet the claim was difficult to deny.

Using his tanks in small groups, vonn Mannstein had struck a series of blows at different places in rapid succession. The German threat reached its climax on the 17th of December, having advanced 36 miles. On Christmas Eve, however, fresh reinforcements had reached the Russians, and they passed immediately to the offensive, and in three days had completed their advance back to their previous positions.

This success was of utmost importance. It assured a Russian victory at Stalingrad.

Koler had also read that Hitler had publicly proclaimed that the Germans would no longer try to break out. He would send an army to break in.

Koler cursed. Empty words. The papers proclaimed that 70,000 Germans were trapped. Koler knew differently. The trapped Sixth Army consisted of a quarter of a million members of the Wehrmacht.

He stepped on a round rock and nearly fell headlong.

Koler knew that Stalingrad was the beginning of the end.

He had his doubts when the Allies had developed a second front in North Africa in November. But at that time the Germans still held the initiative in Russia, even though they were fighting hand-to-hand in the bombed-out city of Stalingrad.

Koler raised an eyebrow. Ja, he thought, the hunter is the hunted.

The thought had been irresistible. As the house neared, his alertness increased. He had never felt this way before. Why? He had hunted in foreign lands before. All had been routine, just as this mission had been.

But he had learned to trust his instinct. There was a curious element about these mountains. There was a cohesiveness among the people here. He would not underestimate them. And had there not been a certain look on the face of Walters in the drug store? Koler trusted his intuition.

He guessed that the time was about six-thirty.

When he was within sixty yards of the house, he stopped, placed one knee on the ground behind a tree, pulled the Winchester from his back, pointed it, and nestled the Bausch and Lombe scope next to his eye.

Through the lighted window he could see the six figures below eating dinner. He moved in closer, his heart pounding with exhilaration.

He thought irresistibly of his own father and mother, perhaps in an air raid shelter in Germany. Times were changing in the homeland with the introduction of allied formation bombing.

But no matter where they were, they would be together, he mused, just as this family is, enjoying what they can, talking about relatives who were stationed in various stations of the world......and his father's face filled him........and eventually they will talk about me.

The light looks pleasant down there, warm, he thought.

He froze. He dove to his belly and again assuming a firing position, pointed the Winchester. Suddenly and inexplicably, the six figures below had calmly stood up as he had begun his second approach, and the lights of the house had been turned off. His mind raced. Now the house was a pale reflection in the moonlight. He could see no one.

Could they have seen me? he thought with a scowl, impossible. In the few minutes that followed, Koler contemplated running. Could it be that someone was behind him? He held his ground and waited.

He heard the creak of a screen door.

There were two men on the back, screened-in porch. He put his eye to the scope. The two figures were dim silhouettes. They seemed to be watching the woods, pretending to have a casual conversation. There could be no question. Somehow they knew he was here.

Slowly he brought the rifle into position. The crosshairs of the scope rested on the visage below, the one with the large nose. The face was unmistakable to Koler. His scope now held the silhouette of Tommy Maxwell.

The dinner table was decorated with a centerpiece of holly, red berries, and pine cones. The table cloth was white with green, embroidered Christmas designs. As always, the Christmas tree sat in the corner of the living room. The same glass angel topped the tree. Thelma Maxwell was hurrying back and forth to the kitchen while everyone else gathered around the table. Mr. Maxwell sat at the head of the table while George, Tommy's brother sat next to him, then George's wife, Rhonda and little, toe-headed Jamie. Maxwell and Thibadeaux sat across from George and Rhonda.

"Turkey again?" shouted Mr. Maxwell, as he dragged his stiff leg into his seat and beamed at the joke.

"Oh hush up," Thelma said from the kitchen.

"Turkey divan is next," George said. He had the same basic features as Tommy except for a softer look, that is, his nose fit the contours of his face and the brow had a smoother, more relaxed appearance.

"Now go easy on that," Mr. Maxwell said as he set the turkey in front of Thibadeaux.

Thibadeaux eyed the plate and said, "Just getting my mind set." Everyone laughed.

Jamie was attended to first, as Mrs. Maxwell leaned over his high chair and cut small portions for him.

"I can do that, mom," Rhonda said.

"No, let me."

"You're gonna spoil me," Rhonda said with a pretty smile.

"That's what grandmothers are for," Mrs. Maxwell said as she cut the baby's turkey, her face beaming with the smile that Maxwell remembered from long ago.

When Thelma was seated, Mr. Maxwell led the prayer.

"Heavenly Father, we thank You so much for this gathering and praise Your holy name. We ask that You will protect those at this gathering as they go their separate ways, so that we can be together again to celebrate this wonderful event. And Heavenly Father, be with our armed forces, with our boys overseas, that Your will can be done......"

At this last sentence Maxwell opened his eyes; Thibadeaux was staring ahead. Their eyes met.

".......and bless this food to the nourishment of our bodies, in Jesus' name, Amen."

For the first few minutes of the meal no one spoke. There was only to be heard the clanking of silver on plates.

"Delicious as usual," Thibadeaux said, breaking the silence at last.

"Thank you," Thelma said. "You're just hungry."

"I know what you're thinking, mom," Maxwell said with a half-full mouth. "Richard will eat anything, and you're right, but this dressing is special."

Rhonda was trying to feed Jamie his beets. First she crushed them in his plate, then spooned up tiny bites only to have him pucker his little mouth and spit them out. This brought loud laughter from all around the table.

"Honestly," Rhonda said, "I can't get him to eat his vegetables."

"Tommy and George were the same way," Mrs. Maxwell beamed. She wore her hair in a bun with a stem of mistletoe in the side.

"Come on, mom," Maxwell said. "George ain't never had trouble eating anything." As he said this, he glanced at the clock near the window. It read 6:24.

"You and Richard clean those rabbits yet?" Mr. Maxwell asked.

"Clean as a whistle. They're in the icebox. Thought we'd whip up some rabbit stew tomorrow."

"Oh please," Michelle said, Maxwell's sister, who wrinkled her pert nose, "I hate rabbit stew. Mom used to fix it once a week during the Depression."

"I thought you liked it," Mrs. Maxwell said sarcastically.

"Rabbit tastes so wild," Michelle said.

"Should be able to hit some deer with this weather so mild," Mr. Maxwell said as he adjusted his glasses.

"We've had our eyes for some," Maxwell said.

"So I noticed," his father said, sarcastically referring to the afternoon activity with Ernest Hammond.

The meal passed quickly. The women cleared the table and served coffee and blueberry cobbler. After finishing his dessert, Mr. Maxwell leaned back in his chair, lit a cigar, and despite the pleas of his wife, knocked ashes into his plate.

"Looks like the Germans are finished in Russia," he said. "Did you hear the radio today?"

Maxwell looked at the clock.

"I heard it," he said.

"Who would ever think the Russians could whip the German army," the old man continued. "But looks like they have."

"It ain't over yet," Thibadeaux said as he lit a cigarette.

"Might as well be from what they say," Mr. Maxwell said.

Since the beginning of the holiday, Maxwell and his father had both made a conscious effort to avoid discussing politics. Nevertheless, his father's curiosity as to Maxwell's activities over the last two years was beginning to get the best of him.

"I'll be drafted within the month," George said with a gleam in his eye. "And if I'm not drafted, I'll sign up."

Both Rhonda and Maxwell had to hide their disgust.

"Your son and your wife need you too," Maxwell said, unable to restrain himself.

"There's lots of people in that boat," George answered with a grin.

"How was Elaine?" Mrs. Maxwell asked, obviously trying to change the subject.

"She's fine," Maxwell said, looking at George. "But none too happy about being separated from her husband."

"You see, George," Rhonda said sharply.

George turned to Rhonda. "Look, war is not a pleasant thing, but we must do our duty."

"Tommy didn't go, so why should you?" Rhonda retorted.

During this discussion Maxwell continued to look at the clock near the back window. Unless one strained to see, the thin piece of line, which ran to the left of the clock down to the window sill and to the right to a single nail on the wall, was completely invisible.

"Elaine said her husband was in the Pacific," Maxwell said with a softer tone.

"Probably getting ready to go to the Philippines with MacArthur," Mr. Maxwell said. "I don't care what anyone says about the Germans, the nips are the toughest enemy."

"You seem almost infatuated with the war," Maxwell said, knitting his brow. "You shouldn't be as naive as everyone else. You've been in combat. Exactly how much action did you actually see?"

"Please, you two," Thelma said, shaking a spoon in the air. "We've had such a nice holiday. Don't spoil it with an argument."

Mr. Maxwell smiled and knocked his ashes. Rhonda was now in the living room with Jamie beside the Christmas tree with little manger figurines.

"Stay out of this, Thelma," Mr. Maxwell said. "A father and son can have a discussion without getting into an argument."

"That's right, mom," Maxwell said.

After helping get the dishes started, Michelle sat again at the table, leaned back, lit a cigarette, and crossed her legs.

"I never used to think so before, Tommy," said his father. "But the more I see of history and of life, the more I'm convinced that God is in control of history."

"Please, dad....."

"No, let me finish. Never have the lines between good and evil been so clearly drawn....."

"Come on, dad. Don't talk to me about God. It's God's will as long as we're winning, right?"

"You think God wants the Nazis to win?"

"I'm not sure He cares. You used to be more concerned with the Communists. Did God change his mind about them? You used to see things more my way."

"You mean as a German sympathizer?" Mr. Maxwell said with anger.

"That's uncalled for. Settle down, both of you," George said, leaning forward. "There were plenty of people fooled by Hitler in the early days, dad."

"No, it's okay, George," Maxwell said, holding up his hand. "I was never fooled. I believed then, as I do now, that all the reasons we give for war are crap. What it amounts to at the instant of combat is unplanned chaos, mass murder."

"According to your Bund," Mr. Maxwell said, and at the word, Maxwell felt a pang in his chest, "peace would only come at the expense of the British Empire."

"Did you hear anything I said, dad?"

"I heard you. Do you still think the British should be defeated?"

"I made mistakes like anyone else," Maxwell admitted, while Thibadeaux shifted uneasily in his chair. "But now, Roosevelt has stuck his foot in his mouth with this talk of unconditional surrender. Churchill's puttin' us in."

"How do you know?" shot Mr. Maxwell.

Maxwell became more animated. His face slightly flushed with the heat of the argument.

"And now that Russia is turning in the Allies' favor," Maxwell said, "the chance for peace is available."

"You're being naive, Tommy," Mr. Maxwell said, and as soon as he said this, Tommy knew it was true. "It's a fight to the end. Do you think that after the bombing attacks on London, that the British will negotiate peace? Do you think that the Russians after losing over a million people are interested in a negotiated peace?"

"You're right," Maxwell stated matter-of-factly. "That's why the Americans should lead the way to negotiations."

"What about Pearl Harbor?" George said.

"Come on, George," Maxwell said, his voice rising. "What more revenge do we need after the Philippines fall? We stand to gain more materiale and money from this war than anyone else. There's the real reason we're fighting. It's the nature of Capitalism, just ask our allies, the Communists."

"The lessor of two evils," his father said. "Negotiations would only buy Germany time to develop more weapons."

Maxwell did not have an answer for this. He leaned back and sipped his coffee.

"If Midway had gone the other way," his father said, stubbing out his cigar, "the Japanese would be in California right now."

"Now who's being naive, dad?" Maxwell said.

At that moment the clock near the window tottered and fell straight down the wall to the floor.

Thibadeaux turned white.

"Well, I'll declare," Mrs. Maxwell stated as she came out of the kitchen.

Maxwell's eyes widened. He stared at the empty space on the wall.

"All right, everyone, listen to me," he said. The sober tone he used got everyone's attention. "Keep talking like normal for a minute, then I want you all to calmly get up and walk into the living room."

"What are you talking about?" George said, laughing nervously.

"Don't ask questions. Just do as I say. I think we have a visitor."

"Why did that clock fall?" Thelma asked sternly. Instead of returning to her dishes, she sat down at the table.

"Believe me," Maxwell said, looking back and forth. "You must trust me. Okay, let's everyone calmly get up.......that's right, Rhonda, keep Jamie in there........okay, Richard, hit the light, Rhonda, unplug the Christmas tree."

Everyone did as Maxwell said. Soon everyone was kneeling or sitting on the living room floor in the darkness.

Jamie began to whimper.

"Try to keep him quiet," Maxwell said, straining to hear anything unusual.

"What is going on?" demanded Thelma, the edge of impatience returning to her voice.

"Just do as he says, Thelma," his father said sarcastically. "We should know by now what to expect. I'm sure it has something to do with the kind of company he's been keeping."

Jamie began whimpering again.

"Who's out there?" Michelle said, her voice trembling.

"Keep everyone calm, dad," Maxwell said. "Richard and I are going to check out the back."

"Be careful," Mr. Maxwell said.

"How close you think he is?" George asked as he started to stand.

"No, stay here," Maxwell said as he and Richard eased to the kitchen door. "If he comes closer than fifty feet, Richard and I will take care of him."

"Tommy Maxwell," Thelma yelled. "I am your mother and I want to know what's going on." She was on the verge of tears.

"Trust me," Maxwell said quietly, gazing sidelong into the kitchen darkness. "It may be nothing at all."

"Tommy," Mr. Maxwell said, his voice now angry, "you've been lying to us again." He could see in a glance how agitated his son had become. "I want the truth and I want it now."

Thibadeaux's legs temporarily buckled near the kitchen entrance.

"You're not just going to ignore our questions," he said.

"Not now, dad," Maxwell said, never once looking from the kitchen, "we'll have our talk later and you can argue till you're blue in the face."

"Don't talk to your father that way," his mother said angrily.

"Sorry," Maxwell said to his mother, then he turned to Thibadeaux. "Richard, come into the kitchen with me."

The two men crept into the kitchen. In a high cupboard they fetched their pistols and were squatted down loading when Mr. Maxwell came in behind them.

With his stiff leg he managed to lean close to Tommy. "Everyone's down in there. Now who's out there?"

Maxwell turned and whispered angrily. "Get back in there, daddy."

"We have guns in the back room."

"Not now. Get back in there. It may be nothing at all."

Patrick Maxwell cursed and moved into the next room.

Maxwell had his P-38 loaded. Thibadeaux was armed with a Colt 45. Maxwell had attached the second alarm to a picture frame in the kitchen. He got a small flashlight out of the hardware drawer. He turned it on and panned it to the picture frame. He heard Thibadeaux breathing behind him.

"Don't worry, Richard, he can't do anything at this distance."

They watched the alarm, nothing.

Maxwell looked at Thibadeaux. "You ready?"

"As I ever be," Thibadeaux replied nervously.

"If the alarm goes, turn on the kitchen light," Maxwell said, pointing to the side door. "I'll take the back porch. Make sure you leave the door open so the light will come through. If he comes in closer, close your eyes, get that door in line and go through it. That way, you won't be blind when you get outside. Got it?"

"Got it," Richard said, looking quickly to the right. "I don't like my back to no window, me."

They watched the alarm. Nothing. Five minutes passed. Maxwell glanced at the picture frame every few seconds. It held.

"Come with me."

They opened the back door and eased out onto the porch. Both men held their pistols in their hands, ready.

They stood looking in the direction the alarm went off. They saw nothing, only the dark woods coming down to the house, above them the mountains, then the twinkling stars and the half moon. The wind moaned from the mountains.

"He's playing cat and mouse," Maxwell said.

"Look like it."

"We'll have to change the game," Maxwell said, the animosity returning to his voice. "Tomorrow we go fishing," he said, removing the clip from the P-38.

Maxwell turned and walked into the dark kitchen.

"Here's what we're going to do," he said, then he stopped himself as if remembering, "first I got to make a couple of phone calls."

"Who you calling?"

"Ernest Hammond for starters."

A half hour later the lights were on. Maxwell instructed everyone to keep the front shades down.

He asked his father if he could use his fishing tackle.

"Tommy," began his father.

"Can I or can't I?" repeated Maxwell.

"Sure," said his father, whose face looked drawn.

"We're going fishing up in the cove. Should be something there. Going to hit the hay early. We want to get there about daylight."

Koler panned the Bausch and Lombe scope from one silhouette to the next. Finally, it rested on the temple of Maxwell. But the assassin was more interested in seeing his prey. There was no way he could get both men without an extended firefight. He was sure his first shot would bring certain death, but after that, he would be at an extreme disadvantage. There were two other men in the house. They would be armed in a matter of minutes. Another thought concerned him. He was on their territory--the same ground on which they had hunted for years. While he would have the edge in the art of killing, they would have every other advantage. They might even have dogs.

He pulled the scope from his eye and began to move back up the hill. The more he walked, the more alert he became. It had been unnerving that he had lost the element of surprise.

Someone at the drug store had tipped Maxwell off.

And how had anyone in the house known of his approach? He was certain he had not been seen. The only answer could be an alarm device, set in the woods, that triggered an indicator in the house.

Never had he had a case like this. His advantage had always been total surprise. He remembered the reports of Maxwell's wherewithal aboard U-168. He frowned, then shrugged his shoulders.

He reached his truck and started the engine.

He shivered from the chill. He drove slowly past the Maxwell house. The lights were on now, but the front shades had been drawn shut. He cursed under his breath.

There could be no more putting off the inevitable.

It will happen tomorrow, he thought, neither man can go to the authorities; that is apparent. If they are not taken tomorrow, the mission could take months.

Koler briefly entertained taking them when they got back to New

York. He quickly dismissed the idea. He had no guarantee that they would return there. Nor could he guarantee that they would be together again. He wanted to expedite matters as much as possible.

He would not divert from his pattern. He would go to the drug store for morning coffee as usual. The drug store seemed to be the center for local information. If Maxwell wanted a confrontation, it would be communicated to Koler at the drug store. That was where the breach had occurred, so it was only logical to assume that it represented the next opportunity.

Maxwell had also lost an element of surprise, Koler thought, now I know that he knows.

He drove into town and entered the room at his hotel.

The more he thought of it, the more certain he was that Maxwell would force a confrontation. Everything in Maxwell's recent history pointed to decisive action. He was not worried. Koler knew that the essential law of nature was in his favor. Once a prey is cornered, he will attack. Maxwell would not be able to live with the thought of being hunted.

If a fight occurs, he thought, they will have no idea what they are up against.

Koler assured himself that he was the best in the world at his craft. His prey had killed before, but never with the same clean skill he possessed. Theirs had been the wanton violence found in the most common gangsters.

The assassin told himself that he had already spent too much time. His anxiety passed. It was just another routine mission.

He went straight to bed.

The next morning Otto Koler entered the drug store at 8:11. He sat down at the first empty table he saw. Mr. Walters waddled over with his order pad.

"Good morning," Koler said.

"Morning," Walters said, who grimaced as he looked down at his watch. "What you have?"

"The same as usual. Coffee and rolls."

"Coming right up." Then Walters looked down and smiled.

Odd, Koler thought, he never smiled at me before. It was as if he forced himself.

He told himself he was getting paranoid. Thoughts of the previous night played through his mind.

He watched Walters as he walked through the door into the back. When Walters returned a few minutes later with the coffee and rolls, Koler was certain by the old man's manner that he was watching him.

Koler pushed the fork into his roll. Again he thought of the previous night. He had been trained to walk noiselessly, yet when he neared the Maxwell house, even before the lights had been extinguished, he had the distinct feeling they knew he was there. He was certain of it when the two men had come out on the back porch.

After an extended period in the back room, Walters emerged to attend to the regulars who lined the counter. The friendly banter had started. After making a round with the coffee pot, Walters walked over to the phone, twisted the handle, and made a brief phone call.

Not five minutes after Walters had hung up the phone, the bell sounded at the front door and Richard Thibadeaux walked in. Koler stiffened. Thibadeaux had walked directly by his table without looking in his direction. He took a seat near the end of the counter.

His hair was wet and slicked back as if having just gotten out of the shower.

"Coffee," Thibadeaux said.

"You up early dis morning," Walters said loudly.

"Yeah," Thibadeaux said, also in a voice loud enough for anyone to hear, "thought I grab a bite. Going fishing with Tommy in 'bout a hour down at Baker's Point."

"Ain't likely to catch nothing this time of year," said a man in overalls. "Fished it the other day and didn't have a bit of luck."

"Nothing else to do," Thibadeaux said loudly. "Besides, I be feeling lucky today."

Although it may have been his imagination, Koler thought that Thibadeaux's long cheeks appeared flushed. He noticed that Thibadeaux constantly knocked ashes from his cigarette into his saucer and appeared extremely nervous.

When Thibadeaux finished his single cup of coffee, he walked over to the wall phone, turned the handle, and made a quick phone call. He talked as briefly as Walters had and hung up. He returned to the counter and paid his bill.

"Thank you," Walters said, who again had emerged after an unusual stay in the back. "Come again."

Thibadeaux walked directly past Koler on his way out.

That's odd, Koler thought, everyone looks around all the time, but not this fellow. It's as though he's deliberately ignoring me.

The bell sounded as Thibadeaux exited the store.

Koler began weighing the evidence that would convince him Walters and Thibadeaux were planning together. He made his decision.

It's a trap, he thought, it's got to be. But what kind? I know where, but how?

He continued sipping his coffee, pondering the question.

After twenty minutes, he rose, paid his bill, and left the drug store.

Three doors down was Coney's Hardware. The counterman was extremely tall, dressed in jeans and a blue jean jacket.

"I need a hundred feet of braided cotton rope," Koler said.

"Right over here. I'll cut it for you."

The rope was placed in a large sack. Koler paid two dollars and left for his room.

By the time he had entered his room, his jaw muscles were working and his eyes widened.

He quickly packed all his belongings into his grip, changed into green pants and a dark shirt, a dark green hunting jacket, and hiking boots. He injected a fresh clip into his 45 ACP, took the length of rope out of the sack and threw it into the suitcase. He paused before leaving the room.

His heart pounded with anticipation. He walked down the steps and checked out of the hotel.

He reached his Chevrolet, which he had brought in town days earlier, and opened the trunk. The Winchester was where he had left it in its case, and the boxes of ammunition were sitting neatly beside it. He threw his grip into the trunk and started out the south highway.

He stopped at a service station and asked directions to Baker's Point.

There was a slight fog in the lower regions of the mountains. And he moved in and out of the fog as the car meandered down the winding road towards the lake. The day would be clear and warm as soon as the fog burned off.

Koler's mind raced as he drove. He would be glad to be out of this area once his job was finished. The rugged and beautiful mountains, the quaint farmhouses, gently dotting the land, the drug store, the hotel--everything had begun to oppress him. He felt suddenly confined, within the jaws of a slowly closing trap. This was no longer an ordinary assignment. The entire community seemed pitted against him. But he was glad of one thing. It would be over soon. The moment had come, the moment for which he had so carefully prepared. It was not on his terms. The Americans had taken the initiative, but with his training and experience, Koler was certain he could regain an advantage.

During the early part of the drive to the cove, he had begun to think of Maxwell with an inkling of respect. At least this adversary had made it interesting. But by the time the car ambled down the final leg of the journey--the bouncing dirt road leading to the cove, an entirely different attitude prevailed.

Koler's eyes had glazed over with cruelty. His mouth pursed in a defiant grimace.

He killed the engine and parked the car. Not fifty yards up the road was the old pickup that had sat in front of the Maxwell home.

Koler got out of the car, opened the trunk, and took out his rifle and cartridge boxes. After loading the Winchester, he threw the coil of rope over his right shoulder, placed the Colt in his side holster, and mounting the scope into place on the Winchester, balanced the rifle in his hands at port arms. He silently closed the trunk and started his descent through the woods to the cove below.

He would have to move slowly so as not to break any twigs or create a disturbance. He stopped periodically and panned around him. His training took over. There was no more thought, only pure reaction and instinct.

Suddenly he hated the Americans. How arrogant they had been in their ill-designed little plot. They had shown him no respect at all. The little scene at the drug store, how infantile and insulting. It would never fool a German. They had no idea with whom they were dealing.

There were two main approaches to the cove--one to the extreme left and one to the right. He chose the right approach. He could hear the sound of a waterfall. As he crept slowly downward, he could occasionally see the sparkle of the green lake below where the sun was already burning off the fog. The closer he got to the bottom, the more quickly he moved. The waterfall below would shield any sound of his approach, just as he knew it shielded the voices of Maxwell and Thibadeaux.

The sun shown down through the woods.

Small patches of light shone on the ground. Koler stopped. He had seen something. He moved two steps to his left. There it was again.

In one of the patches of light his eye had picked up a shimmering thread.

Koler smiled to himself.

A thin piece of fishing line ran taut, across the trail, ankle high. He continued to move to his left. Where the grade became the steepest, down the center of the gorge, the line ran into a patch of trees.

Ingenious, thought Koler.

He moved around until he could see in the thick patch of trees a thin sapling bent down and attached to the line which ran across his path.

Again he smiled. With each passing discovery he gained more respect for his adversaries. They had put up a good fight, but it was all over now. Immediately, he visualized his plan. There would be a series of lures at various depths of the gorge. The trips would trigger an indicator at the bottom of the gorge, telling the Americans he was coming in.

Since there was only one more approach to the gorge, he knew immediately that the same set of lures existed on the other descent. He chastised himself mildly for nearly blundering into the trap a second time. He praised his luck. The line was almost completely invisible. If it had not been for that small patch of sunlight glinting off the string, he would have tripped the indicator. Now he understood how Maxwell had known of his approach to his house. Such a lure would be completely unavoidable at night.

Once devised, his plan was carried out with discipline. He had the demeanor of a skilled craftsman at work.

When he arrived at the place where he had first seen the lure, he stepped gingerly over it. In a half crouch he moved to a large pine tree ten feet in front of the lure. He flashed his hunting knife, which with little difficulty, he managed to plunge into the tree. He could smell the sweet smell of the pine as he drove the knife in. He took the coil of rope from his shoulder and let out fifteen feet. With a large rock he managed to secure the end of the rope, down in front of the tree. He then ran the length of the rope between the tree and the knife, which slanted upwards against the tree at an angle of forty five degrees.

He then moved steadily backwards, stepping carefully again over the fishing line.

The rope now extended precariously over the knife. A gentle twirling of the rope would cause it to fall off the knife and trip the lure. Koler looked above. He would be able to feed the rope some seventy feet before the trees became too forbidding to pan further up.

He backpedaled steadily upwards, careful to keep the length of rope straight and not to let it slip off the knife downwards. The time passed slowly. His legs ached from the constant upwards backpedaling. The rope held. Finally when his back was to a thick patch of trees, he could go no further. He looked quickly to his right and left, plotting his path upwards. He gave the rope a slight tug, saw the white line bob gently up and down. His eyes glared to the left, his white teeth flashing. He felt that delicious feeling, welling into his stomach and chest--the exhilaration of the hunt, the anticipation of the kill. His movements would now be quick and precise.

With a quick upwards motion of his wrist, he caused the loop in the rope to run down to the knife, not enough. The rope had held. On the third effort Koler crooked his arm and twirled the rope. When the descending loop reached the knife, the rope looped over the knife and fell down, tripping the fishing line which went limp.

Now Koler would have to rely on his speed. He sprinted to the summit. His face was scratched as he hurtled through the woods. He fell, jamming his right wrist. His legs immediately churned again as he again ran. He thanked his Order and his training for his conditioning. Not many men could have continued to sprint the height without stopping for a rest, but in three minutes he was at the summit, having covered now what had taken him over an hour to traverse before.

He did not stop when he got to the summit. He unshouldered his rifle and gained the other approach to the cove. Again he ran through the undergrowth, unworried about noise and unconcerned about the cuts and bruises to his body. It was only when the path began to clear that his movements became slow and poised. He held his rifle ready.

He spotted the first lure. He smiled. As he stepped over the line, he could already picture the Americans sprawled with their guns watching the other approach, where his rope had tripped the lure. Now he was coming in directly to their rear. He had to move slowly now, constantly on the alert for the second or third trip.

When he was within two hundred feet of the bottom of the hill, he could see what he anticipated. Maxwell and Thibadeaux were lying sprawled behind a log, their rifles pointed towards the other approach. There were four fishing poles at the bank near the green water. One of the poles was bent to the ground. It was implanted in the ground on one end and straining and trembling, as if fighting a fish, on the other. Four poles meant four lures. He had to watch for the second fishing line. Within one hundred feet of the bottom, he found it. The line was rigged in the same fashion, this time knee high. Koler skipped over it. Now he was clear. In a half crouch he crept to within seventy feet, behind a large tree--sprawled down, found a clear field of fire through the trees and raised his Winchester. The Bausch and Lombe scope touched his eye.

He smiled again. His heart pounded with joy.

Thibadeaux was on the left, Maxwell on the right. He always fired better left to right. He raised the cross hairs until they rested on the back of Richard Thibadeaux's head.

By seven o'clock that morning Tommy Maxwell and Ernest Hammond had finished setting the lines. This time Ernest had showed Maxwell how to rig the lures to four fishing poles, set in the ground on the bank.

When Maxwell thanked Ernest and paid him an additional twenty-five dollars, the old hillbilly offered further assistance.

"Listen, Tommy," he said, a toothpick hanging out the corner of his mouth. "I'll be glad to lend you more help. Ain't too bad with a gun."

Maxwell forced a smile. "Thanks, Ernest, but you've done enough. Besides, it's nothing like that. I'm just playing a joke on a friend."

Hammond took the toothpick out of his mouth and gazed up the hill.

"Twenty-five dollars," he said, "some joke."

Maxwell only looked at him.

Finally Hammond spoke. "Okay, have it your way. Like I say, ain't never been one to pry."

When Ernest left, Maxwell rushed up the hill to his truck. He drove home in a sour mood.

The tension of the last day was taking its toll. Ever since Mr. Walters had tipped him off about the inquisitive stranger, that sick sensation in the pit of his stomach had been present, heightened by the conversation with Cheryl Becken and the realization that Frank had been murdered. He felt exactly as he had felt aboard U-168 during his most tense moments. Rationalize as he would, that yes, perhaps it had been a deer, that had tripped his lure at the back of his house, still he could not allow himself to relax. All the elements of his home, the Christmas tree, his parents, Elaine--all that had previously given him the only peace he had in months--all had turned sour by Walters' revelation. His life was poisoned. He had to act. Even dying in an act would be better than living in the uncertainty of inaction. He had to know. If there was a man specifically assigned the task of assassinating him, he had to know. He could not endure the thought of looking over his shoulder for the duration of the war.

Last night, after he had called Ernest Hammond, he had called Mr. Walters. Walters had granted him a favor.

If the stranger happened to come into the drug store, the old man was to phone the Maxwell number. Thibadeaux would be waiting at a booth for a call from Maxwell. When Thibadeaux entered the drug store, Walters would indicate who the man was. While making sure the man did not leave, Thibadeaux would announce that he and Maxwell were going fishing at Baker's Cove, then call Maxwell to set the plan in action.

The most crucial part of the plan involved Mr. Walters, who had agreed to try to get a photograph of their would-be assassin. He had said that he might manage to take a picture from behind the cracked kitchen door. Walters had always hated "cops" and had been only too glad to oblige.

Mr. Maxwell entered the living room and saw Tommy pacing by the phone. His son was wearing his sidearm holster on his hip with the pearl handle of the Colt 45 visible.

"What are you so nervous about?" his father asked.

"Nothing. Waiting for a phone call."

"Where's Richard?"

"It's not important. The less you know the better."

His father dragged his stiff leg over to his son.

"I thought you had changed, Tommy," he said. "But you're as deceitful as ever. Trust me for once."

"I can't, dad, not now."

His father was enraged, his face splotchy and his eyes bulging as they always did when he was angry.

"I told you it would be this way," he said, snatching his glasses off his face. "Those thugs in the Bund have turned on you, haven't they? Or is it the law?"

"Just can it, dad."

The old man made an effort to slap Tommy. Maxwell blocked the blow and held his father by the wrist, his face inches from the old hawk-like nose and the familiar, porous face. Tommy's eyes welled up.

"Someday I'll tell you everything," Maxwell said, his lower lip trembling. "I love you too much." He let go of the old man's wrist.

"Don't use that ploy with me," his father said, in a softer, resigned voice. "If you're working for Germany now, I don't consider you my son."

The phone rang.

Maxwell picked it up.

"He here," the voice on the other end said. "Leaving now."

Maxwell hung up the phone, looked at his father, started to speak, then frowned and shook his head as he bolted out the door.

"You better put that safety chain on that hitch," his father shouted after him as Tommy climbed back out of the truck, hooked the two safety chains of the trailer hitch, that held an old, wooden fishing boat with an Evinrude motor. Inside the boat were fishing tackle, two shovels, a beer cooler, a large canvass tarp, and two paddles.

"I hope none of us need to go to town today," his father said, dragging his leg nearer to the truck. "You and Richard have managed to occupy both vehicles. What are you taking that tarp for?"

Maxwell stopped at the truck door and turned to face his father.

"I'm not going to feed you any more bullshit, dad," he said, his face sober, his eyes sad and resigned. "You're right, I've lied to you enough. I'll promise you this. If you'll just indulge me this once, when I get back, I'll tell you everything."

Fear shone on his father's face. The manner in which his son now spoke contained an ominous tone. His son's sincerity had touched the old man, who, finding it impossible to speak, merely motioned his hand in the air in a gesture of dismissal.

Maxwell started the truck and sped away.

His destination was Baker's Landing, a place where he could put the boat in, approximately two miles by water from the point where he was to meet Richard.

On the drive his mind raced. He tried to remember if he had forgotten anything. The weapons were in the back of the truck. Richard should just beat him to the cove. He pictured the traps he and Ernest had set. All he and Richard would have to do was watch the four cane fishing poles, which were planted in the ground at the cove. If a trigger at one of the descending trails went off, a fishing pole would be jerked either right or left, depending on which direction the intruder approached.

Maxwell was hesitant to allow his intruder the high ground, but he counted on his own marksmanship and the element of surprise to negate that advantage. Besides, if they had to run for it, there was the last resort of escaping by boat.

Arriving at the Landing, he negotiated the truck and trailer down a bumpy, dirt road until the woods yawned into a clearing at the water's edge. Relieved that no one else was at the Landing, he wheeled the truck around and backed the boat down a concrete ramp into the water. He winched the boat down into the water and tied it off on an exposed root on the bank.

After parking the truck and getting his P-38 and the two rifles into the boat, he shoved out. He had tried the motor several times last night and was relieved that it started on the first pull.

As the back of the boat dipped further down in the green water, Maxwell kept as close as he could to the steep, wooded shoreline on the drive to the Point. He did not want to be visible from too great a distance. A low fog was quickly burning off the water, swirling as the bow of the boat cut it.

When he neared the point, seeing Richard waving his arms at the shoreline, he killed the engine, paddling the rest of the way in. He guided the boat under an overhanging branch and nestled into the brush on the shore. Placed here, the boat would not be visible from the descending trails of the point. Maxwell tied the boat up and handed out the guns, fishing tackle, and tarp to Thibadeaux on the shore.

Like Maxwell, Thibadeaux was dressed in jeans, a plaid shirt, and hunting jacket.

"So how did it go?" Maxwell asked.

Thibadeaux shrugged his shoulders and frowned.

"Like I said, he there all right."

"What did he look like?"

"How I'm gonna get a good look at him. I didn't want to be obvious, but Walters done nodded his head at him-- a big guy with blonde hair."

"A German?"

"How do I know?"

Maxwell's mouth tightened.

"Everything's set," he said. "I see you brought the food."

Richard laughed. "Shit, cher, don't want you to get killed on no empty stomach. I hope this works, me."

"It hasn't failed yet," Maxwell said. He grabbed Thibadeaux's elbow and looked him directly in the eye. "We been this far and we ain't stopping now. Have I ever let you down?"

Thibadeaux rolled his eyes and laughed.

"No, you ain't, but when you crazy ass mind be working, I get the shits."

Maxwell laughed. "Let's get in position and grab a bite to eat."

They walked over to the clearing where they sat with their backs to a large log. Their lunch consisted of sardines, saltine crackers, and tobasco sauce, which they chased with cold water from a shared canteen. The rifles rested on the log beside them. Maxwell gave Richard the Colt pistol for a sidearm while he kept his P-38. Both men had extra cartridge boxes.

Thibadeaux's jaw swelled with a cracker and sardine. "You know, you asshole," he said nervously. "You promised me we see some deer before we lef."

"If we stay here long enough we will. Deer like to come here abouts for water."

"Any snakes around here?"

"You dumbass. Don't you know that snakes hibernate in the winter?"

"Kiss my ass. I ain't no bumpkin, me."

Maxwell laughed and took a drink from the canteen.

"Did you know that a buck deer will kill a rattlesnake?"

Thibadeaux stopped chewing, his long face widened. "The shit you say. Seem like the snake would bite shit out of him."

"If the snake manages to bite the deer, the buck will die within the hour, but that ain't usually the way it works out. A buck deer will attack a rattler by jumping his hoofs on him. A deer's hooves are sharp and will cut the snake to pieces."

"No shit," Thibadeaux said. "Now that's something I like to see."

"Yeah, the old buck will do a little dance on a snake and cut him up."

Thibadeaux grunted. "I had enough to eat. Ain't as good as your mama do. She even got me eating grits."

Maxwell laughed. "So I noticed. You sure you got enough to eat?"

"Sure, man."

"Then get your ass over there and start fishing," Maxwell said with a reassuring smile, "and for Christ's sake, don't go to sleep."

"You think all my bells ain't ringing this morning?" Thibadeaux asked as he walked away.

He made it to his spot at the other end of the clearing where two cane poles were planted in the ground. He pretended to watch for fish.

Maxwell sat at the other end of the exposed shore with his two poles.

He was hoping it was all a mistake. But he was worried. There had been too many coincidences. His stomach churned with anticipation and fear. He leaned his back against a tree. He watched a small waterfall, cascading down a limestone bluff on the other end of the cove. He listened intently for any alien sounds.

The low fog on the lake had burned off. The sun was shining, and the day would be clear. The line on his pole remained still. A fish jumped near the bank, breaking the surface.

He glanced over at Thibadeaux who appeared to be asleep, but Maxwell knew better. Time dragged on. He looked at his watch. Only forty minutes had passed since he had sat down. The sun slowly rose. It started to get warmer, although the air was still crisp. The air warmed slightly. Two hours passed. It was nearing noon.

He was reminded of the excruciating waiting aboard U-168 when he realized that one of the crew had a gun ready for him. This was an identical feeling. If his assassin were really out there, Maxwell surmised that he would not pass up the invitation for a showdown. Maxwell thought briefly of Elaine, Julie, his parents, his entire life. Had it all been wasted? It all came down to this moment. It did not matter. His father was right. Millions were dying in combat all over the world. There would never be peace until one side or the other was annihilated.

He was in a self-imposed daze when one of the poles almost jerked out of the ground. He grabbed it and yelled, "Boy, I must have one that weighs twenty-five pounds. Did you see that?"

He felt the exhilaration of anticipation, as if he were about to burst, exactly like he had felt just before Thibadeaux had kicked open that hatch aboard U-168.

The pole had been jerked to the left, which meant the trip had been on the right approach.

"He's gone around a log or something," Maxwell shouted. "I'm hung up."

But Thibadeaux had already left the bank and was lying behind the log next to the two rifles.

Maxwell joined him, sprawled next to his friend. He pulled the rifle to his shoulder. He was an expert marksman and all he would need was one shot.

His mind raced. Several minutes passed.

If the trip had been on the right approach, where was he? They should be able to see him by now.

"Maybe a bird done hit it," Thibadeaux said, raising up.

"Quiet, let me think," Maxwell said as he started to panic. He panned the rifle once, twice, three times.

The woods were peaceful. Maxwell could see the straightened sapling that was pulling the fishing pole. And the trail ahead was empty. Thibadeaux shifted uneasily.

"Where is he?" Maxwell said, "he had to be......"

Then he heard the shot, and in the next instant, realized he had not been hit. He glanced towards Thibadeaux and knew who the target was.

The bullet had entered Thibadeaux's head, just behind his left ear. Blood exploded out where his right eye had been as Thibadeaux tried to raise up, then fell headlong over the log.

The shot had come from directly behind them.

No! Maxwell thought as he leapt straight into the air simultaneously to the sound of the second shot. Maxwell had landed on the other side of the log, on his back. The top of the log, where he had jumped, was frayed. The bullet must have missed him by inches. He managed to roll to his stomach. Another shot struck the log.

Maxwell peered over the log. He spotted the man, blonde and dressed in green to the left of the large tree. In the leap Maxwell had lost his rifle, which lay on the other side of the log. He pulled the pistol from his belt.

Maxwell raised up and fired three shots quickly. The assailant, who had exposed himself and started confidently forward, leapt behind a tree. He could not have been more than one hundred feet away.

Maxwell pulled the extra clip from his pocket, heard another shot ring off the log, raised up and emptied the gun at the tree, then rapidly re-loaded.

As he was re-loading, he could hear feet running. He looked up and could see the assassin heading up the hill between the trees. He was moving at tremendous speed considering the terrain.

Maxwell leapt over the log, grabbed the rifle and pursued.

At the edge of the clearing he knelt and fired. He had only had a brief glimpse of the green-clad figure before he fired. He was certain he had missed.

He ran after him, got one more glimpse of him as he disappeared through the trees, then thought of Thibadeaux. He went back to his friend.

Koler had placed the crosshairs of his Bausch and Lombe on the back of Thibadeaux's head. He knew a split second before he fired that Thibadeaux was a dead man. It was all a foregone conclusion. The first hit would be a certainty, the second a good chance. The scope was a slight disadvantage for two such quick shots. He briefly entertained taking them with his Colt at such a short distance, then suddenly squeezed off his first shot.

He saw where the bullet had entered Thibadeaux's head, but did not wait to view any further results. He panned quickly to the right. He panned at first too far, then rested the crosshairs on the middle of Maxwell's back. An instant before he fired, Maxwell leapt straight into the air. As the shot was fired, Koler at first thought he had hit Maxwell by the way he had jumped. Koler came from behind his cover and decided to put a bullet through the log to be sure. He fired, saw the top of the log explode in tiny fragments of wood.

Maxwell's rifle lay on the near side of the log, next to Thibadeaux's rifle. Koler smiled to himself. If Maxwell was still alive, he was probably unarmed.

Koler had just started to move forward when he saw Maxwell raise up, a pistol in hand. He froze. He saw the first spurt of yellow flame, the first of three shots. He leapt behind the tree and felt his body quickly to see if he were hit.

Then he felt the most extraordinary sensation. Heat in his crotch. He was horrified. Trembling, he reached down to touch himself and was relieved that he was only urinating in his pants.

His teeth glared and his face showed uncontrollable rage. His rifle moved like the swivel barrel of a tank. He fired quickly, too quickly.

"Damn," he said. He had missed again. Twice he had missed. He could hardly believe it. Then he heard the sound of rapid firing. Fragments flew wildly from the other side of the tree. The man was an expert shot. Suddenly the firing stopped.

Koler's rage turned. Maxwell's sudden reaction surprised him. In the instant that he realized that Maxwell was reloading, the thought hit him.

He bolted headlong for the top of the hill. The trees whisked rapidly by. He knew a shot would come. Then he heard it. He was still running. He was not hit. A new energy seized him. He ran faster. The top of the hill was his goal. By the time he reached the summit, he was breathing hard. He lunged into his truck, started the engine, and without looking back, raced away.

Maxwell darted across the clearing.

He knew that Thibadeaux was beyond help.

He lay draped over the log, his head resting on the ground on the other side. The blood had already begun to coagulate on the back side of his head, but when Maxwell picked up the head by the hair, he could see where the bullet had exited, leaving a large, bloody cavity in the spot that used to be Richard's right eye. Blood flowed in a small creek down to the water.

He turned the body over, put both hands under the armpits and pulled him out of the clearing into the woods in the direction of the boat. Relinquishing his grip, he returned to his rifle and again moved carefully up the trail where he had seen the man run.

He neither saw nor heard anything.

He ran back to the water's edge, cut the fishing lines, and threw the cane poles into the water. Richard's rifle lay by the log. Maxwell ran to the spot, picked it up, and after panning the sites along both descents to the clearing, he threw Richard's rifle as far as he could into the lake. He frantically ran about the clearing, picking up as much as he could--the fishing tackle, the canteen, his rifle, the remains of the food, and both handguns. As quickly as possible, he gathered himself and everything he needed out of the clearing.

He counted on his attacker not knowing about the boat.

With his rifle before him, he crawled on his belly to the edge of the clearing. He lay for a time in the undergrowth, waiting for any sign, any sound of the intruder.

Again the wind blew steadily off the water, the waterfall fell from the limestone bluffs, and the water gently lapped the shore. He heard the cry of a large hawk on up the ridge. His heart pounded.

It cannot be that he is dead, he thought, thinking of his friend Richard, that he was talking and joking to me one minute and now he is........ the thought was impossible. A slight whimper escaped him. No, he thought, not now. I must be strong.

He was fighting the urge to panic, to run screaming up one of the trails, or merely just to scream, to release the overwhelming fear and revulsion welling inside him.

Like a snake, he twisted backwards on his belly until the clearing was invisible through the underbrush.

All of the paraphernalia he had gathered in the clearing lay beside his friend's body. When he looked at the face, its long features still holding the look of surprise, the one good eye opened wide, traces of blood on the long teeth, tufts of dirt and flying gnats now around the coagulated cavity that had been his eye, Maxwell had to fight back his vomit.

Quickly now, he gathered the food, the guns, and his father's fishing tackle and put them in the boat. Placing the Colt and the P-38 in his belt, he lay his own rifle on the shore as he fetched from the bank the tarp and three lengths of rope. He had brought these items to assist him in the burial of the assassin, but now they would have to be used for Richard.

As quietly as possible, he lay the tarp out next to the body and over the three lengths of rope. With considerable effort he rolled Richard onto the tarp face down. He wrapped the tarp around the corpse and fastened it tight, tying one length of rope around the face, just below the nose, another around the lower chest, which would hold the arms to the corpse's side, and one around the legs, just above the knees. He re-tied two of the knots to make them tighter and tucked the tarp down over the top of the head. Now the corpse was a cylindrical mass, hidden by the tarp. Maxwell figured this would keep any passersby on the road from noticing that he was carrying a body.

His heart pounding in his chest, again he reconnoitered the clearing and panned the woods above for any sign of the assailant. Seeing nothing, he returned to the body and placing two hands on the rope around Richard's knees, he pulled the body as he backed up through the underbrush to the water's edge and the boat.

Fetching his rifle and placing it in the boat, he now began the task of lifting the corpse and hopefully placing it in the empty deck of the fishing boat. He squatted down and lifted with his legs, getting his hips under the trunk as quickly as possible. It was extremely heavy, and as he staggered over to the water's edge, his foot slipped and in one motion as he fell into the water, he managed to throw the body in the direction of the boat, Tommy landing waist deep in the water and Richard's head laying over the edge of the rocking boat and exposed out of the tarp. A lap of water ran up one side of his surprised face.

"Goddammit," Maxwell cursed, as he untied the boat, rearranged the tarp to cover the face, and lay the body longwise in the boat. A blanket under the driver's seat covered a collapsible shovel. He lay the blanket over the tarp, got into the boat, and shoved out.

He did not dare start the motor, and he wanted to remain as close to shore as possible. He began paddling.

In the expanse of lake to his left there was nothing but water and the far bank. But he kept his attention on the near shoreline with his rifle close at hand.

If he saw someone or someone began shooting, he knew he would be in a real jam. He would have to almost simultaneously return fire and start the engine. But there was no way for the man to know about the boat, and even if he did, would he risk walking blindly through the woods in search of his prey, especially after running the length of the trail upwards?

The longer Maxwell paddled, the safer he felt. Finally, he decided to start the motor.

He pulled once as the Evinrude sputtered, pulled again as it coughed out its blue-gray smoke, then a third time.

"Goddamn fucking machines," he said, beginning to panic and knowing that anyone close could hear the motor as he cranked it. He watched the shore; still nothing. He cut down the gas on the choke so he would not flood the engine and pulled again. This time the motor roared.

He pushed the boat to full speed, feeling the elation of the wind in his face, now seeing the vibrating shore move back, retreating from the mass of green water. Richard's body vibrated on the deck.

Two miles from the Point, Maxwell finally felt safe. He breathed a deep sigh of both relief and resignation to the task that still lay ahead.

He could see the Landing now. If his friend was still alive and they had been burying their enemy, here Maxwell would have let Richard out near the landing to make sure no one else was putting in. Now with only himself to count on, Maxwell would have to check the Landing first himself, and even then, he would never be certain someone would not drive up as he was hitching up the boat.

He looked down at the blanketed body and decided it was

inconspicuous enough. He would take the chance. He wanted to get the rig hitched and be on the road as soon as possible.

Within fifty yards of the Landing he killed the engine and guided the boat to the concrete ramp with his paddle. He was lucky. There was no one in sight. The truck sat undisturbed where he had parked it. He grounded the boat, got his rifle out of the boat, sprinted to his truck and backed it down to the ramp. In quick order he had the boat hitched up and he was ready to go.

He decided to leave the body in the boat, thinking it just as inconspicuous there as in the back of the truck.

Before getting in and beginning the journey, he took another look at the blanket. He fought back the horror of the realization as to what lay beneath the blanket, swallowed, and got into the truck and started the engine.

As he drove over the potholes up the dirt road, he was careful not to jar the trailer. He constantly checked his rearview mirror. Everything was riding fine.

Finally he was on Highway 19. He passed only three cars as he detoured around Murphy through backroads at times no wider than a cow trail, and re-joined Highway 19 as it climbed into the great Smoky Mountains.

Again he had to re-think his plans. If two men had been carrying a body, they could have climbed on foot to Pinknell's Bald. But now, knowing that the burial must take place at least a mile into the wilderness, off the highway, he decided that he would have to climb higher into the mountains by truck and if he moved the body any distance, it would have to be downhill.

He decided to do it close to Chimney Rock, which was almost two hours away.

He slipped into a daze. Time lost all meaning. He could have driven an hour for all he knew, or it could have been only minutes.

The car and the trailer began their ascent, the bare woods on both sides.

He thought of Richard's ashen face earlier when he had said, "You think this will work?"

There was no sign of anyone, no cars, nothing. The temperature was dropping rapidly. Clouds were rushing in from the west. By the time he had wound around Mitchell's Bluff, it had begun to snow. The road began to climb into the Smoky Mountains near Cherokee. The higher the elevation the more treacherous the road became, especially pulling the trailer.

He looked down at his clothing when he could. There were traces of coagulated blood on his hunting jacket. Now that the corpse was not in contact with him, he began to think more logically, but he was still on the edge of panic.

What was the likelihood of the body being found? If the forecasts were right about the blizzard coming, and if Maxwell buried Thibadeaux in the right spot, the chances of finding a body in these mountains would be slim.

The snow slanted down in earnest now. Maxwell turned on his headlights.

And where was his assassin? Was he on this same road?

Maxwell's eyes grew small with hatred. The idea that they had been hunted down like common animals, by the same nation for which they had prepared to work, enraged him. Frick had been right.

By the time Maxwell reached the wide trail leading to the Chimney's, there was an inch of snow on the road. The temperature had dropped twenty degrees in the last hour. Dusk was upon him.

He pulled the truck and trailer to the shoulder of the road, overlooking a steep descent of woods. As he got out of the truck, the mountain air on his face woke him up.

Thibadeaux's body lay stiff in the bottom of the boat. His head had inexplicably escaped the tarp, at an odd angle to his shoulder. Again Maxwell cursed, covered the head, and with a tremendous effort, lifted the body onto his shoulder, and dumped it among the trees out of sight of the road.

Maxwell took the blanket and the shovel out. He managed to work the blanket under the body by untying the top rope, then re-tying it around the blanket. Now he could pull the body behind him with the blanket, an act which would be aided by the slick, snow-covered ground beneath him and the wet, slick tarp. He took one look over the expanse beneath him. If it had been a clear day, he was sure the view would have been spectacular, but now, instead of fold after fold of mountain, he only saw white, from the clouds below, above him, and the snow. When he started his steep descent through the silent woods, it was not yet four o'clock.

Moving as fast as possible, avoiding trees and rhododendron, his legs aching with the strain of the steep descent, he managed to make good time. In fact at one point he moved at such a quick clip that he tripped and fell several feet, the body coming down just behind him, lodging next to his right shoulder.

"Goddammit," he screamed, his voice echoing emptily off the acoustics of the snow-covered woods. "Goddammit, let's go," he again screamed, merely because it released so much of the tension that had built inside him.

He walked in this fashion for almost an hour until he found a perfect spot.

A wave of pity hit him as he pulled Richard into a gully where the snow had only dappled the brown ground, so thick were the bare limbs of the trees above. The wind changed now as the flakes slanted to the right, the wind moaning from the mountains beyond.

Maxwell threw the body down. If he could dig a six foot hole and the snow drifted into the culvert like he thought it would, the body might never be found.

He lay the body in a sitting position against the bank and started to dig.

As he dug, he tried not to whimper or curse; somehow silence seemed appropriate, and most of all he tried not to look at the cylindrical shape of the tarp. The only sound for what seemed an hour was the wailing wind in the mountains beyond, the sound of the shovel on rock and dirt, and Maxwell's breathing.

The strain of the work seemed to help as he dug deep, frantic with anger, frustration, hatred. At times thoughts could not help but intrude.

Should have been me instead of him, he thought, Jesus, I am an asshole. It's all my fault, just like I had killed him, everything I touch is dying or dead. Goddammit, what has happened to me?

He thought of the time they had tried to visit Richard's mother in New Jersey. He remembered the joke his family had on Richard about taking all the turkey. What would Maxwell tell them? He cursed himself for worrying about his own safety. He deserved to die after what had happened.

Maxwell stabbed the spade downward and snorted in disgust. He remembered Richard once saying, "You and you conscience be the death of me yet."

Maxwell kicked the ground in disgust. Thibadeaux had been right. If Maxwell had not caused the mutiny aboard U-168, none of this would have happened. They could have taken the money and run. The money was still in his valise back at the house. He cursed himself for even thinking of it.

Light was failing fast. At last the hole seemed big enough.

Maxwell rolled the body beside the grave, face up. He untied the three knots which held the tarp together. Pulling the blanket free, he spread it longways in the bottom of the grave. Summoning his courage, he pulled the tarp open.

The oncoming darkness partially shrouded the mangled face of his friend. Maxwell closed the good eye and the gaping mouth, resisted the futile urge to put a covering over the horrible cavity where his eye had been blown out, and with trembling fingers, began emptying the pockets.

He found the keys to the other truck in Richard's hunting jacket. He removed his wallet and looked through it--forty dollars cash, a social security card, driver's license, an old picture of a girl. He ripped up the identification cards and putting the truck keys in his pocket, replaced everything else.

Finally, he got on the opposite side of the grave and with both hands pulled the tarp so that Richard's body fell, back down, into the five foot hole. Maxwell managed to pull the tarp free and covered the face and the entire length of the body with it. He began throwing the dirt over his friend.

My father would pray now, he thought irresistibly, no, not now, silence is the only thing now, besides what is there to say, only silence and........what is he seeing now......anything?......or is it only darkness....... void.......he knows now or else he knows nothing........Jesus........no, I won't pray.

The mountains' winds blew in the distance.

Soon the task was complete, and nothing of the body could be seen. He piled several loose rocks over the grave to ward off scavengers, and finally covered the mound with dirt.

He gathered his gear and started up. He did not look back. There was barely enough daylight left to make out the way ahead. His legs ached with the climb, and he broke into a fresh sweat.

He knew he would never have a friend like Thibadeaux again. Certainly he would never know anyone with whom he would have shared as much.

He remembered the early days at Nordland, the first day they had hunted together, the year in Morgan City, the early days aboard U-168, Lorient, Paris, Berlin, Hanau, and finally this week.

He climbed for a time more. He was close to the top when he froze. He dove to his belly.

He listened again. There could be no mistake. The woods thrashed above him. Someone was coming down. He pulled out his P-38.

Jesus Christ, he thought, someone has seen the truck and now how will I explain, or could it be him, no, impossible.

With two stiff arms he pulled the gun and took aim in the direction of the descending sound.

Suddenly a huge buck deer glided out of the trees, not thirty feet above him. Its large rack held erect in the air, its winter, brown-green coat just visible in the failing light, the buck sniffed the air.

Maxwell shifted and rose. The deer churned the snow and effortlessly sped into the undergrowth to Maxwell's left, leaving behind him a bobbing bush and muddy dents in the snow.

Maxwell fell to his face and wept. How long he lay there he could not say, but when he got up, it was completely dark. He struggled up the hill, blindly grabbing trees and limbs to help his progress.

It was over. Richard Thibadeaux was gone. But as Maxwell climbed the trail, another thought began to prevail. There could be only one thing that would keep him going. He would never rest until he found him. It might be long after the war was over, but it would never leave his mind.

This was his resolve as he emerged from the dark woods and found his truck.

He started the engine, turned on the lights, and slowly managed to turn the truck and trailer around. He headed down the road, using his lower gear and only occasionally touching the brakes.

Maxwell arrived home well after dinner. He made his apologies to his mother, who was obviously hurt and subdued, and sought out his father, who was sitting in his rocker by the fireplace.

Maxwell, looking considerably lame and haggard, picked up the poker and stoked the fire. "What was for supper?" he asked, obviously searching for something to say.

His father stopped rocking. He did not answer.

Maxwell's jeans were soiled through at the knees and tiny tufts of dirt still clung to his heavy wool shirt.

Two of the children came running in the front door.

"Jess hit me with a snowball," Donna said. She was six years old, her little brother four.

Mr. Maxwell studied his son. "Where's Richard?" he asked.

"He decided to go home for a couple of days," Maxwell said, never taking his eyes from the fire. "He's gonna meet me back in Jersey. I took him down to Cleveland to catch a bus. He said to tell everyone he enjoyed the visit. One of those spur of the moment things."

Donna, who had come running up with flakes of snow in her blonde hair, heard Maxwell.

"Is he coming back someday?" she asked anxiously.

Thibadeaux had showed her a good bit of attention over the holiday.

"Sure," Maxwell answered, still staring at the fire, "first chance he gets."

His father looked at him. "Tommy, let's walk up by the spring. I got something I want to show you."

"Sure, why not," Maxwell said.

Both men put on their coats, walked off the porch and up the hill to the side of the house. The snow still slanted down. Maxwell's feet crunched in the fresh snow as the old man's leg made a muted, dragging sound. They moved up the same path as they had during Christmas 1939.

"I've been thinking about putting in a pump by the spring," his father said. He was carefully watching the reactions of his son. Tommy's face looked haggard and drawn. "Pumping water to the house, you know. You're pretty good at those things."

"It's been a long time," Maxwell said in a soft voice.

"Maybe you can give me a hand."

They walked further towards the spring.

"If you put in a pump," Maxwell said, "those kids will run that spring dry the first day. It gives them something to do, carrying the water to the house."

"I wasn't thinking about the kids," his father said. "I was thinking about your mother and sister having to carry water all day while we're gone. They shouldn't have to do that."

They arrived at the spring and continued to talk. Maxwell strained to see the mountains, white against the low sky.

He knew what his father was thinking.

The old man reached down, picked up a stick, got out a knife, knocked the snow crystals off it, and began whittling. He looked over his glasses at Maxwell with his kind, old eyes.

"All right," he said. "Where's Richard? Just give it to me straight and don't put in any of that double talk you like to use."

At that moment Maxwell loved him more than he ever had.

"Dad, I told you I'd tell you everything," Tommy said slowly, "and I will. Let's do it as we drive. It's a long story, and I prefer to be warm."

"Drive where?"

"To Baker's Cove to get the other truck."

"All right, let's get started."

"We'll take our guns," Tommy added.

His father did not answer, but his old face contained a sad look--a look it held in the gingerly ride over the slick, deserted roads on the way to the Cove. As the trees whisked by, covered in their white lace, as the flakes swirled in a steady slant down through the headlight beams, the story of Tommy Maxwell's past two years took its sway, seeming fantastic in that it contrasted in its convulsive violence to the white, silent peace of the surrounding mountain darkness.

The truck sat where he had left it under a cushion of snow.

As Tommy prepared to scrape the snow off the truck and start it up, the old man hobbled behind him. During the entire drive he had let Tommy talk; had not interrupted him once, not even during the story of burying Richard. He had not asked him exactly where he was buried.

Tommy was scraping the snow off the truck's windshield when he felt his father's hand on his shoulder. The old voice was muted, barely audible against the silence of the falling snow.

"Guess there was nothing else you could do," the old man said wearily.

Tommy shrugged his shoulders and got into the truck. It started on the first turn.

"Take it slow driving back," his father said. "I'll be right behind you."

The next morning Maxwell drove to Murphy and went straight to the drug store.

The bell rang as the door opened, and Mr. Walters brought him a cup of coffee.

"How's it going?" Walters asked, looking at Maxwell with significance.

Maxwell managed a smile. "Couldn't be better," he said.

Maxwell sipped at his coffee. Walters went about serving the other customers. An hour passed. His coffee had been re-filled and now was cold. The traffic around the counter thinned until only Maxwell was left. He stared blankly into his coffee cup.

When Walters approached, he looked up. "Did you get it?" Maxwell asked.

"Shoo. All of it. Want it now?"

"Yeah, might as well get on with it."

Walters waddled into the back room and reappeared with a small package.

"I put it in a box. Wouldn't want any of the locals to know what's going on. Hope it turns out good."

"I'm sure you did a good job," Maxwell replied.

"Two dollars ought to cover it."

Maxwell handed him the two dollar bill, plus a dime for the coffee, thanked him again and walked out.

An hour later he was in Cleveland, Tennessee. He drove around town until he found the little shop he was looking for. He parked the truck and walked into the shop.

A red headed woman was at the counter.

Maxwell took the camera out of the box.

"I don't know much about these things," he said. "Could you take the film out and get it developed?"

The woman smiled. She had a slight gap in her two front teeth. "Sure," she said.

"When can I get them back?"

"Day after tomorrow," she said.

"That's fine."

Maxwell collected his receipt and walked out. He took a deep breath.

In two days he would know what the man looked like. He would see the face of the man, who had hunted them down like bountied wolves. He would know the look of the assailant who had murdered Richard Thibadeaux, and for all Maxwell knew, was still hunting for the victim he had missed.

Maxwell could already picture his own reaction when he finally viewed that face. He knew that a long road lay before him. For once seen, that face would never leave him. There would be no turning back. He would go anywhere, spare no expense to find him. No matter where he went or what he did, he would always be looking for him. He knew that the chances of finding him were slim. By now he was probably on his way out of the country.

When Maxwell left the camera shop, he drove back to Murphy. He paid Ernest Hammond a visit and bought a batch of homemade whiskey.

He was feeling no pain when he arrived home.

His father was on the front porch when Maxwell arrived.

"Lots warmer today," his father said. "Snow's nearly melted off."

"Yeah," Maxwell said, looking up at the white mountains, "at least in the valley, but February is still ahead of us."

"Longest month of the year," Mr. Maxwell said.

The old man sat for a time, whittling and looking over the front yard out to the highway.

"Dad, when I got here for Christmas, I was going to stay. Start over. After what's happened, though, I'm going to have to move on. Don't ask me where? But I can't stay here."

The old man looked up at him. The eyes seemed to look older each time Maxwell saw him.

"You got to go somewhere."

"I'll go somewhere."

"Where?"

"Fishing," Tommy said.

The old man's eyes squinted as he removed his glasses, now rubbing his eyes.

"Believe it or not," Mr. Maxwell said. "I didn't want this for you. I wanted your life to be different."

"Different from what?"

His father put his glasses back on, looking directly up into his son's eyes. "I didn't want you to live your life haunted by the past. Believe me, I speak from experience. It ain't worth it."

Maxwell smiled and patted his father on the shoulder.

"Looks like we've both come full circle. But what do you mean, you speak from experience?'"

The old man gazed up at the snow-topped mountains.

"Tommy, I'm going to tell you something that no one else knows, not even your mother. It's a thing that has bothered me for years........"

"It's all right, dad....."

"No, let me finish. The other night you said I was infatuated with the war. I got mad, as usual. Hell, you were right. After listening to what you told me last night, I felt ashamed. You been through ten times what I went through in the damned war. Hell, everybody for years thinks I was injured in the trenches at Lyons by a shell. I let everyone think it. Truth is I wasn't hit by a shell at all. I was marching in my platoon near Lyons, that's true. But our outfit was green. We were heading in an armored column toward the lines. In the distance we could hear the shelling of the German guns. I was so scared that I was sipping whiskey out of a bottle in my field jacket. I was drunk. Anyway, to make a long story short, a shell hit to the right of the road. Everybody but me dove off the road. A troop truck swerved from where the shell had hit. I slipped and it ran over my damned leg. Broke it. It got infected and they ended up having to fuse my knee. Hell, Tommy, nurses saw more action than me. And all these years people thought of me as a hero. I got the damned purple heart, but what does it mean? I got shipped home early because I had been drunk. I don't know how the story got started, maybe I told it, I don't remember. It's something I had to tell you."

Tommy laughed and again patted both his father's shoulders, now massaging them.

"Dad, that's ridiculous. You're still as much of a hero as any of the other assholes that went, even Sergeant York."

"Don't say that."

"It's the truth, dad. It's just a thing that you've made bigger than it is."

"I suppose I was ashamed to be disabled in such a way, to have people's respect for that."

"I'm telling you it doesn't matter," Tommy said, raising his voice. "It's all a fucking accident. The whole war is one slaughterous mess. No heroes. No causes. Just bodies."

The old man grabbed his son's wrist. "Stay here, Tommy. Start over. Forget it. This thing about going fishing. Give it up. It ain't worth it."

"I can't stay here, dad. It's not fair to you or the family. It's too dangerous......"

"Give it up."

Maxwell looked directly into his eyes. He saw himself reflected in his father's spectacles.

"It ain't worth it," the old man added.

"Maybe not, but I won't give it up," he said.

"Wonder how it's going to end," his father said reflectively. He lowered his head, as if in physical pain. "The war to end all wars. That's what they said about our war. Nobody won last time and nobody will win this one. The only thing that changes are the weapons. In my day it was the machine gun. Now it's the tank. Who knows what tomorrow will bring. It's just the machines that improve. Don't guess what I say matters. Guess I was the same way as a boy. Hell, yes, I was. I'm getting old, boy. You go away for very long and you won't see me again, just some name on some old headstone."

Maxwell laughed. "Come on now, dad. You still got a couple of kicks left in you."

"You won't change your mind?"

"I can't dad, not now, maybe some day."

The old man looked up again, sighing deeply.

"You got to do this then. You have to tell some story to your mother. Don't tell her why you're going. And find a way to write her now and again. No matter what you do, you got to find a way to do that. She puts an awful lot of store in you, boy." He hesitated a moment. "And so do I," he said.

"I promise."

"And by God, you better keep it too, or I'll personally find you and tan your ass."

Tommy leaned down and kissed the old man's rough cheek.

"Damn," he said. "What a way to start the new year."

THE RESULT

The crisp morning sun shone down on an ornate, octagonal building with wings jutting out on two sides. The building was the Burgtheater, one of several federal theaters in Vienna. The front of the building contained three Greek cornices of mythological heroes, which overlooked the beautiful shrubs, green lawns, and florid gardens of the Volksgarten in the Inner City.

Behind the theater were two prominent office buildings, which block off the corners of two city blocks, facing one another. Beyond these office buildings stretched the Viennese ghetto, the same ghetto that housed a young Adolf Hitler in the prime of his youth.

In the eastern office building a tall man, carrying a briefcase, entered, read the directory in the lobby, and rode the dumb waiter to the fourth floor.

In Room 8 was the Documentation Center of Vienna. The tall man spoke to the pretty blonde secretary.

"I want to speak to Herr Wiesenthal."

"May I tell him who is calling?"

"My name is Tommy Maxwell. Herr Wiesenthal is not expecting me."

The girl excused herself and disappeared into a back hallway. After a short wait, she returned, and Maxwell was ushered into a small office at the end of the hallway.

A quaint man, dressed in gray serge, sat behind a desk, which was covered with mounds of documents. The man sat in front of a large bay window, overlooking the street. When the man stood to shake hands, Maxwell noticed the surprising height, nearly as tall as himself, and the apparent Jewish features.

"Herr Maxwell," he said as he sat down and lit a pipe, "what can I do for you?"

"First of all," Maxwell said as he lit a cigarette. "I want to say it is a pleasure to meet you. I wholly support your work and will do anything I can to aid you."

"Aid me in doing what? Have you any identification?"

"Of course," Maxwell stood up and quickly handed over his passport.

"An American. What brings you to Austria?"

"I have just returned, like yourself, from Germany. I have been there since Nuremberg, fulfilling the requirements of a university grant."

"Who gave you my name?"

"A man named Friedman. He is with British intelligence. Here is a letter of introduction." Maxwell handed over a folded letter.

Peering over small reading glasses, the old man read the letter carefully, only once emitting a small expression of a smile, but not with the eyes. He removed his glasses, sighed, and said, "Erich Friedman, ja. Now, I repeat, what can I do for you?"

"Help me find this man." Maxwell slid a faded photograph across the desk.

"An old photograph. Who is he?"

"He went by an alias of Simon Ballard at one time."

"This is all you know? Then you don't even know for sure that he is German, nor do you know his real name."

"That's what I want you to tell me. I have reason to believe that he was a member of the SS or SD, somewhere in late 1942 or early '43. He was operating in America during this time."

The old man stared at the photograph, frowned and handed it back. "In what capacity?"

"Assassin."

Wiesenthal took a long draw from his pipe and leaned back in his plush, leather chair to get a second look at the stranger.

"You have been in Germany since Nuremberg. Where do you get your funds? Such an undertaking can be expensive."

"I haven't had to worry about money for quite some time now," Maxwell said, shifting uncomfortably. "I have invested wisely."

"And what were you doing in Nuremberg?"

"Attending the trials, what else?"

"To what end?"

"I wanted to find this man."

"This was the object of your grant?"

"Well, no, I am a teacher of history at the University of Tennessee in the United States. My grant to attend Nuremberg listed me as a scholarly observer."

"You had only a picture and you wanted to locate this man in Nuremberg?" The old man leaned back and laughed.

"I sought an audience with Karl Doenitz."

Wiesenthal sat up. "Hitler's successor? Did you succeed?"

"No, I tried first at Nuremberg, then later at Spandau. I was denied access."

Wiesenthal leaned forward. "Enough of this. What do you want with this man, and why would Doenitz be able to help you?"

Maxwell paused before answering. "This man killed my friend in New York in 1942."

Wiesenthal smiled. "And what reason do you have to believe he was SS?"

"A hunch, I guess. I suspect he had previous connections with Reinhardt Heydrich."

"The Butcher of Prague."

Wiesenthal stood up and paced to the window. He turned around.

"And what right do you feel you have in finding this man?" he asked.

Maxwell stubbed out his cigarette in the ashtray.

"The same right as any citizen of any nation. The same right as you. Nuremberg decreed that any member of Himmler's SS was a member of a criminal organization. An organization bent on the extermination of Jews, slave labor, and atrocities in occupied territories."

Wiesenthal smiled. "But none of these categories include you."

"Let's just say I'm holding a grudge."

Wiesenthal lifted his chin in laughter. Finally, when it was apparent that Maxwell was becoming miffed, the old man picked up his glasses, pointed them, and leaned forward.

"At Nuremberg it was ascertained that SS and Einsatzgrouppen units were responsible for the mass deaths of over 5 million people. Believe me, there are many more people on both sides of the iron curtain, who have far more reason for a grudge than yourself, my friend."

Maxwell did not waver. "Can you help me or not?"

Wiesenthal frowned. "You hand me a picture and ask if I can help you. My answer must certainly be no. Even if I could find a name to attach to a picture, the name would surely no longer exist. More likely than not, the only thing I could trace would be a very cold trail indeed."

"Anything is better than what I have now."

The old man sat back and looked at the younger man sideways. He saw the determination on his face.

"First of all, I must believe your story."

"What do you mean? Why would I lie? I cannot be more specific about my involvement with this man. But as far as checking on me and my origins-- that I would welcome. If you decide you cannot help me, someone will."

"All right. If we assume that this man was SS, and if we assume he was on a type of foreign intelligence mission, then perhaps we could narrow the search to Amt 6."

"Amt 6?"

Wiesenthal chuckled. "My but you are a novice. If your man was a member of the SS in late 1942, then he was under the administration of the RSHA. The RSHA was divided into six Amts.

Amt Six was foreign intelligence."

"Yes," Maxwell said calmly. "Amt Six most certainly."

Again Wiesenthal chuckled. "And what do you hope to find?"

"I want to find this man."

"Ja, and I want to find Mengele and Eichmann."

"Will you help me?"

Wiesenthal lit his pipe.

"I will pay you well," Maxwell added.

"I accept no money. I am a very busy man," Wiesenthal said as he rubbed his chin. "First of all, nothing you say can be accepted at face value. You seem sincere enough, but this must be verified. If you check out and I decide to help you, you will be contacted. I will need information as to your present address in the United States."

"All pertinent information is in the letter."

The old man looked up and smiled. "I will need the photograph," he said.

"Take this one. I have another."

"My search will be confined to a picture check in Amt Six. I will go no further than that. If the search yields any results, I will send you the findings. This will include a rundown of any general areas of escape your man may have made in 1945. There were several general routes, and more of the SS escaped than any other branch of the armed forces. The Wehrmacht did not fare as well."

Maxwell smiled and reached into the inside pocket of his coat.

"I insist on paying you for your trouble."

"This is more than is necessary."

"Please take it."

Wiesenthal smiled, accepted the sum of three hundred American dollars in U.S. notes, and bowed slightly before speaking. "You will not contact me. I will contact you. If you are who you say you are, and there is any reason to follow up, a messenger will show up at your home or place of business. Probably there will be nothing worth following, and in that event I will mail this sum back to you with no comment."

"How will I know this messenger?"

"He will have the photo you gave me in his possession," he said, as he began writing on a pad of yellow paper. "What was this man's alias again?"

"Simon Ballard."

"Yes. All right. As I say, there will probably be nothing to report. Now if there is nothing else......."

Maxwell stood up and shook the old man's hand. Before walking out the door, Maxwell turned.

"I'm curious," he said. "I have been all over Europe, looking for someone who would help me. Why you?"

Wiesenthal smiled. "Actually, I don't know. You seem like a serious man, and as you say, I too hold a grudge."

June 2, 1949

The girl was blonde, her hair tied in the top with a white bow, her skirt plaid, and her white blouse bounced slightly as she bobbed up in her chair, her slender arm raised in the air. She sat by the window in Ayers Hall at the University of Tennessee, and she ignored the beautiful pink blossoms of the dogwood tree, which bloomed just outside the window.

"Mr. Maxwell," she said excitedly, "exactly what are you going to ask on the discussion question?"

The classroom erupted with laughter when the instructor, wearing a tweed, brown coat, comically took off his glasses and peered at the flirtatious co-ed.

"'Exactly,' 'Exactly,' Miss Flynn? I don't know if my answer will be as precise as you would like."

The girl smiled, her large, sparkling eyes enjoying the interplay with the graduate student-teacher with whom she had a crush the entire quarter. "Well, tomorrow is quarter exams, you know."

Again the class laughed at the teacher's reaction.

"I am well aware of that, Miss Flynn," as he moved back and forth in front of the large map of the world, that hung from the board. "And, let me see, what discussion question would be appropriate? How about this one? It will have to do with the causes and results of the Second World War," he said in his booming voice. "Let's kick it around a bit." He pointed to the back row, "Mr. Moran, give me one benefit to Mankind, that was produced as a result of the Second World War."

The burr headed student, who had been almost asleep, appeared stunned. Again the class laughed as hands began to pop up around the room.

"Come now, Mr. Moran, this war ended less than five years ago. Surely you can think of something."

The instructor only gave the student a few seconds; then he pointed at another girl in the middle of the class.

"Miss Fagan, can you help Mr. Moran out?"

"How about the Salk vaccine?"

"A very good answer, Miss Fagan. Certainly that would be one. We had a President die of polio. Hopefully, we can avoid that in the future. Another one, Mr. Belk."

"The discovery of nuclear power."

"Very good, Mr. Belk. And wasn't it nice of the Japanese to serve as unwilling guinea pigs for the dangers of nuclear power. But a very good answer indeed." Now the laughter was slightly tense.

"What else, Miss Mandrell?"

"What about ending the Depression?"

"It certainly worked to that effect. Mr. Turnley, you have had your hand up for quite some time."

The well-built lad with the thick glasses leaned forward as he spoke; Maxwell had recognized him early in the quarter as a young idealist.

"Not only did the Second World War rid us of Fascism; it helped us understand the nature and true colors of worldwide Communist aggression."

"Ah, at last," shouted the instructor, darting quickly between the first two rows of seats. "Controversy at last." The class laughed and buzzed. "Mr. Turnley," he said laughing and gesturing broadly with his arms, "forever harping on the situation in Korea."

"It's a fight to the finish, you'll see," said the student.

"It is quite interesting, Mr. Turnley, that you talk of the defeat of Fascism and the hatred of the Communists in the same breath. Did Hitler not also justify everything he did early on, as a reaction to the Communists?"

"Are you a Communist, Mr. Maxwell?" Mr. Turnley said, receiving a jolt on the arm from a fellow student. The room buzzed nervously.

"Is that supposed to intimidate me, Mr. Turnley?" the instructor said, without flinching. "But the answer to your question is no, I am no Communist."

Maxwell paced to the board and grabbed up a piece of chalk. "But Mr. Turnley's observation brings up an interesting piece of review for tomorrow's discussion question. The Nazi's program had three major divisions in their early political appeals."

Now Mr. Maxwell turned his back to the class and wrote the following on the board:

1. Nationalism
2. Racism
3. Anti-Marxism

"It is important to note," the instructor spoke to the class, while pacing, "that many Germans were brought under the wing of the Nazi's by the appeal of one of these three issues. Many people, even in this country, hated Communists, yet had nothing against the Jews. Many supported Germany's Nationalistic goals, especially regarding gaining lost ground respective to the Versailles Treaty, but still did not hate Jews. Very few of the early converts to Nazism hated Jewry. But they soon found out that if you accepted the party, you accepted all of its treatises. There was no such thing as partial commitment. So, in many ways it was the Germans' own fear of Communism, much like the fears we now have in this country, which led to their fall."

"You seem to be arguing a Communist viewpoint, Mr. Maxwell," the zealous student insisted, his voice rising in agitation. "Are you defensive?"

"No, Mr. Turnley," Mr. Maxwell said with a warm smile, "are you?"

The look that the instructor gave the student caused the class to burst into nervous laughter.

"Don't forget, students, that Russia lost more people in the war than all the other combatants combined. Some of their military buildups are mere overflow from their defense against the Germans. Let's change the subject slightly. Miss Flynn, what difficulties do Americans now have in judging the effects of World War Two on the modern world?"

When the girl appeared completely stumped, the instructor again wrote on the board.

"I see these two elements as having clouded our perspective on the effects of the war in Europe. Point number one points out that we are now too close to the war to give it fair historical weight. Point number two points out the differences between us, the only real winners of the war in the material sense, and the rest of the world. You kids are even different than my generation. We were idealists. You kids only care about getting a new car, wife or husband, fifteen thousand dollars a year, kids, and I almost forgot......a ranch house."

At this generalization the room erupted with laughter, protests, hands popping into the air, and loud comments. Maxwell loved to whip this fine class of students into an emotional lather. He looked at his watch. Class was to have ended three minutes ago.

"All right," he said, holding up his hands. "Be on time in the morning. Be thoroughly prepared. I promise you the exam will challenge you."

Students rushed out of the class, anxious to get into the Spring sunshine. Miss Flynn, who had invented a question as an excuse to see Mr. Maxwell alone, frowned when she saw Turnley in a heated and long discussion with the instructor. She shrugged her prim shoulders, sighed, and strutted out of the room.

"You don't see my point?" the heated student asked.

"Of course I do," Maxwell said with more of a scholarly tone. "But all I am trying to say is that you must keep your views in perspective. Remember, the Nazi's were a product of a Democratic process, pure and simple."

"That sounds unpatriotic."

The teacher reached out and touched the young man's shoulder. His sober words seemed to have a soothing effect on the young student, who hung on every word, as if it were the most desperate information on earth.

"Don't let political considerations at your age become so rigid and concrete," the instructor said. "Although you're mature enough now, don't cling to only one view. Keep your mind open. You might find that with age, your views will be altered. Believe me, I speak from experience."

When Turnley finally left, Maxwell leaned out the window.

Ayers Hall at the University of Tennessee was at the top of the Hill, as it was called, that overlooked the rolling hills of the campus to the west and Shields-Watkins field, the football field, to the south. Bordering the field was the Tennessee River.

Maxwell remembered how last fall the field must have been packed for the Tennessee-Alabama game, matching two of the most powerful schools in the nation. He pictured what it must have looked like--the shifting mass of students filling the stands, the bouncing cheerleaders, the bands, the colors, the crimson and orange jerseys.

How beautifully naive Americans were. He had been naive, too.

Maxwell had missed last football season.

He had been in Nuremberg on the grant. As he stared out the window, he contemplated the interplay and tension between the limbo of campus life, the suspended sense of reality, and the hard facts of the outside world.

Nuremberg existed in his memory in a gray, hazy light. And as much as he revelled in the joys he took from teaching, he could never wholly escape that gray light.

The trial had proved to be a vast sideshow to the war. The remaining figures paraded before the tribunal-- Doenitz, Speer, and the remarkable Hermann Goering. Of all the war criminals prosecuted, during the entire proceeding Goering was the most entertaining. Maxwell could not keep his eyes off his face. His large, moonlike, sensuous visage betrayed its every emotion. At times he could be seen openly weeping, at others laughing hysterically, the spectrum of emotions, running roughshod across his face.

Not a day passed that he did not think of these events.

He picked up his brief case, turned off the lights, closed and locked the classroom door and moved down the hall. To his right a corpulent man with a downturned moustache leaned against the wall. The man smoked a pipe, which he took from his mouth and pointed at Maxwell.

"Mr. Maxwell," the man said, placing the pipe back in his mouth and extending his right hand. "My name is Ed Lindbergh. I was told I could find you here."

In the man's left hand was a bound packet, which after shaking hands, he opened. "I believe this item belongs to you."

From the packet, the man, who stood a full six inches shorter than Maxwell, extracted the faded black and white photograph, that had been given to Simon Wiesenthal.

The man's rosy cheeks puffed up around his moustache. "I believe we have a mutual friend. There is more information available than originally thought. Could we perhaps have dinner? Are you free?"

Maxwell was stunned. He flushed to the roots of his hair.

"Of course, I know just the place."

The two men walked to Daras Restaurant at the edge of the campus. 'Mr. Maxwell' as he was known, was a regular and he was seated, as requested, in a very private, corner booth in the back dining room.

Maxwell ordered a carafe of the house wine, and finding Lindbergh amenable to Italian cuisine, ordered the veal for both of them. They spoke very little during the meal and did not get down to business until the lime sherbet was served as the dessert.

"That was delicious," Mr. Lindbergh said, beaming with his flushed, prominent cheekbones.

"Glad you enjoyed it," Maxwell replied, lighting a cigarette. "Now I believe you said we had a mutual acquaintance."

Lindbergh lit his pipe before speaking.

"As you were saying, being a college professor must be the best. Good intellectual stimulation and job freedom."

"That's right."

Lindbergh smiled. "And what about those young girls. I saw a couple of them as they left class," and at this Lindbergh leaned over and with a stiff arm slapped Maxwell's shoulder. "How in the hell do you do it?"

"How do I do it?" Maxwell said with a sly grin. "It's quite easy."

"Yup, I bet it is," Lindbergh said. This had not been the first time he had employed the expression "yup", as if making fun of southern accents.

"So it's obvious you have a pleasant life. You have furthered your education after the war, all free on the G.I. bill, and now you have your Masters' Degree. By the way, what branch of the service were you in?"

Maxwell frowned and stared across the table as he shifted uneasily. "There was no G. I. Bill. I was not in the service-- a shipbuilder."

"Federal Shipbuilding, wasn't it?"

Again Maxwell shifted. "That's right. How did you know?"

Lindbergh smiled. "That was a great dinner. Do you mind if we get down to business?" Lindbergh's smile, as he took from a satchel a leather notebook binder, did not fool Maxwell.

He braced himself. "Let's drop the cordial bullshit," Maxwell said.

Lindbergh laughed. "Oh bluntness. Yup, let's be blunt.

My, my, what courage. Fine then, you worked at Federal Shipbuilding for three months. The war lasted five years. It's in my notes here. What did you do the rest of the time?"

"I was a hobo on freight trains," Maxwell replied. "In other words, none of your goddamned business."

"A hobo, how amusing. According to my notes here, there is a likelihood that you belonged to the German American Bund before the war. Your war time activities would have nothing to do with that, would it?"

Maxwell ran his fingers through his hair. "Exactly who are you?" he asked.

"Who am I? Who is anybody? You understand my skepticism concerning you. You mysteriously appear to the Nazi hunter Wiesenthal with some cock-and-bull story about an SD assassin, nameless...."

"I gave you a name......"

"Yup. Simon Ballard, it says here in the notebook. It might as well have been John Smith. Still, you expect strangers to help you find this man, when you give no reason for your appearance. You admit to no war experience. You tell us nothing. How do you expect us to trust you?"

"Who is 'us'? Who are you?"

"Oh, I see, this is a little game is it? Who are you? Who am I? Be completely honest with me. Don't lie. I get tired of liars in my profession. The truth is just as easy. The truth will make you free."

"Jews going around quoting Jesus."

"Jews can say anything they want. Do you hate Jews?"

"Not in the least."

"If you were working for Germany during the war, why don't you just say so?"

Maxwell flushed. The stranger's brashness, in addition to his knowledge of his past had disarmed him. Suddenly, he felt it would be foolish to lie.

"Are you with the Mossad, Mr. Lindbergh?"

Lindbergh smiled. "No," he said.

"Of course not," Maxwell said. "Let's get this much straight. I intend to tell you nothing. I will not incriminate myself for you or anyone else. If you have allegations that you want to prove legally against me, then that is your right....."

"Let's stop this," Lindbergh said. "Yes, I have friends in the Mossad......"

"Friends."

"And yes, I know you worked for Germany during the war....."

"You know shit."

"Yup, yup," Lindbergh said in mock southern. "I know shit."

Maxwell shook his head and looked down.

"Would it be fair to say you had friends in the SS?"

Maxwell turned pale. "Fuck you," he muttered.

"You take offense at the assumption," Lindbergh said.

"Would you take offense if I asked you that question?"

Lindbergh shrugged. "No, I would simply say it is not true."

"Then you do not hate the SS?"

"Hate them," Lindbergh said with a smile. "Absolutely, I hate them like I hate rats."

"Why rats?"

"As you say, let's cut the bullshit," Lindbergh continued. "I have extremely interesting information for you concerning this Simon Ballard. But you must give us something in return. We can have no illusions. Yes, I am from the Mossad, that should be apparent. Now who are you, and what is your connection to this Ballard? Do not lie."

"If I had been inclined to work for Germany during the war, it would not have been for scum like Himmler or Eichmann. Men like Doenitz and Canaris were different."

"You were a pawn. You worked for whoever paid you. Do not try to lie to me."

Maxwell's still face was silent.

Lindbergh beamed. "Yup, Wilhelm Canaris. Superspy. Head of Intelligence for the Abwehr. Hanged in April 1945 by the SS for treason. At Riga, I believe."

Maxwell continued. "For complicity in the Hitler assassination attempt and for negotiating secretly with the Allies."

"Through the Vatican", he said, flicking his ashes, raising and lowering his eyebrows like Groucho Marx, "the good old Vatican, yup, let out the SS after the war too. They helped a good bit, all good Catholics, you know."

"Many people were like Canaris," Maxwell said.

"Like what?"

"Disenchanted with Germany, when they discovered the nature of the SS."

"Get out the photo I gave back to you."

From his shirt pocket Maxwell dropped the photo taken in the Murphy Drug Store years ago.

"An interesting face, I must say."

Lindbergh's words were the heighth of understatement. How many times Maxwell had stared at that face could not be counted.

Both in those days of hiding in the west, during the war, after the death of Thibadeaux, working odd jobs, living under an alias and moving constantly, from town to town, afraid, no contact with home or friends--and in the days immediately following the war--trying to pick up his academic life, back to his real name, during his trip to Europe, in the college classroom, library, bathroom, anywhere, whenever his mind was idle--he had pondered that face--a face no longer belonging only to another, but now part of Maxwell himself--forever subliminal, pervading all. Every nuance of the square jaw, the slightly perceptible smile playing around the lips, jaw, and eyes. And the look of alertness, the slight bulge of the left eye, making it larger than the right, all this had run through Maxwell's mind hundreds of times. And all the time that he stared at the photograph, his mind screaming, "Where is he now? What did he have for dinner? What is he thinking?"

Lindbergh produced from his satchel a document, which he threw flat, just beside the photo, on the table.

"We got this from the picture check of Amt 6," he said.

Otto Koler

Rank--Haupsturmfuhrer

Prior distinction--
Obergruppenfuhrer Waffen SS

Hails from Stuttgart
Assigned to Amt 6 in 1940
by Ernst Kaltenbrunner

Function of a highly
classified nature--
Believed to be SD assassin

Expert with all types of
firearms, knives, and
poisons

Last seen in Germany in
1945 with Waffen SS
detachments near Berlin

Maxwell read the dossier several times and leaned back.
"Is that it?"

"Of course not. There is considerably more."

Lindbergh glared across at his subject. "You say you worked for Canaris?" he probed.

"I said nothing of the kind."

Lindbergh leaned forward.

"If you want more information," he said, "you must tell me the complete truth."

Maxwell jerked his head in anger.

"How bad do you want to know?" Lindbergh pressed. "You must answer this question, and you must not lie."

Maxwell took a deep breath, looked up, then down, resolved.

"What the hell," he said. "You've got to trust someone sometime."

As he had done seven years ago with his father, Maxwell told his entire story, sparing few details, except for the money he and Thibadeaux had taken. He had resolved never to tell anyone about the money. Nor did he divulge the specific place where Thibadeaux was buried. The story, told as briefly as humanly possible, filled a full fifteen minutes.

When the story ended, Lindbergh signaled for the waiter.

"Bring us two more drinks. What would you like?"

"Bourbon and ginger with a twist of lime."

The two men were silent until the drinks came.

"That is a most fascinating story. Absolutely fascinating."

"I hope you are not being sarcastic."

"No, no, absolutely not," Lindbergh said, this time looking over his pipe at Maxwell with more respect. "And I can now understand your motives. Your story has the ring of truth."

"It is the truth."

Seeing the agitation now showing on Maxwell's face, Lindbergh held up both palms as if to say, "calm down."

"Okay, I believe you," he said. "It is that simple."

"You said you had further information."

"I shall consult a good deal of notes, as I speak, I hope you don't mind."

"Shoot."

"In the last year of the war, especially on the Eastern front, thousands of soldiers from the Wehrmacht were hanged for desertion. The chief culprits of these atrocities were, as you might guess, the SS. More than just executing deserters, the SS had an ulterior motive in slowing the Russian advance. As you know, by this time in the war, the situation was hopeless from the ordinary Wehrmacht foot soldier's point of view. The SS prolonged the war with their terror on the Wehrmacht by a good six months."

"What was the ulterior motive?"

"To, as much as possible, hide what they had done to the Jews and to prepare for their massive escape and disappearance. As you well know, more than any other branch of the service, the SS escaped. Not just escaped, but raped Germany of all her remaining wealth. Millions of dollars worth of gold bars are now stored beneath the streets of Switzerland and Lichstenstein in steel vaults. As I am sure you know, most of the SS routed from safe house to safe house through Italy and with the help of many good Christian Catholics, yup, yup, escaped Europe. Most went to South America, particularly Peronist Argentina. Some used international Red Cross passports. Some were even transported to the South American coast via submarine."

Maxwell permitted himself a smile. He nodded.

"Since you went to Nuremberg, you saw that those of the SS that remain in captivity are what you Americans call 'small potatoes.' Himmler was captured by the British and cheated the gallows with a cyanide pill. Eichmann, Mengele, Barbie, all of the big boys are still at large......."

"Again, you have told me nothing that I don't already know."

"Be patient. In the last couple of years the hunting has continued, but not with the same fervor as immediately followed the war. Israel has only now become a sovereign nation. And I suspect the SS fugitives are hiding, beginning to absorb themselves into the various societies in which they reside."

"And what have been the Mossad's efforts at finding these men?"

"Mostly following leads. People like yourself. People come to us all the time with stories that they have recognized someone or other. Mostly these are hoaxes and rarely pan out."

"You speak of the SS as if they were still in existence, still organized."

"Precisely. And they are organized much more than you would like to think. Odessa, I'm sure you have heard of them."

"The SS escape network."

"A network designed to serve and protect SS fugitives. This is the area in which we believe your Mr. Ballard or Koler, as you see he is called, is still employed."

Lindbergh did not look up to see the stunned look on Maxwell's face.

"Funny," Maxwell managed to say. "I figured he was just off, living somewhere, remaining inconspicuous."

"Oh, I'm certain he is. But his own brand of expertise is still in high demand with Odessa. In fact, we know this to be so."

"I'm listening."

"In 1946, we received a tip that a Frenchman, a former SS officer had seen a fugitive. I might as well be specific. He saw Klaus Barbie near Lyons, France. Before we could contact this man, he was found dead, killed in a local park, the result of an apparent mugging. Since this time, another murder of this nature occurred in Bolivia to another SS informant--Bolivia is where it is believed Barbie now resides. Both of these murders had the same basic modus operandi as you just described with your friend, Frank Becken, the same basic knife wound, the same method of hiding the body. In 1946 a routine check of hotel registries in Lyons turned up the name Simon Bular. Since your visit to Vienna, we thought it enough like Ballard to warrant a further search. Argentina has been a Mecca for SS fugitives. Naturally, we have several active agents there. Our people in Buenos Aires, did a thorough search of local banks and found an interesting item in a small town near Buenos Aires. The town is called Peron. In this bank was a very active account of a man named Simon Ballard. We discovered that three hundred thousand dollars in Swiss notes had arrived two days before the murder in Lyons. The money had been received at Peron, one hundred thousand of which had been wired to a Chase Manhattan Bank in New York City. The name on the receiving account was Ernest Miller."

Had it not been dim in the restaurant, Lindbergh would have noticed the pallor on Maxwell's face.

"Who is Ernest Miller? Is it Ballard?"

"That we don't know. But if my guess is correct, this person is probably someone who hasn't much to fear, as far as Nazi hunters are concerned. He was not one of the high profile butchers of the concentration camps. Our best guess is that he is provided with rewards by Odessa for liquidating anyone, who proves too embarrassing."

"I'm still puzzled. Why do all these murders occur regarding only one SS criminal--Barbie?"

"An intelligent question. We feel now that Barbie is untouchable."

"Why--if you know where he is?"

"Because he is now being employed by the C.I.A."

"You're joking."

"Absolutely not. The Mossad has made it a practice to communicate with Allied intelligence agencies regarding people like Barbie. Since the deaths of these previous informants, the Mossad has remained silent regarding the discoveries of any new fugitives."

"You are telling me the leak came from the C.I.A.?"

"I'm telling you only what we suspect."

"Why would the C.I.A. employ trash like Barbie?"

"They are interested in protecting the hemisphere from Communists. They can use a man of Barbie's organizational skills in Bolivia. It's not all that unusual or surprising."

"It is to me."

"Don't be naive. We certainly are not. We do not trust anyone in German embassies or the CIA, even some British intelligence. There seems to be a great cover-up afoot. No one wants to open old closets. The attitude is to let sleeping dogs lie, don't rock the boat. The world is sick of being reminded of what happened. They want to close the book on World War II and build a new world."

"But why does Ballard protect only Barbie?"

"Who can say? Our guess is that maybe from an organizational view, Odessa has perhaps assigned bodyguards or assassins to their most high-profile fugitives."

Maxwell leaned back and sighed. He was almost sorry he was hearing this.

"What do you want from me?"

Lindbergh took three puffs from his pipe and looked around before answering. "What are your inclinations concerning this?"

"My inclination is to go to Buenos Aires, find this Ballard or Koler, and kill the son of a bitch."

"We don't want that. We have a man inside the bank at Peron now. It will be only a matter of time before Ballard surfaces. When he does, we will let you know. What we need is a run-down on this Ernest Mitchell in New York. We need someone to find out who he is and what he does."

"And that someone is me, right?"

"Only if you agree."

"What should I do?"

"Move to New York. Settle in. Apply for a job at the bank. Whatever it takes. Find this Ernest Mitchell."

"And then what?"

"You will report in, of course."

"How?"

"Leave that to me. All that would be necessary is to move to New York. We have a man in the local Post Office. Move and leave a forwarding address. You will be contacted."

"My father, rest in peace," Maxwell said, "had an old expression. He said, 'you can piss in my face, but you can't convince me it's raining.'"

"What does that mean?"

"What do you get out of the deal? You're not doing this just to help me."

"We need loyal American agents......"

"And doing this would make me a Mossad agent?"

"Let's take things a step at a time."

Maxwell stared off.

"We need a reliable informant. Perhaps this Miller, if he is implicated, would be someone with whom we can deal."

"You need a double agent."

"Obviously, he is somehow connected to Simon Ballard. Assuming

Ballard is Koler, it would be interesting to talk to this man. He might know the exact whereabouts of Eichmann or Barbie."

"Look, I sympathize with your cause, but you must understand that I am through crusading. I don't give a shit where Eichmann or Mengele are. I want Koler. If I ever find him, there won't be a lot of discussion."

"You wouldn't want him brought to trial?"

Maxwell laughed. "Are you kidding? Look, Lindbergh, don't play me for a fool. What I have told you tonight is to remain confidential. If there is any word given to the authorities...."

"Now why would that occur?"

"Just hear me out."

"I'm listening."

"If anything is spilled to the Feds, you can forget everything. I want Koler. I'll try to dig up this Mitchell character for you. There is someone in New York I'd like to see anyway. But I want this understood. While I'm running around in the States, looking for Mitchell, if your boys run across this Ballard or Koler, I want to know about it. I want the first crack at him. If it wasn't for me, I don't think you guys would have a clue as to this "Bular" guy in France, so I think you owe me that much."

"Agreed. If we find Koler, you will be the first to know."

Maxwell let his hand fall forcefully to the table. "No, sir, that won't do. I don't want to be the first to know. I want to be the one that brings him in. Understand?"

"Of course. Now, we want something of you. Find out all you can about Ernest Mitchell. Use whatever means you can. But under no circumstances are you to follow him or approach him. We will be in touch approximately thirty days after you hit New York. Simply find the man and compile information. By the way, when do you anticipate leaving?"

"As soon as the semester ends and I receive money for expenses. I'll leave for New York immediately after."

Lindbergh smiled, his puffy cheeks around his pipe flushing red.

"Mr. Wiesenthal confided to me that you were a man of some means."

Maxwell smiled. "Wrong," he said.

"How is one thousand dollars cash, for starters," Lindbergh said, matter-of-factly, as he got out his billfold and began counting out onto the table one hundred dollar bills.

Maxwell smiled again. "Since you are feeling so generous, I consider it my civic duty to pick up the tab for dinner."

"You're too kind."

The two men stood and shook hands. "Good hunting," Lindbergh said, as he turned and strode out of the restaurant.

The next evening after exams, Maxwell climbed the hill to his apartment. He heard the sound of female laughter, coming from the upstairs apartment, then saw something white floating down from the window. The girl screamed with laughter. When the object hit the ground, Maxwell laughed to himself. The condom lay helplessly on the asphalt.

Maxwell sighed. College life.

He climbed the steps to his small, sparsely furnished apartment.

After eating a small supper, he finally moved again to the coffee table. The paper, that Lindbergh had left, detailing briefly the background of Otto Koler, still lay on the table. Maxwell picked it up. Butterflies cut his stomach.

His face had aged. His forehead was lined with wrinkles; and his teeth, previously pearly white, were slightly stained from cigarette smoke.

He examined the contents of the package for an hour, having read the documents seven times.

He got up and went to the bathroom. He stood in front of the mirror. Yes, the strain of the last few years was showing, he thought. He remembered his words to Richard Thibadeaux: "We've been this far together; ain't turning back now." Then he recalled his own words, in a different situation: "What if it was one of your friends?"

He watched his face in the mirror. He was puzzled by his lack of reaction to the package's contents. He walked back to the sofa, lit another cigarette, and examined the documents once again.

He sighed and looked through the Venetian blinds. The sun was streaming in the window in orange shoots. How many years had it been now? He heard the girl's shrieking laughter in the apartment above.

She is in love, he thought, and why ain't I up there with her instead of that ugly stiff of a boyfriend she's got? How many years wasted?

After the war his obsession for revenge had taken him all over the country and finally to Europe, in search of any trace of the man that had called himself Simon Ballard.

He looked out the blinds, which cut his face in orange and black horizontal lines of light. Light blue in the fading distance were the feint lines of the Smoky Mountains of Tennessee. He oftimes made out their contours on the horizon from the window of his classroom. Those mountains would range into North Carolina, his home, a place where he had not gone since he had last returned surreptitiously to the Murphy Hotel to find the name of "Ballard" on the hotel register. On that same trip he had snuck a trip to Ernest Hammond. Securing a promise that the old hillbilly would tell no one of his presence, Maxwell learned that his father had died some six months before, apparently of a heart attack.

Home offered nothing now. There was his mother and siblings, but Maxwell avoided seeing them, only writing occasionally.

Maxwell's research had led many places. At one juncture he had asked Naval Archives in Washington for all de-classified information on U-boats during the last three years of the war. One engagement leapt off the page.

U-168 had met her fate on January 18, 1944 when she was spotted by a British patrol plane off the Gibraltar Straits and subsequently sunk by a British destroyer. There were no known survivors.

Now Maxwell had concerned himself with teaching at the university and obtaining his Doctorate in History.

He walked over to the coffee table and gazed down at the documents once again.

By the time Maxwell finished reading the paper for the ninth time, he was exhausted.

"Koler," he said aloud. "Otto Koler."

It was just as Wiesenthal had said; the name had produced nothing.

Maxwell stood up and walked to the window. He peered again through the blinds. The sky was violet now in the west with streaks of orange, like brightened veins in a deep bruise.

And what am I to do now, he thought, go to Stuttgart or Argentina with my crumpled picture? Am I like Turnley, who is dying to go off and get killed in a foreign country?

No, he would stick to his resolve. He had determined in just the last weeks that if Wiesenthal's evidence produced nothing substantial, he would quit his search. He would do this last deed. He would find this "Ernest Mitchell." He longed to put an end to the entire matter, quickly. The war had been over for millions for years now; it was time it was over for him.

He walked to the liquor cabinet and opened a bottle of his best bourbon. He poured himself a stiff drink. Strange as it may seem, his obsession seemed calmed. He felt lighter; like celebrating. He shoved the drink down his throat and felt it burn his chest. He had suddenly decided to try and see Julie. He would move to New York if necessary. Exams would be over in two days and he could be gone in three. He was tired of isolation. He had to see her one more time.

Over the years he had corresponded with one of her friends, a Marjorie Adams. Marjorie had always liked Tommy and had kept him abreast of Julie's situation. Since the war, she had been engaged twice, and both times she had backed out of the situation. Somehow this had not surprised Maxwell. As far as men were concerned, Julie bore old scars, which rendered her quite vulnerable. Their relationship had understood these scars, as Maxwell had familiarized her with his own.

And more than anything else, there was about Julie an implicit understanding--exactly what it was, he could not say, for it went deeper than words--but over the years, she had come to represent to him some emotional and spiritual milestone, as if she alone, because of her proximity to those early days and friends, could make sense of his life and obsession. And remarkable as it may seem, since she was anything but an intellectual, Maxwell had been convinced of this fact through the most tortuous moments of his obsessive search for the man in the faded photograph, the fact that somehow she could make sense of it all.

It was an overwhelming instinctual urge that led him to her again, and like love, an urge that defied all logic.

June 7

At Thompson's Diner on West 71st, Julie Miller was serving two businessmen when the manager came up behind her. As he saw her shapely hips strain against her pink waitress' uniform, he was affected as he always was. She finished distributing the home fries and turned to face him. Her breasts filled her blouse nicely, her large eyes danced with animation, and her honey-colored hair, which she wore up, shone off the morning light.

"Julie, when you get a chance, the customer in booth three wants to see you."

"Who is it?" she said with a quick glance, catching the back of a middle-aged man's head. All she could see was that the man wore glasses.

"I don't know, but make sure your customers' coffee cups are full before you go."

"Don't worry about it, Frank."

"Hell, I should hire ugly girls, the pretty ones always attract loiterers."

"Dry up," she said.

She rushed over to get the coffee pot. She decided to catch the stranger first. When she walked to the other side of the booth and saw the man's face, she almost dropped the coffee.

"Hello Julie," he said, taking off his wire-rimmed glasses.

"My God, Tommy," she slammed the coffee pot onto the table and crawled over the table to hug him. He kissed her on the mouth. At once he was reminded of the softness of her lips.

"You're as beautiful as ever," he said.

"How did you know... where have you been!" she gasped, and by the blush on her cheeks and the beautiful light in her eyes it was apparent that she was glad to see him.

Maxwell laughed and held up a hand. "Marjorie Adams told me where you were, and as for where I've been, it's not important. What is important is where I will be on your first day off. When is it?"

"Tomorrow," she said.

"So the important thing is that I'll be with you on the beach at Cape Cod tomorrow."

She smiled with adoration and tilted her head slightly.

"My, but you're sure of yourself. How do you know I'm even available?"

He smiled. "Are you?"

"Tuna fish sandwiches and beer?" she asked, reminding him of an old joke.

"Tuna fish sandwiches and beer," he confirmed.

"Hey, Julie, get over here," her manager yelled.

"Stick it, Frank, I'm coming."

The day was clear. It had been months since he had seen the sea. He made it a point never to stay away too long. The gentle rhythm of the waves, the white caps breaking five miles out, the gliding gulls in suspended animation over the waves.

They sat on a towel, while drinking beer and eating tuna fish.

She wore a yellow one piece bathing suit and looked remarkably good for a woman in her mid-thirties. Her sandy blonde hair had strands of gray showing, but her legs were still sleek and her face with its golden tan, large eyes, and plump mouth was as beautiful as ever.

"You look nice with your glasses," she said.

"Is that a hint to put them back on?"

"No, stupid, I was only paying you a compliment."

"Tuna fish needs some mayonnaise."

"You always were particular about the things I cooked."

"Come on, now. I loved your cooking."

"You know and I know," she said, her head touching the inside of his arm and setting him aflame, "that I hardly ever cooked for you."

Maxwell shrugged and smiled. "That's just it. It was a real event."

"Yeah, an event all right. Remember when I tried to make homemade pizza?"

Maxwell rocked back with laughter.

"Yeah, you didn't cook the meat first before putting it in the oven."

"And I'll never forget how sweet you were for trying to eat it. The dough wasn't even done. I could see it stringing between your teeth."

Maxwell stopped laughing and touched her cheek.

"Those were good times."

"So, Tommy Maxwell," she said, licking a piece of tuna off her forefinger. "What brings you back? You're always so mysterious."

He looked her straight in the eye. "I've come to marry you."

She stopped opening her beer, took a deep breath that nearly lifted her large breasts from the top of her suit, put her finger to her ear, leaned forward and said, "Is this the Tommy Maxwell I know?"

He laughed and grabbed her hands. "No, it isn't."

"You're crazy," she said, her face beaming with happiness. "You just don't dart in after years' absence and ask a girl to get married."

"Why not?"

She giggled. "You just don't."

"You know me," he said. "Never much one for social propriety." The sea played behind her head, moaning and churning with the wind. Wisps of her hair twirled in the breeze.

"Honestly, Tommy, you take the cake." But she could not hide the joyous animation that played in her eyes.

"Before, when we were together, I never really told you what I thought," he said, "either because I was too scared or stupid. This time if I lose you, I don't want it to be because there are any doubts as to my intentions."

"Lose me?" she managed to say.

He leaned over and kissed her softly.

"I haven't been with anyone special now for over three years," he said, "and I guess I've lost my polish. Might as well be blunt about it."

"It's been so long," she protested meekly. "You have no idea what I've done or anything. We can't just leap into it. God knows, I've had my chances to get married. At least three times, but something always went wrong. Guys can get cold feet. Maybe I'm not the marrying kind."

"We won't leap into anything," he said, lifting her hands to his lips. "You like long engagements, then we'll have one, just as long as you keep one thing in mind."

With his right hand he held her behind her neck.

"What are we going to keep in mind?" she whispered.

"That I am in love with you," he said. "I've always been in love with you. Even before we met. I want to grow old with you. I want you to have my children."

He stopped. Tears trickled silently down her cheeks. They kissed with the gentle warmth of young people in love. He tasted the salt on her cheeks.

That night they lay in a hotel much like the Breakers. The Cape Cod Hotel overlooked the sea. They made love three times before finally exhausted.

Her beautiful white breasts heaved up and down from her breathing. He draped one of his legs around her and touched her soft cheek with his finger.

"Do you remember the Breakers on Pearl Harbor night?" he asked.

She laughed softly and put her head against his shoulder. He felt her hot breath.

"Of course," she said. "I'll never forget that."

"You remember how you told me that something extraordinary would happen to me?"

"Yes. And I was right, wasn't I?"

He smiled and kissed her again. "Yes. You were right. You always were. For the most extraordinary thing that has happened to me was you."

She giggled. "Tommy, please, you're embarrassing me."

He put his finger to her lips. "And you said that we would meet again. Before the war you said that, remember?"

She tilted her head. He felt himself rushing again. "I told you that I knew," she said. "I always knew it would happen. And I'll tell you something else. I knew you would come back and marry me. You laughed and called me a little witch."

Maxwell was stunned. It was true. There had always been an element about Julie that seemed fated. He remembered what she had said at the Breakers that night, that people were continually on the same orbits, that coincidence lost definition between these people, that Time rarely prevented them from making contact again and again.

"And tell me this," she said, already laughing at her joke. "Are all our kids going to be born with that crooked nose of yours?"

"That's right," he said, wrinkling his nose. "All scruffy and mean like me. Let's see, how does about seven sons sound?"

She laughed, throwing her head back. "I love little boys, but knowing you, I'll be lucky to get away with less than a dozen."

He kissed her and rolled on top of her. "Let's get to work on it right now," he said.

"Tommy," she said, giggling and reaching down between his legs, "you're insatiable."

Strange as it may seem, Tommy Maxwell had forgotten what it was like to be in love. From the first moment he had kissed Julie, a renewal of those old feelings, a fluttering in his chest, reminded him of his youth.

The summer had been one long celebration of these feelings. When he was away from her in the mornings, the fluttering in his stomach only increased at the thought of her.

In these times, in her absence, at the same time as he went about his daily affairs, he tried to imagine what she was doing, her every gesture, the people with whom she came into contact.

He and Julie would oftentimes spend lazy, summer afternoons, picnicking with beer and sandwiches and worshipping the sun.

On a particular day they had gone to Connecticut. They had reclined in a park by a lake, drunk beer, massaged each other with lazy, warm suntan oils, swam. They had embraced and kissed on the blankets. When they sought more privacy, they had managed to drive up a small path off the main road. The path ended at a small, country graveyard. Tommy parked the car, got an air mattress and blankets out of the trunk, and proceeded to recline with Julie in front of the car, their heads nearly under the bumper and the tombstones to the right.

Soon naked, Maxwell felt the warm sun on his butt as he thrust into her.

They both laughed at the noise they had made and commented that the dead in the graveyard had not seemed to mind.

Their early courtship was often like this, that is, they seemed completely enveloped within each other, excluding the rest of the world.

This feeling of mutual exclusion was especially a comfort for Tommy. The war had left him for the longest time--with his obsession--dead. Normal human feelings, such as love of family, love for women (he had plenty of uninvolved sex in the past couple of years), the desire for a family, all of these things had been sublimated by the fear and hatred of what had happened during 1942-43.

And whereas pangs of the past occasionally assaulted him, like a bad habit, he disciplined himself to drown these thoughts with thoughts of her.

Now it happened that when they finally set a date for marriage--November 30--that sense of mutual exclusion, that feeling of existing in union together to the exclusion of the rest of the world, began to wane. Maxwell found that as soon as talk of the act of marrying, as a definite and predictable date ensued, the sense of peace between himself and Julie was diluted. Among the talk of a dress, the church, the flower arrangements, the guest list, a trousseau, ushers, bridesmaids, accommodations for out-of-town guests, the composition of the punch, the reception champagne--among all of this, part of his feeling became lost.

To his dismay, he discovered that he could not marry only Julie; he had to marry her family as well. Particularly disturbing to him was his first visit to her parents' house in Virginia. He would cringe, remembering the first impressions he had of her parents--the mother, domineering, gray, and talkative--the father, cadaverous, thin, stiff, sanctimonious. Moreover, Julie seemed uncomfortable around her parents. Early in their relationship, she had told Tommy of her embittered family history, and it was apparent that, at least for her, the old scars still remained.

Maxwell's visit to Murphy was even worse. As he had promised his father, he had written to his mother on occasion.

On introducing his mother to Julie, he had immediately sensed, despite his mother's polite expressions, a rivalry between the two women. As his brother later told him, since their father's death, their mother had not been the same.

Elaine Cory and her husband had moved to Kansas.

The mountains had held their old sway over Maxwell, but the old nostalgic feeling was tinged with bitterness when Maxwell visited Baker's Point.

He had been shocked to find that the Army Corps of Engineers had bought the shoreline at the point, and that the place where he and Thibadeaux had hidden behind the log, was now a picnic area--a shelter with a stone barbecue pit, and a concrete slab on which a shuffle board lane had been painted.

Several times, once when he had been driving Julie through the mountains, he had been tempted to visit the hidden gravesight of Richard Thibadeaux--he was anxious to see if he could even find it again--but he quickly dismissed this idea. The mountains had swallowed Thibadeaux much as he hoped Julie would destroy any memory of Maxwell's embittered past. To take Julie to Baker's Point, or to walk her to the burial site, strange as it sounds, would be to defile her in his mind. Besides Maxwell's loving her genuinely as a person, Julie represented not only a sense of idealistic youth in the life of Tommy Maxwell, but also an entity that was separate from his bitterest memories.

Although she was a part of his past, she must, at the same time, remain separate from his sad obsession. It was his only chance of survival.

Maxwell did manage to visit one grave, however--the grave of his father. In a quaint family cemetery, in the woods above the house, above the spring with the newly installed pump, lay his father. On arriving at the gravesite, Maxwell removed a bouquet of faded flowers, replacing it with a handful of wild, mountain flowers of various colors, picked from the edge of the encroaching woods.

He knelt beside the stone, which read:

PATRICK MAXWELL
1878-1946

Maxwell was barraged with memories. He remembered the night in the sheriff's office as a boy, his father on a tractor, plowing a tobacco field, remembered him walking in the woods, dragging his stiff leg--and more dominant than anything else, the conversation they had after the burial of Thibadeaux, and his father's ridiculous confession.

For the first time in years, Maxwell wept.

He left North Carolina, glad to rid himself of the past, determined to make a new start, and resolved that after the wedding, he and Julie would again find the bliss of solitude.

Despite all his previous cynicism, he began to believe that Fate had brought them together for a reason--perhaps to raise children.

But Maxwell was soon to take a drastically different view regarding the elements of Julie, the significance of what she called "Fate," and the nature of coincidence.

Like most dramatic revelations in life, this huge event, which would soon consume him, was cloaked within the daily affairs of living--all the more devastating in its proximity to the realm of the mundane.

July 3

It happened on a hot afternoon at the University of Tennessee, with the sounds of firecrackers already popping a day ahead of time from the dormitories, and the secretaries in the faculty mail room lounging over coffee and discussing plans for the upcoming holiday, that Tommy Maxwell ran across two notes in his mailbox, needing immediate attention. Maxwell was in town to turn in his resignation to the Dean regarding his teaching post.He was going to clean out his apartment and check into how many of his graduate credits would transfer to Long Island University.

One of the notes was dated June 14 and marked URGENT from the desk of Dean Stevens. The other note, dated June 13, was from Sam:

WHERE IN HELL YOU BEEN? GET OVER
TO MY PLACE NOW OR GIVE ME A CALL.

Maxwell was perplexed at both the urgency of these two notes and the closeness of the two dates. He surmised that Dean Stevens had been contacted by Long Island University as a teaching reference, but since Maxwell had asked Long Island to hold off until August, so that he could formally resign his post at U.T. he was further perplexed.

He decided to call Sam first.

"Where the hell you been?"

"I've been in New York, Sam. I'm getting married."

"You asshole. All kinds of people been looking for you."

"What's up?"

"I ain't talking about it on the phone."

"What do you mean?"

"Meet me at Sydney's Tavern. How soon can you get there?"

"Ten minutes."

Sydney's was located on Tennessee Boulevard just off campus and next to the Campus Book Store. The inside of the tavern overlooked the busy sidewalk, where students and shoppers ambled by, fighting the heat. Maxwell got his favorite table next to the window, overlooking the sidewalk and the busy street. He was halfway into a cold beer when Sam arrived.

"Bring us two more," Maxwell shouted to the bartender.

Sam, his face considerably more tanned and streamed with sweat, sat down and chugged down half his beer before speaking.

"I got your note from about three weeks ago," Maxwell said. "What's up?"

"You are, you asshole."

"What in the Sam Hill are you talking about?"

"You heard about George Weller in the Chemistry Department, didn't you?"

"No, I told you, I haven't been in town, didn't you notice?"

Sam grabbed Maxwell's forearm on the table. "Brace yourself, pal, he's dead."

Maxwell looked at Sam, tilting his head and shrugging, "He's dead; he's dead; okay, so what. I barely knew the guy. I'm sorry to hear it, but what's the big deal?"

Sam's eyes did not waver in their seriousness. "It was suicide. He blew his head off in his study. They said it made a hell of a mess. Did you get a note from Dean Stevens?"

"Yeah, how do you know? He wants to see me. It was dated the day after the note you sent me."

"Right, right, June 14, the same time Weller got his note."

"Goddammit, Sam, would you stop beating around the bush?

If you got something to say, say it."

"You ain't been paying attention to the news? I ain't talking local........"

"You mean about the war?"

"No, asshole, about Joseph McCarthy. The Senate investigations."

"Sure. McCarthy is investigating what they call Communist infiltration in the State Department."

"Bullshit," Sam said, his face the color of a tomato. "It's going farther than that. Now they're looking into educators. I talked to my friend in Ohio. The same shit is happening up there. Resignations are rampant. The F.B.I. is investigating everybody. Anyone to the left of Atilla the Hun is being labeled a Communist."

"Right, okay," Maxwell answered, withdrawing his arm. "I read the papers. So what does this have to do with me?"

"There was a complaint. From some snot-nose kid. Turnip? Turner?"

"Turnley?"

Sam pounded the table. "Hell, yes, apparently the punk reads the papers too. He's claimed you're a Communist."

Maxwell's stomach fell.

"Stevens has been asking around for you."

"You're shitting me."

Sam leaned back and smiled. "Do I look like I'm shitting you?"

Maxwell took a sip of beer and leaned back in silence.

"I thought I'd let you know, man. Stevens talked to Weller on the 15th of June. They say the old guy was sick anyway, but he killed himself on the 16th. Now all the kids are saying that proves he's a Communist."

"Fuck the kids," Maxwell said heatedly. "You know better than that. Nothing could be further from the truth. Me, a Communist, Jesus."

"You know that and I know that, but how can you prove otherwise? What's this Turnley kid talking about?"

Maxwell shrugged and shook his head. "Who the hell knows? We had some words during class at times. I was just teaching. He's another one of these Gung Ho's who can't wait to get drafted into Korea and get his balls shot off."

"That explains it, then."

Maxwell stared out the window. The stores across the street had already hung out American flags on the front window in preparation for the annual Fourth of July parade.

Maxwell reached into his pocket and handed Sam a typed letter.

"Do me a favor and give this to Stevens," Maxwell said, as he finished his beer and called for the bartender.

"I was going to give it to him myself today, but under the circumstances, I'd just as soon send it to him. Give me that pencil. Here's my new address in New York. Keep me abreast of what's shaking down here."

Sam leaned over and shook Maxwell's hand. "Sorry to be the bearer of bad news, man."

"Forget it," Maxwell said, forcing a smile. "Look, I appreciate everything."

"Man, you got to be feeling pressure."

Again Maxwell laughed. "Bullshit, Sam, pressure is when you're in a foxhole and some asshole is trying to blow your head off. That's pressure."

"How would you know?"

Maxwell smiled. "Besides," he added, "I'm in love. Damned if anything can change that."

"Good luck."

Sam watched Maxwell walk down the sidewalk, saw him disappear between two buildings, then ordered another beer.

The summer wore on, and eventually Maxwell stopped worrying about the Turnley complaint. He had decided that worry would solve nothing, and he also surmised that perhaps he would not get the Long Island graduate assistant's job, if Stevens gave him a bad recommendation.

This would not be an insurmountable obstacle. Surely the powers-that-be could not keep him from pursuing his Doctorate Degree, no matter how hysterical the times were. His financial situation was more than stable, since he had invested very successfully in the stock market and had well over two hundred thousand dollars in a Swiss bank account, a matter he had taken care of on his trip to Europe.

But he followed the events of the McCarthy hearings with more than a passing interest. The conservative Congressional forces had been targeting educators and people inside the defense industry as Communist infiltrators. Careers were being ruined in a roughshod fashion as the witch hunt gathered momentum.

Maxwell told himself that the McCarthy Era would be a passing fancy, and he predicted to close friends that the hysteria would wane with the end of the Korean War.

He immersed himself in the details of living.

His marriage was imminent, and the second summer session at Long Island University had started, and Tommy was taking a full load.

When he was married, he had planned to take Julie to Hawaii for their honeymoon. He was going to stay out of school the fall quarter so that he and Julie could buy a house and set up housekeeping without a lot of distractions. He had not decided firmly where he would live.

In the mean time, Maxwell began frequenting the Chase Manhattan Bank. He opened a checking and savings account there, making it a point to visit the plush bank lobby with its marble pillars and floors at least three times a week. He frequented the bank at different parts of the day, changing his pattern, but never seeing anyone he recognized. As luck would have it, Julie had a friend, who had a friend, that was a teller at the bank. Through a vague excuse of Maxwell's invention, that he wanted to find out about a unique bond that Chase Manhattan was offering, he had Julie supply him with the girl's phone number and name. Maxwell finally reached this Alice Hogan late one afternoon, explaining who he was and how he knew her. He broached the subject of improving his credit rating, and when Mrs. Hogan politely offered to refer him to a loan officer, Maxwell answered her objection by stating that if she wouldn't mind, he had rather talk first to someone he knew. Flustered and unable to make heads or tails of Maxwell's double talk, Miss Hogan finally agreed to have lunch with Tommy.

"Just come by tomorrow at eleven thirty. We'll go somewhere close. I only have an hour."

"Thank you so much," Maxwell replied. "Julie told me I could talk to you. I know it seems strange, but when I explain, I'm sure you will understand."

The voice on the other end hesitated before answering. "Okay, then, I'll see you tomorrow."

The day was bright and sunny, and the atmosphere in the spacious lobby of the Chase Manhattan Bank reflected the day outside.

The lobby was huge with marble floors and great marble pillars to a transparent ceiling of brown, stained glass, which covered a dome, where the sunlight illuminated the lobby below. The marble floor echoed merrily the thousands of shoes that struck it, its expanse punctuated with desks, where bank officers interviewed customers in elegant leather chairs. On one end of the great floor were the interior offices; on the other end were the tellers' windows and vaults.

Maxwell meandered down the great row of tellers' windows until he saw the gold name plate, which read: Miss Alice Hogan.

A tall woman with light brown hair and a pretty smile, stood behind the window. Maxwell watched her friendly demeanor as she dealt with four customers in a line before he approached her.

"Miss Hogan, my name is Tommy Maxwell."

The woman, apparently relieved at Maxwell's non-threatening appearance, smiled and said: "I'll be off for lunch in five minutes. You can wait over there," she said, indicating a row of leather chairs across the way.

When Maxwell saw her move across the lobby towards him, he stood up and extended his hand.

"It is awfully nice of you to see me. Where would you like to eat?"

The woman shrugged and said, "As I said on the phone, I only have a short time....."

"How about Maurie's across the street."

They moved into the bright sunshine, crossed the street, waited in line for fifteen minutes before they were seated and received their menus.

Promptly ordering sandwiches, Maxwell sipped on an iced tea after the lady refused his offer for a drink.

"So you are Julie's fiancée," the woman said, feeling the situation out.

"Yes."

"She is a lovely girl. I don't know her as well as Shelley does, but judging from appearances, I would say you are one lucky fellow."

"I agree completely. Are you married?"

"I'm engaged as well."

"Congratulations. When is the big day?"

"November 14."

"I'm sure you are wondering why I insisted on seeing you instead of a bank officer."

"Frankly," Miss Hogan said, shifting in her seat, "I couldn't figure it out. I started to call and cancel."

Maxwell reached inside his sweater and handed her an envelope.

"Take this and put it in your purse. Consider it a wedding present."

"What is it?"

"You will find five hundred dollars in cash inside. You can buy your fiancée something nice."

The woman frowned as Maxwell smiled and slid across the table a faded black and white photograph.

"Have you ever seen this man?"

She picked up the photo, glanced at it briefly, then put it down. "No," she said. "Should I have?"

"No."

"What is this all about," she said, pausing as the waiter brought two hamburgers. "Complete strangers don't go around giving away money....."

"I am an investigator, a private investigator. I need some confidential information concerning one of your depositors. His name is Ernest Mitchell. Whereas I could probably subpoena the information, I don't want to bring the authorities into the picture. All I want is to find out the history of his account, when it was opened, a history of his deposits and withdrawals, things like that."

"We are not allowed to divulge information concerning accounts. I could lose my job."

Maxwell smiled and lit a cigarette. "How's your hamburger?"

"It's fine."

"I am aware that I'm asking a lot, but then again, the information is pretty harmless. After all, I am not trying to rob the bank. The information is available if I am willing to go through proper channels, which I am not."

Alice raised an eyebrow. "You say the information is harmless. You hand me five hundred dollars for practically nothing. What is this all about?"

"If I could tell you that, it would not be worth five hundred dollars. It's a simple favor. Will you do it?"

Again she frowned. "Does Julie know about this?"

"Absolutely not. This will be our secret. No one will know."

"I'll need a couple of weeks. I can't just go plunging through records all of a sudden, but since there is no harm...."

"I assure you there is not. I have a client who is trying to trace some stolen money. It is worth it to me to know if I'm barking up the wrong tree or not. Could you meet me for lunch again in say, two weeks?"

"I suppose so. Are you sure this is okay?"

"You have my word. I will be here at this time two weeks from today."

Alice smiled and shrugged. "Easiest money I ever made," she said.

The two weeks passed quickly, and at the appointed time Maxwell again stood in the waiting line at Maurie's. Alice was sitting at a table in the center of the dining area.

Maxwell walked past the waiting area and sat down across from her.

"How have you been?" he said, shaking her hand.

"I'm fine," she said, handing him a folded envelope. "I would prefer you not open this here. It would make me nervous."

"Of course not," he said with a slight bow of the head. "I'll read it at home."

Again she frowned. "I must say, it is an extremely active account. I hope you find it interesting."

"I can't thank you enough."

"Don't mention it," she said.

Maxwell smiled and stood up to leave.

"And when I say, 'don't mention it,' that's exactly what I mean."

"Relax," Maxwell said, "thanks again."

Upon arriving at his apartment, Maxwell plunged into the document, written in a female handwriting, detailing the activities of the account under the name of Ernest Mitchell, address--560 Fifth Avenue-Park Penthouse Building.

The current balance was two hundred and fifty eight thousand dollars in savings and over twenty-one hundred dollars in checking. Whereas Maxwell was relieved to find an active checking account, verifying that this Mitchell was not only having money received in New York but was actually living here, he was disappointed that Miss Hogan had not detailed any information as to specific checks that had been written. The savings account, however, reflected several fascinating transactions. Large sums of money had been regularly sent in and out of the account. Especially interesting and causing those familiar butterflies in Maxwell's stomach were the transactions on two dates--June 18, 1947-deposit-one hundred thousand dollars-source-Peron, Argentina--December 19, 1948-deposit-one hundred and fifty thousand dollars--source--Peron, Argentina. There were several other smaller deposits from banks in both Buenaventura, Colombia and La Paz, Bolivia. These deposits were smaller sums of forty-two hundred dollars and twenty-eight hundred. Of course the Argentinean deposits were interesting from two points of view. First, Lindbergh had mentioned two murders of Mossad informants and the two deposits from Argentina that roughly coincided with these dates. Second, the sums of one hundred thousand and one hundred and fifty thousand were nice round figures, which might indicate that they represented an agreed-upon fee.

By the time that Maxwell had finished reading the document, he had a pounding headache. There was one other thing that remained to be done.

He immediately picked up the phone and dialed the number of Alice Hogan.

"Hello."

"Hi, Alice, this is Tommy Maxwell."

There was an uncomfortable pause on the other end.

"Yes," the voice finally said.

"Look, the information you provided me has been of great help, but there is only one more little detail I need to clear up before we part company for good."

Again the pause. "What is it?" she said coldly.

"I noticed that the account of Ernest Mitchell was opened in April 1947. Tell me this. Is there any legal way a person can change a name on an existing account?"

"You mean change the name of the depositor?"

"Yes."

"No, not unless proper identification and documentation is provided, in other words, not unless the person's name was actually changed."

Maxwell had noticed the edge to her voice. "Look, Alice, I know this is an imposition. But there is just one more favor I'd like to ask......"

"Tommy, I agreed to do only........"

"There will be an additional three hundred dollars for you. Call it honeymoon money."

Again there was an uncomfortable pause on the other end, then: "What is it?"

"I need to know if there is an active account under the name of Simon Ballard. Do you have a pencil?"

"Yeah, I got it."

"Simon Ballard. And if there is not a current account of Simon Ballard, I'd like to know if there ever was an account under that name. What I'd like to know especially is whether or not an account under the name of Ballard was closed near the same time the Mitchell account was opened."

Maxwell heard a deep sigh on the other end. "You say you are a private investigator."

"That's right."

"Do you hire secretaries?"

Maxwell adjusted the phone on his ear. "Well, yes, I have one now. Why do you ask?"

"Because you might need to hire me when I get fired."

Maxwell laughed. "Let's not let that happen, now."

"I'll need more time for this. You see, normally I don't have access to these records. If I go snooping around this next week, it will look suspicious."

"Take all the time you need," Maxwell said, smiling to himself. "And thanks again, when shall I get the money to you?"

"Don't come by the bank again. Some of the girls know Charlie and might think we're having a fling. You can pay me when I get you the information. I want you to understand this. This is the last thing I'm doing, Tommy."

"I understand. Goodbye."

Two days later Maxwell received a phone call. A deep male voice announced: "Tom Maxwell? I am calling in behalf of Ed Lindbergh."

"Yes?"

"Can we meet somewhere or should I come by your place?"

"Neither," Maxwell said, "I will meet or talk to no one other than Lindbergh himself."

"Very well, then." The caller hung up.

In three days Lindbergh called, and Maxwell agreed to meet him at the Tavern On the Green Restaurant near Central Park.

Maxwell entered the plush, darkened dining area and spotted Lindbergh, sitting over by the window, smoking his pipe.

Maxwell re-thought his strategy.

His plan was to inform the Mossad only partially.

He would keep them one or two steps behind in the investigation of Ernest Mitchell. He wanted no one stepping in now or interfering with his own plans.

"How have you been?" Lindbergh said, as Maxwell sat down and extended his hand.

As had happened previously, as if now it were part of a code of ethics, neither man engaged in any conversation other than chit chat until dessert and after dinner drinks were served. It was only then that they got down to business.

"I was surprised that you had someone other than yourself call me," Maxwell said.

"My apologies," Lindbergh said, a genuinely worried look on his face. "It was careless. I was not immediately available."

Maxwell lit a cigarette as he spoke. "You are my direct link to Simon Wiesenthal. I deal only with you and will trust no one else. Understood?"

"Of course. Now what have you to report?"

"Not a whole lot. I've become engaged since my arrival...."

"Congratulations."

"Thanks. So much of my time has been spent getting settled, going to school, and planning for the wedding. I finally managed to contact a person inside the bank, and I am hoping to hear from her quite soon. She says she can most likely provide me with an address and further account information in a couple of weeks."

"A couple of weeks."

"Is there a huge rush?"

"Not really," Lindbergh said. "Is the account still active?"

"Like I said, I don't know yet. It was hard as hell just finding a person inside the bank and contacting her was something else."

"Who is this person?"

"I will not tell you that. I promised confidentiality.

Besides, I insist on full control of this investigation."

Lindbergh put his pipe down, apparently disgusted. "What do you mean?"

"I mean that I don't want your boys stepping in and contacting my informant."

"Why would that occur? You were chosen for this. We have put our faith in you. You should treat us with the same respect."

"Give me three or four weeks, and I should have everything about this Mitchell clown that you need. What about your end? Has Ballard surfaced?"

"Nothing new to report from Argentina. The Peron account still exists, but there has been no new activity."

"So this guy has conveniently disappeared again," Maxwell said.

"No one stays gone forever," Lindbergh said, leaning back and puffing his pipe again with confidence. "The world is a very small place. Eventually everyone surfaces."

"I'll need a bit more time."

"Very well. We'll contact you in another thirty days. Hopefully, you will have something more substantial to report."

The next day Maxwell made an afternoon phone call.

"Hill Detective Agency," a squeaky female voice announced.

"I would like to speak to Mr. Hill."

"One moment, please."

After a short wait the deep male voice answered: "Jeffery Hill."

"Mr. Hill, my name is Tommy Maxwell. I have reason to believe that a man has been seeing my wife. I want him tailed.

You do engage in surveillance work."

"Of course. But you'll have to come into the office. We don't set up transactions over the phone."

"Fine. How about this afternoon?"

"Let me check with my secretary." After a pause the voice returned. "How about two o'clock?"

"That's fine. See you then."

File 20 The man entered the East 63rd St. Grocery, obtained one of the shopping carts, and started down the aisle. But for a barely perceptible limp in his right leg and an Americanized part on the left side of his blonde head, he looked the same.

The left eye still bulged slightly, especially when he saw that cabbage had gone up three cents. He bought cabbage, tomatoes, scallions, carrots, and a head of both spinach and leaf lettuce. Roxanne loved his salads.

He so enjoyed New York grocery stores, especially the delicatessens. He bought olive oil, tomato paste, cloves of garlic, red peppers, egg plant, red wine, ground beef, bread crumbs, and finally, spicy Italian sausage. He would make his spaghetti sauce for Roxanne tonight. She loved his cooking.

Ernest Mitchell smiled with his white, even rows of teeth as the fat Jewish man with white hair, which stuck out like cotton candy beneath his butcher's cap, threw in the customary extra quarter pound of sausage and winked.

"Butcher's dozen," Mitchell said with a smile.

The old Jew smiled and said: "One pig more or less. What the hell, Mr. Mitchell. We'd just throw it away."

As Ernest Mitchell limped down the aisle to the cash register, he laughed at the two fat Italian women ahead of him, apparently engrossed in lively gossip as they whispered confidentially, all the time gesticulating with their hands in punctuation to each utterance.

How ironic, he thought, it's the ethnicity that I most enjoy. Something that was always verboten in the past.

The plump Italian girl at the cash register smiled as she counted up the groceries and took the check.

He walked in the bright sunshine and planned his day. Roxanne would be over at approximately seven. If he got home, got the garlic, sausage, and meat cooked, he could make the sauce; leave it simmering, and it would be ripe by eight o'clock. They could enjoy two highballs each by that time. Wine of course with the meal. And not to forget the bread.

Of all the elements of his past that he had shed, the one thing he had retained, had been his precision. He still enjoyed it.

He drove to his penthouse apartment on Fifth, greeted his fox terrier, Bandit, who leapt and barked upon seeing his master, indicating he was ready for a walk.

"Wait now, little Tiger," the master said. "Sauce first, then our walk."

The little dog obediently sat on the kitchen floor as the master turned on the gas burner and began first cooking the garlic cloves in olive oil. He stirred the diced cloves twice in the pan before going to his balcony to inspect the planters.

The sun streamed down on his evenly tanned face as he inspected the planters. He was growing gardenias, roses, which climbed a white lattice near the railing, and yellow tulips.

He watered the black dirt of the planters and actually scowled at the absence of weeds. He missed weeding; it reminded him of the old days, made him think of his father.

No matter, he could get all of his gardening instincts satisfied when he went to Connecticut in three weeks with Roxanne. Her parents were transplanted farmers, who adored Mitchell almost as much as did their daughter. Roxanne's father, a man who loved working the raspberry patches this time of year, often commented at the delicate precision that his daughter's fiancée showed in working around the farm.

"It's such a shame you were always a city boy," he would say, marveling at how an executive of an overseas arms concern and a lobbyist in Washington could have such a natural talent at planting, nurturing, and harvesting.

Turning his attention from the planters, he gazed at the city's skyline, heard the moan of the traffic, and finally let rest his gaze upon the visual respite of green, that stretched for miles, below the concrete canyons of Manhattan skyscrapers--Central Park.

He went back into his apartment, cooked the sausage and ground beef, molded the bread crumbs into the meat balls, cooked them, and placed the entire concoction into the deep pot, to which he added tomato paste, tomato sauce, the cooked garlic cloves, parsley, generous red pepper, one and a half cups of red wine, and chunks of eggplant and mushrooms. Upon several tastings and stirrings, he was finally satisfied as he lowered the temperature to a slow simmer. He placed the lid over the top and then attended to Bandit.

To the leaping and barking joy of the dog, he got out the leash and attached it to his collar. In a large black satchel he kept his easel, brushes, and paints. The time was right, the sauce was on, and the sun would be perfect. After a short walk, he would work on his landscape painting. He could go to the knoll today. The light would be just right.

He took the black satchel under his left armpit and the leash in his right hand. The elevator was empty, and soon, he and the excited terrier were traversing the beautiful penthouse lobby with its shiny, hardwood floors, elegant squares of Arabian carpet, and antique fixtures. He nodded to the boy at the paper stand and indicated that he would get a paper on his way back in.

Outside the revolving door stood Adrian, the corpulent, uniformed doorman.

"How are you today, Mr. Mitchell?"

"Fine, Adrian, what's new?"

The doorman shrugged and smiled, at first ignoring the question, then saying, "Guess old Wiley's got some news across the street."

He nodded at the thin man, dressed in a blue work suit, briskly sweeping the sidewalk.

Mitchell paused and smiled, ignoring the urgent tugs on the leash of Bandit, who mildly protested the delay.

"And what could possibly be of interest across the street?"

The doorman frowned in a confidential manner, as if he were imparting the most vital information in the world.

"Wiley over there. Piece of work. He sweeps that walk with energy, doesn't he? Anyway, he tells me today that some clown is looking into buying that piece of shit."

The "piece of shit" referred to the dark, red brick tenement building across the street. Recent efforts by the penthouse owners to have the building condemned had been stalled. To the ritzy neighborhood, everyone considered the Shelborne Towers, as they were called, an eyesore.

"Yeah, Wiley claims some prospective renter has laid a deposit on him. They are even talking of buying the place."

"They'll buy it to tear it down," confided Mitchell.

"No, no that ain't the story. The buyer, according to Wiley, is talking renovation. Renovation, shit. Hell, I hear the roaches are riding bareback on the bigger roaches' backs. Simmons says the buyers are moving into one of the apartments temporarily. About everybody else that lived in the dump is gone. I'll bet there ain't three apartments occupied."

Mitchell smiled, but only a block away his smile turned.

No, he thought, it is mere paranoia. But who would rent that place with the idea of buying it? One look at the outside or the interior would have to convince a buyer that the building must be condemned. And renovation? Impossible. Who would be that stupid?

With a shake of his broad shoulders, he submerged the thought and attended to the business at hand.

Within fifteen minutes he had reached the park. He walked as always with a slow, deliberate pace, to savor the faces and infinite variety of the passersby. He passed the knoll, which overlooked the duckpond and paddleboats and seeing that a few artists had already mounted the knoll, continued to walk the dog down the bridle path. It was on these paths that he loved to walk at nights. Only here and only at nights would the dark and murky images of his past visit him like a recurring dream. Only here would he remember that he had been Otto Koler.

Ernest Mitchell had come to the United States a year and a half ago. He was an executive of Brunewald Armaments out of Switzerland. He negotiated arms deals with various international concerns and was even a lobbyist against gun controls in Washington.

Otto Koler had come by his talents for this type of negotiations honestly, for his father, Klaus Koler, had for years been an executive of Krupp, the German armaments concern.

It made Koler sad to think of his father, for his memory was always of that horrible day in 1943 when he arrived back in his homeland, after his American "excursion."

At his father's home at Hamburg, Koler had been shocked at his country's devastation, which had seemingly occurred overnight. Allied bombing raids had increased to the point that Hamburg was diminished into one huge ruin.

His father, who normally resided in the country, had been called to Hamburg for administrative duties. He and his wife had rented an apartment on Hagelstrasse. When Koler arrived at the address, he discovered that the building had been long since demolished into rubble. The bombing raid had come at night. Upon inquiring as to survivors, Koler had discovered that both his mother and father had been killed.

This, coupled with the shame he had felt at his fear of being fired upon in North Carolina, led him to request transfer from Amt Six of RSHA to a combat unit of the Waffen SS.

The death of his family, a realization of his own cowardice, and the heartbreak of seeing everything in his country being systematically destroyed--all of these things drove him to combat duty. And whereas he found in those last days in 1945, that his fear still existed, it was tempered by both rage at the Allies and at himself. He no longer clung to life with the same zeal as before, in fact, he saw it as a foregone conclusion that he would be killed in combat.

Assigned as an officer of the Leibstandarte, Waffen SS units under the command of the famous Sepp Dietrich, Koler was among the five infantry and four armored divisions that spearheaded the last desperate drive from the Ardennes to Antwerp in December 1944.

In the last great attack of the German Army, the initial thrust met with success. But by the 17th Dietrich's units met with stubborn American resistance.

Koler had believed that the resistance had been stiffened due to what he had seen on the 15th, under the command of group commandante Peiper. Ninety American prisoners had been machine-gunned in a meadow outside of Malmedy.

For Koler this was the last straw. Risking a charge of treason, he and several of his officers complained bitterly to Dietrich.

By 24 December the weather cleared and Allied air power hurled the Germans back.

The last engagement of the Leibstandarte involved Hitler's last, although limited, offensive in Hungary. The mission was to save oil reserves from advancing Russian columns near Lake Balaton. Just as in the Battle of the Bulge, the initial SS thrust was successful, but was finally repelled by the superior numbers of the Red Army.

Ignoring Hitler's orders to hold until the last man, the battered Leibstandarte fell back. Realizing the war to be lost, Hitler raved that the Leibstandarte and Hitler Jugend units were all cowards and should be charged with treason.

Thrice decorated for valor on the fronts, Koler, along with scores of his comrades in the Leibstandarte, mailed his decorations to Hitler in a chamber pot.

It was the final refutation, exposing the last illusion and the great lie that had been the basis of Otto Koler's life. The superiority of the Aryan race over all others, the deification of Hitler as the greatest mind of all time, the thousand year Reich--all had been blasted to oblivion.

In those last days, as the Russian army entered Berlin, and it was rumored that Hitler was dead, Koler along with two other men, deserted with Sepp Dietrich's blessing.

Chaos reigned everywhere. Taking Wehrmacht uniforms off three deserters, who had been hanged by other SS units, Koler and his two comrades were to rendezvous in Fleche and ship to South America. Instead they were captured by British units 100 miles south of Berlin. Koler's two comrades had been killed as they tried to flee, Koler shot in the right calf.

He was given medical treatment and taken to a makeshift British camp for refugees and prisoners of war. Hungry, injured, and dejected, he was routinely questioned after a week of captivity.

"What was your position in the Wehrmacht?"

"Supply officer."

"Are you a member of the Nazi party?"

"No."

"Have you been a member of the Hitler Youth or any other party affiliations?"

"No."

And with the final denunciation that night, his memory swooned into that primeval past that had been his youth.

Hours on end spent in Hitler Youth classrooms, learning the pretexts of Nazism--being told of the inferiority of other races, apprised as to the superiority of his own. The physical training. His initiation ceremony, the great castle at Hamburg. The lit candles, the flickering faces, the regalia--a copy of Mein Kampf, the silver SS dagger, lying side by side on the table over the red flag, the Swastika, the prayerful oath of allegiance, the oath of Blood and Honor, the oath of sacrifice to Adolf Hitler and the Fatherland. The rites of the sacred Order of the SS. SS marriages, SS funeral ceremonies, the comradery and the mournfully sanctimonious dinners held in those great stone halls, the flutter of the candles, the iron cups of wine, the beautiful black dress uniforms, the torchlight ceremonies, SS breeding halls.

All of these images swooned before him like a series of rapidly flickering dreams.

His refuge had been his craft.

He had been the best. Had taken pride in his art. The arrogance with which he had enacted the art of killing now shocked him. It had been the murder of Thibadeaux and the response by Maxwell that had jolted him back into reality.

He was no better than his butcher-brothers in the extermination camps, and just as cowardly. His nights on the front had been filled with nightmares--phantasmagoric fantasies of blood and decay. He had heard of it happening to the coldest of executioners--madness. It would start with an inability to sleep, then a distortion of waking reality, often ending in suicide.

Combat had saved him that fate. It had blunted his disillusionment and guilt in the exhausting effort for mere survival.

After two months of captivity, he made his escape from the detention camp beneath a barbed wire roll of fence. Hidden by farmers in the countryside, he finally managed to hop a freight train, off of which he jumped near Hamburg.

Making contact with old SS friends there, he was finally able to gain a new identity under the name of Ernst Bruner.

The months, that followed, brought about amazing changes in Germany.

The Allies and the Russians were jockeying for position in Berlin and throughout Germany. C.I.C. units were more concerned with combating communist agents than with identifying ex-Nazis.

Finally, a remarkable occurrence. The C.I.C. which later developed into the American C.I.A. began recruiting ex-Nazi intelligence personnel into their ranks.

Klaus Barbie, the infamous butcher of Lyons, former Gestapo police chief and reputed sadist, had been hired by the C.I.C. to inform on communist agents in Germany. Barbie's contacts and organizational skills were invaluable to the C.I.C. During this time, acting on the advice of a former S.S. intelligence officer, Barbie contacted Otto Koler or Ernst Bruner, as he was known.

A French journalist was on the verge of publishing a story, exposing Barbie's atrocities. Barbie had heard of Koler and had offered him the same deal the C.I.C. was offering --"perform this deed and eventually receive safe passage out of Germany." More than safe passage, a sum of one hundred and fifty thousand dollars was to be deposited into an account in Peron, Argentina under the name of Simon Ballard.

To his eventual repulsion Koler accepted Barbie's commission and liquidated the journalist. (He still heard the man's death rattle in his sleep.)

Eventually Koler was assigned by ODESSA to become Barbie's bodyguard.

After Barbie performed great services for the C.I.C. the heat concerning Barbie's activities in Lyons was rendering him ineffective in Germany. It was arranged that Barbie and his entourage, which included Koler, be transferred to La Paz, Bolivia, where the communists were also gaining a foothold.

Safe passage was arranged to La Paz where Koler lived for over a year. Barbie lived sumptuously and was now an agent for the C.I.A. Subsequently Barbie was largely responsible for the destruction of numerous communist cells in Bolivia.

During this period Koler had been given only one "assignment." It was his final violent job. The final knife thrust, the urgent scream, in the hot darkness of La Paz. He informed both Barbie and ODESSA that he had lost his stomach for killing and was going to retire. Barbie, in no position to argue the point, gave Koler his leave and even helped arrange safe passage to America and a position as an agent for Brunewald Armaments.

Koler's success in negotiating a huge arms deal to the Bolivian military landed him a position in New York, a place to which he had longed to return, as a lobbyist and sales agent.

Here Koler sought to blend into semi-retirement and hopefully forgetfulness.

Suicide had seemed a real possibility until he met Roxanne. She had been introduced to him at a dinner party, and the most incomprehensible thing occurred--he fell in love.

Magically, their plans for the future and her motherly affection were beginning to heal him. They talked often of children and their imminent life together.

Suicide was no longer necessary. For Roxanne was taking away the past. Within her beautiful dark eyes, her perfume, her family--the identity of Otto Koler had been swallowed up and the birth of Ernest Mitchell consummated. Otto Koler was dead. The past was dead. All the lies were gone. The direction was forward.

Koler finished his painting on the knoll and headed towards his penthouse. Across from his residence, he paused briefly to watch three men unloading black cases from a moving van into Shelborne Towers.

Apparently new renters, he thought.

The fluttering sense of emptiness swam up in his gut. That old instinct, which was most always mere paranoia and which he tried to suppress.

Bandit tugged on his leash.

"All right, all right, Tiger, I'm coming."

The three men, whom Ernest Mitchell had observed loading encasements into Shelborne Towers, worked for the Hill detective agency. The exorbitant fee of $25,000 paid by one Tommy Maxwell was to cover a one month, 24 hours surveillance of Ernest Mitchell.

Hill Detective Agency had never been offered such a fee. It had been deemed worth the risk of offering the owner of the tenement building a deposit towards possible purchase of Shelborne Towers, in order to insure absolute security during the surveillance.

Twenty-four hour shifts were arranged. Cameras set up in both cars on the street and windows at Shelborne Towers. After a month's surveillance, Hill was to cease its activities and report their findings to their client.

The sun was brilliant over the fields of Norman Farms in Covered Bridge, Connecticut.

Having spent the morning tending Roxanne's parents' gardens, Ernest Mitchell and his fiancée arrived at Norman Farms at three o'clock. Their errand was to purchase and transplant flowers and shrubs for her parents.

The farm was known for its beautifully cultivated gardens, its trout farm, and fresh vegetables, which were sold to tourists as well as natives.

When Mitchell and Roxanne arrived, they parked their cars beside the others. Dust moved in stagnant sheets through the bright summer light as cars were continually ambling in and out of the field.

Under a partition sat three old men and a woman, who supervised the sale of fresh vegetables and keepsakes, such as quilts. Mitchell and Roxanne wandered leisurely in the bizarre.

Roxanne bought a crate of tomatoes, Mitchell a jar of spicy Chow Chow.

Next they partook in the hay ride in an ambling truck bed around a winding dirt road to the shrubbery and flower crops on the hill. As the truck bounced gently along, the air was redolent of dust and hay. A young mother clutched to two young boys at each of her hips, mediating between the boys' efforts to paw at one another and at the same time delighted at their excited giggling.

"Be still, you two wiggle worms, or you'll fall off."

Mitchell's strong hand gripped Roxanne's waist, and staring into her deep, brown eyes, which shone with the most beautiful light in response to the laughter of the children, they both had the same thought, as Mitchell kissed her softly on the lips.

This was the last time he would see her until the wedding. He had an extended business trip in Washington scheduled.

"I don't think I can stand not seeing you for two weeks," he said.

"You'll stand it fine. And after that, when we're old and feeble, you'll probably look forward to two weeks of freedom."

"We'll have grandchildren all about."

"You think so?"

"Sure. Why not?"

The truck finally ground to a halt on the beautiful ridge, which dazzled the eyes with a blend of bright sunlight and colors. Rows of white, crimson, and yellow flowers, along with shrubs, decorated the landscape.

"This would make a beautiful painting," Mitchell said as he was given a shovel by an old man in coveralls.

"You ought to paint it," Roxanne said. "Look," pointing to a row of bushes with white blossoms, "dad wanted three of those. Do you think you can manage it?"

"Of course."

She stayed and chatted with a matronly woman in a faded, checkered dress as Mitchell climbed the hill, chose his first shrub, and began digging.

As the shovel plunged into the soft, black dirt, the smell of fresh earth filled him. Making sure his shovel went deep enough, he maneuvered the spade beneath the roots and pried the bush up.

Looking below, he admired the rows of flowers that descended to Roxanne.

He dug up two more bushes, paid for them, and placed them on the truck.

They stayed until the sun's rays were long and slanting. He and Roxanne balanced the plants as the truck ambled slowly down the hill.

He had dreamed of flowers the previous three nights. And he

had awakened each night after these dreams with the strangest, most inexplicable foreboding.

He attributed this feeling to his anxiety over Roxanne's impending absence.

July 14

July passed into August and August to September. Maxwell had determined in this time that he needed forty hours to achieve his Degree, and he had embarked on the summer term with enthusiasm. He changed his mind about staying out of school the fall quarter and signed up for only nine hours. He had already formulated his treatise for his thesis: "Germany's Future Role in the Co-Existence of Socialism and Democracy."

Despite all the problems that Sam had informed him of, he began to see the world in a much more positive light. World War Two had seen the best and worst of Mankind in the forties. Russia and the United States represented two economic systems on opposite poles. Maxwell saw these two extreme polarities as mixing inextricably in the twenty-first century into a single Socialist-Democratic movement. He would use the Second World War as an example of how the U.S. and Soviet systems were actually the same system and working for the same end. He hoped to cite economic conditions in Germany as a basis for his thesis. He was not certain if his ideas had merit or if they were clouded by Julie. Ever since he had again laid eyes on her, every phase of his life seemed, no matter what kind of external problems existed, tinted by the most beautiful, positive, golden light.

With the wedding only six weeks away, Julie quit her job, saying that she had too much to do in preparing invitations, shopping for clothes, and making the necessary arrangements. Maxwell insisted on buying her anything she wanted, something that made her uncomfortable, especially since the money seemed to have no end, and more importantly, no determinable source.

Maxwell had assured her not to worry, that most of his money was tied up in the stock market and where the original money came from was not important. He assured her that they would always have plenty "to spoil you and our dozen children." The investigation concerning Ernest Mitchell only occupied the back of his mind. At the forefront of all his activities was Julie and the happiness that she represented. The Ernest Mitchell affair took the role of an obsessive hobby, and whereas emotionally he admitted its importance, intellectually, he could not bring himself to believe anything would come of it.

Most of all, he wanted the intrigues to stop. He wanted to marry Julie and forget his past. The Hill surveillance would be his last effort; if fruitless, he would forget the whole thing.

It was with a sense of both dread and surprise that he answered the phone to the voice of Alice Hogan.

"I have the information you wanted," she said simply.

She had caught him at a bad time. "Look, Alice, I'm on my way out the door. I'm late. Can you meet me at the White Elephant Cafe on Times Square. I'm meeting Julie there. I've got your money on me."

"What time?"

"We'll be there all afternoon."

"All right."

September 15

They sat in a small cafe on Times Square. Maxwell ordered a Philadelphia beef and cheese; Julie a Rueben. While eating their sandwiches and sipping beer, they began reminiscing about the old days in the apartment above the laundry.

"You know, it's like we've already been married once," she said.

He laughed. "I hope our marriage will be more conventional."

Her eyes widened. "If it's like when we lived together, we'll be the talk of the town."

"You remember the night the pool hall got raided?"

She laughed until tears came to her eyes. "You were a real sight, running out the door with your overcoat and no socks."

"With reason, baby, believe me."

They spent time talking about the old days, then amused themselves guessing at the names of people as they walked in and out of the restaurant.

A man with purple hair, a beret, and a cigarette holder walked by.

"There's Alvin," she said, attaching a fictitious name to the stranger.

"Greenwich Village all the way," Maxwell said, shaking his head. "Only in New York."

"Where shall we live, Tommy?"

"I told you, San Francisco is supposed to be the most beautiful place in the country. After I finish school here, who knows? We'll investigate the west coast on our way to Hawaii."

The conversation drifted to what they did during the war. When Maxwell made up his story, he had only to extend his stay in Morgan City, Louisiana to his days in Kearney, to hide the truth.

"My career was important to me," she said, looking past him, as if at something in the air, "but after a while art becomes frivolous."

"You mean with the war and all," he said, prompting her onward.

"Jacques, you know, the actor I lived with," she said without shame. "He used to say there were only two ways to defeat death."

Maxwell was awed at her shamelessness. It was an element of her that had always attracted him. She accepted her past as it was; no apologies.

"What did he used to say?" Maxwell said.

"He said that if you presented a work of art, a play or a movie, and people remembered your performance, that it defeated death, because people remembered you after you were gone."

"And what was the other way?"

She reached across the table and grabbed his hand.

"Children," she said.

The sound of silverware on plates and the gentle murmur of the surrounding people were like music.

"Is Kay coming by?" he asked.

"She said she was."

"So what did you do when you finally gave up acting?"

Suddenly she blushed and looked quickly to the side.

"What's wrong?" he said.

"I worked down at the Fuzzy Duck."

"The strip joint?"

Her little shoulders hunched up around her chin. "Please say you can forgive me."

"Forgive you for what?"

"I was desperate. At an all time low. The things I did in those days were......."

"Stop," he said. "It doesn't matter. Don't ever express guilt around me. Believe me, I don't want to hear about it. Whatever you've done could never be as bad as what I've done. So forget it."

"I love you," she said.

"By the way," he said. "What did you do?" They both broke up laughing.

"No other man would say what you just said," she said tenderly.

"I understand that none of that matters," he said.

"Why do you keep bringing up this something that happened to you?" she said. "Don't be so mysterious. Don't you know that I can tell when you're hiding something?"

He leaned back and looked at her. "We have all the time in the world," he said. "I'll tell you about it some day. Right now is just too soon."

She smiled. Her eyes shone with the adoration of a loving mother.

"So what did you do at the Duck?"

She blushed all the way down her elegant neck. "I stripped for a small while. I hated it. Then I danced." She had uttered this last word so silently that he could barely hear her.

"You what?"

"Back then, it was one of those clubs where a guy could come in and pay for a dance."

"I see."

She sighed and looked off as if re-living a painful memory.

"So what was the clientele like?" he asked.

"All kinds. Sailors on leave mostly. I don't know. I guess I felt sorry for them or something. And believe it or not, I often thought of you."

"Me? Why?"

When she looked at him, her gaze was one of strength. It was a look that hardened her features a hint; only adding to her beauty.

"Because I knew you were involved with the war somewhere.

And I knew that you were lonely."

He leaned over the table and kissed her cheek. "You're remarkable," he said.

"I always knew we would be," she said, tilting her head slightly, apparently taken with the phrase.

"Did things ever get rough there?......at the Duck, I mean."

"Occasionally," she said, "but we had this giant of a bouncer."

She tilted her head again, as she always did when trying to remember.

"Speaking of weird people," she said. "This one was a strange one. I meant to tell you about it the other day. I was working at the Fuzzy Duck, let's see, it must have been in 1942, when this tall blonde, good-looking guy comes in and buys a dance. He said he knew you. Anyway, these sailor boys didn't like him horning in......"

Maxwell sat straight up. "Go on," he said.

At that moment Kay, a thin, pristine girl, who was dressed in a dark suit with a hat and black lace over her face, walked in.

Julie stood up and waved.

"I'll tell you about it later," she said.

Kay was an old friend from the theatre days, and the three of them spent the rest of the afternoon getting tipsy and talking over old times.

By four o'clock Kay left them, feeling no pain, saying she was late for her bus.

"Honestly, Tommy Maxwell, you've got me drinking too much again," Julie said.

He smiled and leaned forward. "Are you saying I'm not good for you?"

Her face was inches from his as she leaned forward and kissed him. "No," she whispered, "I never said that."

He leaned back after a time, picked up the bill, rubbed the side of his face. Now he was trying to remember.

"Before Kay walked up, you said some guy knew me in '42. Something about dancing with you and some sailors."

"Oh yeah, right, right, well this Joe dances with me see......and anyway to make a long story short, he knew that we used to live together, so I figured he knew about us and so forth. Anyway, when I told him how special you were to me, he got real hot under the collar. He even shoved me."

Maxwell put the bill down. "What did you say he looked like?"

"He was tall and good looking, blonde hair combed straight back..... anyway there was nearly trouble. When he shoved me, it was the strangest thing, maybe he was one of the regulars at the pool hall or something, 'cause he kept saying, 'What's so special about Maxwell?' and on and on. He was creepy."

Maxwell turned slightly pale. "You seem to remember him well," he said. "You say he was good-looking. Let's see," he added as casually as possible. "In '42, that was when Frank was killed, wasn't it?"

Julie jumped. She always became over-stimulated when drunk.

"Yeah, that's right," she said. "In fact, I read it or heard about it a week after that. What a memory you have."

She sucked her lips into her mouth, then released them.

"Is there something else?" Maxwell managed to say.

"Do you feel all right?" Julie said. "Is there something wrong?"

"No, it's nothing, guess I just had too much to drink."

Maxwell leaned back, shoved his glasses onto his face, and ran both hands through his hair.

"You look a little green around the gills," Julie said.

"That's enough," he said shortly.

"Why are you mad at me?" she said. "Look, the thing at the dance hall happened a long time ago. I doubt if the lug would even remember."

"Never mind."

"What is it? Is it because I worked at the Duck? You said that stuff didn't matter any more."

"It doesn't," he said, forcing a smile and sipping from his beer. "Everything's fine."

He had another drink with Julie before he noticed Alice Hogan enter the bar. Alice averted her eyes from either he or Julie, and took a seat at a corner table.

Presently Julie went to the Ladies room, and it was at this time that Alice, waving her fingers at Maxwell and advancing to his table, made herself visible.

"I've been sitting at that table over there for an hour," she said. "Didn't you see me?"

"Yes I did."

"I didn't want Julie to see me. I'm not particularly proud of this. Here's your information."

She handed him a sealed envelope, and he reciprocated by handing her his own envelope.

"Remember," she said, quickly stuffing the envelope into her purse. "This is the last time."

"Aren't you going to count it?"

"No, I'm leaving before Julie gets back. There's no telling what she would think. People do talk, you know."

He watched her exit the bar as he opened the envelope.

He blanched. All was confirmed. A "Simon Ballard" account had been closed only two days before the "Ernest Mitchell" account had been opened.

On his way home he stopped by Hill Detective Agency. Only three days ago they had terminated their one month surveillance of one Ernest Mitchell, detailing his activities, daily habits, and movements. Maxwell paid the balance of his bill and left with a thick file folder.

Maxwell arrived at his apartment. He had intended to go to his desk and resume work on a paper he was writing, but as he entered his bedroom, he walked by the bureau as if it had not existed. He lay on the bed for an hour and stared at the ceiling. He was aware of a single object in the room, a briefcase containing Nazi memorabilia in the closet under his clothes. He had packed the case up two months ago. With meeting Julie again and asking her to marry him, the tortuous elements of the last three years seemed shoved away forever, just as the objects in that briefcase had been filed away for future disposal.

A feeling of nausea settled in his stomach.

Could it be? he thought. He continued to tell himself it was impossible.

He tried to work on his project for NYU for an hour, and quit, distracted. Deciding to turn in early, he figured that he was merely tired, that things were always worse when tired. Unable to sleep, he bolted upright in the bed at 2:14 in the morning. He struggled with the bedside lamp, turned it on, and went over to his closet and got out the old valise. He laid it on the bed.

In the valise were two SS daggers, Wehrmacht and U boat medals, patch insignias of various Nazi branches. He rummaged through the contents of memorabilia into which he had plunged himself in the last years, until he found at the very bottom of the case an envelope. In the envelope was the information Wiesenthal had sent him. The last thing in the envelope was a single, faded photograph.

He took the picture out and studied it. Could it possibly be? The features on the photograph seemed to have darkened and blurred with time. He compared the old photo with those he had just picked up-- the slick four by ten glossy photos, showing the man from all angles--here seen from a distance, moving down a crowded sidewalk, here at Child's Restaurant, now seen with a young woman, and his face always the same, looking somehow different, the hair parted differently, the face, strikingly different, not the same ruthless, hungry look as before. Could this possibly be the same man? How can one change that much in so short a time? he thought. And yet as Hill had pointed out, the major facial points of identification fit the old photograph, the high forehead with two prominent bone lobes over the eyes, one of which had the appearance of the slightest bulge. It has to be the same man, he thought. But what if it is all a mistake; all a huge coincidence. Perhaps I am losing my mind.

His mind wandered to the incredible conversation that Julie and he had just before Alice Hogan had arrived.

He flipped through the Hill dossiers which detailed the subjects movements and personal habits.

Interesting that he apparently likes the Park quite well, he thought. I must see him myself. I have to be sure.

He knew immediately what he had to do. He would take his time. He figured it was all a mistake, but he had to know.

Tomorrow was Sunday, and Maxwell was going to Central Park. Once he had determined that it was all merely a sick mistake, he could go on with the business of living.

Sunday--September 1949

It was a bright, crisp day in New York City. The air already had a touch of autumn.

Maxwell lived close to Greenwich Village on 9th Avenue. To get to Central Park he drove up 8th Avenue to W.72nd Street and turned into the entrance to the park. On his right he could see The Tavern On the Green Restaurant. As he followed the curving road towards the fountain, he watched the people on the bridle path. He parked near the knoll above the fountain, got out, walked back towards the fountain. He descended the steps which ran underneath an observation deck and continued downwards.

The fountain was located in the center of a round, paved area. The fountain was round and had four levels with white water cascading down in the center of a pond. People sat on a small wall, which ran around the pond.

Straight ahead from the fountain lay a larger pond. Ducks swam on top of the sparkling water, amid the rented paddle boats. The boat house was to the right. Along the edge of the bank a couple dangled their feet in the water. Two young boys were playing with small sailboats while their parents watched. A corpulent man was selling balloons from a small stand.

Maxwell walked past the fountain and near the water's edge. He leaned against a tree. He looked to his left. On the slight knoll above the pond several artists had set up their easels and were painting the landscape.

He strained to see each face. He saw no one that looked familiar.

Maybe I'm too early, he thought.

He smoked a cigarette while he watched the children and the boats. He decided to go for a walk.

He moved along the edge of the pond, strolled across the bridge. As the day wore on, more people came to the park. Everywhere people were coming and going. He walked down to the 59th Street entrance, located at Columbus Circle. Along the way he noted people of all types--elderly people feeding the pigeons, nurses strolling along with baby carriages, lovers walking arm in arm. On both sides of the park he could see the high rise buildings where the affluent lived.

He strolled for over an hour, bought a hot dog and Coke and ate a leisurely snack while sitting on the grass.

He looked at his watch. It was ten minutes till one. He decided to make one more trip to the fountain before returning home.

As he walked, he thought that perhaps it all had been a mistake. In a strange way, he felt relieved.

He enjoyed Central Park. Its leisurely pace was in direct contrast to the city surrounding it. He thanked whatever luck had it, that he had invested his money wisely before the Internal Revenue Service had come into being or its present level of proficiency. He and Julie would not have to be subject to New York's rat race. They could live in California perhaps. Maybe even have a cottage by the sea.

He walked past the knoll without looking up and sat at the edge of the pond. He lit a cigarette. He took three deep drags as he watched the paddle boats move past. He looked up to his left. His expression changed. He jerked the cigarette from his mouth and flipped it angrily into the water.

Amid the other artists he saw him. The man sat cross-legged on the knoll with his canvas on his lap, his easel next to him. Maxwell put his hand over his eyes to compensate for the glare. He took out his sunglasses and put them on.

He walked by a Coke stand and up the steps to the observation deck, where he could observe the knoll from above. As he had passed the knoll, he saw the face again, intent on the canvass and completely unaware of Maxwell's presence. Once above the knoll, Maxwell could watch the man more intently. There could be no mistake.

He trembled visibly as he fed nickel after nickel into the round, observation scope on the deck. Designed for viewing the skyline and the landscape, the scope buzzed and whirred as Maxwell perused every line of the face that had haunted him for seven years. The scope would whir, until the time ran out and the vision went black with a slamming sound, demanding another nickel to continue.

The face was slightly aged from the visage of the old photograph and more relaxed. His hair was parted on the left, just as the Hill agency's photos revealed. The flesh on his jaws was slightly loose compared to the tautness of the photograph. His eyes had the same alert gaze, one slightly larger than the other.

Maxwell watched him from different locations for more than two hours. He felt entranced, as if with the sight of that face, all present worries, plans, responsibilities, all the various objects which were part of daily existence--all fell away from that face. In fact, at times he so fixed his vision on the face that the entire landscape, the trees, the greenery, the passersby, the paddleboats, the bridle path--all revolved around the visage, so hard did he stare.

Just after 6:30 the man gathered up his paraphernalia and descended the knoll.

Maxwell followed at a safe distance, his knees at first buckling, like when he had sea legs.

At a small parking area near a clump of trees the man got into a new Maroon Oldsmobile.

As the car pulled away, Maxwell stared at the license plate.

17-Y-3506. Out of his left shirt pocket he pulled out a small notepad and a pen. He scrawled down the number.

He lit a cigarette and strolled out of the park the same way he had come.

September 18

The overhead fan in Dean Wilkins' office caused the dust particles to swirl like a blizzard as Maxwell stared out the window.

"So you see, with everything to consider, Tommy, I want you to know that it has nothing to do with your qualifications to teach. After talking to Stevens at the University of Tennessee, I have no doubts about that."

Wilkins paused and noticed the distracted look on the young man's face. As serious as the matter was, Maxwell did not appear to care; appeared distracted, as if wanting to speak of another matter.

"As I told a colleague yesterday, Tommy, these are strange times, in a way the strangest I have seen in this country."

"You mean Korea? Strange because this country's at war?"

Wilkins hesitated and ran his hand over his bald head.

"Yes. And of course I see the relevance of this to our conversation. McCarthy is a direct result of what is happening in Korea."

"And you say that Stevens put nothing on my record, regarding my resignation--nothing about the student's complaint."

"Nothing. He accepted your resignation on the grounds that you were preparing to get married."

Maxwell snorted and again stared out the window. "Yeah, he did me a giant favor there."

Wilkins immediately picked up the sarcasm. Before he spoke his calculated and erudite answer, he noticed that the young man before him continually glanced at his watch, as if timing the conversation.

"As I stated before, your position is a perfect one. You are not an established college educator. You can pursue your studies without interference. The Macarthy boys are going after established figures, like Tony Neely in the Physics Department. So I am convinced that in the future, once this idiotic period passes and McCarthy is seen for what he is, a fine educator as yourself can continue on. The sky's the limit," he added with a self-satisfied smile.

Maxwell uncrossed his legs, looked at the dust swirling in the large, bay window's sunlight, and with a look of condescending indulgence and veiled disgust, he said, "But Dean Wilkins, you forgot to ask me one question."

"What's that?"

"You forgot to ask me if I am really a Communist."

Maxwell took his glasses off, leaned forward, and peered into the older man's eyes.

"Well, what should I say?" Wilkins said, flushing.

"Ask me."

The words came out reluctantly. "Are you?"

"Am I what?"

Wilkins cleared his throat. "Are you a Communist?" he managed to say.

Maxwell leaned back, bursting into laughter. "Why hell yes, Dean. You should see me. I sit on the toilet every night and jerk off to a picture of Vladimir Lenin."

Wilkins flushed even more, speechless. "I see."

Maxwell bolted up. "Thanks," he said curtly, then started out.

"One thing more," Wilkins added as an afterthought, stunned and slightly afraid of the turn the conversation had taken. "If you repeat any of the things I have said in here about the hearings, you understand that I must deny having said them."

When Maxwell turned, he seemed to tremble, so hard was he trying to suppress his amusement. "Of course you will, you god-damned jerkoff." He walked out.

Maxwell moved through the students on the walkway with a bowed head and fixed stare.

Why did I say that to him? he thought, I burned my bridges with him. He was only trying to be nice.

Since he had received the packet from Hill three weeks ago, Maxwell had the strangest compulsion to be short with everyone with whom he came into contact--especially Julie.

Isn't that what I want, he thought, to burn all bridges.....all connections to my screwed up existence in this screwed up town....... or should I become one of the mainstream, one of these propagandized robots.......need to get my new car.....a wife with a bouffant hairdo......a new house......Christ, what hypocrites.

As he strode past Simmons Hall, an ivy-covered building where he was supposed to attend class, he barely gave the building a token look. During the last three weeks, his attendance in his classes had dropped to nothing. He was purposefully failing everything.

On the outskirts of the campus he caught the Fifth Ave. bus. In his mind, he had already arrived at the dilapidated apartment building of dark, red brick, soon-to-be-condemned under the city's new urban renewal zoning law, the building which faced the new Fifth Avenue Penthouse Building. The penthouse building was constructed in the style of the times--a skyscraper of sixty floors, designed for the wealthy urbanites of New York.

Maxwell moved as far to the back of the bus as possible.

He would have sat in the very back, but all of these seats were customarily occupied by Negroes or people of Puerto Rican extraction.

Maxwell watched his dim reflection in the bus window--his visage still, amid the buildings and the rivers of people on the sidewalk, people with tunnel vision, a city dweller's stare, that excluded any peripheral perception, staring only straight ahead, ignoring the hundreds of empty faces on both sides.

When Maxwell arrived at the shabby apartment building, the landlord, Mr. Wiley, a thin man in a blue work suit noticed him. The landlord did not bother to speak; merely continued to sweep the front walk.

The new tenant had been far from friendly. He had rented a one room kitchenette three weeks ago and as far as the landlord could tell, had never moved one piece of furniture in. It did not matter. He had paid his damage deposit and two months' rent in advance, in cash.

When Maxwell climbed the stairs and turned the key, entering the darkness again, the musty smell of the kitchenette consumed him. Before a tall stool, on which stood a pair of binoculars, was a bright rectangle of a window with opened Venetian blinds, which he had brought and installed from his other apartment. He spent little time in his other place now, going there only to sleep and collect the mail.

He sat on the stool, lit a cigarette, and began his vigil. The time was 4:30 p.m. He still had over an hour before the man would come in from work, a taller figure than most, a figure that would move up the short walk, past the uniformed doorman, into the plush penthouse lobby.

Ever since Maxwell had obtained the packet from Hill, he had kept this vigil daily, watching the man come in from work at approximately six o'clock and leave for supper an hour later.

It never failed. No matter how many times Maxwell watched him walk, perused every nuance of his determined gait, noticed the smooth swing of the briefcase, watched the sun shine orange off the lapels of his suit--no matter how many times he saw him, each time he expected him to be different. Each time he was surprised that this man, who now called himself Ernest Mitchell, was like all the other city dwellers. Consistently, he went to work, ate, had a girl friend that visited him on occasion--he even had a dog, a small white terrier.

Several days passed.

He continued to stalk his prey.

Twice he had followed his target--once to Wycoff's Delicatessen, then to Child's Restaurant and Central Park.

Like most city dwellers, Koler had become a creature of habit. During the week, he had two places where he ate dinner. Bickford's Restaurant on the corner of W. 47th St and 8th Avenue and Wycoff's Delicatessen on 8th Avenue.

On weekdays after dinner, he walked a small white poodle around his neighborhood. On Saturdays he would take the car and dog and drive to Child's Restaurant on Broadway near Times Square. After his meal he would stroll with the dog in Central Park.

He would walk south past the fountain towards 59th Street. As one moved away from the fountain area, the paths became more secluded and the trees thicker. At times as the weather permitted, people would spend the night in the park--couples oftentimes lying on blankets on the knolls, the patrolling police officers generally looking the other way.

On Sundays, as a rule, Koler would leave the dog at home and go to the park with his easel and painting paraphernalia.

Again, on a Thursday, as on every week day, Maxwell watched the walkway to the plush, executive penthouse. He noticed every figure that entered the building--mostly men, all dressed in suits, as if it were a required uniform, and finally him--Mitchell--wearing a salt and pepper, gabardine, three piece suit; his gait strong, the swing of the briefcase confident, the blonde hair immaculately combed.

It was a Friday night.

Maxwell had taken a quick walk to a local deli, and now he munched on a Rueben sandwich as he watched for the girl's car--a blue Plymouth. Two days ago he had seen Koler kiss her in the private parking lot behind the building. He had seen Koler hold the car door for her.

At 6:33 the car appeared again. She would now be pulling behind the building, now talking to the attendant, who no doubt had been informed by the penthouse dweller, that she would be visiting. Now she would be admitted in the back entrance, now riding the elevator to his floor, he touching her now as he had tried to touch Julie years ago.

Soon they would emerge for a night on the town.

Shortly after 7 o'clock Maxwell saw them, standing on the threshold, under the awning while the uniformed doorman hailed a cab on the busy, four lane boulevard. He watched the couple climb into the cab, their heads close in the back seat, the cab speeding away, left onto 55th Street.

Maxwell moved over to the cabinet in the kitchenette, and finding a small, pen-shaped flashlight, moved down the hall and out into the street.

The air was cool as he walked, the night filled with the sounds of the moaning traffic and car horns.

As he moved past the parking attendant, who was laughingly threatening a wino, who had wondered near the front gate of the lot, it was no trouble for Maxwell to quickly hop the fence of black, ornamental iron and get among the rows of well-kept cars.

Finally, he found the blue Plymouth. Squatting down by the back bumper, he shone his flashlight onto the tag. 19-G-4907. Quickly he scrawled the number down on his small notepad.

Moving to the fence, he noticed the attendant, now in his booth, reading a book. In one motion Maxwell was over the fence and back onto the street.

A trip to Hill Detective Agency with the girl's license number would soon produce her name and address.

Four days later when Koler's Oldsmobile was not found in the lot and when he was not seen going to and from work, Maxwell became concerned. Either his target had left the Penthouse Building permanently or he was temporarily out of town.

He began to stalk the girl.

September 24

Her name was Roxanne Buvonne.

On a fine fall afternoon she and a girlfriend caught the Webster Avenue bus, which headed towards Yankee Stadium.

Roxanne and her friend Jill, a plump brunette, were both dressed in knee-length skirts and sleeveless blouses.

They entered the folding doors at the front of the bus, and since they were obviously in expansive moods, giggling and nustling each others' shoulders as they laughed, they did not notice the tall man follow them to the bus stop, entering the bus by the back folding doors.

The sun played in happy, bright rectangles over the buzzing passengers as the bus moved towards Yankee Stadium. The Yankees had already clinched the American League pennant, but many New Yorkers would attend the game to see the great Ted Williams for the last time this year.

Maxwell followed the girls at a safe distance, getting directly behind them at the ticket window.

They purchased general admission.

As he followed them up the ramp on the first base side of the stadium, he stopped. An old man with baggy pants held his hands over the eyes of a young boy, his face covered with freckles, and his Yankee hat turned backwards on his head.

446

"Close your eyes now, Jeremy, and don't open them until I say."

Maxwell could smell the fresh roasted peanuts.

As he moved past the boy, he could not resist seeing the child open his eyes to Yankee Stadium for the first time. His eyes widening and his mouth drooping open, the child's freckled face frozen in wonder.

Maxwell shook himself and hurried down the aisle, taking a seat directly beside the two girls.

Everywhere the crowd buzzed with excitement. He leaned forward, as best he could, to hear the two girls' conversation.

The national anthem was played, and finally the Yankees took the field to the thunderous roar.

All during the game the girls talked about anything but baseball.

By the fourth inning, when the girls' conversation waned, Maxwell left his seat, walking up the aisle. He eyed from the height the empty, green seat next to the girl, and then, pausing to watch the great Ted Williams fly out to center, he descended the steps again and slid in next to her.

Two innings later he finally worked up the courage to speak.

"Is that kid warming up over there a rookie? Or do you know?"

Roxanne, her pony tail bobbing as her head turned, giggled, looked over at Jill, and shrugged her shoulders.

Maxwell decided to press on.

"And what are two lovely ladies like you doing here unescorted? What do your husbands do?"

Again both girls laughed. Jill spoke. "My husband is a lawyer. And Roxanne is single."

Seeing Roxanne nudge Jill and flush with embarrassment, Maxwell said, "Single, huh? That's hard to believe. I'll bet you've got a boyfriend though."

"That's right," Roxanne said, in a tone of a woman who does not want to be bothered.

"Well, if her husband's a lawyer, let me guess, I'll bet you're dating a doctor."

Roxanne smiled now at Maxwell, feeling less threatened by his obviously friendly banter.

"No, as a matter of fact, he is a lobbyist here and in Washington."

Maxwell feigned surprise, leaned back and clapped his hands one time. "Great, then, that means he's out of town a lot."

Roxanne smiled again, deciding to give the friendly stranger the coup de gras. "You're right, but he gets back in tomorrow......"

Jill leaned in. "Yeah, buddy, and he's a big guy too, so watch yourself."

Both girls laughed.

Maxwell shrugged his shoulders comically. "You can't blame a guy for trying," he said. "Listen, I'm going for hot dogs. Can I treat?"

When both girls declined, he again ascended the steps of the aisle. He paused at the exit ramp to look again at the happy, sun-drenched crowd.

As a high, pop fly fell foul behind the first base dugout, four boys scrambled in the aisle for the ball, one of them jumping up and holding the ball aloft in a sign of triumph.

Reluctantly, Maxwell left the stadium.

When he caught the bus away from the Stadium, he realized that his self-imposed exile from humanity, both in the past and in the past several days, was a natural preface for his preparation. A preparation for what? he thought. In the ball-park he had felt for an instant the old feeling he had as a kid, a feeling of forgetfulness, a feeling of celebration for the immediacy of summer. It had been a brief moment of weakness.

Even as he sat by Koler's girlfriend, even as he had quickly and skillfully obtained the information he had sought as to his target's whereabouts, he had felt at the ballgame happy, for a short instant linked with the great crowd.

That is all I want now, he thought, as the bus struggled through the traffic, to forget, to be normal, to live my life as if none of that ever happened.

But he knew he could never do this until he had confronted him. He did not know what he would do when it happened, but it had to happen.

At that moment, on the bus, moving away from the stadium, it occurred to him that he could not go through with the marriage. He could at least do Julie that favor. All their talk about Fate bringing them together, a notion that he used to entertain as possibly being true, now inundated him with bitterness. If Fate had brought Maxwell to Julie, then Julie had been only a vehicle towards Koler. It now seemed incredible that Maxwell could ever have thought of marrying her. The fact that she had met Koler, the fact that he had touched her, danced and talked with her, somehow poisoned everything for Tommy. It dramatized the fact that Julie was as much a part of his past as Frank Becken, Richard Thibadeaux, or anything connected with those torturous years.

It's not her fault, he thought, but it doesn't matter.

Nothing matters anymore. To hell with it all.

He would tell her tomorrow. It had to be done. There was no other way.

September 25

Julie had begun to panic days ago. Ever since the day at the cafe, Tommy had been conspicuously unavailable. When she called or went by his apartment late at nights, he was not in. And when she called him during the day, the phone was off the hook. He had been involved in a mysterious activity on a regular basis at nights for nearly four weeks now. Whenever she managed to get hold of him, asking him of his whereabouts, he became testy and short.

It was only seven weeks before the planned wedding, but already she had an omen. When he called on Thursday morning and asked her to meet him at the Liberty Island Ferry, she knew to expect the worst.

At the station Maxwell was sitting on a bench, reading a newspaper. His face was dark with a half beard, and his eyes were red with huge black circles under them.

"You look terrible," she said. She wore a light blue summer jacket over her yellow dress.

He leapt up and took her hand. "Come on."

He led her so quickly to the ticket window that she had to run in quick, little steps to keep from falling.

"What's the matter with you?" she asked.

"I don't want to miss the ferry," he said. At the ticket window he had bought one round trip ticket and the other one way.

"You made a mistake with the tickets," she said, but he ignored her words.

"Come on," he said, pulling her through the crowd. "Let's get by the rail."

They got their position and leaned over as the ferry shoved off. They watched the skyline march back from the boat. The morning was brisk and bright. Tiny white caps appeared before the Statue of Liberty in the distance. The chatter of New Yorkers' voices served as the background for the churning engine and the lap of the waves against the hull.

A recorded spiel on a loudspeaker over the Ferry cabin began to play.

"Welcome to the Liberty Island Ferry. Liberty Island, formerly called Bedloe's Island, houses the famous Statue of Liberty. Majestically overlooking New York harbor, her proper name is 'Liberty Enlightening the World.' The statue was a gift from the French government in 1884. The French donated 250,000 dollars for Lady Liberty's construction, and the Americans donated 280,000 dollars for the pedestal. She is the largest statue ever made, measuring 151 feet from her sandals to her torch and has come to represent freedom and hope for all peoples world wide."

Maxwell barely looked at Julie. He leaned over the railing and smoked.

Her eyes welled with tears. "It's over," she said. "That's what you're doing. You've planned this little trip to tell me it's over."

He flipped his cigarette, only half-smoked, into the waves. She was surprised to see his own eyes welling. "Yes, it's over," he said, "and I can't even tell you why."

A small gasp escaped her, and she slapped his face. "You bastard," she screamed. "You gutless son of a bitch."

A lady grabbed her little girl's hand and hurried away.

"I'm sorry," he said, looking past her face, "but there's something I have to do, and I can't involve you. You might be hurt."

"Shutup," she sobbed. "Don't make it sound so noble. You dart in and out of my life...." and she was so overcome with sobs that she could not finish.

He reached out to her.

"Don't touch me," she screamed.

"Julie, I'm sorry," he said.

"Sorry, sorry, you say. How can you even say that? Why did you even bother to find me again? Couldn't you find an easy lay somewhere else?"

"The Statue is an example of repousee molding or hammering metal over a shaped mold. Made of 300 sheets of copper, the entire work weighs 450,000 pounds."

"Julie, I love you," he said, jerking to the side and leaning over the waves. "You must know that. You must feel it."

"Men are all the same," she said. "Why must we learn it over and over again that all of you are nothing but selfish children.......little boys with the facade of manhood. And you had the nerve to talk about children."

"I meant it, Julie. I meant every word."

She laughed bitterly. "Yeah, sure, you meant it, all right." Then she looked at him.

"What is it? Can't you let whatever it is go?"

"I'll never have children," he said bitterly, staring over the waves. "Not now. It's not you, Julie. I'll never find another woman like you. I know that. You'll....."

"Just shut the hell up. Don't bother to lie to me."

"I've never lied to you," he said, turning to her. "Not really. This is the hardest thing I've ever had to do."

Two gulls sped by over the waves. A pocket of laughter escaped the other side of the boat.

"It's not fair," she said, staring at his chest. "Don't I deserve happiness as much as anyone else?"

"Yes, you do," he said, gently touching her chin and raising her face to his. "And you'll find it. You'll find someone far better than me. You'll have to. If you knew what I was going to do, what was going to happen, you would understand."

She stared at him with widened eyes. "I can't believe it. I actually believe you. I must be the most gullible idiot walking the earth."

"I love you, Julie. That's all I can say."

A pouch of people, having overheard the conversation, moved away from them.

"A crown of huge spikes, affecting sun rays, rests on her head. Most people never notice that at her feet is a broken shackle, symbolizing the overthrow of tyranny."

She gazed searchingly into his eyes. "If you loved me," she said, "how could you do this to me?"

He held her arms and pulled her closer. "You know I love you," he said. "You feel it. I know you do."

When she answered him, her voice held the most pathetic hint of hope. "I thought I knew it. I was as sure of it as anything I had ever thought."

"It's got nothing to do with you," he said, turning from her and gripping the rail so hard that his knuckles turned white. "You must believe that. It just can't be, not with what's going to happen."

"Quit talking in riddles. Tell me what's happening. If you're in trouble, I don't care. Is it the money? I don't care about that. We'll make it."

"It's nothing you could ever guess," he said, his eyes small as he looked at her. Suddenly his look gave her a cold chill. He trembled oddly at the top of his frame. His eyes contained a gray cloud, and she felt cold.

Yes, something had happened in his eyes in the last few days. She gazed into them. The life seemed gone, choked out by a more dominant emotion.

"What is it that you hate, Tommy Maxwell? Who are you going to kill?" she said, stepping back one step as if to get a better look at him. "Suddenly, I'm very frightened of you."

"I'm not going to kill anyone," he said, then his cruel mouth turned into a sneer, "but I won't marry you, Julie. Nothing you can say will change my mind. I can't cause anyone else misery. You have to take my word for it."

"Quit trying to hide your cowardice with a noble tone," she sobbed. "You're a son of a bitch for doing this to me. Why?" She put her head down on the rail.

He watched her cry, her back heaving up and down with her sobs.

"I'm sorry, Julie, I truly am."

The waves moved by in slow succession. The Statue of Liberty shone green in the morning sun. The ferry sounded its whistle. The crush towards the ramp had already started.

Julie had stopped crying now. She stared at the waves as if mesmerized.

She allowed him to come up behind her and put his arms around her. He kissed her neck and whispered in her ear.

"I love you. Whatever happens to me, whether you believe it or not, it's true. Meet someone else, Julie. If I didn't love you so much, I would marry you. But something terrible has happened. I can't help it," his voice cracked. "I never lied to you and I'm not lying now."

She turned to face him. "Tommy....." He kissed her hard on the mouth. And with an effort, still tasting the salt of her tears, pushed away.

He looked into her face, into her huge glistening eyes. With his right hand he gently touched her face.

"I'll never forget you," he said.

She watched him walk to the ramp. He was getting off. She had her return ticket. When the boat was loaded, she saw his form lean over the rail at the brink of the Island, watching the ferry re-cross the channel. She watched him until he was only a small, black speck on the other side of the churning water.

Saturday--October 23

In a small bedroom in his apartment, Tommy Maxwell sat on the side of the bed. He leaned over a white wooden table. On the bed behind him was a packed suitcase, an overcoat, and a wide-brimmed hat. With a cigarette hanging out his mouth, he leaned over an ashtray. In the ashtray were various letters and documents, including two faded photographs. He screwed up his eyes at the pile in the ash tray before lighting a match to the pile and watching the resulting flame flirt dangerously with the bottom of the lamp shade. He watched the visage on the top photo melt into brown nothingness.

On the white bedside table were four objects--the lamp, the ashtray, a P-38 revolver, and the last of the Nazi memorabilia, a sheathed SS dagger.

Maxwell stubbed the cigarette out and unsheathed the dagger. His eyes widened as the shiny silver blade with its handsome engravings played off the light. He held the dagger before his face, balancing it in his hand.

He looked at his watch--3:12. He had three hours.

For five straight nights now, he had left his apartment at 6:20 and made the same drive to Central Park. He knew within minutes how long it would take him to arrive in the now familiar neighborhood.

He trembled slightly at the top of his frame. He had not eaten all day, and he felt dizzy and feverish.

He turned the knife in the light again, touching its edge with his finger. He kept the knife as sharp as a razor. He read its inscription, carved into the blade.

"Blood and Honor," he repeated aloud.

The blade remained fixed in his gaze. His head had hurt all day, and now it throbbed.

Fleeting thoughts of Julie ran across his mind. He thought of her unhappiness. Hatred welled up inside him.

Not only did he hunt me down like a dog, he thought, not only did he kill Richard and Frank, but he actually touched her that night. Danced with her. Incredible.

He made a violent motion with the knife, stood up, and walked into the bathroom. The fluorescent light over the mirror blinked frantically, alternating his face in the mirror between sheets of light and darkness.

Maxwell remembered the day down near Atlanta when he had seen children running to soldiers at a convoy. He remembered that he had vowed that he would never kill again. Yet less than two months from that day in Georgia, he lay in the hollow by the Ocoee Lake, waiting for the assailant to come into his sights. Could he kill again after all these years, after feeling responsible for the deaths of Mickey, Rosenberg, Steinhoff, and now Frank Becken and Richard Thibadeaux? He wasn't sure he had the stomach for it.

Maxwell pounded the sink with his fist.

When he had called an end to his engagement with Julie, Maxwell had known that he must act. The end of Julie had colored his entire perspective. Her tears had torn him in two. He felt dead himself already. The SS and Otto Koler had reached into his life, years after the war.

He walked back into the bedroom. He sheathed the dagger.

On the floor lay a small alarm clock, which he set to go off in two hours. Fully clothed, he stretched out on the bed. For a long time he did not close his eyes, but merely stared at the white ceiling. Many conflicting thoughts were coming to him at once.

Children, he thought, a wife, respectability, nothing will belong to me.

He closed his eyes and felt his eyelids throb. Soon he fell into an uneasy sleep.

He began to dream.

He dreamed he was a child again. He was in a boat late at night, on the lake near Murphy. The mountains were black against the night sky. There were two other men in the boat. The lake was dark and smooth like a great mirror. At first the two men with him were Richard Thibadeaux and Frank Becken. He stared forward. They neared the bank; flashlights panned the bank in pale avenues of light. The boat drifted forward. Then he spotted them; two dots of orange light on the bank.

When he turned around to get his frog gig, the two men had changed. His father and grandfather were in the boat with him. He remembered now. This was the time they had gone frog-gigging when he was a child.

The boat eased in. "Just keep it steady," he heard his father say.

Then, underneath the overhanging branches, on the bank by the waterline, he saw the white belly of the frog. The gig had almost touched the frog when he lunged forward. He felt the bursting of the soft flesh at the end of the gig.

The frog was placed on the side of the boat, onto a paddle, the feel of the knife in his hand, his grip trembling, the hesitancy as the knife descended when the boy realized he would actually cut the frog's legs off, the coaxing of his father, then the feel of the knife as he applied the pressure downward, the writhing of the frog, the dark blood against the paddle, and finally the dull cracking of the bones. The legs removed, the frog was thrown into the black water, where even without its legs and amid its last death throes, it tried to swim.

The boat motor started. The breeze cold on the boy's arms. Then the landing. Wasson's Landing on Ocoee Lake. He turned to make sure the two men with him are still his father and grandfather. He was relieved to see they are.

They arrived at the dock.

Then suddenly they were in the bright dining cabin. The long tables and wooden floors like those at Camp Nordland. He went into the kitchen. Miraculously, three women were already cooking the frog legs. Julie, Elaine, and his mother were cooking the legs in the skillet.

"See how they move in the skillet?" his mother said.

Then another room. The light shows Julie, tied to a giant wooden cross, which lay flat on the floor. She is wearing a short, sack cloth dress, on the cross backwards, her hands tied to each hand of the mandala, her feet at the base. As if by a sudden breeze, her sackcloth dress blooms upwards, over her shoulders, her clouded, large brown eyes, half opened, looking behind her.

"Kiss my back," she says, and he sees his black-gloved hand, pulling down as she wriggled out of her panties, his hand now holding the whip, now lashing down on her uprising and already revolving buttocks. She emits a small scream of pain and indisguisable pleasure. Her ass rising and moving in a small circle.

Then the darkness and the shoot of white light. His climax now a shimmering gray beneath his flickering eyelids.

Maxwell bolted upright. He was in a cold sweat. The knocking on the door sounded again. The knocking apparently had awakened him. He felt dizzy. After quickly changing his underwear and re-dressing, he staggered up out of the bedroom and into the bare living room.

"Come on, Tommy, open up."

"Just a minute." Maxwell recognized the voice of his friend Carl from school. Before opening the door, he rushed back into the bedroom, grabbed the gun, suitcase, hat, overcoat, and dagger and quickly thrust it all under the bed. The little clock on the floor read 4:22. He rushed back into the living room.

He cursed his luck. What did Carl want? He only had an hour. He had to get rid of him.

He opened the door.

"Hey, kiddo," Carl said, a tall man with sandy hair, a thin mouth, and eyes that always appeared half open. "I thought you were dead in here."

"Come on in," Maxwell said. "I was asleep."

"You look kind of pale. Are you sick?"

They walked into the modest living room, which consisted of two crates, an old radio, two chairs and a coffee table.

"I asked if you're sick."

"Yeah. Must be some kind of bug going around. I think I have a fever."

Carl sat down in the opposite chair and lit a cigarette. He offered Maxwell one.

"No thanks, trying to cut down."

Carl laughed. "Yeah, like hell you are. Did you finish with your paper? I finished mine."

Maxwell pulled nervously at his ear. "No, it'll be late, I guess."

"Late? You know Morgan won't accept late papers."

"Guess he won't get one then."

Carl leaned back and took a long drag of his cigarette. "What in hell is wrong with you?"

Maxwell did not answer.

"You're not even going to try to get it done?"

"Something's come up," Maxwell said.

Carl laughed. "What in hell could come up?"

When he got no answer, Carl pressed on.

"Where have you been lately? I've been trying to call you for days. You've missed five straight classes."

Maxwell took a deep breath and sighed. "I had personal business," he said.

"What kind of business?"

Maxwell bolted out of his chair. "What is this, an interrogation?" He began pacing back and forth.

"Easy, big fella," Carl said. "Nobody's going to hurt you. I suppose Morgan will accept illness."

"I don't give a damn what he accepts," Maxwell said as he continued to pace.

Carl pushed his cigarette into the ashtray and put his hands behind his head.

"Sounds like you're giving up the old academic ghost," Carl said.

"You always did like mixed metaphors."

"Are you doing anything for that fever? Stop pacing will you? What are you so keyed up about?"

Maxwell stopped, screwed up his eyes at his friend. A look of unmitigated rage swept across his face, followed by resignation. He went back to his chair and sank heavily into it.

"What's the matter with you?" Carl asked.

"Who are you, the question man?"

Carl scratched his head. "Yeah, that's right, pal. I'm just worried about you, that's all."

"Look, I'm sorry," Maxwell said. "Waking up so fast and all makes me ornery. I had the strangest dream."

"Oh yeah? Well, brother, you know I'm a great psychoanalyst. Let me take a stab at it."

"Never mind."

Carl laughed and put his hands back behind his head. "Boy, it must have been a lulu."

Ever since Carl had arrived, he had been trying to make Maxwell laugh, but the normal sense of humor was not there.

"You really believe all that psychoanalysis nonsense?"

"It's proven theory," Carl laughed. "The dream is a reflection of your subconscience, your true feelings. It expresses your innermost desires and concerns."

"Have you tried analyzing yourself?"

"I never remember my dreams," Carl said, beaming at Maxwell's feeble attempt at a joke, "but by the look on your face when I came in the door, I'd say you remember yours."

"Yeah?" Maxwell said, who casually lit a cigarette, blowing the first smoke in two parallel streams out his nose. "What did I look like?"

"Like you had just seen a ghost."

"Maybe I did," Maxwell said with a thin smile.

"Oh, come now," Carl said. "I do believe in God, but not ghosts."

"God, huh?" Maxwell snorted. "Now what has happened in the last thirty years that would make you believe in anything?"

"We've covered this before, old boy. Without a belief in some type of moral order to the universe, Man cannot survive. For all your cynicism, you believe in an order too, a good southern boy like you. You know as well as I do that there is something guiding our destinies, now don't you?"

"Whatever you say, Carl," Maxwell said with a stony look.

"You love to be mysterious, don't you?"

"You're the second person to tell me that."

"Yeah? Who was the other?"

"Never mind."

"Yeah, let me analyze that dream. Let's uncover what Shakespeare called.........let's see..........how did he put it? Oh yeah. That 'vicious mole of nature' that some men have. What do you say?"

"Let's just drop it."

Carl frowned. "You got any coffee? Better still, let's go grab a bite. I'll treat. How does Mario's sound?"

Maxwell jerked quickly to the side as if just remembering something.

"Can't do that," Maxwell said. "I'll take a rain check, though."

"Why not?" Carl asked, shrugging his shoulders. "All right, you talked me into it. I'll let you buy."

"Haven't got time. I have something to do."

"What could you have that's more important than a meal at Mario's?"

"I don't want to be rude," Maxwell said, gesturing with his cigarette, "but I'm going to have to ask you to leave."

"Well, Tommy, don't sugarcoat it, just come out and say it," Carl said, raising out of the chair. "Okay, I can tell you're sick and don't want any company. I don't mind that."

He walked directly towards the door, then turned and smiled. "But if you're hiding any of that famous love life of yours, I'll be pissed. I've been living vicariously through those stories of yours for quite a while. That Julie, she deserves better. Oh well, guess I'll just have to settle with being brilliant."

"I'll give you a call, Carl."

Carl turned just before the door closed. "You do look terrible," he said. "You ought to see a doctor."

Maxwell locked the door, went directly to the bedroom, got the articles out from under the bed and again sat down in front of the white table. He was thinking about the dream. Again he took out the dagger and held it before his eyes. He pictured the neighborhood on Fifth Ave.

His target would be preparing to go to dinner now.

Maxwell stared straight ahead. A revelation was lurking just below the surface of his thoughts. He knew he would soon get up and go one final time to Central Park. He knew his victim as well as he knew himself. In fact, he had begun to feel with his alienation to Koler, paradoxically, an affinity with him. He knew of the Order. He too could show discipline. He too had become a hunter for a man's blood, he too had killed.

But something else bothered him. Could it be the dream? Some connection with the dream and the conversation with Carl had gelled. He started.

In an instant everything became clear--the dream fully interpreted.

His head continued to pound. He put his head into his hands.

Is it possible that I can do such a thing? he thought. And the answer followed immediately. Of course, I can. For he and I are no longer different. We merely wore different clothes and came from different countries. The drive was always the same.

Maxwell's life in the normal sense would be over, just as Koler's would be.

Yes, the dream makes it all quite clear, Maxwell thought.

Underneath the carefully laid overcoat was a shoulder holster and a belt with a key holder device. Maxwell sheathed the dagger, attached a small chain at the top of the sheath to the key holder and put on the belt. He then tucked in his shirt tail, carefully put on the shoulder holster, placed the P-38 in his holster and put on the overcoat and brim hat.

He picked up the cigarettes and suitcase and walked out the door. He did not bother to lock it. He would not be returning here.

Maxwell was in a daze as he drove down W.72nd Street. He remembered on the previous Saturday night, having followed the maroon Oldsmobile to Child's Restaurant. Night after night he had stayed with his vigil, always trailing at a safe distance, seeing the twin red eyes of the tail lights, like spiders' eyes, meander in and out of traffic.

Maxwell rubbed the right side of his head. The headache was getting worse.

As he entered Central Park and drove past the Tavern On the Green Restaurant, he lit another cigarette. He told himself that he had smoked twice as much in the last few days, especially during the interminable waits outside his target's penthouse. He remembered straining his eyes at the revolving door to recognize what had now become the familiar gait of the tall, blonde man. Hours on end he would wait until the man emerged, usually with a small white dog at heel. Unlike the other city dwellers, who hurried by, this man seemed oblivious to the pace. His walk was that of a man of leisure, not lazy, but poised and controlled.

With that same attitude of poise, Maxwell drove slowly through the winding curves of Central Park towards the fountain. It was nearly dusk. People were still abundant on the bridle path. Maxwell stopped his car near the knoll and the fountain.

His victim would walk down the steps where a thin woman now walked. He would descend the steps, which ran underneath the observation deck and down to the round, paved fountain area.

Maxwell could see the duck pond with the paddle boats. He saw the boathouse. The pond was directly across from the fountain. The pace would again be leisurely as his victim made his way between the pond and the fountain, the small terrier obedient, accustomed to the routine of relieving himself only when he had reached the wooded path, which lead to Columbus Circle. The path wound in and out of patches of woods, beside several steep knolls.

Maxwell turned his car around and presently re-entered the park at 59th Street and Columbus Circle. After a considerable drive, he parked in a gravel parking area south of the fountain.

He got out of the car and headed towards the fountain. The night was warm enough to be without a coat, but cool enough not to attract attention by wearing one. The coat would serve its purpose, hiding the gun and the knife.

Soon he could see the fountain, the pond, and the boathouse.

Was this really happening? he asked himself. He walked over to the edge of the fountain and sat down. A hot dog vendor below the observation deck was cleaning his stand. Maxwell watched the little man wipe down the small counter, then roll the stand away to the right.

Three children ran past him to the edge of the pond. He reached inside his right overcoat pocket and pulled out two neatly folded red and white handkerchiefs. He balanced the handkerchiefs on his fingertips, then placed them back into his coat pocket.

He strolled back towards his car, taking what was sure to be his victim's path. He tried to walk at the same pace and attitude that his victim would take, picturing every detail of his movements. He had rehearsed this walk endlessly over the last three nights.

A fat woman waddled past him.

Presently he was back to his car. He started back for the final time. It would take him fifteen minutes to reach the pond again.

The trees moved slowly past his field of vision. Again the question occurred. Was this really happening? Could he summon up the courage to do it?

It is already done, he told himself with resolve, the dream decided everything, all is clear.

But until he saw him, until he actually confronted him, he could not be sure what he would do.

No, you idiot, he chastised himself, one cannot hesitate. He wouldn't. He didn't.

He remembered the half-face of Richard Thibadeaux, seconds before he threw the dirt over him.

Why can't I confront reality, he thought, as he bit his lower lip, why do I doubt myself? When I was a child, I heard about the great war to end all wars. I remember how my father told me the reason he had fought. So there would be no more war. And I believed that. The idea that there would be another war was unthinkable. Yes, the unthinkable always comes to pass. The next war is unthinkable, right, tell me another funny story.

But no matter how Maxwell rationalized his actions, he was unsure as to whether he could go through with it.

Two youths jogged by.

He had killed before without hesitation, but it was different then. He had been in an impossible situation. His choice had been to kill or be killed. Tonight was different. His life was not threatened, rather he felt as if he were driving himself towards a precipice. Tonight was the last night of his life. If he went through with things, nothing would be the same.

He could hear people's voices bouncing off the trees. He could not be far from the pond now.

His head throbbed. All logic was muddled. Nothing made sense. He was going to act, that is all. He was going to step willingly over that precipice. Whether to avenge the death of his friends, to atone for all those years of vigilant search, or to seek retribution for the earlier years of torturous hiding --whether any of these things mattered anymore, he could not say.

The path yawned into the fountain area. The pain in his head worsened. He felt dizzy and his vision was closing into a tunnel.

There was nothing left to think about, nothing left to say.

The gravel crunched beneath his feet. He walked slowly, with his hands in his pockets, in the attitude of a man on a casual stroll. He turned around and headed back towards the trees.

"Stop it, Mikey," screamed one of the children at the pond. The older kid laughed and picked up a larger rock and threw it into the pond, the splash drenching the right leg of the younger boy.

"I'm telling," and when the younger boy started to run, the older grabbed him by the arm, leaned down and spoke to him.

"I don't care."

"Go on then, you little baby."

He passed an older couple, neither of whom looked at him as he passed. He moved along the walkway where smooth brown rocks lined the path.

A mother's voice called a child from a distance. He entered the part of the path just before the hill where the trees encroached deep shadows already on the walkway. Darkness sifted down. He looked to either side of him, left the path, and entered the shadows of the trees. He squatted down.

He strained his eyes to see his watch. 8:15. If the routine followed, Koler would leave the restaurant in the next five minutes. Time passed slowly. His heart pounded.

Then he heard footsteps. He wheeled around. Footsteps coming from the top of the hill.

He cursed to himself. He had missed his opportunity. Koler had already been to the hill. He quickly unbuttoned his overcoat and pulled out the P-38. He crept towards the path. Then he saw them. He squatted down and burrowed his head down between his legs in the shadow. He was lost. His only chance of not being seen was to remain perfectly still in the shadow.

"Come on, Betty," said a young male voice.

"No," said the female.

"Just this one time." They stopped not ten feet from Maxwell. He heard the girl giggle, then could hear them embracing and kissing.

"See, that's not so bad, is it?" the youth whispered.

"Just for a minute, then."

Maxwell cursed his luck. His lips trembled. A cold chill ran up and down his spine. He was certain he had a fever. The pain seared his throbbing temples. Suddenly he felt nauseous.

"I told you to stop that."

"Just a little bit more."

"No."

"Hush, someone will hear."

"I hope they do," she whispered.

"Let's go back to the top," he said.

"No, it's too dark."

"Will you meet me here tomorrow?" he asked as the steps moved away.

She giggled. "If you behave yourself."

Maxwell raised his head. It had been a miracle that the couple had not seen him.

He heard the faint crunch of gravel by the pond. It seemed that all his senses were heightened. His eyes were adjusted to the darkness. The shadows deepened. It was absolutely quiet. He walked onto the path. He returned to his previous vantage point. No wonder the couple had not seen him. The trees were completely blackened with shadow.

He watched the couple move away, hand in hand. They moved

down past the pond. Perhaps Koler could now see them as he descended the knoll towards Maxwell's position. Or perhaps he was still at the restaurant.

Maxwell watched the tall youth drape his arm behind the girl's neck. The girl wore a pony tail. The boy leaned over the girl and kissed her.

Maxwell waited. The couple passed out of sight. Traffic moaned in the distance. He could hear the ducks quacking by the pond and the sounds of the paddleboats in the water.

A man in an undershirt and a woman with a red dress stopped by the pond. It was almost too dark to see, but as Maxwell watched, he could determine that these two people were arguing. The man paced back and forth while the woman waved one arm up and down as she spoke. Finally they moved out of sight.

Maxwell did whatever he could to pass the time.

Occasionally voices swam into the edge of his hearing. Sounds carried much farther at night.

By 9:00 darkness was complete, and no one could be seen in either direction. Everything was normal.

He thought of the two couples he had just seen.

It occurred to him for an instant that he could still have all the normal things--a sleepy little house, a nice square yard, a wife and kids. Perhaps there was still time to reconsider.

His head was splitting with pain. He placed his fingers on his throbbing temples.

The wind kicked up. Maxwell lit a cigarette. A dog barked in the distance. He raised his eyes. He dropped the cigarette and smashed it out on the ground.

The dog barked again; this time closer.

He pictured the man and the dog, descending the knoll towards the fountain.

Maxwell raised up fast. He felt the blood rush from his head. Then his vision sharpened. There was no rush. It would take the walker six minutes to arrive at the appointed spot on the path below.

When Maxwell reached the level spot on the path, he cut to the left fifteen feet off the walkway. A tree was directly to his left, blocking view of the walker who would approach. He reached beneath his left armpit and pulled out the P-38. He waited.

He strained occasionally to look at his watch, but it was too dark. The only sound in the park was the wind rustling the trees.

Time passed. Perhaps he was not coming. He had deviated from the pattern. Maxwell would have to try another night.

No, he is coming, Maxwell thought. He was certain of it. His victim was a methodical man. He knew his prey. His victim was a worshipper of method, of discipline. He worshipped achievement for achievement's sake. Discipline was achievement.

Maxwell's head throbbed. He quickly checked his pockets.

He heard the crunch of the gravel near the pond. Quiet footsteps approached on the walkway, accompanied by the rhythmic clicking of the dog's claws on the path.

His heart pounded up into his ears, and his vision blurred. Then within ten feet of the tree the dog started barking frantically.

"What is it?" said the quiet voice on the pathway.

The dog continued to bark. "Easy, easy, my little tiger," the serene voice said.

The pair continued forward. Maxwell carefully kept the tree between him and the passersby as he silently sidestepped around the large trunk. When he emerged, he could see the tall blonde man's back, as he held the straining leash. The dog must have been fooled by the scent, for he was straining to break loose and run forward on the path.

The shrill barking of the dog shielded Maxwell's footsteps as he came up directly behind the man. His temples pounded.

He was within ten feet when he took the P-38 and pointed it directly at the man's back.

"Herr Koler," Maxwell said.

The leash fell from the man's hand, and the little dog scampered away down the path.

The stranger did not move, apparently not used to hearing the name.

"Herr Koler," Maxwell repeated, holding the gun steady.

"Ja," the man said, frozen, without turning around.

"Guten Tag."

"Wie heissen Sie?"

Maxwell's chest expanded. "Ich heisse Maxwell," he said.

"Maxwell?" the stranger said.

"Ja, vom Nord Caroline."

The man stiffened. Maxwell held the gun steady. The dog was barking ahead on the slight hill.

"Don't move."

"I speak English, Maxwell."

"I know."

"What do you want? The war is over."

"Mine isn't," Maxwell said.

Koler started to turn around.

"Don't move," Maxwell said.

Koler stopped, his back still to Maxwell.

He spoke now in a low, mocking tone. "You obviously want to talk to me."

"You killed two of my friends."

Now the man's voice was insistent, as if talking to a subordinate. "I only followed orders," he said.

"I know, like everyone else, but they're still dead," Maxwell said, surprised at the fluttering feeling in his chest.

"What do you intend to do?" Koler asked.

"Rachen."

"Rachen?"

"Ja."

"Kill me?" and now there was, for the first time, true fear in the voice. And with that note of fear, Maxwell's hatred only intensified.

"Nein," Maxwell said.

"Was?"

"'Dead' in English is spelled D.E.A.D. 'Dead' in German is spelled T.O.T. But there are other ways to be dead."

"I don't understand."

"You will, let's go," Maxwell said.

"Wo?"

"Da entlang. Gerdeaus, dann links und oben."

Maxwell had directed him to walk straight ahead, left, and up. "Don't turn around," he said. "Move it."

Koler started forward. They moved up the path. Maxwell's vision remained fixed on the back of Koler's head. He had not yet seen the face.

As they walked, Maxwell gradually drew closer to his prey. He was sure his target was planning a move. He had thought it all out previously. Koler was a trained killer. He would be just as lethal in a hand-to-hand fight as with a gun or knife. Maxwell had rehearsed this walk for hours on end. Koler was probably thinking that after the path turned left, they would go as Maxwell had directed, up the steep hill. It was all logical enough. A shot would be more muted at a greater height. When they began their ascent, Koler would make his move. Maxwell could feel his thoughts. Once starting up the hill, the victim would be on slightly higher ground than the assailant. Koler would start a conversation, distracting the man only for a split instant. Then it would happen. He would make his wheeling move and either run or attack. As Maxwell drew within an arm's length, he knew he ran a risk. If Koler wheeled fast enough, they would be in a hand-to-hand fight.

Maxwell had already pictured this as they made the left turn and started up the wooded knoll. Koler's steps were more sure now. He had decided on a plan.

Koler began to speak.

"What do you want?"

Maxwell did not answer.

"At least I was following orders," Koler said.

Maxwell was still silent.

"How are you different than me?" Koler asked.

Maxwell paused, stunned at the question.

"You have killed men," Koler continued as he walked. "You have done things you are ashamed of. We are very much alike. We were both pawns, part of the machine. We were both used. Don't you see that? Neither of us had a choice in anything we did. You see that as well as I. Think about it."

"Don't say 'we' when you talk to me, you fucking bastard," Maxwell said, his frame trembling and his face livid.

Koler stopped.

"Keep moving," Maxwell shouted, suddenly afraid, in a half crouch. "Move up the hill."

"How are you so different?" Koler said again as he ignored Maxwell's command. "Tell me that, Maxwell."

Maxwell went blind with anger. He began to tremble at the top of his frame.

"It is so laughable," continued Koler. "All of you look down at us for what happened with these moral platitudes when you are no different...........no different."

"Blood and Honor," Maxwell said.

Again Koler stiffened.

"When you took the oath, you promised to be willing to die for your Fuhrer. Right?"

Koler paused. "What has he got to do with anything?"

Maxwell raised his sights to the back of Koler's head.

"You never answered my question," Koler said. "How can you judge, Maxwell? How are you different?"

Maxwell's vision cleared. When he spoke, his voice was cold and even.

"I am no different," he said. "Never claimed to be."

There were several seconds of silence. Koler shrugged slightly.

"I said move it," Maxwell said.

Koler slowly started upwards.

Maxwell waited until Koler had taken three steps before following. Again Koler spoke.

"You know," he said, his voice softer, confidential. "In a way, I had hoped we would meet someday. I........."

"Shutup," Maxwell screamed. "You open your goddamned mouth again and I'll blow your fucking head off."

As they neared the top of the hill, Maxwell began to slightly decrease the distance between them. Now he was afraid.

Within fifteen feet of the top, the incline of the hill decreased, the gun barrel almost touching the back of Koler's head.

Strange as it seemed, once Koler had begun to speak, Maxwell had fought the sound of his voice. It actually sounded ambiguously pleasant. At least this man knew Maxwell, knew many of the things Maxwell had felt over the years.

In the oddest sense Maxwell now had a gnawing curiosity to know what Koler would say further. What had been his thoughts during the preparations and the action? What had his superiors said about the mutiny? The statement Koler had made, "I had hoped we would meet someday," for all its seeming, initial falsehood, began to ring as the truth.

Maxwell was pressed to talk further.

No, he thought, words mean nothing now. What's done is finished..... nothing to say.

And then the oddest thought came to him: Besides, it would be unprofessional.

Maxwell drew the gun back and struck forward with speed and accuracy. The heel of the P-38 slammed into Koler's temple. The legs buckled. He fell onto the ground. As he had done with Danet, Maxwell then kicked Koler in the head three times for good measure.

Rolling Koler over, he brought the heel of the P-38 down again, just under the left eye.

He was out. Maxwell knew he only had a few seconds. The dog was still barking below. He threw the P-38 into the holster, and straddled him.

He unsheathed and brandished the SS dagger. He quickly cut the buttons of the victim's overcoat, then his belt buckle and pants. He ripped the pants and underwear aside.

And with the image of the boyhood dream reeling before him, that night on the lake with the writhing frog on the paddle and the dark blood, he pulled the dagger slightly up. He paused for a split instant, then with his left hand gathered into his palm his victim's penis, his testicles, and struck.

The cutting required one viscous blow downward, then one slicing motion to the left. He remembered the cracking of the frog's bones.

Koler's trunk jerked about, struggled with consciousness; then he shuddered, and fainted.

The dark blood ran through Maxwell's fingers, down his left arm, staining his white shirt.

His mouth gaped. He dropped the knife on his victim's chest. He held the parts up, gazing at what he had done.

Then he reached down into his right overcoat pocket and pulled out the two red and white railroad handkerchiefs.

The nausea was rising in his upper stomach. He placed the severed parts in one handkerchief on the victim's chest, just beside the dagger. He tied the four corners of the handkerchief together, leaving a neat pouch on Koler's chest. He laid the other handkerchief over the wound to help the blood coagulate. He wiped the blood off his hands as best he could on Koler's wheezing chest, which now rose and fell at a much faster rate. Koler was on the verge of consciousness. The barking was closer now.

Maxwell leapt to his feet, astride the man. He released the dagger sheath from his belt and let it fall.

He turned and walked away.

When he had moved a few feet lower, he stopped for one last look. The sound of scurrying feet and a blur of white in the darkness. The white terrier had discovered his master. The dog was smelling the red pouch when Maxwell turned for the last time.

He had told himself that he would not run. Such had been the plan.

But suddenly the horror of what lay just above him on the knoll, of what he had done, weighed down on him. His legs began to move, and he was running, feeling the wind in his face, bolting headlong down the hill. He felt as if he would throw up. He knew that policemen made rounds in the park at night. What if an officer saw him running? He knew that logic demanded that he calmly walk away. But he was unable to control himself. Near the bottom of the path his leg hit the side of a tree and he fell, landing face down just to the side of the deserted path.

No one was in sight. He had been lucky. He froze on all fours to listen. Nothing. Then as he started to rise, he vomited, heaving on all fours, like a sick dog, until his stomach was empty.

Finally he rose, wiped a small piece of food off his cheek, and began walking along the path towards his car.

When he reached the gravel parking area, he unlocked his car and slid into the seat. As the door opened, the interior light came on. Seeing himself in the rear view mirror, Maxwell was stunned. His white shirt showed brown droplets of blood and there was still brown matter from his stomach on his right cheek.

Quickly he shut the door, rolled the window halfway down, hurriedly took off his shirt and started the car.

Remarkably, despite all that had just happened, it was the sound of the car engine starting which horrified him the most. With tremendous effort he refrained from screaming at the top of his lungs.

When the car began to move, his breathing became calmer. He pulled out of the driveway and slowly drove away.

October 28

On a deserted beach, just below Portland, Maine, the radio blared from a parked red Chevrolet.

It was a clear night. The stars shone brightly over the sea. The moon cut an avenue of gold down the horizon.

Tommy Maxwell stood on the beach at the edge of the water. A newly lit cigarette hung from the corner of his mouth.

He looked back at his parked car.

The car had performed well. The states had hurtled past-- Connecticut, Massachusetts, New Hampshire, and now Maine.

He had kept his radio tuned to any news broadcast he could hear, and nothing had been reported about any incident in Central Park. There had been no reference to the incident in the newspapers. It was probably working out like he had figured.

If his victim had not died of shock, which was unlikely, he would live. He had been on the verge of consciousness when Maxwell had left him. No major arteries had been cut, and unless he had been found, Maxwell figured the crime would go unreported. The last thing Koler would want would be a check into his real identity.

Maxwell knew of the effects of castration on human behavior.

The eunuch becomes pacifist with the cessation of the former flow of hormones. All forms of ambition and aggressiveness vanish. Any form of passion would cease. The eunuch would live to normal life expectancy, but he would never be the same. The jaw muscles would relax, and the formerly sharp eyes would become placid. His days would reflect a living death.

Years later, he would perhaps be a fat, droopy man, gingerly walking along a park path, a small dog at heel.

Maxwell gazed at the sea. The long road to his revenge was over, but a new one was beginning. Tomorrow he would turn north and cross the Canadian border.

Maxwell walked towards the starlit horizon until the tide lapped over his shoes. He loved the sea. Even in his days on the submarine, there was comfort in the empty, churning expanse of water, undefined and unrestrained by any trace of land.

As he smoked a cigarette, the orange glow lighting his face as he inhaled the harsh smoke, he relished the feel of the wind and the constant sound of the incoming waves. Far over that horizon lay lands he had visited once, lands he might go to again. His forefathers, whoever they were, had stared at a horizon before, seeking a new home, seeking escape from their previous definition, in a sense, seeking a new self.

Whatever was to happen, one thing was sure. The Tommy Maxwell, who had grown up and worked in Murphy, North Carolina, was dead. Whatever he was to become could contain no traces of his past. His mother, brother, and sister were gone for him. There could never be a return to them, nor to the mountains. As far as Julie and Elaine were concerned, he would become for them only a memory--lost in the details of their lives, in the love of their husbands, and the nurturance of children.

Maxwell dragged on his last cigarette and flipped the smoldering butt into the sea.

He watched for a time a lighthouse, far out on the peninsula to the right, shooting its pale beam over the black waters as it signaled a freighter.

He thought for a time of his comrades in arms, who lay in a metal tube at the bottom of the sea, somewhere off Gibraltar.

He turned and headed up the beach, his feet deep into the sand. Reaching his car and the sound of Big Band music blaring out of the radio, he turned for one last look at the horizon.

In the brilliant firmament above, a shooting star launched upwards like a rocket.

He walked around the car and got in. Turning on the interior light, he got a map out of the glove compartment and perused it. Soon he folded the map up and put it away. He cut off the inside light and started the engine. He pushed down on the gas while still in neutral, feeling the pleasant vibration of the engine. He put the car into gear. He had better get going. It was a long way to Ottawa.